Praise for
No Comfort for the Lost

"Herriman's historical details provide a rich framework for a gripping mystery and engaging characters."
— Alyssa Maxwell, author of the Gilded Newport Mysteries

"Herriman skillfully brings 1867 San Francisco to life in all its beauty and treachery. Weaving together an intriguing mystery and a fascinating clash of cultures, *No Comfort for the Lost* will keep readers turning the pages long into the night."
— Anna Lee Huber, national bestselling author of the Lady Darby Mysteries

"You'll be transported back to old San Francisco as you walk those dangerous streets with Celia Davies, who has dedicated herself to saving lives but ends up seeking justice for the helpless."
— Victoria Thompson, national bestselling author of the Gaslight Mysteries

No Comfort
for the Lost

A Mystery of Old San Francisco

NANCY HERRIMAN

AN OBSIDIAN MYSTERY

OBSIDIAN
Published by the Penguin Group
Penguin Group (USA) LLC, 375 Hudson Street,
New York, New York 10014

(penguin logo)

USA | Canada | UK | Ireland | Australia | New Zealand | India | South Africa | China
penguin.com
A Penguin Random House Company

First published by Obsidian, an imprint of New American Library,
a division of Penguin Group (USA) LLC

First Printing, August 2015

LIBRARY OF CONGRESS CATALOGING-IN-PUBLICATION DATA:

Herriman, Nancy.
No comfort for the lost: a mystery of old San Francisco / Nancy Herriman.
pages cm
ISBN 978-0-451-47489-6
I. Title.
PS3608.E7753N6 2015
813'.6—dc23   2015006890

Printed in the United States of America
10 9 8 7 6 5 4 3 2 1

Set in Goudy Old Style
Designed by Spring Hoteling

To Phil, Nathan, and Will—
your tireless support means everything to me.

No Comfort
for the Lost

CHAPTER 1

San Francisco, March 1867

The Chinese believed that some days were inauspicious, the ill tidings written in the passage of the heavenly bodies. Celia Davies gazed down at her patient, a delicate Chinese girl whose skin displayed more bruises than unblemished flesh, and wondered if today would prove to be one of those days.

"You heal." The old woman who'd been watching from the doorway flapped wrinkled hands, causing the lengthy twist of her silver-tinged ebony hair to swing across her chest. "You heal!"

"I shall try," Celia answered. "I shall try my best."

Celia leaned over the girl, a bead of perspiration trickling down her spine. It was stifling and gloomy in this airless room no larger than a closet, devoid of any furnishings beyond a washstand, a rickety bamboo stool, and the miserable cot the girl lay upon.

A room as tight and dark as a coffin.

"I have come to help you," Celia said, though the prostitute likely could not hear or understand. There was a purple bruise along her collarbone, just above the neckband of her blue cotton sacque, and several more along her chin and cheekbone. One skinny arm was wrapped in filthy, bloodstained bandages. The girl's face was sticky with dried sweat, and she whimpered drowsily. Undoubtedly, she had been dosed with opium for the pain. Celia rested a hand upon the girl's forehead. Hot but not dangerously so. Not yet.

"She may have inflammation from her wounds. It is bad. *Yau peng*," she said to the old woman waiting by the open door with its lattice-barred window.

The brothel owner's hands had returned to the wide sleeves of her high-necked silk tunic, and her features creased with a frown. How much, Celia wondered, did this girl owe her in exchange for passage from China? Two hundred dollars? Three? Her freedom had been signed away in a contract she probably had not been able to read and might never escape. These girls came here by the dozens, sometimes sold by their own desperately poor families in China who thought they were sending their daughters to a better world, to Gam Saan, the Golden Mountain. Instead they were gathered at the docks and locked in barracoons, stripped and sold at auction, and relegated to the worst servitude a female could endure.

Celia settled onto the bamboo stool and undid the latch on the black leather portmanteau she used as a medical bag. More droplets of sweat collected beneath her collar, in the pits of her arms, and along her ribs where her corset hugged. She longed for a breath of air.

"When did this happen?" she asked, feeling for a pulse in the girl's wrist. Weak and fast. Not unexpected. "How many days? *Yat.*"

"*Saam yat.*"

Did she mean three entire days? Celia wished Barbara were here to talk to the woman. But her half-Chinese cousin had not been home when Celia had been summoned and had rushed to the stews in China Alley with only her portmanteau as company.

"You should have sent for me before now," she said.

The Chinese woman's expression, stoic and implacable, hardened. "You heal or you go."

"I do not intend to let her die."

Swiping the cuff of her sleeve across her forehead, Celia set out the clean cloth she'd had the foresight to bring and spread her tools upon it—a small pair of scissors and forceps. Fresh muslin and linen for the dressing. Carbolic acid for cleaning the lacerations.

Celia unwound the bandage covering the girl's arm. It adhered to the wound, which stank when she peeled the last of the cloth away. The wound was extensive, suppurating, its edges jagged. The tissue was brown instead of healthy pink, and clotted with blood. Bits of torn clothing were stuck in the gashes.

Gently, she turned the girl's arm over, looking for redness along its length, the sign of a dangerous spread of purulent matter in the blood. In the shadowy gloom the extent of the inflammation was difficult to determine, the angry purple bruises too many and too great. She must have attempted to fend off the blows. Celia suspected she would also find bruises on the girl's torso. The strikes her customer had landed—with a heavy belt buckle, if Celia had to guess—had been unrelenting and could have killed her immediately. Might still kill her, despite Celia's best efforts.

A young woman had appeared in the doorway. Two long braids hung beneath a dirty gingham handkerchief tied over her hair, and her hands plucked anxiously at the hem of her shabby tunic. The girl—small boned, pretty—was another of the many prostitutes imprisoned within this building.

"I need clean water," Celia said to her. *"Ts'eng shui."* Given the stench of sewage wafting through the open door, she might as well ask for the moon.

The prostitute gathered the filthy bandages and scurried off to fetch water.

Celia brushed her patient's hair away from her face. The girl groaned and twisted away from her touch.

"Shh," said Celia. "I am here to help you."

"You heal or you go," the old woman repeated.

"Yes, I shall try," she answered firmly. That was all she'd ever sought to do—help, heal. But a brothel in Chinatown was worlds away from her childhood home in England and her youthful attempts to bandage the scrapes suffered by the neighbor's barn cat or mend the broken wings of birds.

"Here. Water."

The other young woman had returned with a tin basin, water sloshing over the rim. She set it on the floor next to Celia's feet and stood back. There were tears in her eyes as she looked down at Celia's patient. It would be hard to be a friend in this place. Hard when life was so uncertain and far too short.

Celia started to work, first cleaning the wound as best she could, flushing it with generous amounts of water to remove the loose debris and pus. The runoff splashed onto the dirt floor at her feet, splattering her boots, dirtying her stockings. The prostitute standing in the doorway murmured to the elderly woman, sounding distressed. Her anxiety for her friend received a sharp reprimand. There was no pity to be found here, and less room for affection.

"Unh." The patient's eyelids fluttered as she tried to open them.

"Hurt?" asked her friend, shuffling forward.

"What I am doing hurts only a little," Celia reassured her. "The flesh is too decayed to have much feeling in it."

Using her forceps to grasp the diseased tissue, she retrieved the scissors and cut away as much flesh as she could manage. The wound began to bleed anew, which she took as a good sign. The other prostitute decided she could stand no more and ran off, her footsteps echoing down the alleyway. When Celia finished, she cleaned the gash with the carbolic and packed the wound with a pad of linen. She would not stitch it closed or cover it with a plaster. It needed a chance to heal, and sealing in the putrefaction would only guarantee the girl's death.

"It must be kept clean. Wash it. *Sai*," she said to the elderly woman as she bandaged the arm. "Change the dressing every day." From her bag, Celia extracted a small envelope. "This is quinine. She must be given a grain every three to four hours." She held up fingers, trying to explain. "For the fever."

The woman took the envelope and tucked it into a pocket hidden beneath her tunic.

"Send a message if she worsens," Celia added.

"You go now," the brothel owner demanded, and stalked off.

Celia stared at the empty doorway, saw a drunk laborer shuffle past and down the alleyway, heard the call of prostitutes. No matter how long she stared, though, the woman would not be reappearing, her concern limited for a girl she considered little more than damaged merchandise.

Celia washed her hands and returned her supplies to the medical bag. Collecting her bonnet, she glanced at her patient one last time before hastening out into the alleyway.

The incessant spring winds had died down, leaving the air heavy with the reek of clogged sewer drains and the cloying sweetness of incense burning in a nearby joss house. She could hold her breath, but she couldn't avoid hearing the muffled noises emanating from behind the closed doors that lined the passageway.

The alley widened as Celia walked on, the prostitutes' rooms replaced by apartments and small shops. Overnight rain had left muddy puddles in the street. Hoisting her skirts, she hopped from one dry spot to the next. A porter squeezed past, the bamboo pole he'd slung over his shoulders curving from heavily laden baskets on either end. She skidded as she attempted to jump out of his path, her feet sinking to her ankles in slimy water.

"Gad!" *Brilliant, Celia.*

At the sound of her voice, the local constable who always offered to act as an escort straightened from where he had been leaning against a telegraph pole. He pulled the cigarette he'd been smoking from his mouth.

"You done, ma'am?" he asked.

"Yes, Constable." She stepped up to him, her feet squelching in her boots. "Thank you for waiting."

They headed for Washington Street, the constable eyeing every Chinese person they passed. "Ain't smart to come here."

"I do believe, Constable, that makes the tenth time you have made that observation," she said, with a slight smile. He meant no harm.

"I keep hopin' you'll get some sense."

"Most of these women are uncomfortable leaving China-town, so I have to come to them," Celia explained. "I do not know what else I could do."

The look he gave her suggested he could think of a whole host of things a proper lady should be doing besides tending prostitutes, and Celestials at that. It was not the first time he had given her that look, either.

They reached Washington Street. "I will be safe from here, Constable. Again, thank you."

He nodded and strolled off, his head swiveling as he peered into every doorway, searching for drunks or gamblers to apprehend. The farther he walked without finding any, the more his shoulders sagged with disappointment.

Celia took one last glance back at the alleyway. In the distance, the old woman leaned through a ground-floor window, checking that Celia had left without taking any of the girls with her. As if there were someplace Celia could readily hide a girl from the owner who controlled her life.

As if there were someplace safe for any of them.

*C*elia hailed the horsecar running along the rails laid down on Stockton, its yellow coach a bright splash of color against the brick buildings and gray macadam. A ride when she was less than a mile from home was a real treat, but as her housekeeper would say in her Scottish brogue, "We didna come to America to kill ourselves."

It was nearly seven years to the day since she had arrived in America with a husband and a dream. She had lost one. She clung fiercely to the other.

The driver reined in the horse, bringing the omnibus to a

halt. She waited for the steps to clear of departing passengers and idly observed the busy streets around her. Across the way, the corner tobacconist closed his shop, shoving back the awning with a bang, and a newspaper boy called out the last copies of the *Evening Bulletin*. An elderly Chinese woman clattered past in her satin shoes with thick soles of felt and wood, silver anklets jangling. She disappeared into the shadows of the alley Celia had just left. The day's activities were winding down, while soon the restaurants, *lagerbier* saloons, and gambling dens of the Barbary would be in full swing. And in the morning there might be new patients like the girl Celia had left moaning on a filthy cot.

Celia climbed aboard and paid her five cents to the conductor, who recorded her payment with his gang punch. The car was as crowded as ever, having come from the businesses along Market Street, and noisy with voices speaking a myriad of tongues. Several men stood hanging on to straps suspended from the ceiling. One or two eyed her outfit and the portmanteau in her hand. She could almost hear their thoughts: *One of that sort of women, looking for rights. Next they'll be asking for the vote, too, just like the negroes.*

Gazing coolly at them, she noticed that a gentleman in a stovepipe hat had risen to offer her a seat. He, apparently, was not alarmed by a woman toting a medical bag. Celia thanked him and sank onto the bench between a matron whose hooped dress spread across two spaces and a man fast asleep. The woman pursed her lips as her regard settled on Celia's muddy boots. Hastily, Celia tucked them beneath the hem of her equally muddy petticoats.

She had closed her eyes for only a second, it seemed, when someone called her name.

"Signora Davies. You come from a patient?"

Her neighbor, Maria Cascarino, occupied the bench opposite. Celia must have been exhausted to have missed her, a stout woman wearing a floral print skirt, her usual bright red shawl tucked around her white blouse. Perhaps Celia had not noticed Mrs. Cascarino without all of her children clinging to her skirts. Today only her youngest boy, Angelo, was at her side, kicking his heels.

"Yes, I have done, Mrs. Cascarino. I am sorry I did not notice you. It has been a very long and tiring day."

"It is fine. I know you work hard." She ruffled the mop of dark hair atop Angelo's head. He must have misplaced his cap again. "We come from the city to buy shoes." She motioned toward the scuffed brogans on the young boy's feet. They looked far too large for a six-year-old. "Seventy-five cents. For old shoes! We cannot buy better."

Celia's gaze lingered on Maria Cascarino's hand. It had come to rest upon Angelo's shoulder, drawing his warm body snug against her side, the familiar itch of his wool jacket beneath her fingers. Celia buffed a thumb across her wedding band and felt an empty, hollow longing, which she quickly snuffed.

"Your shoes look very sturdy and fine, Angelo," said Celia, making the boy grin and kick his heels faster.

Mrs. Cascarino smiled at her, crinkling the skin around her eyes. She often smiled, though she and her husband both claimed they had seen horrible things during the Risorgimento, the wars of Italian independence from Austria, which were still being fought, and the reason they had fled Italy almost twenty years ago, an infant girl in tow.

"But your patient, she is better?" the other woman asked.

"I have done what I could for her."

"*Sì.* You always do the best." She glanced down at Angelo, whose large eyes blinked at Celia, and her smile faltered. "Do you see my daughter?"

"I was in the Chinese quarter, Signora Cascarino. Not near her place of employment."

Mrs. Cascarino clicked her tongue against her teeth. "That Mina," she said. "We worry for her."

I would worry for her, too, if she were my daughter. As far as Celia knew, however, Mina Cascarino did nothing more than sing at the saloon where she worked. A situation far better than what other girls like Mina could claim.

"Mina is a good girl," said Celia.

Mrs. Cascarino eyed her. "My Mina? You are kind to say, but . . ." She looked out the window behind Celia's back and yanked the cord strung overhead, ringing the bell to signal the driver to stop. "You come for dinner tonight. You and Miss Barbara. You talk to my husband and tell him Mina is good. We pray every day."

"We would be delighted to come . . ." *Oh no.* Celia consulted the Ellery watch pinned to her waistband. She'd completely forgotten that she and Barbara were attending a meeting at the Ladies' Society of Christian Aid in less than an hour. Celia was scheduled to give a talk urging the group to extend support to the Chinese women, and she expected opposition. "Actually, we cannot. We have a prior engagement this evening."

"One day soon."

"Indeed."

The horsecar arrived at their destination, and they both alighted. Angelo noticed a friend across the street and dashed over the muddy road to join him.

"Good day, Signora," Celia called, leaving the woman shouting at her son from the corner of Vallejo Street as the streetcar rattled off.

She hurried up the steep wooden pavement that lined both sides of the street. Telegraph Hill rose to her left, the white building and its unused signal pole at its peak. A horse and rider pulling a water cask on wheels slogged up the hill, the dirt road slick from last night's shower. There would be fog tonight because of the damp. The water carrier tipped his hat to her as she reached her house, two stories tall and sturdily built of brick, wedged between clapboard dwellings that stairstepped the incline. From here, the city flowed over hills in all directions, buildings crowding out the chaparral that still clung to the sides of Telegraph Hill and Russian Hill looming to the west. She wondered if she would ever grow accustomed to the drifts of tawny sand that clogged the streets when the wind blew hard, or to the overwhelming brownness of it all during the summer months. At least there was the bay and the green, green mountains to the east to ease her homesickness.

Celia climbed the flight of stone steps and passed beneath the sign suspended from the overhang that read FEMALES' FREE CLINIC and was repeated in Chinese and every other language she had been able to think of. Optimism had encouraged her to add the Chinese characters when she'd first opened the clinic two years ago. To date, only one Chinese girl had found her way there.

Mrs. Cascarino had collected Angelo and was ascending the road with him as Celia entered the house. She gave them a parting wave. Hearing the front door open, Addie Ferguson wandered into the vestibule from the parlor, her attention fixed on the day's copy of the *Daily Alta California.*

"Men looking for positions and men looking for houses to let, but not a one looking for a wife! I'm wasting my time . . ." She glanced up and caught sight of Celia, who had dropped into the chair by the door and began wrestling off her boots. "Och, look at your feet! And those stockings . . . I'll ne'er get that muck out of them."

Lean and strong, with snapping hazel eyes and curly brown hair pinned beneath a cap, Addie conveyed her disapproval—and concern—with the hastiest of frowns. Despite being younger than Celia and on the wrong side of the servant-mistress relationship, Addie never hesitated to express her opinion. The tendency had irritated Celia's husband, whose broad shoulders and Irish wit hadn't impressed the strong-minded Scottish maid the same way they had impressed an impetuous young nurse with a wounded heart. Patrick had demanded Addie be dismissed within a month of Celia's employing her. All this time later, though, she was still with Celia.

And Patrick Davies was the one who had left.

"Has Barbara returned from checking on the girl down the street?" asked Celia, worried for the young woman, who'd burned herself cooking.

Addie caught Celia's boots before they landed on the floor.

"Miss Barbara's been home near to an hour now, ma'am. She's been reading on the back porch. That Dickens book you assigned her. And grumbling all the while," Addie added, holding the grimy footwear away from her hopsack apron, the newspaper tucked under her other arm. "I suppose this rush means you've no plans to eat?"

"I do not have time, Addie."

"'Tisn't my place, ma'am, but starving will do you no good."

"I shall not starve. I'll eat when we return from the meeting." Celia headed for the oak staircase in the center of the house, her fingers working the buttons of her crimson flannel garibaldi. The style of blouse had been named for a hero of the Italian independence movement, she recalled, thinking again of the Cascarinos and their chanteuse daughter.

"And please tell Miss Barbara to be ready to leave in fifteen minutes," she added.

"Aye, ma'am." The newspaper crackled as Addie withdrew it, ready to return to scanning its pages in her hunt for a man seeking a spouse. In all honesty, there were so many unattached males in San Francisco that if Addie really wanted a man, all she need do was step onto the street and snag one. "She's none too happy about having to go."

"Well, I'm none too happy about having to go, either, but we must. For the sake of the women we are trying to help," said Celia, climbing the steps.

"By the by, ma'am, Miss Li didna come for dinner this afternoon."

Celia paused and looked down at Addie. Li Sha, the lone Chinese girl who'd found her way to the clinic—and a way out of her life of prostitution—regularly came for dinner at Celia's invitation. She had never missed a meal before. "Did she send a note?"

"Nae a word."

"That is not like her." Not in the least. "Li Sha will have a good reason for her absence, and we are silly to fret."

"I am certain you're right, ma'am," answered Addie, sounding none too certain at all.

"We have always been generous," Celia said, her gaze sweeping the women seated in the meeting room in the church's basement. This evening the numbers were fewer than usual. "We can afford to be generous again in support of these girls, who have nowhere else to turn."

At the back, a woman rose, gathered her things, and exited the room. Mrs. Douglass, the chairwoman of the Ladies' Society of Christian Aid, intercepted her before she reached the door. The woman, however, was not dissuaded from leaving. Heads leaned together as others debated following her lead.

"I know this is a difficult choice to make," Celia continued, "given how sentiment has turned against the Chinese who labor among us."

"Taking away jobs," someone muttered, generating more restless shuffling of delaine and poplin skirts, more whispers.

Celia studied each face; most of the women in the room had ceased meeting her gaze. "The Chinese should not be allowed to fall victim to prejudice. These girls require assistance now more than ever."

Her cousin, seated in the front row, stared down at her hands folded in her lap. It was because of Barbara that Celia had become so passionate about the Chinese women of this city. A sentiment clearly not shared by most of those gathered here.

"There already is a Chinese Mission House in the city, Mrs. Davies," pointed out a matron in plaid taffeta, a beribboned hat perched upon her graying hair. "The society doesn't need to stretch its meager budget to provide charity to Chinese prostitutes when they already have an avenue toward a proper life."

Her comment received a flutter of applause.

"Many of them cannot get to the mission, even if they wished to," responded Celia. "They do not feel safe in the streets, and their own culture discourages them from leaving their homes and accommodations."

"Brothels, you mean."

"The society has supported other prostitutes who wished to turn their lives around. How are these women different?"

"It's obvious! They're Chinese!" said the woman. Frowning, she slid her glance toward Barbara, whose hands were clasped so tightly that her knuckles were turning white. A young lady seated next to her took a chair farther away.

It had been a mistake to bring her cousin here, Celia realized. In the past, these same women had always welcomed Barbara. Tonight, however, she was learning how readily professions of friendship could hide the bitterness of bigotry.

Celia rapped a fist against the podium, her anger mounting. "And it is because they are Chinese that we must act as a force for good in this city, a city that is becoming obsessed with dangerous hatred."

"You're mistaken, Mrs. Davies. We can't afford to support these women," said a third woman, who stood to leave, taking a friend with her.

The grumbling increased. Mrs. Douglass, sensing serious trouble, swept forward between the chairs and stopped in front of the podium.

"Thank you so much, Mrs. Davies. Perhaps at another time we can discuss extending support to the Chinese girls in this town." She clapped politely and signaled for the next speaker to come up.

Seething, Celia stepped out from behind the podium. She

collected the reticule she had left on her chair and clasped Barbara's elbow. "Come, it's time to leave."

Tears in her dark eyes, her cousin rose awkwardly to her feet.

"Keep your chin up, Barbara. They must not defeat us," Celia whispered, marching out of the room while every eye remained on them.

"Cousin Celia, please wait!" Barbara called, hobbling into the stairwell. Her left foot, disfigured since birth, made it difficult for her to walk quickly.

Celia slowed and helped her climb the stairs that led to the church's vestibule.

"I shouldn't have dashed off like that, but I was angry," Celia said by way of apology. "It was a mistake to bring you here."

"I hate them!" Barbara spat, all of her youth exposed in the angry outburst.

Her cousin was only sixteen and not much different from Celia at that age—sensitive, awkward, baffled by the world. To be half-Chinese and afflicted with a clubfoot made life that much more difficult.

"At the moment, Barbara, I feel precisely the same," said Celia, stepping through the church's main doors and descending onto the street. The sun had set, and the corner streetlamp puddled light over the pavement. A man across the road shot Barbara a black look. Celia hoped her cousin hadn't noticed.

Celia hailed a hackney coming up the cobbled road. They climbed into the dark, quiet interior and the carriage pulled away from the curb.

"How could those ladies be so mean?" Barbara asked, her voice breaking on a sob. "It's just like when Papa sent me to that school and everybody made fun of me."

Celia wrapped an arm around her cousin's shoulders, drawing her close. Barbara rarely allowed such attention, and Celia relished it.

"Shh," she murmured. "We must stay strong, you and I, because there will be times when strength is all we have to rely on."

Her words only made Barbara cry harder.

Celia sighed and let her weep. *We are both pitiful.* A reluctant daughter and an inexperienced guardian who could not replace the parents Barbara had lost. They both had so much to learn.

"*I*t's a bad 'un, Mr. Greaves."

Detective Nicholas Greaves shifted his gaze from the crumpled pile of indigo cotton and black hair tangled in the staves of a discarded broken barrel to stare at the policeman. He squinted against the morning sun. "When, exactly, aren't they, Taylor?"

The man frowned. Lifting his hat, Taylor pulled out a handkerchief to wipe the sweat beading his forehead. It was turning into a typical San Francisco spring day—cool, a breeze off the water climbing the hills, chasing off the fog. The weather wasn't making Taylor sweat. The dead body was.

"Give me the details," Nick requested. His assistant had a weak stomach and probably shouldn't have been on the detective force, but he was thorough in his work. Nick would forgive a lot for thoroughness.

Taylor retrieved a small notebook from the inner pocket of his knee-length gray coat and consulted it. Out in the bay a few yards distant, a seagull bobbed on the waves while its companions swirled overhead. Behind Nick, at the land side of the quay, a crowd had gathered—warehouse workers and longshoremen in shirtsleeves, a couple of chapped-skinned Italian fishermen in blue serge coats, neighbors and nearby shopkeepers. Their gossiping voices rose and fell as children roamed among them, their eyes wide. Where were the parents to keep them away? No one needed to see this, certainly not a child.

Nick rubbed his left arm where it always ached, clenched and unclenched his fist to ease the tingling in his fingers, and nodded to Taylor, who'd waited for his attention.

"Chinese female. Young, maybe in her early twenties. Given that her feet were never bound, she wasn't from one of their higher classes. A prostitute, I'd guess, especially considering the face paint. Though the regular sorta dress she's wearing don't make sense. Sliced across the torso. Deep gash in her right hand, cuts on her forearms. From fighting off her attacker, maybe. Another wound at the back of the head, like something smashed against it."

Nick crouched at the girl's side while Taylor continued his litany of observations and guesses. She hadn't been murdered here; there was no blood on the wharf planks, though last night's rain might have washed it away. Bruises marred her face. The man who had found her in the water bumping against a timber pile had left her in a heap, her bare legs tangled in her skirt, her right arm bent awkwardly beneath her. Nick cast his gaze down the length of the girl's body, at the bloodstained bodice and skirts that stuck to her, revealing her soft curves, the gentle bulge of her belly. A few months pregnant, it seemed, and wearing an oversized dress to accommodate—or hide—the increasing swell. That the gown wasn't the cheap cotton sacque most prostitutes wore indicated something, but what? Nick wondered why her hair wasn't braided into the long pigtail the

Chinese—both men and women—favored. He wondered where her shoes had been left. Perhaps they had fallen off in the water. One thing Taylor hadn't mentioned was how lovely she was beneath the bruises and the clinging tendrils of hair.

Nick swept the lush blue-black mass out of her eyes and off her high cheekbones, piling the tresses at the base of her neck and trying not to think of Meg. One day he'd stop seeing his sister's face in that of every fallen woman. One day he'd stop feeling guilty for having failed her.

One day.

"Don't you think, Mr. Greaves, sir?"

He glanced up. "Don't I think what, Taylor?"

"I said bad luck for him that when he tossed her off the pier her clothes snagged and she didn't sink."

"She would've shown up eventually, in these shallow waters," said Nick, standing. "And we don't know that whoever tossed her in was a *he*."

A flush joined the sweat on the policeman's face. "Yes, sir."

"I've told you that you don't need to call me 'sir.'"

"Can't help myself, sir. Em, sorry . . . Mr. Greaves."

"It's okay, Taylor."

Nick looked out at the water. Goat Island was a rocky outcrop in the bay, and the Contra Costa hills rose in the distance. The nine-o'clock ferry was chugging toward Oakland, creating a wake. Several three-masted ships and steamers were angling into nearby piers, the slap of paddle wheels and the clink of rigging carrying across the water. Stacks belched streams of smoke into the sky, reminding him of the girl's long black hair. It wasn't likely she had been in the water long, even though this particular wharf wasn't one of the busier ones and currently sat empty of any ships. A harbor official had rowed out to intercept a schooner making for the quay, halting it before the boat could dock and add to the confusion.

"When was she found?" Nick asked.

Taylor eyed the workers assembled ten yards distant. "Sunrise this morning. When the workers arrived for their shift. Two ships are due in today, one from Panama. It was that one that found her. A customhouse inspector." He nodded toward a man who was slouched in a dark coat and drawn-down cap and stood apart from the crowd.

"Perfect evening last night to commit a crime like this," observed Taylor, "what with the rain keeping folks indoors." He made the mistake of looking down at the girl's body and blanched.

"Agreed, Taylor."

"And a good spot to dump a body. Wharf hasn't been very busy these past coupla weeks." Taylor used the butt end of his notebook to scratch at his neck above his collar. He studied the book's contents one last time before restoring it to the breast pocket of his coat. "From what I've been told."

"Yes, a good spot," Nick said absently, scanning the ground nearby.

He poked among the bits of detritus, barrels marked SODA ASH and TAR OIL, casks of crockery and fire clay, piles of lumber. No handy footprints were visible. No bits of cloth or dropped cheroot butts to collect as evidence. No incriminating weapon hiding among the stacked crates.

"Don't think I missed anything, sir," said Taylor, sounding uncertain.

"I'm sure you didn't."

Straightening, Nick brushed his hands together and sighed.

"I know you, Mr. Greaves, sir," said Taylor brightly, misunderstanding his superior's exhalation. "You'll get to the bottom of this quick as a wink. Even if the captain isn't gonna want us bothering about some murdered Chinese girl."

"When have I ever not bothered, Taylor?"

"Well . . . never, sir."

Nick removed his coat and draped it over the girl. The gawkers had seen enough. "Bring that one"—he gestured at the customhouse inspector who had found the body—"into the station as soon as you can get him there. Send for the coroner, if you haven't already. He'll need to assemble a jury for his inquest, and they'll want to see the body. Also, put the news out on the street that we're looking for information about her. Somebody will claim her and then we'll learn more."

"No Chinaman's gonna claim one of his girls. They don't care once they're done with them."

Nick glanced over, the raw sea breeze piercing his shirtsleeves.

"This one's different, Taylor," he said, wanting to believe it. "Trust me. Someone will turn up for her." Because they *had* to.

Because he needed them to.

CHAPTER 2

"You did your best Monday evening to be persuasive, Mrs. Davies. I appreciate that," Mrs. Douglass said, perching her cup of pekoe tea atop her melon-and-maroon plaid skirt. She regarded Celia with the intense gaze that had made her such a successful chairwoman. "But you saw how some of the ladies feel."

Celia tapped a fingernail against her own teacup and glanced up at the portrait of Barbara's father that hung above the brocatelle-covered settee. The artist had captured him with a grin on his mustachioed face, his thumbs tucked into the pockets of his silk waistcoat. Plump and prosperous and pleased, he'd been a successful miner who had married a Chinese woman, only to lose her when Barbara was nine years of age. Celia knew what he would say about how "the ladies feel," and the words would not be complimentary.

I miss you, Uncle. Nearly as much as Barbara does.

"Indeed, I did see how they feel, Mrs. Douglass. As did my cousin."

"I am sorry if Miss Barbara was uncomfortable."

Was she sorry? Celia wondered. "Nonetheless, I am surprised the ladies have permitted current sentiment to affect them."

Hardly a day passed without a newspaper article calling for men and women to join anti-coolie groups that were organizing to stem the flow of Chinese immigrants into California. People had had few concerns so long as the Chinese stayed within their own communities. But when the woolen mills had begun replacing white laborers with cheaper Chinese workers, anger and hatred had started to swell.

The anger had spilled out a few weeks ago. A mob of unemployed men, primarily Irish, had assaulted dozens of Chinese laborers who were grading a road and burned their temporary shelters to the ground. Only through the intervention of the police had no one died. Barbara had been afraid to leave the house for days afterward, in case the rage was turned toward every Chinese person.

"I expect," said Mrs. Douglass, "and the ladies expect, that there will be more violence."

"The men responsible for that riot were punished, Mrs. Douglass." Three months in jail and a five-hundred-dollar fine had been handed out, inflaming the locals who had sympathized with the men. "The Chinese of this city stand nothing to gain by retaliating."

"I am not speaking of the Chinese causing violence, Mrs. Davies."

"Then what are you speaking of?"

"I was approached after the meeting and yet again yesterday afternoon by a number of women whose husbands own businesses in this city. I won't share their names; it's not necessary." Mrs. Douglass set her cup of cold tea on a side table. "Their husbands have been visited by members of an investigating committee. This committee has been given the task of collecting the names of any white men found employing Chinese labor. As I'm sure you know, several of our members' husbands utilize Celestials. They are good workers."

"And inexpensive."

Mrs. Douglass ignored Celia's comment. "But now these same members are alarmed. This is not the time for the society to provide financial assistance to your work with the Chinese . . . females of this town, Mrs. Davies. We shouldn't be drawing attention to ourselves in this fashion. It is simply too dangerous. Perhaps in a few months, once the situation has had a chance to calm. It is a worthy cause, but let us wait for a better time."

"A few months, Mrs. Douglass? Do you honestly believe that the workingmen behind these attacks, these meetings, this intimidation, will be pacified in a few months? The women need our help now, not when these men finally decide to stop rioting and assaulting the Chinese."

"I have informed you of the situation, Mrs. Davies," said Mrs. Douglass, rising to her feet. "I won't be scheduling you to speak again on this topic for the near future."

Celia stood as well. "I also presume these same ladies will no longer be providing support for my clinic." She couldn't afford to lose their donations; Uncle Walford had left her a stipend for the clinic in his will, but the money never went far enough.

"How they decide to distribute their charity is up to them, Mrs. Davies. Good—"

"Cousin!" Barbara burst into the parlor, her face as white as chalk, startling Celia, who spilled tea onto the red-and-gold-patterned carpet beneath her feet. "I'm sorry to interrupt, but there's awful news in the paper."

She thrust the newspaper into Celia's hands. "There. Right there." Barbara jabbed a trembling forefinger at an article. "It's got to be Li Sha. It's got to be!"

The headline screamed CHINESE GIRL FOUND DEAD.

Celia lifted her gaze to an ashen Barbara. "Dear God, no."

"*H*ere he is, Mr. Greaves," announced Officer Mullahey. Nick looked up from his desk. Mullahey pressed a beefy hand to the back of the customhouse worker, thrusting him into the office Nick shared with one other detective. Who, thankfully, was currently away.

"Glad you could come talk to us again, Mr. Wagner," said Nick, gesturing for the man to take a seat. Thomas Wagner. Average height, average weight, average looking. Above-average temper. Already, a vein in his neck was bulging. He wore a black suit of high quality over all that averageness. Working as an inspector for the U.S. Custom House must pay better than Nick realized.

"Didn't give me much choice, Detective Greaves," Wagner muttered, dropping into the chair.

"Need me to stay?" asked Mullahey.

"No. Thank you," said Nick, waiting to proceed until the officer had closed the door once again.

He leaned back in his chair and stared at Wagner, the

rattle of carriage wheels on the street outside the basement-level office the only sound in the room. That and the whistle of Wagner's breathing, which was getting louder and more rapid as each second ticked past.

"Well?" the man asked. "Are you just going to stare at me?"

"I might."

"I already told you people all I did was spot that Chinese girl in the water. And then that dockworker came along to help me pull her out. That's it! I didn't have anything to do with killing her."

"Yes, I know that's what you said to Officer Taylor." Wagner had claimed to have never seen the girl before he'd arrived at work Tuesday morning to inspect a vessel and found her bobbing in the water. It might be the truth. Might not.

"So you don't need to talk to me anymore," said Wagner.

"What did she do?" asked Nick. "Did the girl spurn your advances, and you got angry?"

"I don't go to Chinese prostitutes."

"Ah, I see. Of course not. It's also come to my attention"—Nick consulted a paper on his desk—"that you were arrested last year for assaulting a Mexican sailor. Not far from the wharf where that Chinese girl was dumped."

"I was let off. Besides, he started it," he answered, sounding like an eight-year-old accused of a spat with a neighbor kid.

"Still, it seems you don't much care for foreigners. Maybe you can tell me how much you hate the Chinese. All that grumbling among the Irish laborers. Lots of folks agree with them. Maybe you do, too."

"Unlike those Paddies, I've got a job, a good one. I don't hate Celestials. Don't have any reason to."

"You sure?"

"You think I'd kill that girl?" Now Wagner was sweating. He yanked a handkerchief from an inner coat pocket and mopped his forehead. "I was home with my wife. Didn't your officer talk to her? She'll tell ya!"

"She did say something to that effect. But my officer also spotted a newspaper on a table at your place. Open to an article about an anti-coolie meeting planned for a few days from now." Nick rested his elbows on his desk and leaned over them. "So perhaps you can tell me just how much you hate the Chinese."

"When will you be back from the police station?" asked Barbara, looking over at Celia from where she sat at the dining room table.

"As quickly as I can," said Celia, tying the ribbons of her low-brim spoon bonnet beneath her chin. "Get back to your sums. The work should distract you while I am gone."

Barbara scowled at her workbook of mathematical computations. "But I can't concentrate."

"Miss Barbara, 'tis best to carry on when awful things happen," said Addie, who was cleaning the walnut sideboard, the feather duster repeating its circuit across the polished surface for the third or fourth time. She seemed adhered to her spot on the dining room rug, as if moving too far might disturb the heavens and cause more unhappiness to rain down. "As my father would say, nothing is so difficult but may be overcome with perseverance. And that includes sorrows."

"The Palmers would never make Em do schoolwork if she was upset," retorted Barbara.

"They might do," said Celia. Invoking the wisdom of the

wealthy and influential Palmers, acquaintances who had be-friended Barbara, was one of the girl's favored tactics. And tire-some, at a time like this. "They dote on Emmeline, but not at the expense of her education."

Barbara sighed loudly but picked up her pencil.

"I was thinking mulligatawny for supper, ma'am. Something light," said Addie. The feather duster made another pass across the sideboard.

"A good idea, Addie," Celia said. "Here is hoping I have good news when I return."

Celia set out for Portsmouth Square, where city hall and the police station were located. It was a short walk, all down-hill, and she arrived within minutes. She dodged the traffic along Kearney, the hackney carriages discharging passengers, others waiting for fares near the iron fence that surrounded the square. The wind whirling across the road snatched at the rib-bons of Celia's bonnet, and she caught her breath as a gust spat sand against her cheek.

Pausing, she stared up at the three-story, sandstone-fronted structure that housed both city hall and the police station, gath-ering her nerve against what she might learn inside its walls.

Please, let it not be Li Sha.

She climbed the short flight of steps at the same time that a woman in a striped dress with a low-cut bodice strolled through the front doors.

"What's your hurry, darlin'?" she asked Celia, wafting the aroma of alcohol.

Celia brushed past her and stepped inside. The entry area was dim and quiet and retained vestiges of the building's past life as the Jenny Lind Theatre, though most of the interior had been gutted during the renovation. Ornate moldings decorated doors and ceilings, and a broad staircase led to other floors. Hallways sprouted offices with closed doors, the sounds of a commotion coming from behind one of them. Three men in black frock coats exited a room to her right and crossed to climb the stairs, their footfalls echoing. They didn't halt their conversation or notice her attempts to hail them. Frowning, she examined the signs tacked to the farthest wall and realized the police station was located in the basement with the jail cells.

The staircase descended into an open room jammed with chairs and desks, gas lamps flickering to chase away the gloom. Cigar smoke hung in the air, the source of the smoke hunched over a desk shoved into the farthest corner, his gray policeman's coat with its black buttons and velvet collar and star thrown over his chair. Though every window was propped open, Celia could hardly breathe for the appalling stench coming from the direction of the jail cells, guarded by a barred door. The stink likely explained why most of the room was empty.

Off to one side, a man argued with an officer, stammering on about not being involved in smuggling. At the nearest desk, another policeman glanced up, his eyes widening. She suspected it was not every day that a reasonably well-dressed woman found her way here.

"Ma'am?" he inquired, her wedding ring having been observed.

"I need to speak to an officer." She took a quick, small breath; the stink made her head swim. "About the Chinese girl discovered dead yesterday morning."

"Detective Greaves is busy."

Detective. If a detective was involved, Li Sha had not met with some sort of accident, as she'd hoped despite what the newspaper article had implied.

She felt light-headed. She should sit and collect herself. She reached for the nearest chair and collapsed onto it, a mound of crinoline and heavy skirts. The alleged smuggler stopped arguing to gawk.

The policeman jumped up. "Ma'am?"

"I shall be fine," she assured him.

"I'll fetch water anyhow," he said, and scurried off through a side door, leaving it ajar.

To ease light-headedness, she would advise a patient to put her head between her knees, but Celia's corset kept her as upright as if she had been strapped to the chair back. *Wretched cage.*

She breathed in carefully. She had fainted only once before, even through everything she had experienced in the army hospitals—the putrefying wounds, the hacked-off limbs, the sickness and disease that took as many as the damage caused by men's bullets and bayonets. Only once, and that had been when they had brought in Harry, her brother, delirious from fever. She must not faint now. They would never take her to see Li Sha if she fainted.

The policeman returned and thrust a chipped glass at her. "Here."

"Thank you, Officer . . ."

"Mullahey."

"Thank you, Officer Mullahey. I'm sorry to have alarmed you." Celia took a sip and handed back the glass. "So, might I see the detective?"

The officer scrunched his nose, which was crooked from a

long-ago break. "Detective Greaves don't take to bein' disturbed when he's interviewin' folks."

"In that case, is there someone else I might speak to?" When he hesitated, she sat taller and looked him straight in the face. "I shall wait here as long as is required."

"I kin tell."

"Then you have no reason not to permit me to speak with someone immediately."

The smuggler, eavesdropping, laughed aloud. His enjoyment of the spectacle she was making prompted a cuff on the shoulder from the constable beside him, which generated another argument.

"Hey, Taylor, you busy?" the officer called to the policeman smoking in the corner. "This here lady wants to talk to someone about that Chinese prostitute—"

"If the girl is who I think she is," Celia interrupted, "she was not a prostitute." Not any longer.

He smirked. "Anyways, Taylor, can you talk to her about that girl found on the wharf? While she waits for your boss. If'n he even agrees to meet with her."

Officer Taylor glanced over, his eyebrows lifting, and hastily stubbed out his cigar. He stood and pulled a second chair close to his desk. "Miss."

Celia crossed the room while Officer Mullahey went in search of the uninterruptible Detective Greaves. The smuggler lost his argument and was hauled off through the door with the barred window. The portal thudded shut behind him, settling the room into a sudden quiet.

"Not miss," she said. "Mrs. Davies."

"Sorry, ma'am." With a gentle smile, Officer Taylor waited until she seated herself to retake his chair. "So, you think you might know the girl who was found yesterday?"

"I would have to see the body, obviously, to be certain."

He went crimson, having the sort of pale skin that reddened easily. "Well, now, ma'am, that's a mighty unpleasant thing you're suggesting—"

"I have seen dead bodies before, Officer Taylor. More than you can imagine." She *must* see the girl they had found. "More than you likely have, unless you served during your war."

His blush spread across his face, and he jutted out his chin. The gesture made him look far younger than her own nine-and-twenty years. "I didn't have a chance to fight, but I would've if I could've."

"I am sorry. I did not mean to question your patriotism or your courage," she replied, regretting her brusqueness. "I still insist, however, on seeing the body. I must know whether or not it is Li Sha."

"A dead body isn't a sight for any lady," he said curtly, her apology rebuffed. "She was cut all over. It was awful."

Murdered?

"If she was murdered, then I absolutely insist on seeing the body. I must know."

"Detective Greaves won't—"

"I shall speak to him myself."

She stood and marched back across the station room, headed for the door through which Officer Mullahey had vanished.

"Ma'am!" Officer Taylor shouted. "Come back here!"

With one motion, Celia stepped over the threshold and plowed straight into a very solid chest.

$\mathcal{N}$ ick grabbed the woman's arms before she lost her balance. "I told you she was obstinate as all get-out," said Mullahey from within the office.

"I see that."

"You may let go," the woman said, her voice as cultured and smooth as English cream. The impact with his chest had dislodged her bonnet, which tilted on her honey-colored hair.

She had even features and was as pretty as Mullahey had also claimed. She smelled good, too, fresh with the scent of strong soap and lavender, though any scent was better than the station's reek. The beat police, who worked out of their homes, were lucky they hardly ever had to come here.

And her eyes . . . well, they were a gray-blue like the sheen of ice on a winter's lake. About as damned lovely as any eyes he'd ever seen.

"I am Detective Nicholas Greaves," he said. "I understand from Officer Mullahey you wanted to speak to me about the Chinese woman who was found yesterday morning."

"I do." Those eyes lowered to look at his hands, still gripped around her arms. "And you may release your clutch on me, Detective."

"Excuse me, miss," he said, letting go.

"Mrs. Davies," she corrected, and brushed her hands down the sleeves of her jacket. A wedding band glinted on her left hand.

"So, whatever you've got to say about that girl, I'm listening, Mrs. Davies."

Inside the detectives' office, Wagner got up from the chair. "Can I go now?"

"Mullahey, get him out of here." The man had stuck to his story, despite Nick's attempts to force him to confess.

Mullahey complied, dragging the man toward Mrs. Davies, whose wide skirts were blocking the aisle. She moved aside.

"I must see her." Mrs. Davies felt for her bonnet and rearranged it upon her head. One tendril escaped her efforts to contain her hair, and the strand quivered against her cheek. He didn't suggest she fix it. "I must know if it is my friend who has been murdered."

"That isn't possible."

Taylor had come to stand nearby and was shaking his head. "She'll insist," he murmured.

"Thank you, Taylor." Nick focused on Mrs. Davies. Definitely very pretty. "Let me describe her for you. She was wearing a dark blue dress and—"

"And had black hair and Chinese features, I do suppose?"

Her superior-sounding accent made her sarcasm all the more pointed. "Mrs. Davies—"

"I know you must think me forward to come here and make these demands," she interrupted again. "But I have to see the body. Li Sha was a close friend, and I feel responsible for her."

"I am not taking you to view the body, ma'am."

"If you will not take me to her, then I shall go and speak to the coroner and have him show me," she said. "I am no delicate creature who will faint at the sight, if that is what you are worried about."

"I might've been having thoughts along those lines."

"Then I have reassured you."

She squared her shoulders, calling to mind all of his dead sister's fierce determination, puncturing his resolve.

"All right," he conceded, startling Taylor, whose brows leapt up his forehead. "I'll take you to the undertaker's where the body has been stored for the coroner."

He reached for her arm again, but she evaded his grasp. "I can make my way upstairs on my own, Mr. Greaves."

To prove it, she nodded to Taylor and started for the stairs.

"We can use . . ." *Never mind telling her to use the side door out into the alley.* She was already halfway up the other steps, her back as flat as a board and her skirts swishing as she moved quickly out of sight. Delicate? She was as delicate as a chunk of granite.

Watch yourself, Nick.

"If the captain asks where I am, Taylor, tell him I'm with the coroner." Grabbing his hat off the rack just inside the doorway, he bounded after her.

She felt a fool.

Celia bolted across the foyer of city hall, startling a clerk carrying an armful of papers, and burst through the front doors. She pressed a hand to her side and gulped in air. She had been unnerved by a handsome detective whose every finger she could still feel upon her arms and had let her response vex her into rudeness.

Such a fool.

"Oh, Celia, do calm down," she grumbled, slowing to take the few steps down to street level.

"Celia? What a fine name."

It was that detective, the uninterruptible one with the spaniel brown eyes, his hair a thick sable wave. She wanted to touch it. That was what she had been thinking while his hands had clutched her arms. She wanted to touch that gorgeous hair.

"Do you always sneak up on ladies?" she asked, lifting her chin to hide her embarrassment at having been caught talking to herself.

"Not always." With a slow scan of the street around them—was he always watchful? she wondered—he joined her on the pavement.

"Just sometimes," she said.

"If the need arises," he responded.

A tall man, he looked down at her. His eyes, shaded by the brim of his clove brown flat-crowned hat, did not blink. He must intimidate criminals with that gaze. It strayed to the bit of hair trailing down her face, and she stuffed the errant strand back into the chignon at the nape of her neck.

"I was named after my mother," she explained. Cecilia Eglinton Walford. Her mother's name was one of the few things she remembered about the woman, a blurry face and form from her childhood.

"Celia is not a common name," said Mr. Greaves. "Short for Cecilia, I'd guess?"

"You guess correctly, Detective," she said, "but even in America, only my closest friends address me as Celia."

"I might be an uncouth American, Mrs. Davies, but I don't make a habit of calling ladies by their first names," he said. "Are you ready to go to the undertaker's or have you changed your mind?"

"I intend to go. Stubborn as a government mule, is that not what you Americans say?"

One corner of his mouth quirked. "Only a blind man would compare you to a mule."

Leaving her dumbstruck, he stepped out smartly, heading south to where the buildings closed in about the road, their awnings stretching over the pavement. She hurried to match his pace, her boot heels rapping against the planks. He walked so rapidly she feared they would crash into the customers and businessmen crowding the walkway.

"Whereabouts in England are you from?" he asked, not the first query she had anticipated from him. Perhaps he intended to distract her from the task that loomed ahead.

"Do you know the regions of England?"

"I might. Try me."

"Hertfordshire."

"Hmm. Can't say I've heard of that one," he admitted, not slowing his pace. A pair of Jewish men in long beards and sober black clothes, busy discussing commerce, were forced to hop out of their path.

"It is a lovely area," she said. "You should visit sometime."

He laughed. "Don't see that ever happening."

So many years had passed since Celia had seen Hertfordshire's gentle hills dotted with sheep, the hedgerows and low stone walls, bluebells in the woods, the sparkle of sunlight upon winding streams. So many years since she'd heard her father's rumbling laughter, smelled her mother's delicate perfume, been the brunt of Harry's quick wit. Now they were gone.

All of them, gone.

"Bad memories?" Mr. Greaves asked, sounding sympathetic. She questioned what she had allowed to show on her face. The pain, perhaps. The loss.

"Many good memories, actually," she replied.

"What brought you to America?"

"My . . ." She hesitated. "My husband, Patrick Davies. He thought we would do better here than in England."

Patrick had been encouraged by his brother to take advantage of the "wonders of America," and she hadn't protested his plans; she had been too eager to leave the past behind.

"Every immigrant's story," Mr. Greaves said.

"I suppose it is," she said. "Patrick ended up serving during your civil war. My husband is Irish, and he responded to the placards seeking recruits from Ireland that plastered virtually every light pole in Philadelphia, where we first moved upon arriving from England. Perhaps the U.S. Army was right about the Irish making good soldiers, because Patrick always did enjoy a fight, and he signed on."

"There isn't a fight going on in San Francisco that I'm aware of," Mr. Greaves said, a trifle sarcastically. "Other than the usual scrapes in the Barbary or down by the docks."

"My husband's interest in the war did not last beyond the time he'd volunteered to serve. Patrick developed gold fever, collected me in Philadelphia, and we came to California three years ago to make our fortune."

He peered at her. "The gold rush is mostly finished, too."

"San Francisco is the proverbial 'land of plenty,' Mr. Greaves. This city bustles with growth and the chance of prosperity." The din of a milk wagon rattling across uneven cobblestones, the cry of a corner huckster proclaiming the healing powers of sarsaparilla, and the pounding of hammers emphasized her point. "The idea of going west and striking it rich appealed to Patrick. Besides, his younger brother was already here."

She frowned as she thought of Tom and his relationship with Li Sha; her death touched too close to home for many reasons.

"Patrick was a restless sort who hated to stay in one place for long," she added. "However, settling in San Francisco did not satisfy him either. Within a few months of our arrival, he took to the sea, finding work on various merchant vessels." He'd been eager to get away. From her.

"You don't seem like a woman who would care for a restless sort, ma'am."

"You do not know me, Detective."

He was watching her closely; she could feel his gaze on her face. She did not care to explain that Patrick had provided her with a reason to awake every morning when, after Harry's death, she'd been far too willing not to bother. She could readily describe the precise shade of her husband's weary blue eyes, the pitch and timbre of his voice, the feel of his fingertips against her warm skin at night. She could recite the exact words she had been unable to speak, the ones he had needed to hear to keep him content. It was far too late to wish both she and Patrick had been less blind to the mistake they were making by marrying; far too late to wish that the hot flush of passion that had once fused them together had not turned to ash.

Far too late to wish she had not been so troublesome, so easy to leave.

They crossed an intersection, dodging carts and runnels of sewage. Detective Greaves took her elbow to help her onto the curb. "Restless or not, your sailor husband shouldn't have let you come to the police station alone. Unless he's off on a boat right now."

"It is a more permanent absence than that, Mr. Greaves," Celia replied stiffly. "He is believed perished off the coast of Mazatlán in a steamer accident."

Mr. Greaves paused, his fingers on her elbow contracting. "My deepest apologies, ma'am."

"However, I'm not certain he is deceased," she said, a knot hard in her chest. "I hired a man to locate him, and he is the one who learned of the accident, which occurred last summer. Apparently, the boiler exploded," she explained, telling the detective more than she had intended. "However, Patrick's name was not on the shipping company's official logs, and his body was not among those recovered."

Leaving her not quite a wife, not quite a widow.

The detective glanced over. Whatever he thought was concealed in his unreadable expression.

"So he might return one day," he said, releasing his hold on her arm.

Like a resurrected Lazarus. Or a bad dream. "It is possible, though unlikely. Nonetheless, I wish to be absolutely certain."

"Until then, you're managing on your own?"

Celia halted. "Detective Greaves, I question how this conversation is relevant to your investigation."

"I'm simply curious, Mrs. Davies. It goes with the job."

"Does it, now."

"Yes, ma'am."

She turned on her heel and continued walking. "I have a small inheritance and am gainfully occupied. I am a trained nurse and run a free medical clinic for females who cannot afford regular care or who have been turned away from hospitals."

"I take it your clinic work is how you meet Chinese girls with whom most ladies would have nothing to do."

She shot him a glance. "I would have to own a very hard heart to ignore their plight, Mr. Greaves."

"I don't know about that, Mrs. Davies. Plenty of others ignore their plight and seem to get along just fine with the condition of their hearts."

They turned toward the harbor, which was bobbing with tall-masted ships and smoke-belching steamers, away from the hills that rose at their backs. The detective stopped before a two-story corner building, its stone facade lined with columns and large windows.

Clasping her bonnet, Celia tilted her head to read the massive sign overhead. ATKINS MASSEY'S COFFIN WAREROOMS.

"We don't have a city morgue. The coroner complains regularly," he explained, pausing to look at her before he opened the door. "It isn't too late to turn back, Mrs. Davies."

"If the girl is indeed Li Sha and she has been murdered, I cannot turn back. For her sake. And for the sake of justice."

His expression shifted unexpectedly to one of admiration, eliciting her surprise. It had been years since any man had admired her, at least in a way that mattered. The shock, the pleasure of his regard, must have registered on her face, for he smiled. Briefly.

"After you, Mrs. Davies," he said, extending his hand.

CHAPTER 3

Inside the coffin warehouse, the noise from the street was muted, and curtains drawn over the windows held back the sunshine as if it had no right to enter such a somber place. Nick dragged his hat from his head and closed the front door behind him, the shop bell's chime disturbing the hush.

He didn't immediately follow Mrs. Davies as she strode forward between the rows of caskets. He had gone too far, asking about her husband, but it interested him that she'd shed no grief-stricken tears over the fellow. Nick reminded himself that her feelings for her husband, whether he was alive or dead, were irrelevant. After she viewed the body, he'd gather some information from her and put the widow who might not be a widow out of his mind.

She looked over her shoulder with her lovely ice gray eyes—eyes that could pin him to the spot. He couldn't afford, however, to be fascinated by somebody connected to a murder investigation.

The undertaker, Atkins Massey, hurried from the back room to greet them, the tails of his frock coat flapping against his legs.

"So sorry to be delayed, Detective Greaves!" Massey swiped a pongee silk handkerchief across his mouth, then stuffed the handkerchief into a pocket. He bowed over Mrs. Davies' fingers, his muttonchop whiskers brushing her skin. "Have you brought a"—his gaze swept over her—"a person who has affection for that sad girl?"

"Mrs. Davies is here to view the body but not to pick out coffins, if that's the direction your thoughts are heading, Mr. Massey."

"If the girl is Li Sha," she said, "I intend to pay for a coffin as well as obtain a space for her at Lone Mountain Cemetery."

"In that case, we have an excellent selection to choose from. We can even provide the latest in metallic caskets, if you so wish." Arms spread wide, the undertaker pointed out the caskets on display, their varnish gleaming.

"Mrs. Davies can deal with caskets later, if that proves necessary," said Nick. "Is the coroner here?"

"Dr. Harris is conducting a postmortem, Detective Greaves." His attention shifted to Mrs. Davies. "Such a dreadful business. If you require smelling salts, I am at your service."

She looked offended by the suggestion. "That will not be necessary, Mr. Massey."

"I'll be right back, Mrs. Davies," said Nick.

He headed for the rear ground-floor area where the undertaker tended to those without kin—a large portion of men in this town—or those who'd died of contagious diseases. Everybody else would be looked after by their families in their own homes.

The coroner was at work in the room he borrowed to conduct

postmortem examinations. Bowls, jars, and medical instruments glinted on shelves, and the astringent tang of disinfectant drifted on the air. Pairs of scales and glass beakers and a brass microscope stood on a bench against the far wall, the tools of the man's trade. The law didn't require that the coroner be a doctor. In fact he could be anybody who ran for the office, so long as the public voted him in. But Harris was a physician and a good one, and the city was lucky to have him.

Harris was bent over the corpse of a balding male whose purplish feet protruded from beneath a cloth. Fortunately, the coroner's body blocked the view that might have revealed exactly what he was doing. In his lifetime, Nick had seen plenty of torn flesh and spilled guts, but autopsies always raised his gorge.

"Dr. Harris," he said, drawing the man's attention from the corpse. A large incision in the man's torso was hastily covered. They must have examined Meg like this after they'd found her. It was the thought Nick had every time he saw Harris at work. A thought he wished he could strike from his brain.

"Detective Greaves," the coroner said with a smile. "You must be here about that Chinese girl."

"I've brought someone who might be able to identify her."

"Good. The inquest is this afternoon, and I'd like to have a name for the paperwork." Harris dropped his scalpel into a nearby bowl, then rinsed his hands in another. He wiped them across the clean corner of the bloodied apron tied over his clothes. "Brought in as a drowning victim," he said, noting that Nick was staring at the male corpse. "Second one this week. Looks to be an accident. Considering the state of his liver, I'd say he was drunk as a loon when he fell into the bay."

Harris strode across the room and past Nick, shutting the

door to the sights within. "So who have you brought? The brothel owner?"

"A nurse who runs a medical clinic for poor women. She sometimes treats the Chinese."

"Ah." Harris dragged his fingertips through his beard, which was bristling with gray, and chuckled. "Mrs. Davies, is it?"

"I was hoping you'd know her."

"Know *of* her is more like it."

"And what do you know?"

"Well, she's been in San Francisco for only a few years—"

"Three, she told me," Nick interrupted.

"Sounds right," said Harris. "Her clinic's just outside the Barbary, and I gather she served in the Crimea and in an army hospital back east during the war, not sure which one. And I believe she trained at the Female Medical College in Philadelphia, very solid credentials. Lives with a half-Chinese girl—the daughter of a deceased gold miner, I hear, and some sort of relative." He scratched at his beard. "I've also heard that her passion for her female patients has led to plenty of disputes with some of the physicians in town. Personally, I've never had the pleasure of meeting Mrs. Davies. Doctors' wives can be"—he paused, his smile apologetic—"particular in who they invite to social events."

"Because she's had disputes with the local physicians, or because she has a half-Chinese relative?"

"Both, I suppose," he admitted. "And her tendency toward bluntness does her no favors."

Blunt and stubborn. A perfect description. "Mind if we take a look at the girl now?"

"She's in the basement. There's no one else down there at

the moment, so you don't have to worry about Mrs. Davies seeing too much."

Before Nick could leave, Harris stopped him. "What's Eagan got to say about this? I'm surprised he's letting any of his detectives spend time on this case."

"What my boss doesn't know won't hurt him," answered Nick.

Harris chuckled again, and Nick returned to the main room. Massey had made use of Nick's absence to show Mrs. Davies his array of funerary trappings—black plumes to decorate the hearse and the horses that drew it, swaths of ebony cloth for draping over caskets or wagons or just about anything, velvet if a person wanted extra luxury. Extravagances meant to awe the living, because they certainly wouldn't impress the dead.

"Mrs. Davies, please come with me," said Nick.

"Excuse me, Mr. Massey." She accompanied Nick to the basement stairs, gripping the railing as she descended. It was cold down here, perfect for slowing decay, and gloomy. Spare caskets were propped against one of the walls, and a floor-to-ceiling curtain blocked off the area where bodies awaiting identification were kept. The smell of death filled every corner, seeped out of every stone. This was no place for a lady, even one with as much grit as Celia Davies.

She paused at the bottom step. "Where to now, Mr. Greaves?"

"Back here."

He parted the curtain. Daylight coming through a set of windows illuminated the three marble slabs that occupied the space. The girl had been laid upon the center one, a length of dark fabric draped over her body.

Mrs. Davies stepped slowly forward. Nick peeled back the cloth, just enough to reveal the girl's face with all its bruises, along with the abrasion that traced a pink line across her neck.

"Yes." She nodded. "That is Li Sha."

"Thank you." Nick flicked the fabric back into place too hastily, accidentally revealing the girl's right arm and the lacerations that had torn the skin.

"Sliced by a bayonet?" Mrs. Davies clapped a hand to her mouth.

He grabbed the cloth and re-covered the body. "Let's get you out of here."

Nick led her up the stairs and past Massey, who was clutching a bottle of smelling salts. "Mrs. Davies?" He unstoppered the bottle and waved it beneath her nose.

"I am perfectly fine."

"She'll select a coffin some other time, Mr. Massey," said Nick, refusing to release this woman, fragrant with lavender and strong soap, who felt too right pressed against his side. "And tell Dr. Harris the girl's name is Li Sha."

"I appreciate your assistance, Mr. Greaves," Celia said, disregarding the gawkers passing by as she braced a hand against the nearest telegraph pole, her reticule swinging from her wrist. Until the last moment, she had hoped the police were wrong, hoped she would walk into that cold room and see a different unfortunate girl lying dead. But the body on that slab was Li Sha, the even planes of her lovely face unmistakable though puffy and bruised, the swell of her abdomen holding an unfulfilled promise of new life. How Li Sha had looked forward to becoming a mother.

"You must think I am forever dashing out of buildings for one reason or another, Detective," said Celia.

His mouth twitched with a smile, bringing warmth to his eyes. Though his curt disposition rubbed her raw, she could not deny he was handsome.

"Twice isn't enough for me to draw a conclusion, Mrs. Davies." The hat brim took a turn through Mr. Greaves' fingers, and he squinted against the sunlight. "Would you care to sit down? There's a decent coffeehouse nearby."

She was grateful for the suggestion; answering questions in a coffeehouse would be preferable to doing so in the fetid air of the police station.

"I'd enjoy some coffee, yes, Mr. Greaves. And a sandwich, if they offer food. I should try to eat." Though her hunger had vanished in the coroner's makeshift morgue. "However, I shall not permit you to pay my bill."

He tapped his hat upon his head. "Didn't think you would."

As promised, the coffeehouse was not far. Given the reception he received from the owner, the detective must be a regular customer. Though she preferred tea, the coffee brewing smelled heavenly as they wended their way between tables. There were only a handful of other customers—all male—and plenty of empty seats, but Mr. Greaves chose a table beside the large front window where they could be readily seen. Protecting her reputation, she presumed.

He held her chair as she took a seat. He made a quick scan of the room before settling across from her, facing the door. He was ever watchful, indeed.

They placed their orders, and his expression became sympathetic. "I'm sorry about the girl, Mrs. Davies. Not the way anybody's life should come to an end."

His sentiment did not seem contrived, though Celia expected he'd had to extend similar words to sorrowing families and friends many times before.

"'Tired he sleeps, and life's poor play is o'er,'" she said sadly. "Although in this case, it's a *she*."

"Is that some sort of quote?" he asked.

"Alexander Pope, Mr. Greaves," she said. "Poor Li Sha. A difficult life come to a terrible conclusion. I did not, however, anticipate slashing wounds from a bayonet."

"What makes you think they were bayonet wounds? Harris often reminds me how tough it is to tell what sort of blade has caused a cut on a body."

She considered his observation. "Perhaps I see them where there are none, Detective. A consequence of months spent in army hospitals."

"I am familiar with bayonet wounds, too. I volunteered in an Ohio regiment." Detective Greaves rubbed a spot above his left elbow, then flexed his hand as if testing its ability to function. He noticed the direction of her gaze. "Old war wound." He dropped his hand to the table. "Saw more killing than anybody should have to witness. We all did."

"War is never as grand as it reads in the papers, Mr. Greaves."

"In that we agree, ma'am."

His steady brown eyes watched her without further comment, and she looked away, out the window at the pedestrians and the traffic. A curly-tailed mongrel snuffled at the gutter, and a sunburned boy called out, "Po-ta-toes," at the top of his lungs, competing with the shouts of a particularly dirty fellow in a shabby jacket trying to sell old rags and patched boots. Across the way, a black-haired woman in an indigo dress hurried along the pavement, and Celia momentarily thought she looked familiar. But it was a trick of the mind, and she was forced to recall that Li Sha was gone.

"Officer Mullahey called Li Sha a prostitute," she said, returning her gaze to the detective's face. The coffeehouse was considerably more quiet than the din outside, the volume of conversation having fallen when they entered. She suspected they were being stared at. "She had been, at one time, although not a common one. Because she was unusually lovely, and could sing and play the Chinese two-stringed fiddle, she worked in a parlor house as a concubine."

"A parlor house." Mr. Greaves lifted an eyebrow. "Nicer than the usual cribs."

"It is a discreet establishment and enjoys, I've been told, a higher class of clientele than the stews of China Alley. Rich white men, even." Men who could indulge their taste for the exotic without dirtying their shoes in the worst parts of the Barbary and the Chinese streets.

"But she still wore face paint," Mr. Greaves observed.

"Her one vanity."

"How exactly did you meet her?"

"She was my first Chinese patient. It was last autumn— September, if I am not mistaken—shortly before she stopped working at the parlor house. An abusive customer had injured her, broken a rib, and some of her wounds had festered, though she had attempted to heal them with traditional Chinese medicines. I treated her as best I could and she recovered. But after that assault, she resolved to escape the life she was leading."

Coffee and a ham sandwich arrived, delivered by the proprietor himself, a robust man with an Eastern European accent who lingered too long at the table, until Mr. Greaves frowned at him. Celia gripped her cup, letting it warm her fingers, and resumed speaking.

"Eventually, Li Sha earned enough from selling the gifts customers had given her to pay her way out of her contract. She was one of the fortunate ones, to be able to do so." Celia sipped some of the bitter coffee. "After she left the parlor house, she came to me, seeking help. I was more than happy to do all I could. I considered taking her into our house, but I had to make allowances for my cousin Barbara. She can be anxious around people who are not family, and I also have her reputation to protect."

"The half-Chinese girl you live with is your cousin?" Detective Greaves asked, interrupting. At least she did not see in his eyes the bigotry she so typically encountered in others'.

"You have very quickly gathered information about me, Mr. Greaves."

He gave a slight nod. "And your uncle was a gold miner."

"That he was." Celia smiled. Gregarious, adventurous Uncle Walford. So different from her cautious father. "Sadly, he passed away two summers ago, leaving my cousin an orphan. Her mother, a Chinese woman my uncle had met in a mining camp, had died when Barbara was a child. Barbara was left alone in that big house she'd inherited. She was too young to be on her own, and as her nearest relative, I was appointed her guardian.

"Acquaintances suggested that I send her to a boarding school, but she wouldn't have been happy there. Attending school had never been a good experience for her." Uncle Walford had once attempted to send Barbara to a public school in the city; when she was jeered at and tormented by the other students, she'd been hastily removed. "With her father's encouragement, I had already established my clinic in her house. Taking up residence there, I confess, made my life a great deal easier."

Celia paused to take a bite of the sandwich. It was good, and she was surprised by the return of her appetite. The detective used the break in conversation to scan the room.

He reached inside his coat and extracted a notebook. "When did you last see Li Sha?"

"Wednesday of last week, when she came for dinner, as she often did. She seemed her usual self that day."

"Did you give her the dress she was wearing? You don't usually see Chinese women in Western clothes."

"I did. She wanted to blend in better, and she thought people might stare less if she dressed like everyone else." Li Sha had been so pleased with Celia's present, even though the gown was far too big. She had wanted to conceal the pregnancy for a while and had rebuffed Celia's offers to have the dress properly altered. "I believe people stared more."

He took additional notes, then paused to consider her. "After she left the parlor house, what did she do? A Chinese woman alone would live mighty precariously."

"I tried to find her work, but it was difficult. People in this city might hire Chinese men, but they do not hire Chinese women," said Celia. "I finally did find her a position with my apothecary, Hubert Lange. A good man doing a great favor for me."

"Must have been a pretty big favor, to hire a former prostitute."

"Some time ago, I saved him from a serious scandal. One of his customers fell ill, terribly ill, from a concoction he was selling. It nearly killed the woman, but I nursed her back to health. Mr. Lange has been grateful ever since." And she had taken advantage of that gratitude. He had been good to Li Sha, though, and she had given him no reason to complain about her work or her conduct.

"Li Sha cleaned his shop a few evenings a week," continued Celia. "After the shop had closed, when there were no customers to see her. Nonetheless, the situation was not easy for her. I believe people were harrying her in the streets, provoked by the audacity of a Chinese woman venturing outside the boundaries of Chinatown."

"Any particular threats you know of?"

"None at all."

Someone in the coffeehouse dropped a piece of cutlery, the clank jarring the hushed quiet. The proprietor was attempting to move within earshot again, wiping down tables located progressively nearer to the one where she and Mr. Greaves sat.

"Any idea who might be responsible for her death, Mrs. Davies?" the detective asked.

"A member of the Anti-Coolie Association?" she offered.

He didn't blink at the suggestion; it was not such a foolish idea, then.

"I'd considered them myself," he said. "Even though I can't really see the men who rioted a few weeks back bothering with a prostitute."

"Perhaps they were the ones who'd been harrying her, though." Celia recalled the man on the street who'd glared at Barbara after the meeting Monday night. Would her cousin have been attacked if she'd been alone? "It has to be someone from the Anti-Coolie Association, doesn't it? They're whipping up so much hatred against the Chinese that even my cousin has felt it."

"I don't know, ma'am," he said, "but I'll find out."

"Thank you."

"I'd like to start by talking to anybody who knew Li Sha," he said. "Anyone who might know what happened in her final days. Where was she living?"

"Sometimes she stayed at the Chinese Mission, although she did not like it there. But usually she stayed with Tom."

"Tom?"

"The father of the child she was carrying," Celia answered. "But Tom would never have done this."

"I'll determine that," Mr. Greaves said. "What is Tom's full name, and where can I find him?"

The pencil hovered over Nicholas Greaves' notebook. Celia felt a chill, one that no amount of gripping her coffee cup would warm. "His full name is Tom Davies." She paused. "He is my brother-in-law."

$\mathcal{N}$ick set down his pencil. "You could've told me earlier that Li Sha had been living with a member of your family, Mrs. Davies."

Her eyes had taken on a definite coolness. "He is a member of my husband's family."

Not her family, but her husband's. A distinction that suggested just how well she and Tom Davies got along.

"You've got to admit it looks suspicious that you've been keeping his name from me." He peered at her. Off to their left, the man who owned the coffeehouse was inching close again. "Care to come up with a different answer to who you think might have killed Li Sha?"

Mrs. Davies' cup clinked against the saucer as she set it down. "Just because we are not fast friends does not make Tom a killer. He cared for Li Sha. That much I know about him. He wouldn't hurt her or their child."

"So he wasn't the abusive customer who injured her last summer? Or the man who caused those recent bruises on her face?"

"In the few months they have been together, I have never known him to hit Li Sha."

"Somebody did," Nick said, "and not all that long ago."

Her gaze flickered; apparently she hadn't pondered who'd given the girl the bruises before now. Willful ignorance, maybe.

"I'll have to question him," Nick added.

"Please don't interview Tom without me there," she said. "I owe it to my husband to support his brother as best I can. And I expect Tom will be devastated to hear Li Sha has died. He intended to marry her."

"Men may use these women, Mrs. Davies. They may even believe that they're in love with them. But they never marry them."

"That is not always true."

She had to be thinking of her uncle and the Chinese woman who'd given him a daughter. So they'd married, then. Would've had to, in order for the girl to have inherited the house. But a personal example hardly meant that vague promises by her brother-in-law could be trusted.

"Nonetheless," Nick said, "love can easily turn to jealousy, and jealousy is a powerful—and sometimes violent—emotion."

"What or whom would Tom possibly be jealous of?"

"Perhaps she'd found another man or had threatened to take the baby away. Whatever the reason, I'll find that out, too." Standing, he retrieved coins from a vest pocket and dropped them onto the table. "That ought to cover my part of the bill." He hadn't even touched his coffee.

"Are you going to Tom's right now?"

"I have an investigation to conduct, Mrs. Davies," he said, restoring the notebook to his pocket.

She scrambled to her feet. "You are not going to be rid of me so easily, Mr. Greaves. I intend to be with you when you talk to my brother-in-law, because I will not let you coerce him into some sort of confused confession."

He clenched his jaw. She was too stubborn for her own good. "I'm not giving in this time."

"You cannot stop me from following you. I have made Tom a suspect, and I feel answerable to what might happen as a result."

"And I'll have Taylor arrest you for interfering with an investigation."

"Be practical. Tom will more readily speak to me than to you, as will anyone else who knew Li Sha. Especially if you are considering questioning any of her Chinese acquaintances. I truly did mean what I said about wanting to see justice served, proper justice, and for that to occur I'm convinced you need my help."

He stared at her long and hard. She didn't budge.

"Have I told you yet that you remind me of my little sister?" he said.

"I am trying to imagine you with a younger sister, Mr. Greaves. You must be very protective of her."

"I was," he answered, all the pain of Meg's death as fresh as if he'd received the news yesterday rather than almost three years ago. "Once."

"I am so sorry. I did not realize . . . ," she stammered.

He stepped around her, bound for the door. When she did not immediately make a move to follow, he glanced over his shoulder. "I thought you were coming."

She rummaged through her reticule, left money on the table, and hastened to his side. "You will not be sorry."

"I sure hope not, Mrs. Davies," he said, frowning. "I sure hope not."

CHAPTER 4

"I'll not be believin' she's dead." Tom Davies was defiant. "You're wrong."

Mrs. Davies, seated on a chair across the table from her brother-in-law, slid Nick an uneasy glance. If she suspected he already disliked the man, she was right; Tom Davies was a hot-headed Irishman.

Standing in the shadowed corner of the man's rented room, Nick shifted his weight to the other foot and waited. Davies would eventually calm down enough to be interviewed. Until then, he'd let Mrs. Davies offer condolences, because Nick never did anymore. The consequences from the one time he'd assumed a suspect's innocence when he was a green police officer had eliminated any temptation to make the same mistake twice.

"The detective is not wrong, Tom. I'm sorry."

Davies scowled. He was good-looking in a rough-around-the-edges sort of way, well muscled for a clerk with a desk job. Though it was probably good-paying work, Davies couldn't claim to own many furnishings—just a table, a few chairs, and an oil stove in the opposite corner, a small chest of drawers, a trunk. A folding partition screened off the farthest corner. Dust covered every surface, and a slick of grime blackened the baseboards. If Li Sha had lived here, she hadn't been cleaning Davies' room or leaving feminine touches behind.

The room's two dirty windows were closed tight. Tom Davies lived south of Market, near Tar Flat, which meant breathing the stench from the Donahues' gasworks. Distilling coal into gas produced sludge, and the sludge was piling up thick to the east of the works, exuding stink into the air. Some folks thought the fumes cured lung ailments. Nick was pretty sure the fumes would eventually kill a body.

He shifted his weight again and noticed a stain on the tattered rag rug. It might be from spilled coffee or something else. However, Davies' lodgings were more than a mile from the wharf where Li Sha had been found. If she'd been killed here, that was a long way to haul a body without any means of transportation.

"But I know you're wrong about it bein' her," Davies insisted, and stood. "So thanks for finally comin' to visit, Celia, but you can leave now."

"Sit down, Mr. Davies," said Nick. To his surprise, the man complied. "Mrs. Davies, tell him once more."

"Tom, the Chinese girl who was found in the bay is indeed Li Sha. I saw her body only a couple of hours ago."

Davies' shoulders sagged. "You're wrong," he repeated, but the fight had gone out of him.

Nick stepped farther into the room. He'd commit Davies' responses to memory. With a suspect this jumpy, pulling out his notebook might make the man less willing to talk. "Were you with Li Sha two nights ago?" he asked.

"I wasn't." Davies' gaze leaped between them. "Wait. Why are you askin' me that? You think I'd kill her?"

"No," Mrs. Davies denied it, stretching fingers across the scarred wood surface to touch his hand. "Of course not."

"But *he* does!" Davies accused, pointing at Nick. The man's biceps tensed within his white shirtsleeves. When they'd arrived at the boardinghouse, Davies had just come home from his clerking job and was down to his vest, black neckcloth untied, dark jacket hung on a hook by the door. There was an ink stain on his left cuff, but no old blood that Nick could see. Davies might have two or three shirts, though. "And you think it, too. Don't you, Celia?"

She withdrew her hand. "Tom, please simply answer the detective's questions, so that he can discover who did hurt Li Sha."

Davies slumped into his chair.

Nick asked, "When was the last time you saw Li Sha?"

"A few days past. A week, maybe." He shrugged. "I don't recall."

"I thought she lived here. That the two of you were . . . close." His intentional pause was loaded with meaning.

Davies' eyes narrowed. "I loved her. Maybe that's hard for you to understand."

It wasn't hard at all; he'd once loved where he shouldn't have. "Where was she staying, then, if she hadn't been here? At the Chinese Mission?"

"I don't know where she'd gone to."

To the person who'd killed her?

"Tom, when you did see her last, did Li Sha seem all right?" asked Mrs. Davies.

Nick sighed. "Mrs. Davies, can you let me ask the questions? It is my job." He'd allowed clear, pale eyes and hair that shone like gold in the sunlight to make him foolhardy. He should've sent her home and had Taylor stand guard to keep her out of here, in case she got the idea to show up anyway.

"My apologies, Mr. Greaves."

Her brother-in-law answered her question. "Li Sha was fine when I saw her last."

"Where were you Monday evening?" Nick asked.

"I was at Mitchell's place that night," he answered. "The saloon around the corner."

Mrs. Davies cast Nick another uneasy glance, but she didn't need to worry about Davies' admission. If Nick came to suspect every man who spent his evenings drinking in saloons, he would have to arrest half the town.

"Will anybody remember seeing you at Mitchell's that evening?"

"See? He is thinkin' I killed her. That's why you brought him here, ain't it, Celia? Patrick was right about you. You're a hard woman."

She flushed and dropped her gaze.

"Tell me about that evening, Mr. Davies," said Nick.

Davies looked at him. "I'm not goin' to Mitchell's often. Just an occasional night here or there, you see? A lot of the fellows were drunker than me. One of them bought me a whiskey. Felt sorry for me. But I'm not recallin' who, exactly."

"Why'd he feel sorry for you?"

Davies didn't answer, glancing over at his sister-in-law, whose lips were pressed into a thin, pink line.

Nick made a stab at a probable reason. "Did you think Li Sha had left you and that was why you hadn't seen her for days?"

"I don't know!"

He'd guessed correctly, then. "And you were jealous and angry and went looking for her. Things got out of hand—"

"That's not what happened at all!" A quiver rippled through Davies' body, and he clenched his fists. Nick tried to imagine them clutching a knife in anger. It wouldn't take much for a man of Davies' size to kill a tiny woman. "I loved her, and I wanted her here with me. She was gonna have our baby. I wanted to raise it right."

"You sure the baby was yours?" Nick asked, ignoring the disapproval that flashed across Celia Davies' face.

"Did you tell him it wasn't, Celia?"

"No, Tom." She turned to Nick. "Haven't you learned enough, Mr. Greaves? I will vouch for my brother-in-law's character, if that is what is required."

She intended to vouch for the character of a man she rarely saw. A man who didn't seem to like her.

"So you believed Li Sha's claim that you were the father?" he asked Davies. "You're telling me you don't think she'd been with another man. A man who might have killed her."

"It was *my* baby." He swallowed. "If it was a girl, we were gonna name her Katie. After me ma. She woulda been mine. Me little girl . . ." His voice broke, and he began to sob.

Nick felt pity despite his wish not to. What a god-awful business he'd chosen to be in, following in Uncle Asa's footsteps. His uncle never would've felt pity for a suspect. "What about the bruises on her face? Did you give her those?"

"Must you, Mr. Greaves?" Mrs. Davies accused. "Can you

not cease the questions? Tom is too upset to go on, and clearly not responsible for her death."

The world was not that black or white to him, and nothing about this case was clear. Yet. "I thought you wanted justice for Li Sha. That's all I'm aiming to achieve."

"Of course I want justice." She stood and rested a protective hand on Tom Davies' shoulder. "I also want a measure of compassion."

"I can't afford compassion during a murder investigation, Mrs. Davies," Nick replied, and turned back to Davies. "I need an answer. Did you give Li Sha the bruises on her face?"

"Honestly," Mrs. Davies protested.

"I didn't." The man dragged a hand over his pasty face and looked up. "I would never kill her. I loved her."

As though professed love kept men from killing their women. "So, you were drinking at Mitchell's all evening. What did you do afterward?"

"Came home. Fell asleep. Woke up late for work the next mornin'."

And no one could confirm or deny his whereabouts. "Can I look around a little before we leave?"

"You'll be doin' it whether I say yes or no," answered Davies.

Behind the partition was a narrow bed covered by a patchwork quilt, a washbasin and mirror with a crack in the glass, a lidded chamber pot painted with roses, and a narrow chest of drawers, a pair of muddy boots tucked beside it. A second white shirt, the left cuff also smudged with ink, hung on the wall. Another rag rug much like the one by the table lay next to the bed. Nick pushed it aside with his toe to see if the rug hid any bloodstains. It did not.

When he rejoined them, he noted that Mrs. Davies had moved apart from her brother-in-law and a tense silence filled the room.

"Let's go," he said to her. He'd seen enough.

He grabbed his hat from atop the chest where he'd left it and strode through the door, out into the hallway. Within seconds, he heard Mrs. Davies say good-bye to Tom followed by the rapid tap of her boot heels behind him.

"*T*hank you for not arresting him." Celia jogged to keep pace with the detective's long strides.

Mr. Greaves shot her a look. If she could see the expression in his eyes, shaded by the brim of his hat, she might better understand him. Though on second thought, learning to read this man might prove a dangerous occupation.

"I don't have enough evidence," he said. "But I will check his alibi, even if you are willing to vouch for the character of a man who calls you a hard woman."

"As I have said, we are not close."

"How did Tom and Li Sha meet? You haven't explained."

"It's my understanding that Tom met her at Mr. Lange's," she answered, skirting a grocer hauling crates of gin into his shop. "Tom's office is only a few doors down the road from the apothecary shop. He knew Mr. Lange's daughter, Tessie, and met Li Sha during one of his visits, I presume, and fell in love with her. Their courtship proceeded rapidly. Before I knew it, Li Sha was carrying Tom's child and sharing his room."

When Li Sha had further informed Celia that Tom had offered to marry her, she had been astonished. Perhaps all the Davies men were impulsive when it came to matters of the heart.

"And somewhere along the way, their relationship turned sour," said Mr. Greaves.

"Given that she had moved out, that must be the case."

Likely thinking that was the last to be said on the matter, he removed his notebook from within his coat, along with a pencil, and started scribbling notes, looking up only to avoid colliding with telegraph poles and gaslight posts.

"Do please slow down, Mr. Greaves."

He did not.

"Since you've dismissed the anti-Chinese groups as being responsible for killing Li Sha, whom else do you consider a suspect?" Celia asked as she trotted after the detective. "Because I cannot fathom who would harm her. She really was a gentle, quiet creature."

"I didn't say I've dismissed the anti-Chinese groups, Mrs. Davies."

"Are they your main suspect, or is Tom still the primary one? Or someone else?"

He exhaled loudly; she surmised she was annoying him. "Most times the killer is an acquaintance of the victim, ma'am. An acquaintance has motive and opportunity," he said without taking his gaze off his notebook.

"Which means I might know the killer as well." What a horrible notion.

"It's possible."

"What shall I say to Barbara and my housekeeper about Li Sha?" she asked.

"Whatever you do, don't describe the body. It'll be better that way. Easier for them."

But not so easy for me. "If they have any information or

suspicions, I will let you know. And I will try to discover where Li Sha might have been living since leaving Tom."

"Thank you."

The notebook at last returned to its pocket, Nicholas Greaves paused on the corner in the lee of a bank building, its iron door and shutters locked tight. A party of horsemen and horsewomen galloped down Market Street, laughing and shouting, blocking the road. Based on their accents, they were fellow Englishmen and well-off, their costumes the finest Oxford Street in London could provide. Mr. Greaves watched them pass, appearing unimpressed with their self-satisfied high spirits.

Celia contemplated Nicholas Greaves. His suit of clothes was not of the highest quality, although serviceable and adequately tailored, and his footwear needed a polish. He seemed to be a man who might have pulled himself up by his bootstraps, another saying of the Americans. What might he think of her, though, if he learned she was once as privileged and careless as those riders?

He looked down and caught her staring. Her cheeks warmed and she glanced away. They started across the road.

"Would you like me to speak to Li Sha's former associates in Chinatown?" she asked. "I can take my cousin with me. She speaks their language. And a guard, of course. The local constables help me—"

"This is my job, Mrs. Davies," he interrupted.

"They will not speak to a policeman."

"They won't speak to you, either. Who might they think killed Li Sha? They'll most likely think it was one of their own people. Or a customer. And if they suspect a Caucasian customer, they can't testify," he pointed out unnecessarily, since she was already familiar with the unfair law that prohibited the Chinese from bearing witness against whites.

"Yes, Mr. Greaves, but—"

"Either way," he continued, "the women of Chinatown are in no position to voice their opinions or offer names. They would be risking their necks."

"I cannot do nothing."

"You've given me a direction for my inquiries and provided plenty of information. That's more than enough, ma'am." He looked down the street and halted his steps. "You can take the omnibus from here to where you live."

"You uncovered where I live while you were fact gathering on me?" What else did he know about her?

"Didn't get the exact address, however."

"Which surprises me."

"Don't get any ideas about heading to Chinatown to ask questions, Mrs. Davies." He frowned at her, a further attempt to intimidate. "My advice to you is to go straight home. It'll be dark soon, and I'd rather not hear about you at the morning station briefing."

"Do not tell me you are worried for me, Mr. Greaves."

His eyes searched her face. "Mrs. Davies, I hate to say I am."

The horsecar rolled to a halt, discharging a handful of Germans and Poles from the wharves and Irishmen from just about everywhere else. She watched them as they dispersed along the road, their accents and swagger reminding her of Patrick.

Mr. Greaves helped her board and paid the fare over her protests. "Compensation for your time," he said.

She clung to the railing as passengers shoved past her. When she reached a seat, she lowered the window and leaned out.

Mr. Greaves tapped fingertips to the brim of his hat. "Good evening, Mrs. Davies," he called out from the curb, "and good-bye."

"Good-bye?" She lifted her chin. "I wouldn't be so hopeful, Detective Greaves."

The horsecar lurched forward before she could be sure of his response. But she thought he might have chuckled.

After he'd seen Mrs. Davies off, Nick took a detour through Chinatown before heading home. Until this case, he hadn't paid much attention to the anti-Chinese groups. He'd expected their righteous indignation would soon burn out, once they realized they weren't getting anywhere and the Chinese were in San Francisco to stay. But if Mrs. Davies' half-Chinese cousin was scared . . . well, there might be more heat behind their indignation than he'd thought.

A block shy of the police station, he turned west off Kearney. The Chinese lived and worked along Sacramento and Dupont, and they crowded the streets, mostly men in their silk tunics and wide pants, skullcaps over their pigtailed hair. They watched him as he strode past the tables they'd set up on the sidewalks to hawk their goods—unfamiliar vegetables and painted fans and oriental medicines and bits of just about everything. Red paper lanterns hung over doorways and red signs dangled from protruding balconies. A scrawny dog barked at him and a kid shouted in Chinese. A nearby man shushed the boy and sent him scurrying inside their shop. The man's eyes followed Nick. Did the vendor seem apprehensive or fearful? Neither, it seemed. Maybe Mrs. Davies was wrong.

But Nick wanted to be sure. He didn't want every Chinese person in town wondering who might be murdered next, and if he could find out who'd killed Li Sha, they might begin to feel safe.

He knew that's what Uncle Asa, one of the finest detectives—hell, one of the finest policemen—Nick had ever known, would do. Because his uncle had valued justice like Nick did. And those who needed justice the most were the ones least likely to get it.

He had almost reached Stockton when he heard a shout coming from an alley up ahead and began running toward the sound. Halfway down the passageway, a skinny Chinese laundry boy, his load of clean underclothes spilled into a dirty puddle, had been cornered in a doorway by a handful of white boys in filthy caps and torn duck pants. The kid's lip was bleeding and there were cuts on his face.

"Hey!" Nick sprinted forward, his hat flying off. The cowards scattered like marbles after a good strike.

"Dirty China boy!" shouted one before vanishing around the farthest corner.

With a sob, the little boy dropped to the ground, and Nick changed his mind about chasing the bullies and pummeling them. He returned to the kid.

"Here," he said, extending a hand. "Let me help you to your feet."

The boy looked up at him with tears in his black eyes but no sign of gratitude. He was all of seven or eight and his expression conveyed only hatred.

"No!" a woman screeched, clattering down the alleyway in her high shoes. Angry Chinese words followed, some directed at the boy, some at Nick. She hauled the boy to his feet, gathered the spilled laundry, and thrust it into his arms. Grabbing the boy, she dragged him toward the road without looking back.

Nick collected his hat, brushed it off, and restored it to his head. A glance around revealed faces in doorways and windows, hastily withdrawn. Mrs. Davies was right to worry. Trouble was brewing, and if they weren't all careful, the pot might blow its lid.

"*C*rumpets and orange marmalade this morning, ma'am?" asked Addie, leaning through the doorway into the downstairs room Celia had converted into her clinic. "With some poached eggs?"

"Addie, that sounds wonderful," Celia answered, glancing over from her desk. "And tea. The strongest oolong you can brew."

"Aye, ma'am."

Celia yawned into her fist. She had been called away last night to help a young Mexican woman through childbirth. The infant, a lovely black-haired boy, was stillborn. How his mother had wept. When Celia had finally returned home and collapsed into bed, she had lain awake and thought about Li Sha, whose baby had been likewise cheated of life. Thought about the cruel brevity of man's existence.

She wrapped her crimson shawl with its paisley border more tightly around her shoulders, the cashmere whispering against her neck. She closed her eyes and breathed in. The shawl had been her mother's, and if she tried very hard, Celia could imagine she smelled her mother's jasmine perfume caught up in the warp and weft. A small morsel of comfort.

Perhaps her aunt in Hertfordshire was correct, and nursing was no proper occupation for a lady. Her aunt had never forgiven Celia when she'd reasoned that the quickest way to join Harry in the Crimea was to pretend she was older than her true years and volunteer as a nurse. When she'd learned just how different mending a bird's broken wing was from tending shrapnel-riddled bodies, she'd almost turned back from her chosen path. But she hadn't. She had persevered, seen success, and come to love what she did.

She could not, however, restore a stillborn baby to life or save Li Sha.

"Your tea, ma'am," announced Addie, striding into the room with a tray, bringing Celia back to the here and now.

"Is Barbara awake?" she asked.

"Aye." Addie moved aside Celia's ledgers and set the tray atop her desk. She poured out a cupful of steaming tea. "She was sitting on the porch for a while, catching a chill, but she's in the parlor now. Staring out the window, poor bairn."

After burning her tongue on a quick sip, Celia rose and wandered across the foyer that separated the two front parlors—one now Celia's examination room, the other used as their sitting room.

Barbara had turned one of the upholstered chairs to face the window and fixed her gaze on the street beyond the glass, her damaged foot resting on a low stool. There wasn't much of a view across the stretch of dirt road except for the top story and roof of the house across the way, its ground floor below street level.

"How are you feeling this morning, Barbara?" Celia asked from the doorway.

Barbara had taken the confirmation of Li Sha's death very hard. When Celia had returned from her patient last night, she'd heard her cousin sobbing in her bedchamber. She should have realized that Barbara had grown attached to Li Sha, though she'd rarely shown affection for the girl. Her cousin must have longed for a friend who could comprehend the isolation she endured, halfway between her mother's Chinese world and her father's white one, where people whispered behind their hands and didn't fully accept her.

"How can she be dead?" Barbara's head drooped. "I keep

thinking and thinking, but when Owen came by earlier, he said it's just something that happens to people like him and Li Sha, people nobody wants."

"That isn't true," Celia protested. "Li Sha was wanted. And Owen Cassidy is wanted, too, by those who matter." Having been abandoned by his parents, Owen scraped by, living on the streets and doing odd jobs, just one boy among the many lost souls in this city. "But I can understand his feelings."

Or were they more than feelings? Owen was Irish like many of the men in the anti-coolie groups. What might he know about Li Sha's death? She would ask him the next time he came by.

"It's just awful," said Barbara, toying with the folded lace-edged handkerchief in her lap, running her fingertip across the looping *B* embroidered in vermilion silk.

"Are you afraid that the rioters who attacked those Chinese laborers a few weeks ago might have killed Li Sha?" asked Celia. "Because I am thinking that may be the case."

Barbara glanced over, a tiny crease in her forehead. "The rioters . . . oh yes. Of course. Them."

"I don't want you to be concerned for your own safety," said Celia. She hated to see Barbara upset like this. "I will not let anyone harm you. I promised your father on his deathbed I would take care of you, and I shall."

Barbara chewed her lower lip. "I wish I still had piano lessons with Em so I could talk to Mr. Palmer about what happened to Li Sha. I'm sure he'd have an explanation."

Why did she think that? Joseph Palmer and his family had met Li Sha at a charity event at the Chinese Mission earlier that year, but a casual acquaintance hardly meant Mr. Palmer would have insight into who had killed her.

"But I'm not sure that Mr. Palmer is at home," added Barbara, the crease in her forehead deepening.

"Has he been away?"

"I think so."

"Clearly, I don't know Mr. Palmer's plans," said Celia. Barbara's preoccupation with the man made Celia uneasy. She glanced up at Uncle Walford grinning down from his portrait. Barbara wanted a father. Was charming, handsome Joseph Palmer the substitute she'd settled upon?

"Once I've finished with my patients today, I shall be heading out to visit the Langes," said Celia. "I need to pick up some supplies, and I also wish to see how they have received the news about Li Sha. Mr. Lange was fond of her. Would you like to go with me?"

Barbara's expression darkened. "No. I'd rather not."

"Then perhaps you can visit my patient in Chinatown. I want to know how the wounds to her arm are doing. The constable should be making his rounds"—Celia checked the time on her watch—"in about two hours and should be able to accompany you. If you are uneasy about going alone, you can take Addie."

"All right," Barbara muttered, chewing her lower lip again, as she did when she was agitated.

Celia considered her. "Is there something you're not telling me, Barbara?"

"No."

Celia stepped back from the doorway. "I will have Addie bring you some tea, and a crumpet if you'd like. Some food will help you feel better."

"I'll be fine," Barbara answered. "I just wish . . . she didn't have to die."

CHAPTER 5

Lange's business was located a few blocks south of the police station along a stretch of Pine Street that was thick with stores. Nick scanned the pedestrians, a better class of folks than Li Sha would have interacted with in Chinatown.

He reached the store, where a middle-aged woman had her nose pressed to the window glass.

"Is Mr. Lange in today?" Nick asked her.

She startled. "Why, yes. Seems they are."

"Then maybe you should go in."

"Oh no. No, no, no," she said, retreating from the window. "I heard about that Chinese girl of theirs getting killed and I wouldn't want to disturb them, you see. Though I'm not surprised, you know. Mighty strange goings-on, if you ask me. Mighty strange."

"How so?" Nick asked.

The woman leaned forward as if she were dispensing a great secret. "Peculiar comings and goings at night, you know? Strange men. Must have had something to do with that girl, though, don't you think? She was a prostitute once, wasn't she?" Something behind Nick attracted her attention. "Why, look, there's that nice man at the dry goods store. I think I'll see how he's doing. His rheumatism's been bothering him. Good-bye."

She scurried up the road before Nick could ask her any more questions.

Nick stepped inside the store, the bell overhead jingling. The air was heavy with a pungent mixture of unidentifiable scents. Each wall was lined with tins bearing the names of the compounds they contained—sassafras bark, cochineal, oxide bismuth, flaxseed, poppy leaves. Beneath the tins were rows of dark glass jars containing acids and oils, or patent medicines labeled with doctors' names meant to assure a customer of their curative powers. But the Dr. Richardson of Dr. Richardson's Pectoral Balsam wasn't likely any more a trained doctor than the corner quack who hawked hair restoratives. The same went for Dr. Fak and his Worm Lozenges or the Fahnestock of Fahnestock's Vermifuge, whatever that was.

A massive table occupied the room's center, its surface covered with mortars and pestles, several reference books that looked to contain recipes for medicines, and a large brass weighing scale. From behind the table, a young woman straightened from a crouch, a brush and bin in her hands. The bin held the broken remains of a bottle of Dr. Chase's Anodyne Dysentery Cordial, according to the label attached to a shard of glass.

"Can I help you?" she asked. She was plain but not unattractive, and unusually tall for a woman, with light brown hair and large brown eyes. They watched him with defiant curiosity. "Or you just here to stare?"

"I'm here to ask about a woman who worked here. Li Sha."

"And who are you?"

"Detective Nicholas Greaves. From the San Francisco Police. And you are . . . ?"

"Tessie Lange." Hastily, she set down the bin and brush. "You should talk to my father."

Stepping over the pool of spilled cordial on the floor, she hurried into a back passageway that was separated from the main room by a thick gray curtain. Muffled voices came from the rear of the store, followed by footsteps. Mr. Lange, also tall, with thinning hair and narrow shoulders, pushed the curtain aside.

"Detective Greaves?" he said, giving the *r* a raspy pronunciation. French, then. He peered through the spectacles perched on the bridge of his nose. "Can I help?"

"I'm talking to anybody who knew the Chinese girl who was killed on Monday. I've been told she worked here."

A look of pain crossed Lange's face. He exchanged a glance with his daughter, who'd come into the room behind him. "*Effroyable.* We saw the news in the paper."

Nick had read one of the accounts, an article on page two of the *Morning Call.* MURDERED CHINESE GIRL in bold letters, with enough sordid details of the discovery of the girl's body to shock the reader. The reporter who'd penned the column hadn't wasted space calling on the police to find her killer, though. One less Celestial, and a former prostitute at that; exactly who would care in this town? Not many, besides Celia Davies. And him.

"So, it is true it is Miss Li?" Lange asked. "We thought, but I did not imagine . . ."

Miss Lange's face was stony hard.

"When did you last see her?" Nick asked.

"Her last workday," answered Lange. "Which was . . ."

"Monday, Papa," said Miss Lange, sounding as if she often finished her father's sentences.

"Yes, Monday. Thank you, Thérèse. Monday. The day she . . ." Lange struggled for words. "She does not work on Tuesdays, but she was to come yesterday. Now we know why she did not."

"On Monday did she seem worried? Scared of somebody, maybe? Did she have plans to meet anybody later that night?"

"She said nothing to us."

"She never said much, Detective," explained Tessie Lange. "Came to work. Swept. Tidied. Went home."

"She didn't come here looking for a place to stay sometime last week?" Nick asked, remembering that Li Sha had moved out of Tom Davies' room.

Miss Lange's gaze narrowed. "No," she answered.

"Do you know who killed Miss Li, Detective Greaves?" asked her father.

"We're following some leads. You?"

"Me?" he asked, eyes widening. "Oh! You wonder who I think . . . this I cannot say. I have the customers who learned of her work. They make the complaints, but I do not think they would be so angry as to hurt her. If I had hired a Chinese boy, they might understand. The boys, they are everyplace in the city, no? I have heard of the ladies who prefer them to the Irish girls."

He wiped his hands down his apron and recollected Nick's question. "None would want to hurt her. Miss Li, she was a fine young woman. It is difficult to comprehend how she was ever in that life. Just ask Madame Davies. She will tell you. Miss Li had left the past behind and was now a fine young woman."

Based on the frown on Miss Lange's face, Nick expected she didn't share her father's high opinion.

"I have already spoken to Mrs. Davies," he said. "What about that man she'd been with? The father of her child . . . Tom Davies. Had they fought recently?"

"Child?" Lange seemed startled by the news.

Tessie Lange's brow crinkled for a second, but she didn't seem as shocked as her father was. But then, women had a way of knowing such things.

"She was going to have a child. Didn't you know?" asked Nick. The girl must have been keeping the pregnancy from Lange, hoping to keep her job; no doubt she'd have been let go if Lange had found out.

Lange shook his head. "*Ma foi*, no. No."

"You're not thinking Tom's guilty of killing her, are you?" interrupted Miss Lange.

"Do you know Tom Davies?"

A peculiar expression crossed her face. "He works down the street. We were acquainted. He doesn't seem the type, though."

"Murderers come in all types, miss."

"Tom Davies would not murder anyone, Detective," said Lange firmly. "He has the temper, *c'est vrai*, but is a good boy. He is the brother of Madame Davies' missing husband. She will tell you he would not hurt Miss Li."

"She's said that, too."

"You know, Papa," said Miss Lange, "maybe Li Sha was acting fidgety lately. I think she was afraid of somebody. Folks are pretty upset with the Chinese these days. Maybe she was having trouble, too."

"She never said this to me, Thérèse," said her father.

"Although it could've been one of her former customers bothering her, I guess," continued Miss Lange.

Nick went on, "One of your neighbors mentioned there have been men hanging around, men who possibly wanted to speak to Li Sha. Have either of you noticed them?"

Tessie Lange slid her father a look, then answered for both of them. "Can't say that we have. None besides Tom."

"This is terrible," said Lange. "It must be those horrible people who hate the Chinese. They make such trouble. Our poor Miss Li."

Mr. Lange shoved his spectacles up the bridge of his nose, though Nick wasn't sure they'd slipped down. The man's hand was trembling. The last time he'd seen somebody so shivery, the fellow had been ready to confess to murder.

Nick started to count how many blocks it was to the wharf where Li Sha had been found—nine—and pondered ways Lange or his tall daughter could have hauled her there, or lured her there.

"Where you were on Monday night, Mr. Lange?" he asked.

Lange blinked at him, the motion magnified by his spectacles. "I was here."

"With your daughter?" asked Nick, nodding toward her. Tessie Lange could've been carved out of marble.

"Yes," he replied quickly. "Yes."

"Is it okay if I look around?" asked Nick.

"*Mais oui*," said Lange.

Nick guessed that meant yes.

Down the passageway behind the curtain was a large storage

room. The kitchen, two bedrooms, and a parlor were located upstairs. No evidence he could see that a young Chinese woman had been murdered on the premises.

He returned to the shop front, where Lange and his daughter were whispering together. They stopped when they heard Nick slide the curtain over.

"Thanks. If either of you thinks of anything further, you can contact me at the main police station," Nick said, and turned to leave. Outside on the street, a man with his sleeves rolled up and carrying a broom peered through the window at them. Next to the shopkeeper stood the gossip whom he'd encountered earlier, still straining for a glimpse inside. They caught sight of Nick frowning at them and bolted like a pair of guilty kids.

"And tell your neighbors to contact me or my assistant, Officer Taylor, if they have any information for us."

"Of course," said Lange, nodding, his daughter at his side still as emotionless as a statue.

Out on the porch, Celia waved good-bye to her final patient of the day. The young woman, an actress from the Metropolitan, had come to collect medicines for her monthly pains—an infusion Celia purchased from Mr. Lange composed of gum guaiac, pokeroot, and black cohosh—and was hurrying back to rehearsals. The feathers on the woman's hat bobbed as she sped along the road, her carrot-colored jacket and skirt a bold slash of color.

"She actually paid me, Addie. A dollar." Celia held up the coin as proof.

Addie slapped the entry hall rug against the porch railing, sending dust flying. "Perhaps I'll buy us a treat at Ghirardelli's with that."

Celia smiled and pocketed the coin with a sigh. She was tired, but she still needed to go to the Langes', and after that, she had accounts to review. Her busy day was far from finished. However, she lingered on the porch, savoring the cool breeze against her cheek, the spicy aromas emanating from a neighbor's kitchen, and the azure of the sky overhead. She missed England but she loved this city more.

"Hullo, Miss Ferguson!" Across the street, a deliveryman from a Washington Market butcher stall had finished dropping off meat and noticed Addie on the porch. Tipping his wool cap, he grinned. "Swell day, ain't it? You're looking just swell, too."

Celia glanced over at Addie, whose face had gone as red as pomegranate seeds. "Whisht, go on with you."

"Any Sunday you'd like to go to the Willows with me, you just holler," he shouted.

"You'll be waiting a long time for me to *holler*, you will!"

Laughing, he hopped up onto the delivery wagon seat and drove off, but not without a final grin for Addie.

"The Willows, Addie?" Celia asked. "I've heard it is very lovely there."

"He's a forward one, he is," she replied, busying herself with folding the rug over her arm. "Thinking I'll go on some picnic with the likes of him."

"He is not bad looking, though," Celia said, biting back a smile.

"Och, ma'am! Now you're wanting to see me go!"

"I would never want to see you go, Addie," Celia insisted. "But if you are serious about finding a husband, he seems a promising place to start."

"That one?" She peered at the delivery wagon wheeling down the road. "Canna trust a man who grins so much— Miss Barbara!"

Celia looked to where Addie was staring. Barbara, visibly upset, was rushing up Vallejo as fast as her bad foot allowed.

"Barbara!" Celia hurried down the front steps.

Her cousin stumbled to a halt, and Celia reached out to help her rise.

Barbara shook off her hand. "Don't make me go to China-town alone ever again."

"I told you to take Addie with you."

"I'm sorry, ma'am," said Addie. "But when Miss Barbara wanted to go, I was busy cleaning the kitchen floor and couldna leave right then. I said I would go later."

"So, Barbara—"

"I know, I know, Cousin Celia. It's my fault." Barbara grabbed the stair railing and hauled herself up the last steps to the porch. "They didn't even let me see your patient. That old woman turned me away. So it was a waste of my time. And then . . ." Tears gathered in her eyes.

"What is it?" asked Celia. "What happened? Are you all right?" She started searching for any sign that her cousin had been injured, but she seemed fine aside from her pallid face.

"They said awful things to me. It was horrible."

"Who?" asked Celia. "Who said awful things?"

"It was a bunch of boys. They shouted obscene words at me." Barbara pressed her hands to her face and sobbed. "It's the mid-dle of the day, but nobody stopped them. They frightened me."

"I must tell Mr. Greaves," said Celia. But what could he do without the names of the bullies?

"Maybe Li Sha *was* killed by a nasty group of dirty white men who hate Chinese people. Just like those disgusting boys."

"Oh, Barbara." Celia buffed her hands down her cousin's trembling arms. The hatred was coming too close to home.

"I wonder if Owen knows them," said Barbara. "He knows everybody on the streets. I should've asked him when I saw him a bit ago. He was just around the corner. But I wanted to come home . . ." Barbara sniffled and wiped a hand beneath her nose. "I bet he knows who killed Li Sha. Maybe it's one of them. Maybe it's not . . . It's just about gotta be."

"I'll find Owen and talk to him." Celia looked up the road in search of the boy. "Addie, take Barbara up to her room and see she has something warm to drink."

Addie led Barbara into the house.

Celia caught sight of Owen Cassidy, his wool cap set at a jaunty angle, moving down the street, kicking a stone along the plank pavement. He shot a glance at a scrum of boys, home from school and playing a boisterous game of French and English, trying to pull the opposite line of their mates across a mark scratched in the dirt. He slowed, perhaps hoping they would invite him to join in, and walked on when they did not.

"Owen!" Celia called.

"Aye, Mrs. Davies!" He trotted the rest of the way to the house. "You're not busy now. I came by before and you was with a patient. Didn't want to disturb you then, but I was just wondering how Mr. Smith is doing. You know, looking for my ma and pa."

The anticipation on his face caused her breath to catch. She never had the news Owen most wanted. She had paid Mr. Smith, the strange man she'd hired to seek out news about Patrick, to search for Owen's lost parents as well. He'd had no more luck discovering their whereabouts than he had learning if Patrick was still alive.

"Mr. Smith has not found them yet, Owen," she answered.

The boy's face fell. He had the clearest green eyes, full of weariness and cynicism, emotions no child his age should possess. He claimed he was fourteen; his eyes made him look much older.

"Don't give up hope," she said.

"Right, ma'am," he responded, his courage tugging at her heart.

"I need to ask you something very important," she said. "It might help the police find the person who hurt Li Sha."

"That's awful, ain't it, ma'am? She was nice to me." Kindness was Owen's measure of anyone's worth. "But it's just something that happens to people like me and her, people nobody wants, I guess."

Exactly what he had said to Barbara. "Who was it in particular that might not have wanted Li Sha, Owen? Someone you know?"

He shrugged. "There's all kinda anger out there, ma'am. It don't have to have a name."

All kinds of anger. "Just now, several boys confronted Barbara on her way home from Chinatown. They shouted dreadful things at her."

"Who was it?" Owen asked, tensing. "I'll whup 'em!"

"I do not need you to whup them, Owen," she said. "But I was wondering if you have heard anyone—those who hate the Chinese, I mean—discussing plans for something worse than shouting foul names or beating people up."

His eyes widened. "I kin poke around, try to find out," he offered, happy to have a purpose. "How's that?"

"That would be very helpful, but promise me you'll be careful. Any such men might be dangerous."

"Shucks, ma'am, who'd bother with me?" he asked brightly, suddenly unconcerned by what had happened to Li Sha or to people like him.

He dashed off, a whistle floating on the air behind him.

"What did Harris say, sir . . . Mr. Greaves, sir?"

Taylor followed Nick to the detectives' office and dropped into the chair in front of Nick's desk. Briggs, who shared the office, was out again. To Nick's mind that was like winning the lottery.

Briggs had left behind crumbs from the molasses doughnuts he liked to eat, and a line of ants crawled across the floor. Nick crushed some under his boot and went to sit in his chair, the window at his back, the afternoon breeze stirring papers on his desk. He steepled his fingers and rested them against his chin, which was scratchy with stubble. In a rush to speak with the coroner that morning and visit the Langes, he'd forgotten to shave.

"Dr. Harris concluded what we'd thought, Taylor: Li Sha was definitely dead when she was tossed into the bay; there wasn't any water in her lungs. He also agrees she was murdered elsewhere. Her blood had pooled, indicating she'd lain someplace for a while after death."

The coroner had been clinical as he'd recited his findings. The girl had been sliced by a sharp-edged blade across the stomach just below the ribs. There were multiple cuts on her forearms, indicating she might have attempted to fend off the blows from her attacker. She'd had significant bleeding on the brain and a fracture in the skull where it struck or was struck by an object, the probable cause of death. Also, the multiple bruises on her face had likely been received within a few days of her murder, although she had a misshapen rib from an old injury. A thin abrasion of unknown origin ran along the back of her neck, and she was in general good health, although there were indications she'd had the sorts of diseases prostitutes were prone to.

Lastly, she was around four months pregnant and carrying a female child.

We were gonna name her Katie . . .

"Did you learn anything from the folks living near the wharf?" Nick asked Taylor. "Any unusual wagons in the area that night, or people out of the ordinary hanging around? The murder either occurred very near the wharf or her body was carted there. The perpetrator couldn't have gone completely unnoticed."

"Hard to get much information out of that bunch," Taylor replied. He dragged his notebook from his coat pocket and flipped through the pages. "One of them claimed he saw a gent in a fancy carriage, though, but his friend said he was too liquored up to know his right hand from his left. Another fella commented that it was raining hard around ten or eleven that night and nobody smart was out of doors. That's about it."

It was much as Nick had expected; it was almost impossible to get people to talk in this town, especially the boatmen and longshoremen who lived in the rough shacks near the wharves. "Did you ask at the Chinese Mission if Li Sha had been there lately?"

"The reverend who runs the place said he hadn't seen her for weeks."

"She had to go someplace. I doubt she was sleeping on the street. Too dangerous."

"I'll keep asking around, sir." Taylor scribbled more notes. "When I came into the station this morning, sir, one of the men told me he'd heard some Chinese servant over on Jones Street had been pelted with rocks. Maybe somebody who sympathizes with those anti-Chinese groups forming all over the city got an idea to pick on a girl."

"You might be right," said Nick. "I came across some kids yesterday who were harassing a Chinese laundry boy in a Chinatown alley. Seems things are getting worse out there."

Nick knew somebody who could tell him; it was a long shot that she'd provide answers, though.

"I can't figure out why her, though, sir," said Taylor.

"Neither can I. Maybe Li Sha was killed for a reason we haven't considered. Or maybe simply because she made an easy target. She walked alone at night from Lange's store to wherever she was staying." Tom Davies' lodgings were about half a mile distant, the Chinese Mission as well.

"What did the Langes have to say?" Taylor asked.

"They're blaming the anti-Chinese groups, too." Nick scratched the stubble on his chin. "Strange duo. About as skittish as a pair of unbroken horses."

"Could one of them have killed her?"

Could they? Nick rubbed the ache in his left arm. The pain and numbness had been worse these past couple of days. Maybe it was because of the damp. Or maybe it was because he'd been dreaming about the war.

Dreaming? Having nightmares was more like it.

"They're both tall enough to overpower a tiny Chinese woman," he said. "Even Miss Lange. And they probably have a sharp knife or two in their kitchen."

"But why do it?"

"We'll have to discover a reason, Taylor."

There was a knock on the door, and Mullahey stuck his head through the opening. "Got a moment, Mr. Greaves?"

"Sure."

Mullahey nodded at Taylor and took the other empty chair in the room. "I just got done talkin' to that dockworker. The one who stumbled over Wagner and the body of that Chinese girl. Told me he saw somethin' funny."

"He's only mentioning it now?" asked Nick.

Mullahey shrugged. "Anyway, he says when he first came along the pier, he noticed this fella, Wagner. On his hands and knees on the edge of the pier, which is what got his attention to begin with. Thought it was odd. He claims it looked like Wagner was tryin' to push somethin' down into the water. Didn't realize at first it was a body."

"Whoa," exclaimed Taylor. "But I checked Wagner's story, sir. Wife says he was with her Monday night, all night, and went to work at his usual time. And his boss says he was sent to the pier Tuesday morning to inspect a ship come in from Manila. So he had a good reason to be there."

"Yeah, okay, Taylor," said Mullahey, looking annoyed.

"Maybe Wagner's wife is lying and he did kill her, sir," Taylor said. "Came in extra early for some sort of liaison with the girl that went sour. We know he beat up a Mexican sailor. He might just like to hurt people."

"Wagner told me he doesn't visit Chinese prostitutes," said Nick. Plus, according to Mrs. Davies, Li Sha had left prostitution behind. "How would they have known each other?"

"Wagner could be lying about that, too, Mr. Greaves, sir."

"So when that dockworker came along, Wagner lost his chance to hide his dirty work," said Mullahey, brightening.

"And Wagner claims to have found her body in the bay in order to throw us off!" With his thumb, Taylor crushed an ant crawling along the edge of Nick's desk. "I mean, who'd ever suspect the fellow who found her, aside from us? He mighta thought he'd be in the clear. Plus, he'd know there wasn't much going on all night down at the wharf, wouldn't he? Since it's his job to know when ships are coming in."

"Should I bring him back in, Mr. Greaves?" asked Mullahey.

"Yes. Bring Wagner back in."

Celia turned the corner of the street housing Mr. Lange's apothecary shop. Just a few doors down, she could see all was dark behind the tall windows. She quickened her steps and noticed the CLOSED sign hanging over the roller shade, the blinds partly drawn. Had Mr. Lange forgotten she needed to replenish her supply of gum arabic and had planned to come by? Celia leaned forward to peer through the gaps in the window blinds. Lamplight flickered in the back room, visible beyond the open curtain.

She tapped on the window. "Mr. Lange? Miss Lange?"

A shadow crossed the room's far wall, the motion hasty, furtive, and the lamp was extinguished.

How odd.

Celia considered what to do. It would be a waste of time to have come all this way only to return home without her supplies. Perhaps if she knocked on the door leading to their private residence, they would answer.

She found access to the alleyway that ran behind the row

of buildings and hurried down the passage, scattering rats foraging through garbage as she passed. As she approached the Langes' back door, she saw a figure hunkered within a heavy shawl and deep-brimmed bonnet slip away and take off briskly.

"Miss Lange!" she called to the woman, who did not stop.

Had she been mistaken? Celia counted doors. No, she was not wrong. That was the rear door leading to the Langes' residence above the shop. And the woman had been Tessie Lange. She recognized Tessie's checked brown dress and unusual height. Where was she headed so secretively?

Celia hastened after the woman. Up the road, she spotted Tessie rushing north along Kearney Street, zigzagging through traffic and pedestrians. Was she headed for the police station for some reason? But she hurried past that building without slowing. Celia dashed across an intersection in pursuit, drawing a shout from a produce-wagon driver who reined in his horse to keep it from trampling her.

Tessie glanced over her shoulder and turned right down Jackson. If she continued on this path, she would be heading out of the Barbary Coast and toward the warehouses, the lumberyards, and the docks beyond, where the masts of ships bristled like a forest of denuded trees tethered to the piers.

Celia's heart pounded in her chest. Her hair was coming unwound from beneath her hat, and she was certain she'd kicked mud onto her skirt. Addie would have a fit when Celia got home.

They were approaching Montgomery Street on the Barbary's far edge. A heavy-shouldered stevedore whistled at Celia as she rushed along. Mariners milled about in the streets, headed for the deadfalls and brothels that now lay behind Celia: Kanaka sailors put in on a Sandwich Islands whaler; Canadians off steamers loaded with timber; olive-skinned South Americans from ships loaded with coffee, tobacco, and cocoa. Not the sort of neighborhood Hubert Lange would like his daughter to frequent.

Suddenly, Tessie halted and darted another glance around her. Celia squeezed behind a pile of lumber propped against a wall and pressed a hand to her side where she had gotten a cramp. Two doors down, a tavern girl leaned in a doorway leading into a dim basement liquor den, her arms folded over a turquoise silk dress, its best days long past. She slid Celia a curious look. Beyond the woman, the proprietor shouted at a drunk sprawled on the sawdust-covered floor. With a smile for the girl, whose dark eyes widened, Celia stepped out from her hiding spot and rushed into the alleyway she was certain Tessie had gone down. There, in a shadowy doorway, she was talking with a man—

Suddenly, Celia was grabbed from behind and yanked backward, pain shooting through her shoulders.

Bloody hell.

CHAPTER 6

"What in . . . Don't make me curse, Mrs. Davies," the man's voice hissed in her ear. "But what in God's green earth are you doing here?"

"That hurt, Mr. Greaves." Celia squirmed in his grasp. A pair of men entering a nearby oyster shop looked over.

"Hey!" one shouted, and started toward them. He must have decided Celia wasn't a prostitute or a tavern girl, based on her clothing, and needed rescuing.

Mr. Greaves released his hold. "Just a little misunderstanding," he said, raising his hands.

"Yes. A misunderstanding," Celia grumbled. She forced a smile and thanked her rescuer. The stranger doffed his cap and joined his mate in the oyster shop.

"There was no need to manhandle me, Detective," she protested, straightening her cloak.

"Did you spot the pickpocket following you?" he asked sternly. Celia looked around. "What pickpocket?"

"That's what I figured," he said. "And what are you doing in the Barbary without a guard? I thought you had a whole passel of constables to show you around."

He shifted his stance so his back was to the rough wooden clapboard of the adjacent building. Policemen must always seek to protect their backs, afraid that someone might sneak up behind them and catch them unawares.

"I didn't have time to seek one out," Celia answered in a tone as sarcastic as his, tucking loose hair into the pins holding her chignon in place. "And your attempt at protection made me lose sight of who Tessie Lange was talking with."

His brow furrowed. He did look quite fierce when he did that. "You might want to explain yourself."

"I went to visit the Langes. The shop was closed—earlier than usual—and I spotted Tessie hurrying away. It looked as though she didn't wish to be recognized. Since her actions struck me as odd, I thought to follow her. I did not see the harm."

"You did not see . . ." The detective groaned. "I thought I told you not to go snooping around in Chinatown, Mrs. Davies."

"This is not Chinatown, Mr. Greaves."

He was not amused. "Listen, ma'am, if you have any information or suspicions, you need to share them with me, not chase them down yourself. I am responsible for this investigation, not you. Promise me you'll stop interfering."

She hesitated. She dared not tell him about the request she had made of Owen; he would only grow angrier.

"Promise me," he repeated.

"Mr. Greaves, don't force me to make promises I shan't keep. Li Sha came to me for help, and my brother-in-law appears to be the primary suspect in her death, though he has yet to be arrested." It was only a matter of time until he was; she was certain of it. "I have a responsibility to them both, and I was not attempting to interfere. I followed Tessie because I didn't have time to come to the station to inform you of her behavior. Although apparently I wouldn't have found you there since you are also in the Barbary, skulking down back streets."

"It's my job to skulk," he said, and headed toward the alley exit.

"I cannot help but wonder, though, why Tessie would come here," said Celia.

On the far side of Montgomery loomed great buildings of commerce and shops selling fine goods to the upper crust of San Francisco. Just behind the side they stood on, though, were the stews and taverns. It was no place for a proper young woman. No place for Celia, either. She had not been thinking clearly to have followed Tessie here with evening approaching and no police escort. She was fortunate to have been accosted by Nicholas Greaves and not the pickpocket she hadn't noticed.

"What did the man she was talking to look like?" he asked.

"He had reddish hair, a beard, I think, and the most outlandish yellow-and-red waistcoat. Do you know him?"

"Might be a shock to discover, ma'am, that I don't know every man who lives near the Barbary."

"I shall endeavor to recover from such a revelation, Mr. Greaves." They stepped onto the broad pavement of Montgomery Street, leaving behind the sounds of laughter and arguments, jangling music starting up. "You do realize how very close we are to the wharf where Li Sha was found."

"Yes, I do," he said stiffly.

"Am I annoying you, Mr. Greaves?"

He gazed over at her, an eyebrow arching. "What do you think?"

She continued asking questions anyway. "Have you discovered where Li Sha was staying in the days before her murder?"

"I did just tell you this is my investigation, didn't I?"

"It is a simple question."

He muttered beneath his breath, words she could not discern. "Not at the Chinese Mission and not at the Langes'."

"I'm seeing a patient tomorrow morning, Dora Schneider, who knew Li Sha. They met at a charity event I organized last autumn. Dora talked to Li Sha when everyone else ignored her. Perhaps she will have some information."

Mr. Greaves halted. "Do you ever intend to listen to me, Mrs. Davies?"

"I will let you know what Dora has to tell me. I promise," she added.

"Just like you were going to tell me about Tessie Lange's odd behavior, I suppose."

"Do not say you do not trust me," she responded with a faint smile. "I would be most hurt."

Which made him laugh.

*N*ick watched Mrs. Davies stride up the road. He worked to convince himself he was standing there because he half expected her to take a detour and continue her pursuit of Miss Lange. To be honest, he was actually standing there to catch a final glimpse of her before he continued on his business. She had the sort of carriage women got from balancing books on their heads, but she was spit and fire behind those sophisticated British vowels. And he had a soft spot for spit and fire.

Tugging his hat lower and turning on his heel, he headed for Pacific Street, the destination he'd been bound for before he'd spotted Celia Davies racing along Kearney like a coonhound on a scent.

Nick scanned the road, which was crowded with soaks and gamesters and thieves, noting the dour men who studied him through open doorways and around the edges of faded velvet curtains, prepared to chain and bolt their doors if the cop— they knew he was police even though he didn't wear a gray uniform with an obvious badge—made a move to barge inside and start throwing the law around. Since the chief of police rarely received any complaints about Barbary crime from the folks who mattered to him, the proprietors weren't much at risk from Nick doing any such thing.

He located the saloon he sought, BAUMAN's painted on a wooden sign tacked to the lintel. Unable to choose its neighbors, it was located next door to a brothel with the unoriginal name of Mrs. Brown's House of Joy. One of the brothel residents reclined within the depths of the curtained doorway, smoking a cigarillo, her skirts hitched up to reveal red petticoats and shapely bare ankles, a sliver of early-evening sun warming her skin.

She noticed him stopped on the street and stubbed out the cigarillo on the stone step before scrambling to her feet. She was pretty, young, with thick brown hair and big brown eyes. Part Mexican, he'd guess, and not so long on the streets that she'd grown haggard before her years. She smiled; she had all of her teeth. She wouldn't for long, if she kept smoking cigarillos.

"You looking for company, mister?"

Nick pitied her; he always pitied them. Not that a single one of these street girls wanted pity so much as they wanted cash. Enough cash to get away from the depravity and the squalor, the abusive customers, the drunks and brawlers. He would give her some, but if he pulled out a coin here, he'd be identified as a mark within seconds and pickpocketed before he could even reach for his purse. Besides, every evening she was probably searched by Mrs. Brown or one of her lackeys and stripped of any money found on her.

"You shouldn't be asking me," he said.

"You police?"

He tapped the brim of his hat. "Good day to you," he responded and descended the steps leading into the basement saloon.

A stove warmed the space, and gas lamps lit the tin ceiling. The proprietor was cleaning tables while in the tiny kitchen beyond the main room his wife was frying wurst, preparing for the evening crowd that would turn up around seven and stay until it was kicked out at twelve. This was a nicer saloon than a lot of those in or near the Barbary, with a better clientele.

"Mina?" he asked the girl's boss, a barrel-chested German with a handsome smile.

"She is in back, Detective Greaves," he answered, returning to the walnut bar near the large front window. "Leave the door open."

"You must want to hear the shouting, Bauman."

The German laughed and started stacking clean glasses on shelves.

The saloon was not only nicer than a lot of them; it was bigger, too, with two rooms of living quarters for the Baumans and a spare room for the musicians to rest and prepare for the night's entertainment. Nick nodded to Mrs. Bauman as he went down the hallway adjacent to the kitchen.

He paused in front of the closed door, an uneasy feeling in his chest. Removing his hat, he knocked and didn't wait for her to tell him to come in.

"It's not time yet, Herr Bauman." She looked up. Her dark eyes met Nick's in the mirror propped against the wall over the dressing table where she was seated. Her pink lips, lips he had once thought tasted as good as they looked, fell open. "Nick."

Not *Hello* or *What the hell are you doing here?* Just his name. Which said a whole lot about the months that had elapsed since the last time they'd seen each other. It said even more about all the pain he'd caused when he'd told her it was best he walk out of this room and out of her life.

With a swish of striped purple-and-yellow silk, she spun about on the stool. She'd saved for months to buy the dress, which Nick hadn't realized when he'd made the mistake of asking who the admirer was who had bought it for her. She had a mean slap when she got angry.

"Hullo, Mina."

She was lovely even in the harsh flare of the gas lamps turned up high to help her apply the scant amount of makeup she wore. She had lustrous black hair and skin that was as smooth as silk on every inch he'd ever touched. Her temper could be quick to flare and quicker still to burn out, but she had been able to make him laugh. He'd needed to laugh when they had first fallen in together. After Meg had killed herself.

"I'm busy, Nick." Her face had settled into hard lines. He hadn't exactly expected her to jump into his arms. "I need to finish getting ready so I can have a bite to eat and get some practice in before the place opens. We have a new pianist tonight. Who knows what tempo he's going to take for some of those songs. I'd rather not find out the hard way. Herr Bauman wouldn't like that."

"I won't take long."

"You've already taken too much of my time."

He let that comment go. No point in bringing up old arguments. "What do you know about the anti-coolie groups? Any of them in here complaining, talking about causing trouble?"

"This is about the murder of that Chinese prostitute. That's why you're here." She let out a harsh laugh. "Business first, like ever, eh, Nick? Your blasted work. Always so damned important. More important than anybody or anything else. You never change."

So much for not wanting to bring up old arguments.

He turned his hat in his hands. When he drew in a breath, he inhaled the tuberose perfume she used and recollected a woman who smelled of soap and lavender. A woman who didn't have reasons to despise him.

"I told you then that getting involved with me was a bad idea, Mina."

"And you were right."

"Back to my question." He'd apologized once for breaking her heart; he wasn't going to again. "This is serious, Mina. I need to know if you've heard anything. Might one of them be behind the girl's killing?"

"Hell, Nick." She let out a breath. "I don't remember hearing anything about folks hankering to kill a prostitute, if that's what you're asking. I don't think any of the men who come in here and complain over their beers would go that far. It was probably one of her customers."

Mina sounded indifferent, but he knew she sympathized with the girls on the streets, girls who had it a lot rougher than she did as a woman who didn't have to sell her body in order to survive.

"Ever hear of a man named Wagner? A customs official who likes to beat up people?" He described the man.

"No, Nick. I don't know the man. He's never been in here."

"So that's it?" he asked. "That's all you're going to tell me?"

She licked her lips and contemplated him. He didn't like that he could read concern in her eyes. After all they'd said to each other, she could still care. "I'll let you know if I hear anything. But that's all I can promise. Don't ask me for more."

"Thank you, Mina." Nick placed his hat on his head, leveling the brim with a sweep of his fingertips. "And I'm sorry."

"Don't bother. I don't believe you."

He turned on his heel and strode out into the hallway.

"Be careful, Nick!" she called to his back, proving that his obsession with work wasn't the only thing that never changed.

*C*elia had waited until she was certain Nicholas Greaves hadn't followed her before retracing her steps to Mr. Lange's shop. As she'd hoped, he had returned and was outside on the street, speaking with a man who had his back to Celia.

"Mr. Lange," she called out.

The stranger turned toward her. He caught her eye, frowned, and rushed off. He must not appreciate being interrupted.

Mr. Lange let him go without comment. "Madame Davies. It is good to see you. The news about Miss Li . . ." He shook his head sadly and escorted her inside the shop.

Apparently, the stranger had distracted Mr. Lange while he had been preparing pills. A mahogany pill roller and a bowl of reddish paste bound together by plant gum and glycerine waited on the shop's large table.

"I cannot believe it, either," she said.

"A detective was here to talk to us. Do you think the police believe we are responsible?"

"Of course not. They're merely being thorough."

"Ah. *Oui*." Hubert Lange stepped around the table. "Do you mind if I continue?" He gestured at the pill roller. "It is a most important order."

"Not at all. Please do."

He formed a thin tube out of the reddish paste. "You have come for your gum arabic, no?"

"I have. You were not here when I stopped by earlier."

"Ah yes. I was called away to make a delivery." She noticed his hands were shaking. It was not like him to be so agitated; he must be very upset by Li Sha's death. "Was not Thérèse here?" he asked.

She was glad he asked the question; now she did not have to think up a reason to inquire about Tessie's peculiar actions. "No, she was gone as well."

"I must speak to her about leaving when I am away." He flipped over the mahogany roller, revealing the twenty-four channels carved on the other side, laid the paste tube atop them, and began pressing out pills. "We cannot have the customers going to the other shops because we are not open."

"I was on my way home when I spotted her heading for the Barbary." *A trifle disingenuous, Celia.* "I thought it so unusual, I decided to follow her."

He glanced up then and peered at her through his spectacles. "You follow my daughter?"

Celia flushed. However, in for a pence, in for a pound.

"I'm far too curious at times, I suppose," she said, hoping she sounded as though she realized she'd been silly. She probably had been silly. "I know how much you worry about her, though. So I thought I should tell you that when Tessie was in the Barbary, I saw her talking to a rather unpleasant-looking man."

"A man in the Barbary?" he asked, stroking the flat paddle forcefully across the grooves, the pills dropping into the shallow trough at the end. "Perhaps she did not go to speak to this man you saw, but he stopped her. You know how it is in this city. The men, they can be so . . . what is the word? Brazen?"

Tessie hadn't seemed alarmed by the man's advances, though. "So you don't believe the man was an acquaintance of hers?"

"Not at all. Who would she know in such a place?" asked Mr. Lange, applying a trembling fingertip to his spectacles and sliding them up the bridge of his nose. "I thank you for the concern, Madame Davies, but you do not need to worry. I will tend to Thérèse."

He picked up a labeled jar from the table. "Here is your gum arabic," he said, and waved a hand at his pills. "And as you see, I am most busy, so . . ."

"Yes, of course. I will leave you to your work," she answered, taking the glass jar and leaving behind the money she owed him. "Good day."

She exited the shop, pausing to look back through the window. Mr. Lange returned her gaze, his mouth set in a grim line. She waved jauntily and headed up the street.

"There is something wrong there," she said to herself.

Not only had Tessie's behavior been strange, but her father's agitation was out of character. She'd known the Langes since she and Patrick had arrived in San Francisco and she'd gone to him for medication to relieve some chest congestion. She'd always liked Hubert Lange and had thought him a decent man. Otherwise she wouldn't have asked him to take on Li Sha. She wouldn't have entrusted the girl with someone who would not be good to her.

"I took him for the plainest harmless creature that breathed upon the earth . . ."

"And I may also have been mistaken, Mr. Shakespeare," she said, drawing a quizzical look from a shopkeeper in apron and shirtsleeves who was sweeping his doorstep.

She hurried on, not liking her thoughts.

*N*ick pushed open the door to his rooms and was greeted by a cold, wet nose pressing into the bag in his hand. He grinned. "Hey, hey, hold on there, Riley."

After tossing the bag containing two baked potatoes onto the parlor table, followed by his hat and neckcloth, Nick stooped to ruffle the dog's sloping ears. A shaggy-coated, speckled mix of greyhound and setter, Riley wagged his tail in response.

"You hungry, boy?" Nick asked. "Well, it's just potato peels and oats for your dinner tonight. Sorry."

After taking Riley down the steps and out into the board-inghouse's tiny backyard, he returned alone to his upstairs rooms. He lit the coal oil lamp on the table, keeping dark the rest of his top half of the house—one parlor, one bedroom, one small storage room, and a space his landlady flattered by calling it a kitchen.

"Riley's comin' up!" shouted his landlady, Mrs. Jewett, from the base of the stairs, and Riley trotted through the door Nick had left open. He followed Nick into the kitchen as he prepared a meal for the dog before sitting down to his own.

Back in the parlor, Nick removed his coat and his belt holster and laid his notebook in the pool of light cast by the lamp. He dotted his pile of potatoes with a precious sliver of butter and studied his notes. As was typical at this point in a case, he had very few suspects.

Make a list, Nick. Always make a list. That had been among Uncle Asa's earliest advice. So he did, jotting it down in his notebook.

Tom Davies. Possibly angry Li Sha had moved out. Would be easy for him to lure her to the wharf.

Wagner. Worked at the wharf and had a history of violence aimed at foreigners.

The Langes. Too early to truly suspect them; neither seemed to have a motive, although it appeared Miss Lange hadn't much cared for Li Sha, which he suspected had to do with Tom Davies.

One of the "strange men" whom Lange's neighbor had noticed around the store. Motive or means unknown.

An unidentified member of the Anti-Coolie Association who'd decided Chinese women made good victims, too.

"Not much here, Riley."

The dog lapped up the last scrap of his food and sprawled atop Nick's feet. Nick leaned back in his chair, which creaked beneath him, and kneaded his left arm. The ache suggested he'd probably have another nightmare tonight about the war and a towheaded boy in an oversized gray coat.

Nick tightened his hand around his arm, remembering that battle and that boy. The kid—thirteen? fourteen?—had materialized like a ghost among the smoke and the shattered tree limbs.

The kid had frozen in his tracks, his crudely hemmed coat sleeves dangling over his dirty hands, a piece of twine wrapped around his waist to secure a knife to his side, mismatched shoes on his feet. Nick had wondered that they were sending children to fight. The boy should have been safe at home, not slogging through woods where scraps of combatants were trampled underfoot until the remains of men became indistinguishable from the sticks and leaves and stones. He had wondered that war had come to this. Wondered long enough for the boy to lift his bayoneted Enfield and pierce Nick's arm to the bone.

His closest friend had run to Nick's side and blown a chunk out of the boy's head, but not before he'd taken a bullet meant for Nick. Guilt. Lord, how it had bloomed. Kept him in a hospital longer than he should've stayed. Destroyed the contented man he'd once been. Eaten away part of his soul.

He flipped shut his notebook and stared into the shadows.

"It's nothing, right, ma'am?" Dora Schneider asked Celia the next morning in the clinic.

"I believe you simply have a touch of bronchitis, Dora," said Celia, folding away her stethoscope and returning it to its mahogany box.

"Good, because I can't afford to miss a day of work or they'll sack me for sure. And you know how hard it is to get a job if a woman doesn't want to be a domestic," she said.

Dora must have been fetching once, with her pale blond hair and laughing eyes, before the smallpox had scarred her skin. The disease had not scarred Dora's spirit, however.

"You should recover quickly. You're strong."

The girl coughed, a thick rattle. "But see, I sound like I've got the consumption." She secured her corset over her chemise and tugged on her bodice. "The other girls on the floor stare at me like I'm a leper. I hate being sick."

"You will need to rest more than you probably do, however, if you wish to prevent the cough from worsening." Celia selected a bottle containing an infusion of comfrey root from among her supplies, meticulously arranged on her examination room's shelves. The medication should help thin the secretions in Dora's lungs and speed her recovery. "Take some time to rest this weekend, if at all possible."

"Rest?" Dora laughed, which brought on another bout of coughing. Celia handed her a handkerchief and she blew her nose loudly.

"When am I gonna rest, Mrs. Davies? The boss is trying to get us to learn to use those newfangled Grover and Baker sewing machines, and I just hate the thing! Work all day at the clothing manufactory, then have chores when I get home." She returned the handkerchief to Celia, who dropped it into a basket from which it would be collected by Addie at day's end.

"Dora, I would like to ask you something about Li Sha. The police are trying to discover where she was staying in the days before she was killed."

Death from homicide by person or persons unknown. That was what the report from the coroner's inquest had stated. Detective Greaves' assistant, Officer Taylor, had brought her the news that morning and told her she could claim the body and plan the funeral. "Do you have any idea? Had you seen her?"

"That's easy, ma'am." Dora hopped down from the thigh-high armless bench Celia used as an examining table. Uncle Walford had built the table for her when she'd begun talking about opening a clinic, shortly after Patrick had signed on to a merchant vessel and sailed away for good. Her uncle had done so much to help Celia right her world after it had been upended by a husband who had abandoned her on their eighth wedding anniversary.

"Li Sha was with me," Dora said, brushing her skirt flat over the crinoline with a snap of her wrists. "She begged and begged, and I let her sleep on the floor a couple nights."

Celia could imagine what Dora's grim landlady had thought about having a Chinese woman on the premises.

She handed the bottle of comfrey root to Dora, who tucked it into her net purse. "Why had she left Tom's?" Celia asked.

"Li Sha wouldn't want me to tell, Mrs. Davies," said Dora.

"Li Sha is gone now and beyond fretting over having her secrets revealed."

"But I don't want to say anything bad about your brother-in-law, either, ma'am."

Uneasiness swept over her. "That is all right, too."

Dora's brow puckered. "They'd fought. Weren't the first time. But this time he hit her. Never had before. Broke things before, but never hit her."

"I saw the bruises on Li Sha's face, but I had no idea Tom had caused them." Nicholas Greaves had suspected, however.

"She musta thought it would get better with him. We women are always hoping our men will change one day, aren't we?" Dora asked sadly. "But when Tom had been drinking he could get mighty ornery. He'd promised to stop with the liquor, promised Li Sha because of the baby, but there'd been some sorta worriment at his work and he was upset and took to the whiskey."

"When did this fight occur?"

"A week ago it was. On Friday. Li Sha came from work at the Langes', and Tom started shouting. Hit her hard. Said he didn't believe anymore the baby was his," Dora continued, her words tumbling one over the other in her haste, now that she had decided to speak. "But of course it was his baby. Don't know what made him think it wasn't. Li Sha was true to that ornery cuss. Sorry, ma'am."

"I know he has a temper, Dora." It was the reason she avoided Tom, although Celia had attempted to be cordial to please her husband. "I merely hadn't realized he could be violent."

"He said some other things, ma'am, mean stuff. Threatened her. She was mighty beat up when she showed up at my door with nothing more than a raggedy carpetbag," Dora explained. "I still have her carpetbag at my room. Do you think the police will want it?"

"They might, Dora. I'll ask."

Dora nodded. "Well, as I said, she came to my place and was hopping mad. Said she was done with Tom. Wouldn't ever go back to a man like him. And earlier that night, the night she died, she told me she was gonna get some money. Gonna cut stick and head someplace better to raise her baby."

"I wonder who she thought would give her money." It was important to find that person, who was either the last to see her or the one responsible for the crime. "She didn't mention a name?"

"No. I wish I'da asked, but I was in a hurry that night. Me and a friend were going to Maguire's Opera House to celebrate her birthday, you see. Alice Kingsbury was performing in *Fanchon, the Cricket*. We sat in the gallery and it was lovely." Her eyes shone. A visit to the opera house would be quite a treat for a seamstress, the daughter of German immigrants, who lived in a tiny room in a lodging house. "I didn't get home 'til late. I thought Li Sha would be there, but she wasn't. She never came back."

"Did she ever talk about the people she worked for at the apothecary shop?" Celia asked.

"Talk about what?"

"Did she ever say they were unkind to her?"

Dora scrunched up her nose and looked uncomfortable. "Um . . ."

"You can tell me, Dora."

"It was that daughter of Li Sha's boss. She didn't much like Li Sha. Because of Tom, you know," said Dora. "You did know, didn't you? I think he used to be with that woman, if you know what I mean, before he settled on Li Sha."

"I was aware Tom and Tessie Lange were friends—"

"It was more than friends, ma'am."

"They were lovers?"

Dora blushed. "Well . . ."

"I wonder what else I do not know about my brother-in-law." Dora's information suggested Tessie had been jealous of Li Sha, the woman who had supplanted her in Tom's affection. *And jealousy is a powerful—and sometimes violent—emotion.*

"Thank you for helping, Dora." Celia nodded toward the young woman's net purse. "Sip the infusion twice a day. I want to see you in three days, even if you're feeling better. If you are worse, come sooner."

Dora thanked her, and Celia showed her out. Next door, Barbara was entertaining Angelo with an old battered top that skipped over the Cascarinos' uneven walkway. The boy laughed at her antics. Barbara looked calmer and happier than she had all day.

Celia returned to the examination room and folded the

thin blanket that covered the bench. While she tidied the space, she considered how Li Sha must have felt while working at the shop of a woman who didn't like her. Or worse, might have hated her. She must have been miserable. And who could Li Sha have asked for money? The list of possible people was not long, although there could be friends Celia was unaware of. The list had to include Hubert Lange, despite his daughter's feelings about Li Sha. Celia was certain, though, that Mr. Lange would have mentioned if Li Sha had asked him for money.

Wouldn't he?

She was still standing in the middle of the room, blanket clutched to her chest, when Addie shouldered open the connecting door that led to the kitchen, a tray of tea and biscuits—or cookies, as the Americans called them—in her hands. Her wonderful shortbread, which she always baked to lift Celia's spirits.

"And what did that Dora Schneider have to say about Li Sha?" her housekeeper asked.

"Were you listening at the door?"

Addie didn't even bother to look guilty. "This isna our concern, ma'am. Asking questions and whatnot. We should leave such matters to the police. That is what they're paid to do."

"But I've learned that on the night Li Sha was killed, she went to ask someone for money to leave the city. That's very important information."

"You know what my father would say about all this, ma'am. Of little meddling comes great care."

"Sometimes a little meddling is called for, Addie."

One eyebrow arched. "Nae to my mind."

With that, Addie snatched the blanket from Celia's arms and marched back to the kitchen, head held high.

CHAPTER 7

"I don't know what he thought he saw, but it wasn't like that at all!" Wagner shouted, looking at Nick, then Taylor, and back again.

Nick leaned against the wall of the detectives' office, the wind from the open window at his back ruffling his hair, and folded his arms. "Then what was it like, Mr. Wagner? The dockworker is pretty sure you were trying to sink that Chinese girl's body, not drag it onto the pier."

Seated next to Wagner, Taylor jotted in his notebook, his pencil scratching against the paper.

Wagner glared at him. "What're you writing? You writing I did it?"

"Just taking notes, Mr. Wagner." Taylor licked the tip of his pencil and flipped to a new page. "Just taking notes."

The veins in Wagner's thick neck bulged. "I was not trying to sink her body, Detective Greaves. I was on my knees trying to grab her dress, and it was stuck. I lost my balance and nearly fell into the bay myself. You could've been fishing me outta there, too."

Taylor glanced up, looking for direction on how to proceed. Wagner's story seemed reasonable. It could've happened that way, and the dockworker who'd noticed him with the girl's body could've gotten the wrong idea. Witnesses weren't always reliable, and memories could change to fit what you wanted to see.

"My wife told you I was with her all night," said Wagner. "Right? And I bet you could ask my neighbors if they saw me, too. That woman who lives across the way is pretty nosy. She'd tell you I was at home that night, and I didn't leave early for work, either."

Taylor raised his eyebrows and Nick nodded. Another person to confirm that Wagner hadn't killed Li Sha. A suspect to take off the list.

"Have Mullahey show Mr. Wagner out, Taylor," said Nick. "But don't go too far away, Wagner. We might need to talk to you again."

"And I'll just keep saying what I've said all along—I didn't know her and I didn't kill her."

"Good day, Mr. Wagner."

Nick turned and stared out the window where a gust of wind swirled dust across the street. For a city built on sand, it was a common occurrence.

Chairs scraped back and the door opened, Taylor shouting to Mullahey to get Wagner out of there.

The door closed again, and Nick glanced over his shoulder at his assistant. "I think we can write that one off, Taylor."

Taylor frowned and dropped into the chair he'd just vacated.

"I'll check with his nosy neighbor, but it looks like you're right, sir. Mr. Greaves. Sir."

Nick stalked across the office. It was only fifteen feet by fifteen feet, so it didn't take long to reach the tall oak filing cabinet against the far side. At Briggs' desk, he grabbed a doughnut from a plate of them that the other detective had left behind.

"Tell me you've learned something useful about Tom Davies," he said, setting the doughnut back down; he didn't have an appetite after all.

"Tom Davies was at Mitchell's saloon on Monday evening like he said. The saloonkeeper remembers him. Guess he's there often enough for the fellow to recollect Davies. And that night he was in a mighty sour mood, according to Mitchell. But he wasn't there for long. Left after about an hour or so. If he went anyplace other than home afterward, I haven't been able to find out."

Davies had had time, then, to meet Li Sha that night. Could've killed her, dumped her body, and gone back to his room near Tar Flat with nobody the wiser. But if Li Sha was angry with him, would she have agreed to see him?

"I also went to the Clerks' Relief Society looking for friends of his who might have more to say about Davies," Taylor continued, "but they've never heard of him. And I still haven't figured out where Li Sha was staying before she died."

Dead ends. More dead ends. "Anything else?"

"Yep. When I was out in the station room, I saw that Mrs. Davies is here."

Nick smiled, which raised Taylor's eyebrows. "You don't have to keep looking for where Li Sha was staying, Taylor. I suspect Mrs. Davies has found out for us."

Taylor showed her in.

"I have come to admit I was mistaken, Mr. Greaves," Celia Davies said, her pale eyes steady on his face.

Her accent was more distinct than before. Maybe that was what happened when Englishwomen admitted they were wrong.

"About my brother-in-law," she added.

"Listen, I need to get out of here," said Nick. "The stench is turning my stomach. Care to walk and tell me what you've learned?"

"Are we going anywhere in particular?"

"Anyplace that's not here."

Nick collected his hat from his desk and guided her out. From the doorway, Taylor watched their passage with an irritating smile.

"Taylor, what are you smirking at?" asked Captain Eagan, stepping through the barred door between the main room and the jail cells.

A bear of a man, he had heavy black sideburns that he kept meticulously trimmed and broad shoulders. His irises were so dark you couldn't distinguish them from the pupils, which made him difficult to stare at. The few policemen in the station scrambled out of his path as he wended his way between desks.

"Uh, nothing, sir," Taylor answered, and scuttled to his desk.

"Greaves, I was just coming to talk to you about that Chinese girl's murder," said Eagan.

"We can talk later, Captain. I have a witness to interview."

Eagan scanned Mrs. Davies. "Make it quick. I don't want you wasting time on this case. You've got better things to do."

Eagan's priorities never did include giving a damn about the Chinese.

Nick indicated to Mrs. Davies that she should use the alley door, and he stomped up the steps behind her.

"Your superior?" she asked. The sunshine was glaring, and she squinted as she looked at Nick. "He has quite the most magnificent black whiskers."

"Yep, that's him," said Nick, striding toward Kearney. "But I wouldn't call Eagan's whiskers magnificent."

"Perhaps extravagant is a better word," she said as they wove through the lines of parked hacks and smaller, cheaper one-horse cabs that clogged the street in front of city hall. "Your captain bears a strong resemblance to a physician I knew at the army hospital in Philadelphia. A domineering man who refused to listen to anyone."

"Especially you?"

She smiled ruefully. "Especially me. Although the sister I served under in Scutari, during the war in the Crimea, was even more intimidating than that doctor."

"I can't imagine you being intimidated by anybody, ma'am," he said, guiding her out of the path of a Mexican cowboy who was clomping along the sidewalk, his sombrero flapping and his spurs jangling.

"When I was younger I could be intimidated. Absolutely. I was only seventeen when I went to the Crimea, and pretending to be much older. I was always afraid I'd be found out and sent home to England." The smile faded. "Perhaps I should have been."

He ushered her through a gate in the iron fence surrounding Portsmouth Square. The flag waved on a tall pole, and gravel walkways radiated from the center, where a marble fountain spit water. Across the way, a clutch of eastern tourists in their freshly purchased traveling outfits headed to Chinatown with a policeman as a guide.

"Explain to me about your brother-in-law," he said as they

strolled. The wind teased loose strands of her hair and carried the scent of lavender to him.

She told him what Dora Schneider knew about Li Sha and Tom Davies. That, in the days before she'd been killed, they'd fought about the baby and he had beaten her. That Li Sha had gone to Miss Schneider's for refuge. Mrs. Davies also told him about the girl's quest for money the night she'd died because she'd wanted to leave town.

When Mrs. Davies finished, she turned to stare at him, hoping for . . . hoping for what? That he would ignore the information she'd provided and somehow save Tom Davies?

"I'll have to bring Tom in, Mrs. Davies," he said.

"There could be another explanation," she said. "The person she approached for money might be responsible. Or that person is, at the very least, the last to have seen her alive. He may know who killed her."

"Could be," Nick agreed.

"Furthermore, Li Sha didn't come to me or Barbara, or Dora, not that Miss Schneider has much money to give to anyone. Which leaves a reduced number of individuals to inquire after."

"Such as?"

She paused to think while the bell on a nearby church tolled the hour, followed by another church bell down the road. San Francisco didn't lack for places of worship, which sprouted like weeds. Places for all the sinners who drank and gambled and whored in the Barbary and along the docks to turn back to God. As far as Nick could tell, the effort wasn't working.

"Not Mr. Lange," Mrs. Davies said. "He didn't mention anything about Li Sha asking him for money when I spoke to him yesterday. By the way, Mr. Lange claims Tessie doesn't know anyone in the Barbary."

"He might not want folks to know."

"True." She frowned. "I also learned from Dora that Tessie Lange and my brother-in-law were once involved romantically. At first, I presumed this meant that Li Sha wouldn't ask Tessie for money. But now I suppose Li Sha could have reasoned that Tessie would happily supply funds in order to get her chief rival out of town." She paused and gazed up at him. "But why kill Li Sha if she was already intending to leave?"

He liked the logical way she thought.

"Just because Li Sha currently wanted to leave town doesn't mean that would be the situation forever," he said. "After she had the baby, it was always possible she could change her mind and come back to be with Tom."

"I see."

"Any other folks she might've gone to?" Nick asked.

"She might have gone to the Chinese Mission. They don't usually provide the girls with money, however," she said, looking uncomfortable admitting that the missionaries didn't trust what the Chinese women would do with it.

"When Taylor asked the reverend who runs the mission if Li Sha had stayed there recently, he claimed they hadn't seen her for weeks."

"So, if not them, Li Sha might have approached one of the Palmers. Perhaps Mr. Palmer."

"Who?" he asked. "Mrs. Davies, if you really want to help, the best way is to tell me everything you know about her."

"You have attempted to be rid of me on numerous occasions,

Mr. Greaves," she responded. "I regret I have not previously enumerated her every acquaintance."

"All right, all right. Mr. Palmer."

"You haven't heard of him?"

"You've discovered a gap in my knowledge, Mrs. Davies."

She resumed walking, the gravel crunching beneath her sensible boots. He fell into an easy pace at her side.

"Joseph Palmer is a very successful land speculator and developer. He provides funds for my clinic and many other benevolent organizations in the city. Li Sha met him once, along with his wife and daughter, at a charity event at the Chinese Mission," she said. "Li Sha was well aware he supported my clinic, and Barbara and I spoke of him often in her presence. She might have believed his generosity would extend to providing her with money, if she asked."

"Would he have?"

"It does not matter, because according to my cousin, Mr. Palmer was away from town Monday evening."

"I'll go talk to him anyhow. See what he has to say."

Her steps slowed. "I should warn you that Joseph Palmer will not be happy for the police attention."

"Is he friends with Captain Eagan or Police Chief Crowley?"

"Probably both men. Which is why I'm surprised you had not heard of Mr. Palmer before."

"They don't exactly invite me to their parties." Rich and powerful men, as thick as thieves. Not that Eagan was rich. But if you were a businessman in this town, it didn't hurt to have friends on the police force.

"And Tom?"

"I haven't changed my mind about arresting him."

"I truly hope I didn't miss warning signs that Tom could be violent." She closed her fingers tightly around the straps of her reticule. "Li Sha trusted him because of me. Because he is my husband's brother. I need to believe I could not have prevented her murder. Because I fear if he is responsible, I could have."

"It's not your fault, Mrs. Davies."

"Convince me that is true, Mr. Greaves." Her gaze was unfaltering. Beneath a clear sky, her eyes were more blue than gray. "If you do nothing else, convince me that is true."

A ddie met Celia at the front door just as she arrived home. "Mrs. Palmer is here, ma'am. In the parlor."

Proof hung on the hook in the vestibule—Elizabeth Palmer's massive tartan-plaid burnous scarf, which she used as a morning wrap.

"Did she bring Emmeline?" asked Celia.

"No, the poor bairn must still be ailing," said Addie, collecting Celia's shawl. "Miss Barbara is with Mrs. Palmer. 'Tis odd how they're behaving, though. Usually they're friendly enough, but today they could be sitting on thorns in there." Addie leaned closer and lowered her voice, even though the pocket door to the parlor was shut. "Nae that I can blame Miss Barbara one bit if she's become uncomfortable with that woman."

"Elizabeth is not so bad," Celia said.

"You'd think different, ma'am, if you were in my shoes."

Elizabeth Palmer made nearly everyone uncomfortable, especially servants. Celia had heard that in the past two years alone, the Palmers had engaged four separate housekeepers, a Chinese boy, and one maid of all work. The latest had left just last week, to be replaced by yet another young woman. Elizabeth expected the utmost out of everyone, and sometimes her standards were too high.

High standards that would extend to Celia's dusty boots.

She dropped onto the chair by the door and fumbled with the bootlaces, and ended up tightening the knots rather than loosening them, hindered by the corset, which prevented her from bending down.

"What did the detective have to say?" Addie asked, crouching at Celia's feet and undoing the laces for her.

"He intends to arrest Tom," she answered, leaning back in the chair. "We should be thankful Patrick isn't here. He would be livid."

The Davies temper. She had never before imagined that it could be fierce enough to kill.

"We could talk to Madame Philippe," Addie offered. "She's an astrologer. She could tell us who did it."

"An astrologer, Addie?" Had they already arrived at the point where an astrologer was their best hope for a solution? "You don't believe in such things, do you?"

"Weel, my mother always claimed the auld woman who lived at the edge of the village had the second sight," said Addie. "Besides, Miss Lange sets great store by what the woman tells her. She's mentioned Madame Philippe to me more than once when I've gone to the shop for you. I think it canna hurt to visit the woman."

"Miss Lange uses her?" Celia asked. Here was an interesting turn. She wondered if Tessie had ever spoken to Madame Philippe about Li Sha. It could be worth a visit to find out. "Perhaps we should go, Addie."

"Then I'll make an appointment, ma'am," said Addie, smiling.

Her boots removed, Celia tucked her feet into the soft leather mules lying nearby and stood, smoothing her skirt with her hands. She slid open the door and entered the parlor, where Barbara and Elizabeth Palmer blinked at each other over cooling cups of tea.

"Cousin Celia, there you are!" Barbara said, relief causing her voice to rise. "I told Mrs. Palmer you wouldn't be much longer."

"Good afternoon, Celia," said Elizabeth, who was dressed as perfectly as ever. She wore a gown of dove gray silk appliquéd with ebony velvet, which fell in folds and ruffles that enhanced her fine figure. A beautiful woman with enviable cheekbones, she was several years older than Celia but did not look it.

Celia returned Elizabeth's smile. The Palmers attended political events and magnificent galas during New Year's festivities and had a ten-dollar private box at Maguire's Opera House, unlike Dora and her friend, who were satisfied with the twenty-five-cent gallery seats. Elizabeth Palmer socialized with the grand and great of the city—an impressive elevation from her rumored humble beginnings—but there was an uneasiness in her manner, a fretfulness, as though she feared her world might crumble.

And Celia felt sorry for her.

"I apologize that I wasn't here when you arrived, Elizabeth," she said.

"Your cousin has been as charming as ever, even under these . . . difficult circumstances."

Barbara stared down at her lap.

"Might I refresh your tea?" Celia asked Elizabeth.

"No need," the woman answered, waving her hand toward the full cup on the marble-top rosewood table between the chairs. Celia took the chair opposite her, self-conscious over the condition of her own dress, with its repaired tears and a stain along the hem that Addie hadn't been able to completely remove. At one time, Celia had worn gowns as fine as Elizabeth's. Those days, however, were in the distant past.

"I was just telling your cousin how much we miss her visits." Elizabeth turned her radiant smile on Barbara. "Emmeline asks for you especially, Barbara. But her asthma has been so bad lately that we've had no visitors. She's been ill for several days now, longer than usual. Those doctors are just useless."

The Palmers' fourteen-year-old daughter had always been fragile, with frequent bouts of severe asthma. Celia had offered to examine the girl, but her offers had received cool dismissals. Among the prosperous of San Francisco, male physicians were much preferred over the care of a woman who ran a free clinic.

"I gather Emmeline's illness is what kept you from the society meeting on Monday evening," said Celia. "I was wondering, because Barbara and I always see you there."

"That's how ill Emmeline has been. She hasn't been out of the house in weeks."

"Some fresh air might help in this case," suggested Celia.

"I don't dare take her out," said Elizabeth.

Every other child Elizabeth Palmer had borne had died in infancy, and consequently her only daughter was cosseted and fussed over. More than was good for her, in Celia's opinion. "And it's a good thing I didn't take her to the meeting on Monday. Mrs. Douglass told me that the ladies weren't very welcoming to you, Celia."

"Barbara and I felt compelled to leave, actually."

"Well, I have good news that should take your mind off their unkindness," Elizabeth said. "Mr. Palmer has recommended we help with Li Sha's funeral expenses. Whatever the cost."

"Are you certain? Your husband has been more than generous

to us already." In addition to supporting the clinic, he paid for the piano lessons Barbara received from Emmeline's music tutor, lessons Celia could never have afforded with the stipend Uncle Walford had left her.

"How kind!" Barbara's eyes shone. "Isn't Mr. Palmer just the best of men, Cousin Celia?"

"Yes, he is," said Celia, looking away from the rapt expression on her cousin's face.

Elizabeth waved an elegant hand, pleased by the compliments. "It's nothing, Barbara."

Celia recalled the more elaborate caskets at Atkins Massey's Coffin Warerooms, the trappings they could now afford. Not that Li Sha would have expected trappings or desired an elaborate casket.

"Please extend my thanks to your husband," said Celia.

"I shall." Elizabeth smiled and took a sip of her tea. "I'm sure I don't have to say how shocked we are about Li Sha's death. To think we've met somebody who has been murdered. And I'd had such hopes life would turn out well for that girl. She was a protégée of yours, wasn't she?"

"More than a protégée. A friend."

Elizabeth Palmer's eyes, a pale brown the exact shade of café au lait, peered into Celia's. "Do the police have any idea who might be responsible?"

Celia tensed. Nicholas Greaves would not like her to discuss the case, even though the news of Tom's arrest would soon be in every paper in town. "Why do you ask me?"

"You identified the girl's remains, didn't you? I presume that means you're in close contact with the police."

Celia wondered where Elizabeth had learned she'd been to

the coroner's. It had not been mentioned in the papers. "The police are pursuing several leads, I believe."

"Anybody we know?" Elizabeth always endeavored to be the first to have heard the best gossip.

"I'm not at liberty to say," said Celia, noticing that Barbara had turned pale.

"Of course." Elizabeth looked disappointed.

"However, I have learned that Li Sha planned to leave San Francisco. She intended to meet with someone in particular in order to get the money to do so," she said. It was more than she should have said. "Do you have any idea whom Li Sha might have turned to? Did she ask you or your husband, by any chance?"

"She didn't approach me," Elizabeth said. "And Joseph was down in Santa Clara County looking at some farm property and did not return until midday Tuesday."

"So he *was* gone," said Barbara.

"I hate to say this, Celia, given that he's your brother-in-law, but don't you suppose it's possible Li Sha told Tom Davies of these plans to leave him? And then—I know this is dreadful—but then he killed her in a rage?" Elizabeth lifted a hand to her throat and curled her fingers around the cameo locket pinned to her collar.

It appeared everyone knew of Tom's temper. *Convince me it is not my fault, Mr. Greaves.*

"He would not kill her," said Celia, firmly. "I am certain of that."

"Of course not. I shouldn't have said that," Elizabeth soothed. "Maybe then it's somebody from the Anti-Coolie Association."

"That was my initial thought, too," said Celia. "But her plan to meet with someone that evening has made me reconsider that idea."

"Li Sha likely never made it to her rendezvous with this benefactor, Celia," said Elizabeth, offering a possibility Celia had not considered. "Mrs. Douglass is right to be worried about those awful people. The anti-Chinese groups threaten the peace. Threaten those of us who've simply tried to help the Chinese women. The society needs to focus on the reformable white women of San Francisco and leave the women of Chinatown to fend for themselves, I'm afraid. Maybe the Six Companies will finally take an interest in them and tend to their own."

Celia doubted that would ever happen. The Chinese benevolent societies—there were six, hence their common name— existed to take care of their members, and the prostitutes were not members. The Six Companies seemed to care nearly as little about the women as the average citizen did.

"I will not stop helping the Chinese women where I can," said Celia.

"You should take my advice and steer clear of Chinatown, Celia. You place yourself and your cousin at risk."

"She's right, Cousin Celia," said Barbara.

"We will be cautious, of course," Celia responded. "But I'm confident we will be fine."

Elizabeth studied Celia as if she had never met a person who was so hopelessly naïve. "Li Sha probably thought she'd be fine, too."

"He didn't exactly go peacefully, sir," said Taylor, returning from the street to Tom Davies' room. "In fact, he kicked the constable who was loading him into the wagon to take him to the station."

The front door to the boardinghouse must have been open,

because Nick could hear Davies shouting down on the street, a string of Irish swearwords.

"Idiot," said Nick. Davies' yowling faded.

"Have you found anything else?" asked Taylor. He scratched his neck beneath his ear and looked around at Davies' room. "What with Davies' landlady saying she heard all the shouting and cursing last week, that he'd threatened that Chinese girl, that she'd 'regret it' . . . that's enough, though, right?"

Nick exhaled. Word of the threats and the knife they'd found hidden in Davies' chest of drawers were enough to arrest the man.

"Don't need nothin' else," said Mullahey, righting a cane-seated chair that had been knocked over during their search, before turning his attention to the trunk shoved into the corner, its contents spilled onto the floor.

Nick bent to pick up the Bible at his feet. It was well-thumbed, with notes in the margin. Notes in an inexperienced hand, reminders to learn the meanings of specific words. They might be Li Sha's notes. He recollected the bruised and cut body lying on that cold marble slab in Massey's cellar, her dark hair spilling over the edge. If she'd hoped for God's mercy and protection, it hadn't come.

Gently, Nick placed the book in the bottom of the trunk and covered it with a patchwork quilt that had also been stored there.

"We can take care of cleaning up, sir," said Taylor. "No call for you to be doing that."

"It's okay," Nick said, straightening.

What they'd learned meant the noose was tightening around Tom Davies' neck. It also meant Celia Davies was likely going to feel guilty about Li Sha's tragic relationship with her brother-in-law for a damned long time.

"That China girl shoulda cleared out earlier, huh," said Mullahey, dropping a pair of worn boots into the trunk. "Given what a cuss that feller is."

Nick skirted the folding partition. The rug was rolled back, and the drawers from the chest lay upon the bed, making the hair-stuffed mattress sag. Besides the knife, there hadn't been much in the drawers—a few items of clothing and an albumen carte de visite portrait of a man, woman, and young boy posed beneath a potted palm, its silver frame tarnished. Taylor had also found a letter from Davies' mother, dated five years back, asking him to return home to Ireland. Nick gazed out the nearest window. Davies had propped it open for some reason, as if the stink outside could ever freshen the air inside. Tom Davies wouldn't be going home to his mother anytime soon. He'd been sent to jail and would likely be staying there.

Until he was convicted and hanged for murder, that was.

Nick closed the window, latching it tight, and spared a parting glance for the photograph Taylor had left on the chest of drawers. Another family shattered. Nick could give a lecture on that topic.

"Finish putting everything back in order here," Nick said to the policemen. He'd stop at Joseph Palmer's office on Sutter before returning to the station. "We're done here. On your way to the station, Taylor, visit Dora Schneider's place and pick up the carpetbag Li Sha left with her. In case there's something interesting in it. Mullahey, get to work on that liquor-smuggling case Eagan wants you to handle, since he won't be happy to know I'm making use of two policemen on this case."

"Sure enough, Mr. Greaves," said Mullahey. "Eagan's none too happy any of us are botherin' with this China girl."

"Looks like we can wrap up this case pretty quick, though," said Taylor.

Nick lifted his hat from where he'd left it on the table, right in front of the chair where Celia Davies had sat and comforted her brother-in-law. "I'm not convinced we've got the right man, Taylor. And I don't care if Eagan's happy or not. He can take my job if he doesn't like what I'm doing."

Mullahey hooted with laughter. "Don't be tellin' Eagan that, Mr. Greaves, 'cause he might just take you up on the offer!"

*S*tretching, Celia yawned into her hand. She dug a finger through her skirt and beneath the bottom edge of her corset, attempting and failing to reach an itch. "Gad."

She lowered the wick on the lantern on her desk and stood. The examination room's small china mantel clock showed the time to be half five. The sun would set in thirty minutes. Just enough time to do some gardening before eating a light meal and going to bed early.

Yawning again, Celia clutched her mother's shawl tight about her, the soft fabric comforting, and scanned the shelves, making a quick survey of her supplies. She needed more bandages, but that looked to be all for now.

She crossed the room to shut the window blinds, her hand pausing on the cord. She leaned closer to the glass. A man stood outside, down the road a short distance, and he was looking at their house.

"I thought you might want some tea before you head out to the garden, ma'am," announced Addie, bustling into the examination room.

"Addie, have you noticed a man watching the house?" Celia turned and asked her.

"What?" The tea tray thumped atop the desk, and Addie came to her side. "Where?"

"There." Celia pointed, but the man was no longer lurking in the shadows across the street. "He's gone now. But I thought . . ."

Addie peered around the curtains. "Are you certain you saw someone?"

"It's nothing, Addie. I am mistaken. The strain of the last few days is making me see things." She smiled at her housekeeper. "Or maybe I need spectacles."

"And hide your lovely eyes?" Addie clucked over the idea and returned to the kitchen.

Once she'd gone, Celia scanned the street again. Nothing. With a quick tug of the cord, she snapped the blinds closed.

"Thank you for your time, Mr. Palmer."

"Anything to help the police, Detective Greaves." Joseph Palmer had a deep voice, his consonants soft around the edges. Southern origins, Nick would wager. Palmer gestured toward a man standing near the windows. "This is my associate, Mr. Douglass."

Mr. Douglass, robust and outfitted in a black cassimere frock coat and pants, inclined his head. "Detective." He leaned against a silver-headed walking stick and eyed Nick, not in a friendly fashion.

"You might prefer to speak to me alone, Mr. Palmer," said Nick.

Palmer slid a glance at Douglass. "We shall talk later about this matter."

Douglass nodded. "Good day to you, sir," he said. He exited

the room, his walking stick tapping against the floor, and shut the door behind him.

Palmer pressed his fingertips together while Nick made a circuit of his office, located on the topmost floor of a three-story limestone-faced building. Shelves held books on real estate legal matters and building methods and designs. Maps of California and San Francisco hung on the walls. A red, gold, and blue patterned carpet covered the floor, muting Nick's footfalls. Overlooking Sutter were two floor-to-ceiling arched windows, through which he saw long shadows cast along the road. Nick could just glimpse the onion domes atop the towers of Temple Emanu-el farther up the street. All in all, a pleasant spot.

"You've built up a nice business for yourself," said Nick, continuing his circuit of the room. "How long did that take?"

"Since I and my family arrived in 'sixty-two," he answered. "Hard work, but a man cannot be afraid of that if he wishes to succeed."

"Suppose not."

Palmer folded his hands over the leather blotter atop his mahogany desk, its wood polished to a blinding sheen, and followed Nick with his gaze. His eyes were hawklike, and he wore a suit of clothes as costly as his friend's. A gold watch chain looped across his checked silk vest and a ring glimmered on his left pinkie. Nick had once served under an officer who'd worn a pinkie ring. He'd never thought much of the man.

"Would you care to explain why you might be here, Detective?" Palmer asked.

Pursuing a lead that nobody except me is going to care about, now that Tom Davies has been arrested. "I have some questions about the Chinese girl killed on Monday. I've been told you knew her."

"Ah. Li Sha." He frowned. "She was a poor creature, God rest her soul. The crime in this city. Hmm. But I would not say I knew her. Not really."

"Not really?" Nick asked, arching an eyebrow.

"I do not care for what you are implying, sir."

"So you weren't a client."

The man didn't break a sweat. "What an unseemly suggestion."

"Okay, so you'd only met her once."

"Mrs. Celia Davies introduced us at a Chinese Mission function. She was proud of her efforts to assist Miss Li with her new life and wanted those of us who support her clinic to see that her work could go beyond merely curing ills." Palmer studied him. "I presume Mrs. Davies is the one who told you I had met Miss Li."

Nick straightened a silver inkstand on Palmer's desk, aligning it with the desk's edge. A cedar cigar box occupied another corner of the desk, and the air was sweet with the smell of recently smoked Havanas. Two stubs rested on a brass ashtray. "I've learned that on the night she was murdered, she approached somebody for money in order to leave town. Was that person you?"

"Why, no, Detective Greaves. I was in Santa Clara County that night. Had been for a number of days. Looking at some land I would like to buy, as well as visiting some associates of mine who live in that area. I didn't return home until the next afternoon." He grazed his knuckles over his goatee. He had hands that had never seen manual labor, his wealth earned by cunning rather than brawn. "I was due to return on Monday, but the horse I hired caught a rock in his shoe and pulled up lame. I rested him overnight, then rode on. Mighty inconvenient."

"Where'd you stay?" And would somebody verify his story?

"I camped in a dilapidated old adobe I came across. It was raining. I was awfully lucky to find dry shelter, even though I had to share it with a family of mice."

"Yep. Lucky." Nick eyed letters stacked in a shallow wood tray. One had come from the governor's office. This man had friends in places higher than the police office. "Who do you think murdered her?"

"Why, I have not had the time to consider, Detective. But I am sure I don't know. A woman like that . . ." Palmer shook his head mournfully. "It could have been anyone. There are so many disreputable men in this city. Such a shame."

A shame that Li Sha was dead? Or that there were so many disreputable men?

"I am wondering, though," said Palmer, "why the police are bothering with this case."

"I bother with every single case, Mr. Palmer."

"Do you, now." He pushed back his chair and stood, pulling his gold watch from its pocket and flicking open the engraved lid. Nick recognized the signs that he was about to be dismissed. "I wish I could assist further, but I have a dinner engagement in fifteen minutes, Detective Greaves. I'm obliged to wish you a good evening."

Nick gripped the brim of his hat. "I'll be back if I have more questions."

Joseph Palmer snapped closed the pocket watch lid. "I expect that won't be necessary."

CHAPTER 8

"How are you?" Celia asked the girl the next morning, even though her patient couldn't understand her any better than she had on Monday.

Celia set her black portmanteau on the bamboo stool, which teetered, its legs unsteady on the dirt floor. The girl's eyelids fluttered and her body shook with tremors. This time, her stupor had nothing to do with the opium they'd given her for the pain. This time, the cause was much, much worse. Traumatic sepsis had set in.

The old woman with the long twist of gray-streaked hair watched from the doorway, her face set rigidly, no expression of concern to be read on its broad, flat width.

Celia rested her fingertips on the girl's uninjured arm, lying atop the threadbare blanket that had been thrown over her.

Celia felt for a pulse in the girl's wrist. Weak and quick. She labored for breath, shaking from the chills of fever, and her face was splotched with red. She was fatally ill.

Celia gently unwrapped the bandages from the wounded arm and removed the wad of linen she'd placed there. Five days. They had left it like this for five days. The wound oozed, and redness had spread up the arm to mingle with the purple bruises.

"She's poorly, isn't she?" asked Barbara, entering the room, her limp more noticeable on the uneven ground.

"I wish they had let you see her the other day, because they did not follow my instructions to regularly clean the wound. And now it is too late for her."

Celia recalled a soldier in the Crimea who'd suffered shrapnel wounds on the battlefront, wounds that had been severe but deemed treatable by the field doctor. By the time the soldier had arrived at Scutari hospital, however, he was delirious and shaking with spasms. Celia and the other nurses had looked on helplessly as the man, once so handsome with his blond hair and gray eyes, had succumbed in a matter of hours.

Once sepsis set in, death followed shortly.

"Bring me some water, Barbara."

Celia tossed the filthy linens onto the floor and took fresh ones from her bag. Once her cousin returned, Celia set about cleaning the wound, the girl shivering and moaning the entire time. Celia washed the arm with carbolic acid and wrapped it in fresh bandages.

"Tell the old woman I have brought more quinine for the fever. The inflammation itself . . ." She had nothing that would help at this point. "Tell her I will try to find a surgeon to remove that arm. It is all that might save the girl. Tell the woman that."

Celia would never be allowed to leave Chinatown with her patient and take her to a surgeon. He would have to come here.

Barbara translated for Celia. The elderly woman scowled. A prostitute disfigured by a missing arm was as useless to her as a dead prostitute.

"You bring nobody here!" The old woman said more in Chinese to Barbara, then added, "Go! You no good." She jabbed a thumb in Celia's direction.

"We should leave," whispered Barbara.

The old woman scowled and folded her arms within her sleeves. "You go. You not come back."

"I shall come back. If not to help your girls, then to help the other prostitutes living in these filthy streets." Celia grabbed her medical bag. "And have that arm removed."

Celia marched out of the room and into the alleyway.

Barbara limped as she hurried after her. "Will she die?"

"Possibly. Probably." Celia slowed, all the while feeling eyes upon them, the watchful behind curtained portals and barred doors. "I'll try to find somebody to come and remove her arm, but even if the woman allows a surgeon into the room to do the work, I'm afraid it will be too late."

"Oh."

From their left, a young Chinese woman darted from a doorway, calling out to them. Celia recognized her as her patient's friend.

They paused. From a pocket within her loose cotton trousers, the girl pulled out a bundle of red paper strips covered with Chinese writing and handed them to Barbara.

"What are they?" asked Celia.

"Sayings from Confucius that talk about the vanity of earthly things," said Barbara. "You're supposed to scatter them on the ground in front of Li Sha's funeral procession. They're a sort of prayer."

Barbara thanked the young woman. They started to walk off, but she tugged on Barbara's sleeve and looked anxiously around her. No one seemed to take notice of them, though. Not the merchants calling out descriptions of their wares; or the boy climbing the steps of a nearby basement cigar workshop, carrying a crate in his skinny arms; not even the two gossiping women in brightly colored silks who shuffled past.

Their lack of attention didn't ease the young Chinese woman's apprehension. She spoke too quickly for Celia to make out more than a few words.

"What is she saying, Barbara?" she asked. "She said *yan*, didn't she? That means 'man.' Is she speaking of a particular man?"

But the young woman grew alarmed by Celia's questions and fled through a doorway behind them, disappearing from sight.

"She didn't mean anybody in particular, Cousin Celia." Barbara glanced toward the empty doorway. "She just wanted to know if the police have found the person who killed Li Sha. That's all. I told her they've arrested the father of her child."

She began walking toward Washington Street and the constable who was waiting for them around the corner.

"That was not all, Barbara," said Celia, joining her cousin. "She acted as though she wanted to tell you something important. Something that had alarmed her. If she suspects she knows who killed Li Sha, she has to inform the police."

"Would the police listen to her?"

"Detective Greaves would."

Barbara did not respond.

"If that young woman told you something that Mr. Greaves should know, you must speak up."

Barbara's eyes were hard, making Celia ponder how well she knew the person standing next to her. "It's gossip, Cousin Celia. That's how they are. That's how Li Sha was, too."

That was how many teenaged girls were, Celia wanted to respond, but she didn't, caught off guard by her cousin's manner. "They are your people, too, Barbara."

"No, they're not. I don't have any people," Barbara spat, and she limped away through the traffic, the bits of red paper crushed in her fist.

"*T*om Davies? You can't be serious!"

Tessie Lange's tirade carried clearly through the partly open door to the detectives' office. Nick expected that even if he'd been on the street walking past the station he could've heard her screeching at Taylor.

"Is there somebody in this station with any smarts?" she asked. "Tom isn't guilty of murder."

Taylor was attempting to quiet her. "Now, Miss Lange—"

Nick heard the angry tramp of boots across the floor and he guessed she was out there, pacing. Just as he formed the thought, he saw her swish across the room, then march back.

"Why are you looking at me like I'm crazy?" she shouted at Taylor. "He's not guilty!"

Briggs—in the office for once—shook his head over her tantrum. "Jeminy, that one's madder'n a wet hen!"

"Do you have evidence that would get Davies out?" Taylor was asking, his voice calm. "After all, we did find a knife hidden in his room, and his landlady says he threatened Li Sha—"

"I don't care what you found! Because I was with him that night and I know he didn't do it!"

Briggs stopped midchew and whistled, spewing doughnut crumbs onto his beard. *Here's an interesting turn*, thought Nick. But just as with Wagner, there were always women who were willing to vouch for their menfolk, whether they were guilty or not. Sometimes their willingness came from love. Sometimes it came from fear.

"You sure about that?" Taylor asked Tessie.

"Just let me see him."

"Visiting hours on Saturday are this afternoon at—"

"I want to see him now!"

Taylor's chair legs scraped across the wood floor. "Hold on, miss. I'll talk to somebody about your request."

Nick's assistant entered the office, nodded at Briggs, and closed the office door behind him. "What do you think, sir? Captain won't like it if we let her back there outside of regular hours."

"She's here to see Davies now, and the captain doesn't need to know," Nick answered.

Chuckling, Briggs got up from his desk. "Eagan's not going to like this, Greaves."

"And wouldn't *that* make you happy?" Taylor shot back.

"Bootlicker," Briggs snarled, and lumbered out of the office.

Nick watched him go. Their animosity went back a long way, to the day Nick had been promoted to detective ahead of Briggs. Briggs had credited Nick's uncle Asa with pulling strings with the police chief. He'd never admit the early promotion had come because Nick was a better cop.

"Take her to see Davies," he said to Taylor. "But tell her she only has five minutes to speak to him. I'm going to listen in the cell-house bullpen and see what we might learn."

"Got it, sir . . . Mr. Greaves."

Out in the main station room, Taylor led Tessie Lange off to the jail cells.

"*W*hy are you here, Tessie?" Tom Davies asked, not getting up from where he lay stretched out on the narrow bunk.

Nick eased the cell-block door closed and slipped into the corner of the bullpen. Tessie wouldn't notice him here, obscured by a stack of empty crates, apparently forgotten, that had once held ropes, chains, and stakes for closing off streets. Nick could easily see Davies from here, along with Tessie's hands pressed against the thick iron grate that separated her from the prisoner.

"I wanted to see how you're doing," she said, leaning closer, her face coming into view.

At the far end of the six-foot-wide aisle that divided the two rows of cells, the warden snoozed on his chair, his feet pointed toward the corner stove. At the sound of a new voice, he propped an eye open for a second, then closed it again. He wasn't worried about his prisoners, apparently.

"You've seen me. Now leave."

Davies rolled over on the bunk to face the wall. A white-bearded prisoner across the aisle belched, and his cell mate offered to keep Tessie company when he got out, his lewd suggestions of what they might do together causing the other man to guffaw. Somewhere farther along the cell block, a man was mumbling angrily, when he wasn't shouting obscenities or crying. There were a few women, too, ladies of the night in soiled bright dresses, their hair straggling, kept apart from the men by a thick wall of iron. People could easily die in a place like this, with its cold and damp, the smell of open slop jars and unwashed bodies, and mold darkening the stone walls. At night, rats scuttled about, nibbling. Preachers said hell was a place of fire and brimstone; if they'd ever come down here, they might think differently.

"Tom, I've told them you're not guilty," Tessie said, leaning into the grate until her forehead rested against the metal. "I've told them I was with you."

"Why did you do that?" he snapped. He lurched off the bunk, ducking to avoid hitting his head on the empty bunk above. He walked up to the floor-to-ceiling grate and stared at her. The light from a solitary lantern hanging on the far wall illuminated his face, and the black stubble on his chin made him appear wan and sickly. "Just stay outta this, Tessie, before they begin to suspect you, too."

"I told them that because it's the truth! I don't care what people say about me, Tom, if I can get you out of this place."

"The magistrate has charged me with murder. I can't be bailed and I'll be stayin' in here to rot until I hang."

"You won't hang. I won't let them hang you," insisted Tessie. "I went to see Connor, but he told me not to bother him about Li Sha."

Nick wondered if this Connor fellow was the man she'd gone to visit in the Barbary.

"Course he doesn't want to hear about her!" Davies said. "Hell, *he* probably killed Li Sha, much as he hated her."

"Don't say that, Tom! Connor's your friend."

"Well, he didn't like her at all, now, did he?" Davies slipped a finger through an opening in the grate and pointed at her, grazing the tip of her nose. "And neither did you. You and Connor in it together, then?"

She recoiled from his touch. "No!"

Davies withdrew his hand. "Go home, Tessie. We made a mistake, you and me. 'Tis time to forget it."

"But I love you!"

"Too late to be realizin' that," Davies said, watching her face. "And I loved her."

"How could you have loved a yellow China girl? She wasn't carrying your baby, Tom. There've probably been all sorts of other men since she left that brothel. Don't be an idiot."

The white-bearded prisoner across the way, who'd been hanging on their every word, grunted a sound of pleased surprise. The warden started snoring.

Davies curled a fist and pressed it against the iron grate, inches from her face. "You've been sayin' that just to make me hate her as much as you did. There weren't other men."

Taylor slipped through the cell-block door. "Eagan was out there looking for you," he whispered to Nick. "He wants you up in his office in five minutes or else."

"He doesn't come in on Saturdays," Nick whispered back.

"He did today, and he's mad enough to chew nails and spit rivets. He's heard you went to see Palmer."

Nick cursed under his breath.

"Listen, we can put this behind us," Tessie Lange was saying, with what Nick judged to be foolhardy persistence. "You'll get out and then you can be with me—"

"Stop it, Tessie. I'll not be gettin' outta here," he hissed, stepping backward. "Go home. Just go home. And leave me be."

"I won't give up."

"Then you're a fool, woman." Davies climbed onto his bunk and turned to face the wall again.

"Go get her," ordered Nick, heading to the bullpen door. "And bring her to my office. I need to ask her about a man named Connor."

"Your time's up, Miss Lange," Taylor announced, striding forward. "Time to go."

"I'll get you out, Tom!" she cried. "I swear I will."

The grizzled prisoner found her vow riotously funny, his cackle echoing off the cell-block walls.

*C*elia, still wearing her garibaldi and holland skirt, crouched in the garden. She was pulling weeds among the rosebushes, which were just beginning to put on fresh leaves. Addie liked to shake her head over Celia whenever she came out here. It was not much of a garden and certainly very different from the magnificent flower beds her aunt had maintained in Hertfordshire. All they had in San Francisco was a patch of land with a set of wicker chairs and some rosebushes, two poles with a clothesline stretched between them, and a spot of wet ground where Addie tossed refuse.

But Celia came outside to work in the garden and listen to Mrs. Cascarino singing in her kitchen, to watch for seagulls whirling overhead, and to breathe in the smell of the warm soil. Calming, all of them. And Celia needed calming after the morning she'd had. After she had left her patient, she'd visited five different surgeons, none of whom was willing to make a trip to Chinatown to help a dying Chinese prostitute. She'd approached a sixth and begged him until he claimed he would see what he could do. His promise was the best Celia could accomplish. She'd saw the arm off herself, but she did not have the proper tools or necessary training.

Celia felt the first drops of a rain shower and stood, wiping her gloved hands down the apron she'd borrowed from Addie, and regarded the rosebushes. Her aunt would be appalled by their sickly appearance. Perhaps, though, if Celia paid them some attention this year, they would eventually thrive.

"Oy! Ma'am!"

She spun about to face the voice. "Owen! Good heavens, you startled me!" What a relief to see him, though.

He closed the gate behind him, his left arm hugging his side. "I've got some news."

She peered at him. "Are you hurt?"

Owen glanced down at his side as if he'd just remembered it. "Fell into a ditch. I was listening in, you see—"

"You fell into a ditch?" She peeled off the thick gloves she wore when she worked in the garden and hurried over to him. "Does it hurt to breathe?"

"A little. But it's not bad. The ditch weren't so deep," he said, winking.

She prodded his ribs. "Cough, please." Owen did as ordered, wincing, but she could not feel any bone grating against bone. "Just a bad bruise, I think. Or a tiny fracture."

He grinned at her, revealing a dimple. "That's good, then."

The rain started to fall more steadily. "Come inside and explain to me what caused you to fall into a ditch."

They retreated to the kitchen, interrupting Addie, who was busy making shortbread. The kitchen smelled sweet as Addie pulled the biscuits from the little oven in the Good Samaritan stove.

"Sit," Celia said, pressing Owen into a chair.

He sniffed the air and smiled blissfully. "You're the best cook, Addie, know that?"

"Owen Cassidy, you'd eat anything set before you, so you can save the compliments," she replied, but she looked pleased anyway as she set the biscuits atop the stove to cool.

"So, the ditch?" Celia asked him.

"A bunch of fellas got together last night, you see. To talk about them rioters and how rotten unfair it is they got sent to jail." He watched Addie as she slid shortbread onto a plate. "But I wasn't invited to join them. So I thought I'd just give a listen at the window of the house where they were meeting."

"What did they say?" asked Celia.

"There were talking mean, saying there's a man who's planning trouble for the Chinese, and then they started laughing. Well, it weren't like funnin' laughing, or nothing." Owen scrunched up his face at the recollection. "They want to burn 'em out, Mrs. Davies. Them Chinese and anybody who hires 'em."

Burn them out. "Did you happen to hear this fellow's name?"

"All I heard was *Connor.* But there are dozens of Connors around."

"Yes, I know." It was a popular name among the Irish. But still, this was information to share with Mr. Greaves if he did not already know it.

"Och," muttered Addie, and she set the plate of shortbread in front of Owen, who scooped a biscuit into his mouth.

"And then one of 'em came to the window," said Owen, his mouth full, "and I got scared they'd see me outside and I ran off. But it were already dark and I didn't remember the ditch that'd been cut along the road and I fell in. Banged up my side." He patted his ribs.

"How serious do you think they were about attacking the Chinese?"

"Don't know, ma'am. They do like to talk big, but sometimes they like to cause trouble, too."

Did they also like to slink around in shadows and spy on people? "You did not hear any of these men mention us here, did you, Owen?"

"Nope," he said, looking worried. "You think they might be after Miss Barbara again? I mean, more than what those kids said to her the other day?"

"I was hoping you might be able to tell me."

"I'll give a listen. How's that?" he said.

Oh dear. I have put him in more danger.

"You're a brave laddie, Owen, you are," said Addie. "And for being so good, you may have another biscuit."

The boy happily obliged. "By the way, Addie," he said, dribbling crumbs down his shirt. He licked a finger to catch them up and pop them into his mouth. "I might know somebody who'd like to go walking with you along North Beach some Sunday. Like to meet him?"

Addie colored. "Whisht, lad, what sort of nonsense are you talking? A friend of yours? Whatever gave you such an idea?"

"*You* did. Don't you 'member?"

"No, I dinna remember," she said, and turned back to the stove, slamming a pot onto the hob.

Owen chuckled and jumped up. "Thanks for checking my ribs, Mrs. Davies." He snapped up a handful of shortbread. "I'll be going now."

With a grin, he stuffed two into his mouth and darted out the rear door.

"*J*t's about time you got up here, Greaves," said Captain Eagan, moving aside a stack of papers he'd been reviewing.

Nick stepped into the captain's office, a nicely furnished room with a soft carpet and polished wood paneling. A room that didn't stink like the police station in the basement.

"A woman was visiting Tom Davies," Nick said. "I wanted to hear what they had to say to each other."

Eagan eyed the clock on his desk. "It's outside of visiting hours."

"Have to take advantage of opportunities when they arise."

The captain inhaled, his burnished police badge winking in the glow of the gas chandelier. "It's come to my attention that you've been questioning Joseph Palmer. What the hell's that all about?"

Time to tread carefully, Nick. "I've learned the murdered Chinese girl knew him and might have met with him the night she was killed. She was looking for money to leave town."

Eagan leaned forward. "And you're thinking that Joseph Palmer, one of the most respected men in San Francisco, met this girl and ended up killing her? That's ridiculous."

"It's a lead, sir. I'd be stupid not to follow it."

"No, where you're stupid, Greaves, is messing with him," said Eagan. "Take my advice and leave Palmer alone. Men like him can cause more trouble than it's worth. Trust me."

Nick stared back at his superior. There were days when he despised the captain, even though his uncle had thought the world of Dennis Eagan. *The best police officer you'll ever meet, Nick. Do as he says, and you'll go far.*

Eagan might be the best police officer Nick would ever

meet, but the captain was too cozy with men who liked to throw their weight around. Men like Palmer.

"I'm just doing my job, Captain."

"You're wasting valuable police time on this, Greaves," Eagan shot back. "We have a suspect in jail. And I hear Taylor's involved. Mullahey, too?"

Nick refused to say anything that would get them in trouble. "I'm not convinced Tom Davies is guilty. I want to be sure."

"The chief is unhappy, Greaves," said the captain. "Sure, he doesn't like the violence against the Chinese, but he hates even more the complaints he gets from the good citizens of San Francisco. They pay taxes so we'll keep them and their property safe. They don't expect us to bother with crime among the Celestials, especially the murder of a girl from a bagnio."

"The 'Celestials' pay taxes, too." Hefty ones.

"You need to wrap this case up. I want you done by Tuesday, when the grand jury'll meet. No more police time wasted on a dead Chinese girl after that. Hear me?"

By Tuesday? Who was he kidding? "I want a week at least to concentrate on this case."

"Tuesday," Eagan repeated.

"Nobody could be done by Tuesday, Captain. A week."

Eagan regarded him. Overhead, the gas flames flickered and snapped.

"I only put up with you, Greaves, because your uncle used to be one of the best men on this force," he said. "But I'll only give you until Wednesday. And if I think you're slacking on cases that deserve more attention, you can be damned sure I'll yank you so fast off this one, you won't know which way's up."

Nick strode out of the room. Downstairs in the detectives' office, Taylor was waiting with Tessie Lange.

"Miss Lange," Nick said, sweeping past her. "Thanks for taking the time to talk with me again."

"What do you want, Detective?" she asked.

"I have some more questions for you." Nick settled into his desk chair and gestured for her to sit. "First off, who is this Connor fellow?"

"You were listening."

"Answer the question."

"He's a friend. A good friend of Tom's. They used to work together when Tom first came to San Francisco." She looked at Taylor, who was engaged in his usual note taking. "They took a liking to each other. I met him through Tom."

"A last name?" asked Taylor. "And don't bother to make one up."

She swallowed. "Ahearn. Connor Ahearn."

Irish. *What a coincidence*, thought Nick. "Why did you go to see him about Li Sha?"

Tessie shrugged. "I was being stupid about that. I thought he might know something."

Hmm. "But he didn't?"

"Not that he'd admit."

"And he hated Li Sha for some reason. Why was that?" Nick asked.

"He sympathizes with the Anti-Coolie Association." She narrowed her eyes. "Are you asking me about him because you think he killed her?"

"Do you think it's possible?" asked Nick, kneading the old wound on his left arm.

"It wouldn't be safe for me to say, Detective Greaves."

But if he was the man she'd met in the Barbary, she wasn't all that afraid of him.

"Why did Tom Davies claim you hated Li Sha, too, Miss Lange?" Nick asked. "Were you jealous of her, his new woman?"

She blanched, the recognition that she'd become a suspect dawning. "I wouldn't hurt her."

"You knew she was pregnant. Yet when I came to talk to you at the store, you didn't mention it."

She dropped her gaze. Taylor was writing as fast as he could.

"Where'd you go after you left Davies' room Monday night?" Nick asked.

"Home. Ask my father."

"About what time did you get there?"

"Around eight thirty or nine, I think. I'm not exactly sure. I don't own a pocket watch."

"Rather late for a young lady to be out on the streets by herself," observed Nick, steepling his fingertips and staring over the top of them. "Especially coming from Tar Flat."

"Tom accompanied me part of the way." Tessie raised her head and looked at him. "I was hoping to get Tom back by being with him that night, but it didn't work out. We were together for a short time and then I went home."

"And you didn't meet with Li Sha, pretending you would give her money so she could leave town, but killing her instead?" asked Nick.

"Money? I don't know what you're talking about."

Nick looked at her long and hard. He believed her about the money; the rest . . . he wasn't so sure.

"We're done here, Miss Lange. For now."

In her haste to stand, she knocked over the chair. She ran out of the room like the hounds of hell were after her.

"Maybe?" asked Taylor, lifting an eyebrow.

"Maybe."

"What did Owen have to say when he came by this afternoon?" asked Barbara, standing in the doorway of Celia's examination room. Her hair, in braids, hung down over her mauve cotton wrapper.

At her desk, Celia cleaned the nib of her pen, replaced the lid to the glass inkwell, and closed her notebook. She welcomed the interruption. The lines of her entries, painstakingly recorded symptoms observed and medications dispensed, as well as follow-up questions she needed to ask, had been swimming before her eyes.

"Apparently there is grumbling among those who are sympathetic with the Anti-Coolie Association," said Celia. "They are planning more violence, it seems, and they might also target the employers of Chinese labor." Which was what Mrs. Douglass had also mentioned to Celia. "Owen is not positive they're serious, however."

"Do you think they'll come here and hurt us?"

"No, sweetheart. Not at all. We are safe in our home," Celia said. "Have you finished your schoolwork for the day?"

"I left it on the dining room table for you to check."

"Thank you. Go ahead up to bed. And try not to worry."

Barbara nodded and left, passing Addie, who was on her way into the examination room.

"Your supper's gone cold, ma'am," she said.

"I forgot all about eating." Just then, Celia's stomach rumbled.

"I wish I could be certain I am right to tell Barbara not to worry about what's happening."

"Dinna fash, ma'am. As my father would say, care will kill a cat and she has nine lives. Worry only causes ill."

"But didn't he also say you should not put your hand out farther than your sleeve will reach? We must be cautious. All of us."

"Aye," Addie agreed. "Oh, by the by, there was a note left at the door."

Addie reached into the pocket of her rust calico print skirt, withdrew a folded and sealed piece of paper, and set it on Celia's desk. "If we're all to be cautious, we ought to ask Madame Philippe if Owen's in danger for telling us about that Connor fellow."

"We are going to keep Madame Philippe quite busy with all of our questions, it seems," said Celia.

"Aye, ma'am. She willna mind, I suspect." Addie nodded. "I'll go warm your supper."

Addie departed and Celia picked up the note she'd left behind. The stationery was of poor quality and looked as though it had been torn from a larger piece. She broke the seal and flipped it open.

Her hand began to shake. "Oh!"

Addie rushed back into the room. "Ma'am? What is it?"

"This note. Where did you get it?"

"It was stuck in the back door. Found it earlier, when I went out to the yard to toss the dishwater. Why, ma'am? What does it say?"

Celia looked up at her. "Someone has scribbled 'careful or you'll be next' onto this scrap of paper."

"What?" Addie snatched the paper from Celia's fingers to confirm for herself. "We're going to be next?"

Celia rose. "Show me exactly where you found the note."

"Out here." Addie hastened from the room, Celia behind her. They hurried through the kitchen and opened the rear door. Addie grabbed the kitchen lantern and stepped onto the small porch outside, pointing to the ground. "It was here. I saw it flutter down when I opened the door."

Seizing the lantern, Celia descended the steps and scanned the flagstone path and the bare earth, muddy from an afternoon rain shower, between them and the ground floor of the Cascarinos' house. She swung the lantern to light their minuscule rear yard. She didn't spot any sign of who had left the note, but Celia doubted she would recognize clues even if she saw them.

"He must have come by in the last hour and snuck into the yard while I was busy with your supper," said Addie. "I'd gone out before then and nae seen the note. Besides, the paper is dry and it was raining earlier."

Which meant the person had crept around behind the house while she and Addie and Barbara were inside, unaware. "I wonder if the Cascarinos noticed anyone." She looked up at their windows, but the curtains were drawn shut, the rooms dark.

"Looks verra quiet," Addie said. "For once."

"Do not breathe a word of this to Barbara. She is already worried enough," said Celia. "The note is likely merely a prank. Someone read about Li Sha in the newspapers and decided to have fun at our expense."

"A prank, ma'am," said Addie, looking dubious. "After that stranger you saw watching the house yesterday, you call this a prank? And those hooligans that Owen knows promising to burn out the Chinese? Maybe they mean to burn down our verra home!"

"Those men would not alert us ahead of time," said Celia.

"Then maybe someone's upset by what you've learned through your investigating, ma'am."

"I am not investigating, Addie. Mr. Greaves is."

Addie rolled her eyes. "Weel, *he* wasna the one who chased Tessie Lange all the way to the Barbary, trying to see what she was about. And *he* wasna the one in Chinatown asking scarlet women about Li Sha. And *he* wasna the one asking that Dora Schneider all sorts of questions like someone from the Inquisition, and you ken she likes to gab, ma'am!"

Celia regretted having shared all that with Addie; she would have to be more circumspect in future. "I will inform Detective Greaves, of course."

"Of course."

Celia gathered her skirts and headed to the stairs. "And get the sturdiest padlock you can find and lock the gate. We do not need any more unwanted visitors."

Addie was staring toward the tall gate. "I hope a padlock can keep him out."

"So do I, Addie."

So do I.

CHAPTER 9

"Connor Ahearn?" The widow who owned the boardinghouse where Ahearn lived—a Mrs. Barnes—stared at Nick. "He lives here all right. With his mother and frail sister. In a set of rooms on the third floor."

"Is he there now, Mrs. Barnes?" Nick asked. "I need to speak with him."

"It's Sunday, Detective. He's at that restaurant he likes down the street. Not that he ever treats his family to a nice steak. Just goes by himself. To meet those friends of his," she said, her scornful tone suggesting what she thought of Connor Ahearn's friends.

Mrs. Barnes gave him the name of the restaurant and where Nick could find it. "Do you have time for some questions?" he asked.

"About Mr. Ahearn?"

Nick nodded.

"Come into the parlor. It doesn't pay to be overheard talking too much about him."

She led Nick into the parlor off to their right and slid the pocket doors shut. A hodgepodge of frayed upholstered chairs in clashing colors was scattered about. In one corner a black-and-white cat, its tail flicking, examined them from behind a dying potted palm. The place stank of turpentine cleaning solution, stale cigarette smoke, and something that had burned in the kitchen. It was pretty typical for a boardinghouse in this part of town.

"So, what do you want to know, Detective Greaves?" she asked. "And make it quick. I've got lunch to oversee."

"Do you recall if Mr. Ahearn was in his rooms Monday night?"

"He was here, all right. Came in late, which he does a lot. But this time his mother gave him quite the tongue-lashing." Mrs. Barnes shook her head. "She's got to be the only person who's not afraid of him. He's a big man who scares the colored girl who helps cook and clean for me. He even frightens his poor sister. Thank the Lord he's not here much."

"Could you make out what his mother was shouting at him about?"

"She wanted to know what he'd been up to, coming in so late and soaked to the bone from the rain. He told her to mind her own business. Only he used a few choice words I won't repeat in polite company," she added. "And I didn't have to press my ear to the wall or nothing, Detective. They were shouting so loud, I'd guess everybody heard them."

Interesting. Connor Ahearn, who happened to live a mere four short blocks from the wharf where Li Sha's body was discovered, had been out late Monday evening. And his mother hadn't been pleased about it.

"What about the Chinese?" asked Nick. "How does he feel about them, with what's been going on lately?"

"Oof, he hates those Chinese people! I've heard him going on about how they're taking his friends' jobs and need to be packed up and sent back to China, the lot of them. I think he's been trying to organize one of those Anti-Coolie Association ward chapters," she said. "But you know what, Detective Greaves? I've heard tittle-tattle that he goes to visit those girls in Chinatown."

Those visits might make Connor Ahearn one of Li Sha's former clients. He might've known the girl very well, and not just because she had worked with Tessie Lange and slept with his good friend Tom Davies.

"Any chance I could speak to his mother and sister?" Nick asked.

"They went to church services this morning and aren't back yet. Sometimes they visit with the pastor."

"I see." Nick returned his hat to his head. "Thank you, ma'am. You've been a great help."

He exited the boardinghouse, descending the steps to the deserted street. Except for the random drugstore or restaurant, most establishments were kept closed on Sundays by law. Nick could list any number of proprietors, however, who'd figured out how to conceal a gambling den in the basement of an innocent-appearing coffeehouse. He wondered if Connor Ahearn's favorite restaurant had secrets to hide.

"You watch your back, Detective," called the widow from her front doorway.

"I always watch my back, ma'am."

She lifted her brows and considered him. "As my dear departed husband might say, with some men, though, you can't have enough eyes."

*T*he morning had been cloudy and gloomy, which suited Celia's mood. She'd passed a restless night, lying awake and listening to the sounds filtering through her partly open window. A late-night reveler galloping down Vallejo, whooping to wake the neighbors. A swain serenading the young Chilean woman who lived across the street. The Cascarinos' youngest girl crying from a bad dream. Celia had lain awake and contemplated what last night's note meant, and who could have sent it. If the note was a warning to Barbara, Celia couldn't imagine from whom it had come. Their neighbors, many of them immigrants themselves, had always been kind to her cousin. But then, the women from the society had always been kind as well, yet they'd had a change of heart on Monday evening.

Celia turned up the flame on the examination room's lamp. She unlocked the desk's top drawer and pulled out the note. Spreading the paper flat, she drew the lamp nearer. *Careful or you'll be next.* Five simple, exasperatingly uninformative words. Were they meant for Barbara or for herself? *Because of your investigating,* Addie had said, convinced the note was related to Li Sha's death. Celia had to take the possibility seriously.

If the note was connected to Li Sha's death, the person must believe Celia possessed information that would unmask the killer's identity. It was a disturbing thought.

Did this note have anything to do with the stranger she'd seen watching the house on Friday? It seemed reasonable to presume it did. And also, though she'd been convinced the watcher was a man, given the trousers, broad-brimmed hat, and long coat the person was wearing, Celia had to consider that she might be wrong. Obscured by shadows and seen at such a distance, the person could have been a woman in disguise. If Celia had to take into account every woman and man who knew both her and Li Sha, the list would be a lengthy one.

"Then whittle it down," she murmured.

She retrieved every piece of correspondence stored inside the desk drawers and within her files. She'd had an idea that those five words might reveal who had penned them. Celia stacked invoices from the Langes' shop—how fortunate that one had been compiled by Tessie—atop a list of charges from the greengrocer, written in his heavy hand. For good measure, she included invoices from her butcher and the coal deliveryman. She found notes from several ladies at the society, along with one from Mrs. Douglass and another from her husband. They were thank-you letters for a charity event Celia had hosted at the house last spring, the praise for her efforts effusive. How readily a change in the winds could snuff out Mrs. Douglass' enthusiasm. And as absurd as it was to consider the society's ladies possible suspects, Celia also placed their notes alongside the others.

Next, she tackled the files occupying the bookcase. She found a letter from her minister, welcoming her to the parish and informing her of all the volunteer opportunities available. She tossed it onto the growing pile atop her desk. Everyone, she reminded herself. Everyone she or Li Sha or both of them had ever known that Celia had correspondence from, no matter how preposterous it might be to consider them responsible for the message. Next came messages from the investigator, Mr. Smith, notes about his progress in locating, or not locating,

Patrick. There would be nothing from Owen Cassidy—as far as she knew, he couldn't write—or from any of the neighborhood boys. And nothing from the women in Chinatown, who spoke limited English and surely couldn't have penned the note. Several of the Chinese merchants spoke and wrote passable English, but she had no correspondence from them to compare. She would simply have to omit them from her analysis.

Lastly, she found an old set of letters from the Palmers, both Elizabeth and her husband. They bore dates from 1864, the year Celia and Patrick had first arrived in San Francisco and had met the Palmers at a function at the Chinese Mission, which Patrick had been loath to attend. There was a Christmas letter with a brief postscript in Emmeline's hand, and an invitation to a formal holiday dinner. Patrick had been much happier to attend that event than any fetes at the Chinese Mission. Her husband, a poor Irishman who had suddenly found himself in the middle of proper society, had wanted to cultivate the Palmers' friendship. Regrettably, Patrick had partaken too freely of the champagne that evening. Though Barbara and Celia were still welcome at the Palmers', no more invitations came that had included him.

The front bell rang and Addie hurried through the house to answer it, rousing Celia from her recollections. She put away the files and examined the papers spread beneath the glow of the desk lamp. She set the note at the center of her desk, sat in her chair, and began working through each piece of communication, relegating them to one of three categories: possible, unlikely, and uncertain. If only the note's author had been more verbose; five words were hardly enough when one was comparing the loops and lines of people's penmanship.

"What are you doing?" asked Barbara.

Her cousin still wore her dress from church that morning, the floral-print aqua-on-cream with the beautiful aqua lace trim that was her favorite gown and usually made her smile. She was not smiling now. "It has to do with that note, doesn't it?"

Before church that morning, Barbara had overheard Celia telling Addie to take a message to Mr. Greaves informing him of the warning they'd received. They hadn't succeeded in keeping the news from Barbara for long.

"I am attempting to discover who may have written it by comparing the handwriting," said Celia.

Barbara crossed the room. "Do you think this is wise, Cousin? If we're in danger, we shouldn't be trying to discover who sent the warning. We should tell the police and leave it at that."

"If I do not help the police identify the author, Barbara, what will stop the culprit from returning?" Celia considered the stacks of notes. Two uncertains—a letter from one of the society ladies and an invoice from the coal man—and thirteen unlikelies. She could already see that the remaining two, the notes from the Palmers, would bear no fruit.

Barbara looked over Celia's shoulder. "Have you found a match?"

"Not among our acquaintances, no."

"I guess it's good it didn't come from somebody we know."

"The author still could be someone we know, Barbara," Celia explained. "They simply may be clever enough to disguise their handwriting."

Barbara stared at the warning note. "Maybe we should leave town until Tom's trial is over."

"I cannot leave, Barbara. I have patients who need me."

"Mr. Palmer wouldn't make Em stay if she wanted to leave."

"Now, Barbara—"

"He wouldn't. He's too kind. Kinder than *you*! *You* only care about your patients and nobody else!" Barbara stumbled out of the room, bumping into Addie, who was coming in from the vestibule.

Addie stared after her. "Now, what has provoked her to say such things?"

"This is one of those times, Addie, when I wish that assuming the guardianship of a teenaged girl had come with an instruction manual," said Celia, dropping the Palmers' letters onto the unlikely stack. "She wants to leave town, but it's not possible. My patients rely on me to be here."

"Are you nae worried it would be unsafe to stay, ma'am?"

"I will admit I am a little afraid, but I cannot go."

"Then perhaps the braw policeman I've shown to the side yard might be willing to stand guard," Addie suggested with a wink.

*T*he *braw* policeman was slowly traversing the narrow side yard, inspecting both the flagstone path Uncle Walford had laid down and the dirt on either side of it. How revealing it was that when Addie had mentioned a handsome policeman, Celia had hoped it was Nicholas Greaves.

Addie stood to one side as Celia greeted Officer Taylor. "I was not certain anyone would be at the station on a Sunday to get my message," she said.

"I always come in for a spell on Sundays, ma'am. Don't have a wife or kids at home to mind."

A piece of news that visibly cheered Addie, causing her to fuss with her hair. Officer Taylor wasn't at all bad looking and must earn a nice living. He would be a good catch for Addie, who'd come to America seeking a better life, leaving behind a cramped turf-roofed farmhouse in rural Scotland and the poverty that had starved her and her eight brothers and sisters.

While Officer Taylor scouted the side yard for clues, Celia glanced up and noticed Angelo peeking around the curtain in the Cascarinos' second-story window. Most of the others had gone out for the day, but Angelo must have had another sore throat and been forced to stay behind with his mother. Once the rest of his family returned home, he could boast about getting to watch the policeman do his work at Mrs. Davies' next door.

Officer Taylor squatted on his heels next to a footprint stamped into the ground. City soil was as hard as stone in the summertime, and her uncle had worked in clay and compost in an effort to get anything other than weeds to grow. As it was, only a few shoots of Bermuda grass poked up their heads. The soil was soft, however, from the recent rains, and the passage of feet that had wandered off the flagstones had left clear imprints.

"Who's been through this way recently, Mrs. Davies?" he asked.

Addie spoke before Celia could open her mouth to answer. "Since yesterday's rain, only the lad athwart the way, Officer Taylor. He came by in the afternoon yesterday to deliver some eggs from the chickens his mother keeps in their yard."

"But no men?" He stood again and placed his own foot next to the print, which was an inch or so longer than Officer Taylor's boot.

"You are certain that print was left by a man, Officer Taylor?" Celia asked.

"Yes, ma'am. A workingman's heavy boots, I'd say."

"You do not think it could have been a woman wearing a man's boots?" she asked. Because it would not take much to slip on a pair in order to complete a disguise.

Officer Taylor peered at her warily. "Don't think I've ever heard of somebody doing that, ma'am."

"In that case, to answer your earlier question," said Celia, "it's been some time since a man came through the side yard. Two months ago when we had an oil delivery would be the last."

"Would you like me to fetch the neighbor's laddie to see if his shoes match the print?" Addie asked, surprising Officer Taylor with an understanding of what he was looking for.

"That's mighty kind of you, Miss Ferguson."

Addie smiled coyly and dashed through the side yard, dodging the footprints by staying on the flagstones, and slipped through the gate to the street.

Officer Taylor, fumbling in his coat pockets, cleared his throat and glanced anxiously at Celia.

"I am not going to get light-headed again as I did in the police station," she assured him, "if that is what's concerning you."

"Um, no, ma'am. I mean . . ." He produced a cigar and a friction match, which he struck against the house's brick wall. He lit the cigar and puffed furiously. "I plumb forgot what I was thinking about."

"Here is the note we received, by the way," said Celia, handing it to him.

Officer Taylor studied it for far longer than it took to read five words. "Why do you reckon this fellow wants to warn you that you could be the next victim?" he asked around the cigar clenched in his teeth.

"Possibly because my cousin, Barbara, is half-Chinese and

the anti-coolie folks are after her," she said. "Or because of my relationship with Li Sha. The author might be the killer and believes I have knowledge of his or her identity."

"Hmm. I'll have to ask Mr. Greaves what he thinks, ma'am." Officer Taylor struck a contemplative stance, a stream of smoke issuing from between his lips, and tucked the note into an inner pocket of his overcoat. "Yep."

Celia figured that Nicholas Greaves would have definite thoughts on the matter, and those thoughts would include reminding her that he'd told her not to interfere in his investigation.

Addie returned with the neighbor's boy, his black hair hanging down over his goggling eyes. She guided him into the yard, pointing out to him that he was to avoid stepping in the dirt.

"We just want to see if your feet are the same size as these prints here, Joaquín," said Celia.

"I am not in trouble?" he asked haltingly.

"No," she answered.

He did as asked and confirmed that his kip boots were much smaller than the prints. Which also meant the prints weren't left by Owen, who was no larger than her Chilean neighbor, when he'd come by yesterday.

"Thank you," said Celia. Joaquín ran off. "No one else has been in the yard since last night, Officer Taylor. As a precaution, we locked the gate once we received the note."

"What will you do now, Officer Taylor?" asked Addie. "Can you find this person?"

"Boot prints don't tell us much, Miss Ferguson. Wish they did."

"I've been thinking since last night, ma'am, that the intruder could be one of Owen's mates," Addie said to Celia. "Maybe they discovered Owen was spying on them and told us about their plans!"

Officer Taylor withdrew a notebook. "What's this?"

Celia recounted what Owen had shared yesterday. "I told Addie I doubted those men would warn us, however. I think they would simply go ahead and burn down our house."

"You've got a point there," he agreed. "And we've heard of this Connor fellow. Connor Ahearn is his name. One of your brother-in-law's friends, as it turns out, and tied in tight with the anti-coolie agitators."

A friend of Tom's? Why was she not surprised? Celia thought cynically.

"We're going to see Madame Philippe—she's a famous astrologer—in a couple of days," said Addie. "Think we should ask her who did this?"

"Uh . . ." Officer Taylor was so taken aback by her comment, he forgot to puff his cigar. "An astrologer?" He seemed to struggle not to laugh.

"Thank you so much for your help, Officer Taylor," said Celia before Addie could blurt a caustic retort. "We shall keep the gate and our doors firmly locked at night."

"Good idea, ma'am. And I hear the funeral's tomorrow," he said. "You might want to keep a sharp lookout there for any strangers. I hear sometimes the killers like to spy on their victims' funerals."

"I shall inform you or Mr. Greaves if I notice any such person."

Officer Taylor returned to smoking and headed toward the gate Addie had left open. Celia followed him. Upstairs at the Cascarinos', Angelo had abandoned his post at the window. After Officer Taylor departed, Celia would have to go to see how the boy was feeling. Watching where she stepped so she did not destroy the evidence, Celia passed through the gate ahead of the officer, who held it wide for her.

The family who'd recently moved into a house across the street scurried down their steps, dressed in bright Sunday-picnic colors. Joaquín's mother, her own skirts a kaleidoscope, stood in the middle of the wood pavement and glowered in Celia's direction. She must be upset that a policeman had sent for her son. The family spilled around the Chilean woman like a stream rushing around a boulder, the children running pell-mell down the hill. The street fell quiet again, as it often did on Sundays. A quiet so thorough that Celia found it eerie.

She nodded at Joaquín's mother, who glowered more fiercely and climbed the steps to her house.

"Hey, now, what's this?" Officer Taylor was saying. He bent down to dig something out of a clump of grass. It was the dirty stub of a cigar. He held it between forefinger and thumb and sniffed it. "A good one. And it's not wet. Only been lying here, I'd say, since the rain yesterday."

"Could it have been dropped by the person who left the note?" asked Celia.

"Mighta been." He opened his coat and stashed the butt in an inner pocket. "Know any folks who wear heavy boots and smoke cigars?"

"Besides you, Officer Taylor?"

He flushed. "Other than me, ma'am."

"Any number of men of my acquaintance smoke cigars and cigarillos and cheroots. Maybe even some of Owen's older mates," she added, contradicting her earlier contention that those men would not leave warnings.

"We'll figure it out, ma'am. Me and Mr. Greaves."

"I hope so," she responded. "Because I do not care to have become a target."

"Your landlady told me I could find you here, Mr. Ahearn." Connor Ahearn sat alone at a table enjoying a cut of beef with potatoes and peas, a very nice Sunday meal for a machinist at the ironworks. The two companions who'd been sitting with him when Nick entered the chophouse had retreated to a table by the window. Far enough away to stay out of Connor Ahearn's business, close enough to come to his aid if the need arose.

"Yeah, did she, then?" Ahearn eyed Nick with no apparent concern. A brawny man, he wore a neatly trimmed beard and had short auburn hair beneath the cap he hadn't removed. He also had on a bright yellow-and-red-checked vest, just like the man Celia Davies had seen in the Barbary with Tessie Lange. Finishing off his attire was a leather holster, complete with a bowie knife, which he'd strapped around his waist.

The roar of conversation in the restaurant had quieted to a whispering hum since Nick had walked over to Ahearn's table. Somewhere off to his left, a man stood to leave, his bill paid with a jingle of coins upon the table.

"You're makin' me nervous, Detective. Pull up a chair and rest yer feet, will ya?"

"I'll stand." Nick's elbow bumped against his holstered Colt police revolver.

Ahearn's eyes flicked in the gun's direction. "You gonna shoot me, Detective? I'm just havin' some food here on a fair Sunday, and you're gonna shoot me." He turned to a man seated at an adjacent table. "Faith an' all, he wants to shoot me. And what have I done, I ask you?"

The fellow shrugged, while the proprietor, standing behind the bar where he served beer on other days, gaped. Maybe he was afraid for the large framed mirror hanging on the wall behind him, in case gunfire erupted.

"Tell me about Li Sha," said Nick.

Ahearn let the man at the neighboring table return to his food, though the fellow looked like he no longer wanted to eat. "Who?"

"The Chinese girl who was killed last Monday."

Ahearn sawed at his beef. "Don't know her."

"Well, isn't that funny, because I've heard you hated her."

"Now, who would be sayin' that?" he asked, chewing, the muscles in his heavy jaw flexing.

"What about Thérèse Lange? You know her, don't you?"

Ahearn set down his knife and fork, the handles clinking against the plate, and swiped a napkin over his mouth. The tension rose in the room, turning as thick as the humidity on an Ohio August day. "If I do, that'd be between me and Miss Lange, Detective Greaves."

"You were spotted talking to her on Thursday. What was that about?" Nick asked, wanting Ahearn's version of events.

"Nothing in particular," Ahearn answered calmly.

"You two weren't discussing Li Sha?"

"There you are, askin' me about her again, Detective Greaves."

"If you know Tessie Lange, you have to have known Li Sha, since Tessie's father employed the girl."

"So that's the China girl yer talkin' about!" He went through the motions of looking amazed. "'Tis a small world, then, isn't it?"

"Did you ever happen to use her services when she was a prostitute?"

Ahearn blinked slowly, but his breathing had sped up. "What would my blessed mother have to say about me doin' such a thing?"

"I don't know. Probably nothing good," replied Nick. "What did you think of a Chinese woman, a former prostitute, working in a white man's store?"

"Like a lot of people, I think the Chinese are takin' our work and takin' food from our own mouths."

Ahearn, though, wasn't suffering from a lack of food. "Is that why people say you hated her, or is it because Tessie hated her? She was jealous that Li Sha was with your friend, Tom Davies, her former beau, wasn't she? So the two of you, what? Plotted to lure the girl to someplace near the wharf, killed her, and then dumped her body in the bay. Is that how it worked?"

"Is that what she's sayin'?"

"I'm giving you a chance to help me understand what did happen."

"You know, I would be suggestin' you leave, Detective." Ahearn's hands curled into fists and he pushed his chair away from the table. The proprietor made an anxious noise and started clearing glasses off the bar top, storing them as quickly as he could behind the bulk of the walnut counter.

Ahearn stood and Nick shoved him back into his chair. It rocked on its back legs. "I'm not done yet, Ahearn."

"I think I'll be complainin' about how you're treatin' me here."

He probably would.

"Are you a member of the Anti-Coolie Association? I've heard you're organizing a ward chapter. I wonder what you're planning. Care to tell me?" asked Nick, feeling every eye in the place on them. Some might be hoping he'd pull out his gun and do some shooting, just to liven up a dull Sunday afternoon.

"'Tisn't against the law, now, is it?" Ahearn glanced around the room, his gaze stopping at each set of eyes turned in their direction until each observer found something better to look at. Satisfied that he'd cowed all present in the chophouse, Ahearn picked up his fork again, smashed a lump of potatoes onto the back of the tines, and balanced peas atop it. "And I'm also thinkin' I won't be tellin' you what my plans are for today or any other day. Because I know you're simply fishin', and I'm not so stupid as to be hooked." Without dropping a pea, he shoveled the lot of them into his mouth.

"Maybe you should tell me why you were out unusually late Monday night, Mr. Ahearn. Can anyone vouch for your whereabouts?"

"My friends here will tell you I was with them. Having a good time of it, weren't we, now, fellas?" he asked the two who slouched in their chairs by the window. They both nodded dutifully.

"I wonder if you and your friends would mind coming in to the station to make a statement."

"They just told you what you're needin' to know, Detective." Connor Ahearn eyed him. "And you'll not be pinnin' that girl's murder on me."

"I will if you've done it."

"Well, and isn't that the problem, Detective? I've not done it!"

Connor Ahearn shoveled the last bite of meat into his mouth and chewed, a smug grin on his face. But the bead of sweat trickling down his cheek told a different story.

"*S*orry I've come on a Sunday, ma'am," said Dora, coughing into her handkerchief. "I know your clinic's not usually open, especially this late."

"I told you to return if you did not feel well," said Celia, moving the stethoscope down the young woman's back. "Breathe in, Dora. Deeply."

She did, which triggered another round of coughing.

Celia straightened and removed the stethoscope's earpieces. "Have you been taking the comfrey infusion I gave you?"

Dora turned to face Celia. "Yes."

"And have you tried to rest?"

Dora glanced away. "Well . . ."

"You are not worse, Dora, but you have not improved much, either." Celia folded the stethoscope. "You need to rest for the remainder of the day. And by rest I mean not move a muscle. Also, drink lots of hot lemonade or some other warm beverage to thin the mucus in your lungs. That should help."

Dora retrieved her corset and put it on. "So I'm not too sick to go to work tomorrow?"

"If you rest, you may go to work. I expect by the end of this week, you should feel better." She helped Dora climb down from the bench. "Will you be able to attend Li Sha's funeral in the morning?"

"Not if I'm well enough to work," she answered, slipping her arms into the sleeves of her bodice. "I'm sorry, ma'am. I did want to go, but my boss never understands about that sort of stuff. Probably thinks women don't belong at funerals anyway, causing so much of a fuss with their crying."

Dora rolled her eyes, and Celia moved out of her way to

allow her to finish dressing. Celia heard footsteps across the porch, one of the planks creaking outside the room's front window. Had another patient arrived? Or perhaps it was Mr. Greaves coming to check on them.

"You could also go to the chemist and purchase a poultice for your chest, Dora, if you are having difficulty breathing when you lie down."

"Maybe I will on the way home," she answered, tidying her hair. "I think he's still open at this hour."

Celia paused. The ring of the front bell that she had expected hadn't come. "Excuse me."

She left the examination room and went to open the front door. No one was there, but a scrap of paper poking up between two planks caught her attention.

Celia squatted to retrieve it. *No cops,* it read.

Crushing the note in her fist, she hurried to the edge of the porch and searched the road. But the street was empty.

*N*ick stretched his back and sighed. He'd been standing in the shelter of a dry goods store, watching for Connor Ahearn, for more than an hour now. He'd seen plenty of patrons come and go from the restaurant, including one of Ahearn's friends who'd been eating with him, but not the man himself. Which had to mean he'd slipped out a rear door.

Damn it all.

Nick set off for the alleyway behind the restaurant. There he found a cook seated on an overturned barrel cleaning his fingernails with the tip of a knife. The door to the kitchen stood open, and the smell of frying food poured into the alleyway.

"There was a man in the restaurant," Nick said. "A Connor

Ahearn. Big man with a reddish beard and a bold checked vest. Did he come through the kitchen in the last hour?"

The cook shrank within the greasy apron tied over his clothes and glanced hastily down the alleyway toward the south. "Nope," he answered with a flat expression. "Don't see nobody."

Nick flashed his badge, hidden beneath his coat. "You wouldn't care to answer differently, now, would you?"

"Well, there mighta been some fella who came through the kitchen. 'Bout a half hour ago, mebbe?"

Great.

"He went that way?" Nick asked, pointing to the south and the closed businesses of downtown. Lange's was also in that direction.

"Might've," the cook reluctantly admitted.

Nick took off running. If Ahearn was headed to Lange's store, then he might be thinking of causing trouble for Tessie, whom Nick had rather recklessly allowed Ahearn to believe was accusing him of murder.

He turned up Pine Street. He was very close to Lange's place now, but he didn't see either Ahearn or any of his companions.

Nick arrived at the apothecary's just as the sun slid behind the hills. He peered through the windows, trying to see around the half-closed blinds. No lights were lit in the main room. No light shone around the curtain to the back room, either.

He took the narrow passageway that accessed the alley behind the buildings. Paying attention to the variation in brick and stone that marked the different structures built side by side, he found the sliver of a building that housed Lange's store. Nick scanned the deserted alleyway as he withdrew his Colt and checked the rear door. It was unlocked. He eased it open. Thankfully, the hinges didn't squeal.

The door led to a small vestibule with a flight of stairs straight ahead. He recalled from having searched the place earlier that the door on his left led to a storeroom through which you could reach the store itself. Nick stepped inside the building and listened for voices. Besides the muted rumble of a wagon passing on the street out front, he didn't hear a thing. He considered heading upstairs, but if Ahearn had come here, Nick doubted he was lounging in the second-floor parlor, drinking tea.

Nick stepped over to the storeroom door, which stood a few inches ajar, and paused to listen again. He thought he heard a shaky, indrawn breath. Just one person inside the room? Check that. Possibly just one *living* person inside the room.

Sweat collected at the edge of Nick's neckcloth. The breathing quieted, the building around Nick turning as silent as a tomb. Could be his tomb, in about ten seconds.

Using the barrel of his Colt, he pushed open the door. It didn't get very far when a gunshot exploded, deafening him and jerking him backward like a rag doll. His last thought before he hit the ground was how much he regretted that he'd never get to see Celia Davies again.

CHAPTER 10

"*Mon Dieu!* Detective Greaves!" Hubert Lange stood over Nick, a pistol dangling from his fist. The sharp smell of exploded gunpowder hung in the air. "It is you!"

With a groan, Nick sat up. Lange's shot had gone wide. Shock had kicked Nick backward, not the impact of a bullet. He rubbed the back of his skull where it had smacked against the wall. No significant damage. Couldn't say the plaster and lath had fared as well.

"Who were you expecting?" asked Nick.

The man lowered his weapon and offered his hand to Nick, pulling him to his feet. The walls spun for a moment, then righted themselves. "That *terrible* Connor Ahearn."

"Then he did come here." Cautiously, Nick bent to retrieve his hat and his revolver, which had slid across the floor when he'd dropped it. He was glad he hadn't cocked the pistol, or there'd be another bullet hole someplace besides the one in the banister behind Nick.

"He looked for Thérèse," said Lange. "He shouted she told the police he hated Miss Li and the police wish to accuse him for the death. But how could he know this?"

Nick holstered his revolver and brushed the dust from his hat. "I'm afraid that's my fault, Mr. Lange. I interviewed Ahearn a couple of hours ago and let him believe Tessie thought he was guilty."

Hot anger flashed across Lange's face, the strongest emotion Nick had seen from the man. But then it was gone.

"She is not here, however," said Lange. "She went to the Cliff House with friends today to watch the seals and see the ocean and has not yet returned. This made Ahearn so very angry. He left, but I thought it was he just now who had returned to hurt me. So I stayed quiet in the storeroom with my pistol to wait."

"Why did you think he'd come back to hurt you? Did he threaten you?"

"No words this time. Just the look with the eyes, you know?" Lange was shaking. "Mr. Lange, you should sit," said Nick.

"We may go upstairs."

Nick followed him to the second-floor kitchen. Lange set his gun on the table in the middle of the room and lit a lantern. In one corner stood a sink with a pump handle overhanging it. Alongside was a stove, and hooks and shelves were attached to one wall. Dinged copper pots and pans hung in a tidy arrangement, and tins of cooking staples lined the shelves. Some time ago somebody had fitted out the lone window with gingham curtains, which were faded and tired by now. In fact, most everything looked faded and tired, including Lange.

The druggist dropped into a chair, and Nick took a seat across from him.

"So, tell me when Ahearn has threatened you before," said Nick.

"When he learned I hired Miss Li." Droplets of perspiration were collecting on the inside of his spectacles, and Lange pulled a handkerchief from a vest pocket and swiped it across his sweating forehead. "His sister, he wanted the job for her."

Nick recalled what the boardinghouse owner had said about Ahearn's sister. "The one that's sickly?"

"She is not strong, *oui*. Mr. Davies, Tom Davies, brought her here with Mr. Ahearn one day. To ask about the job. I saw she was too weak. So when Mr. Ahearn learned I hired Miss Li instead, he was angry. He said to me that the anti-Chinese groups would teach me a lesson." He touched the pistol on the table. "I buy this for protection, then."

Lange's employment of Li Sha had given Ahearn another reason to despise the girl, in addition to her ethnicity. "Do you think Ahearn was angry enough to have killed her?"

"I cannot say."

"What about your daughter, Mr. Lange? She was Tom Davies' sweetheart before he took up with Li Sha, wasn't she?"

Lange frowned. "That is true."

"How did Tessie feel about Li Sha after that? She couldn't have liked the situation. Did she and Li Sha ever fight?"

Would her father be honest and admit it if they had?

"Thérèse did complain of the work Miss Li did, but no more."

Nick considered Lange, the sweat on the man's forehead glistening in the lantern light. "Tessie's told us she was with Tom on Monday evening. Is that where she was?"

"She was out, *oui*, but with who I do not know for certain. Ever since her mother passed away, I cannot keep the control on my daughter."

Apparently not. "When did she get home that night, Mr. Lange?"

His shoulders sagged. "Ten, perhaps? I do not recall precisely. Very, very late."

Rather different from the eight thirty or nine that Tessie had claimed. So which of the two was right? And which of the two was lying? "Weren't you worried? I would've been."

"I was. She knew she had done wrong. She knew I would be most upset. As soon as she came in, she ran upstairs to her room and locked the door."

Maybe she'd hurried upstairs to hide blood on her dress. "Did she try to dispose of any clothes the next morning?" Nick asked.

Lange's eyes widened, magnified by his spectacle lenses, and he went about as white as a body could and still be considered alive. "*Mon Dieu*, no! She did not. I swear it!"

"I think I'll ask her myself." Nick stood to leave. "Tell your daughter I want her back in the station tomorrow. And if I or my assistant don't see her there, I'll send a uniformed police officer to haul her over. Which might attract all sorts of embarrassing attention from your neighbors."

"I will." Lange nodded so emphatically, Nick thought he heard the man's teeth rattling.

"Shall we go?" Celia asked Addie the following day. Addie, her bonnet trimmed in a length of black lace, carried a supply of mourning bands to be handed out to the few people who would attend Li Sha's funeral.

"Aye," said Addie. "But I'm worried that dreadful person's out there, watching us."

Celia slipped her hands into her black lace gloves, a pair left over from Uncle Walford's funeral. "Once we return home, I shall take the latest note to the police station and show Mr. Greaves."

"D'you think that'll stop the person, ma'am?"

"It is all I can do." Celia pressed her housekeeper's hand reassuringly. "Come, Addie, Barbara is waiting outside for us."

Addie locked the front door behind them, giving the handle a stern shake to ensure the latch had caught.

Down on the street, Barbara waited beside a hired hack. She turned a somber, tired face in their direction, then looked away when her eyes met Celia's. She hadn't apologized for accusing Celia of only caring for her patients and had maintained a dour silence all morning.

"Am I heartless, Addie?" Celia asked. "Barbara has a good reason to be fearful if the person leaving us messages wishes to harm her."

"No, ma'am, you're nae heartless. And Miss Barbara will come to see that."

They descended the steps. Next door, Mrs. Cascarino, her wool shawl wrapped around her head and shoulders, stood on the porch with Angelo, the boy's face barely clearing the top of the railing.

"A sad day, Signora Davies," she called out.

"Very sad, Mrs. Cascarino," agreed Celia.

Barbara, clutching her reticule bulging with the scraps of paper scrawled with Chinese prayers, climbed into the hack. Even though Mr. Palmer would have paid for it, Celia had refused the cost of a mourning coach.

They took their seats inside, and the driver yelled "get up" to the horse. A child too young for school chased them down the dusty road until he lost interest. They would meet the undertaker's wagon at Lone Mountain Cemetery, where the Chinese were buried. Li Sha, however, had been baptized by the reverend at the Chinese Mission and would sleep eternally in Christian ground nearby the Chinese graves, courtesy of the Palmers' unexpected generosity. She would rest within reach of her people and yet remain removed from them; even in death, Li Sha's place in the world remained unresolved.

The hack turned west toward sandy hills dotted with scrub and grasses. The buildings and houses became increasingly sparse, but the flags and pickets of surveyors marked where the next great development would occur, declaring growth and change. Usually, Celia found the city's energy thrilling. That morning, though, she would readily exchange vibrant progress for the sedate predictability and safety of pastoral Hertfordshire.

Barbara stared out the window, and Celia watched the passing houses as well. Last night she had compared the most recent note to the prior one and concluded that the handwriting was identical. The same person had penned both. But what was the author's motivation? *Is Barbara in danger or am I? Or are all of us?*

"Almost there now, ma'am. I can see the big cross atop Lone Mountain," announced Addie.

A sea of white wooden crosses, stone grave markers, and subdued marble monuments covered the swell of the hill, laurel bushes and squat evergreens filling in what remained of the open ground. The mortuary chapel hugged the road's edge, and Mr. Massey's hearse, festooned in black netting, had taken up a position outside the front door. Another hired carriage stood nearby, along with a buggy that belonged to the Palmers, a small cart she recognized as the Langes', and a riderless horse.

Waiting by the gate in the fence that surrounded the burial ground stood a familiar figure in a flat-crowned hat.

The hired hack halted, and the driver hopped to the ground to open the door. Mr. Greaves, carrying a tattered carpetbag, sprinted over before Celia could descend. After a quick greeting, she introduced him to Barbara and Addie.

Barbara looked alarmed. "Why is he here, Cousin? We were warned to stay away from policemen."

"That is enough, Barbara."

The detective studied Barbara, who lowered her gaze, and set the carpetbag on the bench. "This is the bag Li Sha left at Dora Schneider's, Mrs. Davies. Taylor inventoried the contents, so we're done with it."

Celia released the clasp of the carpetbag. It contained very few items—mostly clothing and a blue bandana tied up like a sack. "What's inside the bandana?" she asked.

"Those are the belongings she had on her when she died. The coroner released them to me this morning."

Celia untied the bandana. Inside, she found the cheap red paste earrings she'd given Li Sha as a gift, some hair combs, and a small purse containing a few pennies.

Barbara was leaning across, peering at the contents. "That's all?" she asked.

"I had the coroner dispose of the clothes she was wearing," said Mr. Greaves. "I figured you wouldn't want them."

They would not; the garments would have been stained with blood.

Celia thanked Mr. Greaves and returned the small bundle

to the carpetbag. He took her fingers in his—Celia wondered if he felt their trembling—and helped her descend to the street. Then he handed down Addie, who looked pleased to be treated like a lady, followed by Barbara, who did not look pleased at all. Addie assisted Barbara over the rough stone path that led to the chapel door, exhibiting considerable restraint by looking back only once to stare at Nicholas Greaves.

He was scrutinizing the conveyances parked along the fence. "Whose are those?"

"The one on the left is the Langes' cart, and the buggy belongs to the Palmers."

"So they both had the means to haul a body to the wharf."

His dispassionate assessment chilled her. "We have received another message, Mr. Greaves," she said. "If I had known you would be here, I would have brought it with me."

"What did it say?"

"'No cops.'"

"That explains your cousin's reaction," he said.

"The watcher had to have seen Officer Taylor at our house yesterday."

"And who is 'the watcher'?"

"On Friday, I noticed someone observing our house. At the time, I convinced myself it was nothing sinister," she said, wrapping the straps of her reticule around her hand. "But after the note on Saturday followed by the latest one, I have been forced to change my mind."

"Could you identify this watcher if you saw him again?"

"I am not certain it is a him, Mr. Greaves. The person wore clothing so loose and oversized, fully concealing their features, that it could have been a woman."

"But not a small woman."

"No, probably not," Celia admitted as she recalled what she had seen last Friday. The watcher had not been small or short. "Could the author be this Connor Ahearn whom Officer Taylor told us about? Because the notes do not appear to have come from anyone we know."

He shot her a look, his eyes shaded by the brim of his hat. "And how can you be so sure about that?"

"I have compared the handwriting to that on all of my correspondence."

"I see." He sounded amused, which was better than angry. "I don't know what Connor Ahearn's role is in all this. He knew Li Sha and had reason to dislike her. He carries a bowie knife, is a confirmed anti-coolieite, and happens to live near where Li Sha's body was found. He has also threatened Mr. Lange, who decided to shoot at me yesterday, thinking I was Ahearn."

"Hubert Lange shot at you?" Had the world gone completely mad?

"Luckily he's got terrible aim," quipped Mr. Greaves. "Plus, Ahearn was the man you saw with Tessie Lange the other day."

"But why would Mr. Ahearn threaten us?" she asked. "He does not know Barbara or me."

"Perhaps your brother-in-law or Miss Lange told him about your friendship with Li Sha."

The straps of her reticule pinched her fingers. "I have no information about him that could be considered incriminating."

"But he doesn't know that."

At the chapel, Mr. Palmer had come to the door and was checking his pocket watch, hung on its heavy gold chain. The minister from Celia's church stood beside him, looking impatient to be under way.

Mr. Greaves dragged his hat from his head, running his fingers through his thick hair, and peered into the chapel's dark interior. "Tell me something," he said. "What else was your cousin expecting to see among Li Sha's belongings?"

"I have no idea." Celia had a fleeting thought, something to do with Li Sha, but it slipped from her grasp before she could seize it.

"All the same," the detective said, "it was a strange comment."

She followed his gaze. The minister was now speaking to Mrs. Douglass, who must have decided to attend as reparation for the treatment Celia had received at the society meeting. Mrs. Douglass' husband—such a surprise to see him there as well—waited to one side. Within the chapel, a sparrow darted among the rafters and then out through the open front door, up into a sky scattered with clouds. At the end of the aisle waited Li Sha's coffin, draped in a simple black pall, the finality of her life contained within wood and brass.

"I wish she had come to me for money that evening, Mr. Greaves, instead of trusting the wrong person."

He didn't answer, the brim of his hat making a circuit through his fingers as he stared into the chapel's shadows.

*W*hy was Palmer's business associate at the funeral of a Chinese girl?

Nick contemplated the reasons while the minister recited Bible verses that were intended to console and instead sounded grim. Douglass' wife, who Mrs. Davies had explained was the head of the Ladies' Society of Christian Aid, must have compelled him to accompany her. Nick considered the back of the woman's head, held rigidly erect. She was no delicate flower who needed her husband to prop her up.

All the Palmers had come, too. Mrs. Palmer fussed with the brooch at her throat and whispered to her daughter. Emmeline wheezed when she inhaled and refused to look at the coffin. Her father kept his Southern gentleman's expression as flat as pond ice.

Hubert Lange sat behind Nick. His daughter, who had yet to make an appearance at the police station, was absent. Lange had assured Nick she was probably there right now. Nick suspected Tessie would find anyplace, even the reeking police offices, preferable to the funeral of her onetime rival.

Nick heard the rap of boot heels against the chapel's stone floor, and Briggs slid into a chair next to him.

Nick groaned. "What in . . . I'm in a house of God, so I won't curse, Briggs, but what are you doing here?"

"Captain wants me to make sure you don't bother Palmer." He craned his neck. "Which one is he?"

The minister paused in his speech and glowered at them.

Nick lowered his voice. "Eagan needs to send you as a watchdog?"

Briggs shrugged.

"If I promise I won't bother Mr. Palmer," said Nick, "will you go back to the station?"

"Why should I trust you?"

"How about I buy your doughnuts for the next week."

Briggs smirked. "Deal."

He clomped out. Propriety restored, the minister completed his words of consolation and indicated that the assembly should gather to follow the casket out to the grave site. Joseph Palmer had offered to serve as pallbearer. He stepped forward when Nick did.

"I am surprised to see you here, Detective Greaves," he said while the minister conferred with Mrs. Davies and her cousin over what would happen next.

"Likewise, Mr. Palmer."

"My wife and I support these girls, sir, the ones trying so valiantly to alter the course of their lives. We are all here to show that we do not forget them, even in death." He gazed at the coffin. "Such a pity."

There wasn't any chance Joseph Palmer looked at that casket and saw what Nick did. Palmer saw a girl not of his class, not of his culture, who'd failed to become a respectable woman. Nick saw a girl who'd lost her way and been trampled underfoot. A pebble drowned in a stream. A broken shell.

"I suppose I should let you know my assistant is checking on your whereabouts last Monday," he said to Palmer. "Just to make sure you were down in Santa Clara County like you've claimed." He'd buy Briggs his doughnuts; he wouldn't leave any possible suspect alone, though.

"I expect you are merely doing your job, Detective Greaves."

"That I am." Nick turned his attention to Mr. Douglass, who was speaking quietly to his wife. "I'm wondering why your associate is here, Mr. Palmer."

"To support his wife, who knew the girl."

"Any possibility Li Sha asked *him* for money?" Nick asked.

"What a suggestion." Palmer glanced over at Douglass and narrowed his eyes. "What a suggestion."

A good suggestion, if Nick read Palmer right. Douglass must have felt them watching him, because he looked over and frowned.

"Let us depart," boomed the minister.

Palmer reached out to lift the casket, his hands encased in good leather gloves. He wore a tailored suit, a beaver top hat, and polished shoes. Nick wondered, though, if the man had a pair of thick-soled boots at home, muddied from tromping through Celia Davies' side yard.

Nick took one corner of the casket, as did a white-faced Lange. Lange shot a look at Palmer, who was studiously ignoring him. Maybe the man didn't care to rub shoulders with a storekeeper. The sexton who'd dug the grave and had been lolling in the doorway was pressed into service, and together they hoisted the coffin and set it on their shoulders. It wasn't heavy, the young woman inside having been barely more than a wisp.

Celia's cousin passed the line of mourners to go to the front, scrutinizing Nick as she went. He could guess what Barbara Walford felt about Li Sha, somebody she had more in common with than she might like to admit. But he couldn't guess what was missing among the girl's belongings that had bothered Miss Walford. When he'd entered the chapel with Mrs. Davies, the girl had been talking to Palmer, Miss Walford excitable, Palmer poker-faced. Nick hadn't overheard what she'd said, but it had been insistent and brief. It seemed everybody wanted to gain the man's attention today.

Palmer cleared his throat. "If everyone is ready, let us proceed," he called out. Not that anyone had asked him to take charge. It must just come naturally.

Nick shuffled along until all the pallbearers settled into a rhythm and plodded outside into the sunshine. The wind snatched at the ladies' black ribbons and scraps of lace they'd pinned to bonnets and gowns. Mrs. Davies was composed and walked arm in arm with her housekeeper, who sniffled into a handkerchief. Up ahead, Miss Walford reached into her net purse and scattered pieces of red paper onto the ground. He'd seen that practice at other Chinese funerals. More commonly, bits of brown paper meant to resemble Chinese money were scattered or burned as supplication to their spirits. He'd guess that wouldn't happen today, and there wouldn't be any offerings of food or smoking incense, either. The minister, frowning at Miss Walford's back, didn't seem to appreciate what the girl was doing. Celia Davies had secured a Christian burial; foreign superstitions had no place there.

The line marched down the hill toward a spot not far from the Chinese burial ground. A few of their graves had been disturbed, dirt roughly mounded over the now empty holes. It was tradition with them that when their bodies had become bones, they would be returned to their home country if the means could be found to pay for the journey. But a former prostitute like Li Sha might lie here for all eternity.

They halted beside an open grave, and the men lowered the casket to the ground. The sexton joined a brawny cemetery worker who was standing nearby. They would finish the task of placing Li Sha in the earth.

Celia Davies came to Nick's side. The black mourning gown she wore turned her skin sallow. She looked worried, and there wasn't much Nick could say to convince her not to be. Two warning notes were two too many.

"Not much longer, ma'am," he said.

She gazed up at him. He'd never been one for pale eyes, but he'd make an exception for hers. "Thank you for being here, Mr. Greaves. Even though you are only here in an official capacity, I appreciate your presence."

"Who said I was only here in an official capacity?" he asked, and she smiled.

They watched the coffin slowly descend into the ground. Nick could smell the salty scent of the ocean three miles to the west and could easily see the gentle hills north of the Golden Gate. This was the most beautiful spot San Francisco could claim and the reason why almost every cemetery in the city was located nearby. It was an ideal place to honor the dead, who were blind to the clouds overhead and unable to feel the wind that rustled the grass growing among the iron fences guarding their tombs.

Nick couldn't stem the memories of a spring in Ohio, where the sky could be the same sort of blue. He could clearly recall Meg stretched out upon a shawl that his twin, Ellie, had spread across the farmyard's clover for their little sister. Meg's shoes and stockings were discarded, her violet gingham skirts hiked around her skinny knees, her toes wiggling. She smiled at the sky overhead, where few clouds broke the endless expanse, her expression full of a peace that only children could manage.

Blue like a robin's egg, she'd say, twirling the first of the dandelions in her fingertips.

Don't you think, Nick? Just like a robin's egg.

No, Meg. Robins' eggs are more greenish.

Poo on you! It's blue like robins' eggs. Right, Ellie? I'm right and he's not!

And Ellie would wag a finger, correcting them both like a parent, and laugh.

Blue like a robin's egg . . .

A broken shell.

Nick pushed away the memories. Next he'd be thinking of that boy in the Wilderness, of the friend who'd saved Nick's life, and of how much he wanted to live those spring days in Ohio all over again.

The minister uttered his final words and shut his Bible. Mrs. Douglass came forward to drop a handful of dirt onto the coffin, the soil clattering against the wood. Others moved to do the same, including Lange and Mr. Palmer, whose wife put a protective arm around her daughter's slumped shoulders and drew the girl to her side. Emmeline leaned against her mother, coughing weakly into her hand.

Celia Davies was the last to stand over the coffin. From beneath her cloak, she brought out a red tulip and dropped it onto the casket. "Farewell, Li Sha."

The cemetery workers began to fill the grave, the *chink* of their shovels hitting the pile of sandy soil louder than the subdued voices of the mourners. Mrs. Douglass' lips moved in prayer, and then she hastily departed with her husband before Nick could make a beeline for them to ask any questions.

Mrs. Davies rejoined Nick. "Do you need a ride back into town, Mr. Greaves? There is room alongside our driver."

"I borrowed a horse."

They were the last besides the undertaker, Atkins Massey, to exit the cemetery, and Mrs. Davies slipped through the gate as Nick swung it wide for her. Lange was long gone, his cart wheeling along the road toward the city. Mrs. Davies' Scottish housekeeper was helping Miss Walford over the rocky path to their hack, the girl apparently needing the assistance. Miss Walford looked toward the Palmers, standing next to their buggy with its red wheels. If she hoped to talk to Mr. Palmer again, Addie Ferguson kept it from happening with a firm tug on the girl's arm.

"I'm wondering something else, Mrs. Davies," he said. "What

did your cousin have to say to Joseph Palmer earlier? Seems strange they'd be talking together, a girl her age and a much older man."

"She was likely thanking him for paying for the funeral. They are on friendly terms," she replied. "Barbara has spent a great deal of time in their home, visiting with Emmeline."

Nick's eyes tracked Mrs. Palmer as she tucked Emmeline's shawl around her shoulders before assisting her into their buggy. Mr. Palmer climbed onto the driver's seat and took one last look at him and Celia Davies before snapping the reins and steering the buggy down the road.

"I plan to speak to the Douglasses about Li Sha's search for money," Nick said.

Mrs. Davies was also watching the Palmers' buggy depart. "Mr. Douglass did not leave the warning notes," she said. "I checked his handwriting, too."

"All the same . . ."

"I can speak with Mrs. Douglass, if you wish," she offered.

"It's best you leave this to me, ma'am." Because she was tangled up in the mess tighter than a burr in a horse's tail and sure to get hurt.

"It is no bother—"

"I insist. You need to be careful, Mrs. Davies. The man watching your house . . . okay, the *person* watching your house," he amended, catching the correction in her hasty glance, "has given you two warnings. I don't like to think what might happen next."

"I shall, of course, be careful, Mr. Greaves, but it seems warnings only make me more determined to learn the truth."

"I guess we're alike in that, Mrs. Davies."

———

"*I* canna help but think Miss Emmeline should have stayed at home with her mother today," said Addie to Celia as the hired hack swayed down the road. "She looked so frail a feather could've toppled her."

"Poor Em. She did look poorly and seemed very upset. More than I expected," said Barbara, the first words she'd uttered since they had arrived at the cemetery. Other than whatever she'd had to say to Mr. Palmer.

"Barbara, what were you speaking to Mr. Palmer about?" Celia asked.

Barbara chewed her lower lip. "About Em, of course. About how upset she was. He was very concerned, too. But then, he's such a good father, what else would he feel?"

"If he's such a good father, Miss Barbara, the bairn should've been left at home," retorted Addie.

Barbara looked ready to begin another enumeration of Mr. Palmer's many virtues, so Celia cut her off. "There is no need to defend him, Barbara," she said. "However, I am curious about something else. When I opened Li Sha's carpetbag, you made a comment that suggested something was missing. What was it?"

"I thought there might be more clothing," Barbara responded.

"You know she owned little more than that one indigo-colored dress." There it was, the memory again, like a flash of light in the dark hastily snuffed. What was she forgetting?

"I wasn't thinking clearly," said Barbara. "You know, you've taken an unnatural interest in solving this murder, Cousin."

"Miss Barbara!" chided Addie.

"And I still want to leave San Francisco. It's not safe here," she added and returned to her glum scrutiny of the passing buildings.

Addie lifted her eyebrows and Celia sighed. The rest of the journey passed in frosty silence.

As the carriage horse labored up the steep incline of Vallejo, Addie squinted out the hack window, her attention fixed ahead of them. "Is that Mr. Smith at the house?"

Celia craned her neck to peer around Addie. A man in a bowler hat and tweed overcoat sat on their porch, a cheap cigarillo clamped between his teeth.

He is here today of all days.

"Maybe he's found your husband, Cousin," said Barbara, who fixed her gaze on Celia. *She is watching my reaction, and I hope she cannot read my feelings on my face.* For dread was an improper response, even though Barbara had no tender feelings for the man who'd never been particularly kind to her. Her cousin would likely be content if Patrick Davies never returned.

Addie was frowning. "Ma'am, I ken that Mr. Smith came well recommended by Mr. Walford's lawyer, but I canna say I like the look of him."

"He makes his living investigating, Addie," said Celia. "I would expect all such men look a trifle . . . shabby."

When the hired carriage halted on the street below, Mr. Smith stubbed out his cigarillo on the stone step and stood.

"Why, there you is, Mrs. Davies," he called out in his booming voice, which echoed off the walls of the Cascarinos' house, drawing the attention of a neighbor tossing dirty water onto the street. "That Irish boy of your'n said you'd be back soon from your funeral." He took in her mourning dress. "Sorry for your loss."

"Owen was here?" Celia asked, grateful to know he was still all right.

Celia climbed down behind Barbara, who hobbled up the

steps. Mr. Smith was gentlemanly enough to doff his hat as she passed. Addie, Li Sha's carpetbag in her arms, harrumphed and unlocked the front door, hustling Barbara inside. The door shut and moments later the blinds at the parlor window cranked open, her housekeeper peeping through.

"The scamp was here just a second ago," said Mr. Smith, who made a show of looking around him. His clothes wafted the smell of cigarillo smoke.

"Do you have news?" Celia asked.

"I do, ma'am," he said, his grin showing tobacco-stained teeth. "But I'm thinkin' . . ." He scratched his chin, then held out his hand.

She reached into her reticule and dropped coins into the man's grimy fist. "Your fee." Another five dollars gone.

The money vanished into an inner pocket of his wool coat, so quickly that the glint of silver in his palm might have been a mirage. "The news?" she asked.

"A steamer from Mexico let in at the Folsom Street wharf this afternoon. Showed around that photograph you give me." Mr. Smith patted the general vicinity of his coat where the coins had gone. She had given Mr. Smith a locket containing a daguerreotype of Patrick, a gift from her husband marking their engagement.

"One of those Jack Tars said he thought he recognized the fella," Mr. Smith was saying. "Said he was down in Mazatlán, bummin' around the docks, lookin' for work."

That sounded like her husband. "Then Patrick is alive?"

"Well, here's the rub. The fella who might be your husband got hisself killed in a knife fight at a saloon."

Celia released the breath she'd been holding. "I need to be certain, Mr. Smith. I cannot continue to live with the doubt."

"I could be more certain the fella was Mr. Davies with more money. Because I'm thinkin' five dollars ain't enough for all the inquirin' I've been doin'. My time's valuable—"

"If that is the case, I no longer require your services," said Celia, making to go around him. "I will speak to my late uncle's lawyer about finding another man who is willing to make inquiries for the fee we agreed upon."

"Whoa, whoa, whoa, ma'am!" Mr. Smith raised his hands in protest. His fingernails were filthy. "No need to tear round like that."

"Five dollars," she insisted.

"Ma'am," he groaned.

"I'm back!" called Owen, drawing Celia's attention. He strolled up the street, his hands thrust into his pockets, seemingly never in a rush to get anywhere. "You here about my ma and pa, Mr. Smith?"

"Kid, I'm never findin' your ma and pa," Mr. Smith replied gruffly. "Why don't you just move in with Mrs. Davies here? Seems to me she's got plenty of room for a scrawny boy like you."

Owen looked over, waiting for Celia to answer, his need for security and his yearning for a family evident in his gaze. But she couldn't accommodate an unrelated male beneath the same roof as Barbara and leave her cousin's reputation intact.

"Owen, you know I cannot offer you a home."

His green eyes showed a hurt so deep it wounded her. He masked the pain by sticking out his chin.

"That's okay, ma'am. Ain't got a need for soft beds and warm meals anyhow. Not when I have my own mates now," he said, and he ran off before the tears could spill down his cheeks.

CHAPTER 11

"The funeral this morning was lovely, Tom," Celia said. "We honored Li Sha as best we could."

Facing the wall, her brother-in-law lay curled up on the cell bunk's torn mattress, a moth-eaten blanket covering his body. Celia pressed her hands against the cold iron grating. The air was fetid, and the sawdust covering the cell floor looked as though it had not been refreshed in weeks, perhaps months. She was glad she had worn her oldest boots.

"More people attended than I expected," she added.

She didn't think Tom was asleep, but he was certainly ignoring her. She looked over at the warden, who shrugged, stretched out his legs, and closed his eyes.

She turned back to Tom. "I have heard the grand jury is set to meet tomorrow. Perhaps they will decide the evidence against you is not strong enough."

Still, he did not move a muscle.

"Tom, I need to talk to you about what happened to Li Sha. Please do not ignore me."

Suddenly he swung his legs over the edge of the bunk and lurched over to the cell door. "Are you expectin' me to be grateful for the visit, Celia? 'Tis your fault I'm in here!"

He slapped a palm against the grate, and she jumped away.

"Hey, Davies!" yelled the warden. "Calm down or you'll lose dinner privileges!"

Tom backed off.

"I am sorry. I did not mean for you to be arrested," Celia said quietly. "And I am doing all I can to free you from this place."

Tom glared at her. Only in the flash of his blue eyes did she see his resemblance to Patrick. Tom had always been scrawnier, more sullen. But he was a hard worker and could be charming and persuasive when he wished. He had succeeded in persuading Patrick to come to America, after all.

"Why would you be botherin', Celia?" he asked. "You chased off me brother with your coldheartedness, and now you'll see me hang. Both Davies men got rid of."

The accusation stung, and she glided her thumb across her wedding band. "Patrick is tragically dead, Tom. We should leave him out of this conversation."

"But you don't believe that, now, do you?" Tom peered at her. "That's why you keep lookin' for him. Wantin' to be sure he's not comin' back."

Celia drew in a long breath and returned his stare. They'd had this conversation before, and there was no favorable conclusion to it. "We have received threatening notes, Tom."

"And what does that have to do with me? Are the coppers

goin' to accuse me of somehow sendin' them?" He waved toward the barred window set high on the brick cell wall. "Maybe I've got magical powers and can fly through these bars like a fairy to leave you notes."

"But that is the point. You could not have left them on my doorstep. It had to be someone else. Someone who either hates Barbara or murdered Li Sha and knows I was her friend. Perhaps this person is afraid I suspect his identity, as well."

Tom scrubbed hands over his face and exhaled. "All right. What do you want?"

"Tell me about Connor Ahearn," she said. "I have heard he is a friend of yours."

"If Connor wanted to warn a body, he'd be more direct than to leave a note."

"You have never mentioned me to him."

"No, I've not."

"What about Tessie Lange?" she asked, much as she hated to link the young woman to the crime. "Might she have told Mr. Ahearn about my friendship with Li Sha? She met him through you, didn't she?"

"You'd have to ask her what she's said to Connor."

Celia's next question would likely inflame Tom. "Do you think Tessie could have killed Li Sha out of jealousy?"

Tom's gaze turned menacing. He leaned in, close enough that Celia could touch his arm if she extended her fingers. His lips were chapped and he reeked of sweat. "She was with me that evenin'."

"Perhaps Connor Ahearn killed Li Sha as a favor to Tessie," Celia continued. Her pulse was racing, which was foolish, because Tom could not hurt her.

"A *favor*, Celia? Like helpin' with chores?" he scoffed.

"He *is* known to despise the Chinese and is organizing a group to possibly burn down their lodgings and businesses, hoping to get the Chinese to leave San Francisco."

"I won't be accusin' either of them, Celia. The coppers have tried to get me to blame Ahearn, but I won't. I'd merely be swappin' one hangin' for another."

"Tom, at least point the police in the proper direction. If you think Tessie or Mr. Ahearn is responsible, tell me."

He pushed back from the grate. "I don't know one way or the other."

"All right, then," she said, changing tack. "If not one of them, who else could it be? You must have some suspicion."

"I think it was one of her customers," he said. "The ones who used to give her all those gifts she got. She kept a few, you know. Her mementos."

But would any of Li Sha's clients have reason to leave threatening notes at Celia's house? "Did she ever tell you the names of these men?"

His expression clouded. "I don't know the names. I don't know anything about them, and I never asked."

She retreated to the center of the aisle and contemplated him. There were secrets everywhere around her, tantalizingly close yet utterly out of reach.

"I will get you out, Tom," she vowed.

He grunted another laugh. "Tessie said the same. And I'm not believin' either of you."

"Mrs. Davies was here dropping off that second note they got. She also decided to visit her brother-in-law, sir," announced Taylor, striding into the detectives' office, a newspaper tucked beneath his arm. He handed the note to Nick and glanced over at Briggs, who was munching a doughnut at his desk.

The detective caught Taylor staring. "What're you looking at?"

"Nothing," said Taylor, rolling his eyes. He dropped into the chair opposite Nick's desk. "Guess you missed her."

"I saw her at the funeral this morning," answered Nick, shoving a file Eagan had left on his desk—reports on confiscated liquor that had been smuggled in from Canada—into a more distant corner.

"Oh, that's right," Taylor repeated, grinning.

"You can stop smirking right now, Taylor," said Nick. Briggs chuckled at that, and Taylor shot him a glare.

"Did you see this today, sir?" Taylor opened the newspaper and pointed to an article. "A report about the female witness— a close personal friend of the defendant—who has provided an alibi for Tom Davies."

Nick glanced at the paper. "They're late. The story was in some of the Sunday editions." Maybe he should interview the reporters; they seemed to know an awful lot. "Who's been talking to the newspapers, I wonder?"

He turned to Briggs.

The detective frowned. "You blaming me?"

"You come to spy on me at funerals. Why not?"

"I don't have to listen to this," said Briggs. Standing, he brushed crumbs from his fingers and stormed out of the office.

Taylor relaxed into the chair and removed a cigar and matches from an inner coat pocket. The tip flared orange as he lit the cigar. "Does Briggs annoy you like he annoys me?"

There was no need to answer that question.

"Has Tessie Lange been in to the station?" asked Nick.

Taylor tilted his head back and blew out a stream of smoke. "Nope."

Damn. "I'll go to Lange's and get her. I wish she wouldn't make this so difficult."

"By the way," said Taylor, "I checked on Palmer's whereabouts Monday. He was in Santa Clara County like he said, sir. And he left for San Francisco that Monday morning, like he also said, but didn't arrive back in town until Tuesday. The man who guards his office door is positive his boss wasn't in the city before then."

Mullahey came through the doorway, pushing Connor Ahearn before him.

"Look who I've brought in, Mr. Greaves," said the policeman. "And he let me borrow his nice bowie knife for a bit."

"A fine afternoon to you, Detective." Ahearn stopped next to Taylor's chair. He towered over Nick's assistant as well as Mullahey, who was shorter by a good head.

"Have a seat, Mr. Ahearn," ordered Nick. "Thank you, Mullahey. Leave the knife on Taylor's desk. Mr. Ahearn can collect it on his way out. If he's leaving today, that is."

Mullahey nodded and shut the door behind him.

Ahearn kicked the empty chair next to Taylor, moving it away from Nick's desk, and sat. "What are you wantin', Detective? I thought we'd talked through everythin' yesterday."

Taylor eyed Ahearn's feet, assessing the size of his boots. "Do you smoke cigars, Mr. Ahearn?"

"Will you be offerin' me one, Officer?" the man asked, smirking.

"No, just asking."

"'Tis a pity. I would be enjoyin' a smoke right now."

Which meant he did smoke cigars, thought Nick. "Where did you go after I spoke with you at the restaurant, Mr. Ahearn?"

Ahearn's gaze scanned the room, stopping on Taylor before alighting on Nick. "Home."

"Not to Celia Davies' house to leave her a threatening note?"

"Would that be Tom Davies' sister-in-law?" asked Ahearn. "Why would I be leavin' her threats, I ask you?"

Nick tucked his thumbs into his vest pockets. "It's come to my attention that you've threatened Hubert Lange because he hired Li Sha instead of your sister. Is that what made you and your friends decide to kill the girl? The last straw, eh?"

"Just sad you are, Detective." Ahearn snorted derisively. "And a pity it is you can't see there are a plentiful crop of men in this town hidin' behind their good deeds when their mothers should be prayin' for their black souls. Maybe you should be lookin' at them, and not at an honest workin'man like me."

The door banged open and Eagan strode through, a stack of papers in his hands. "Connor Ahearn?" He threw the stack of papers onto Nick's desk, generating a breeze. Taylor attempted to disappear into his chair. "What are you doing here?"

Oh, damn, thought Nick, sitting up straight in his chair.

"Havin' a fine chat with two of your men."

"Sorry about your father's passing," said Eagan, resting a hand on Ahearn's shoulder. "Wish I could've made the funeral. He was a good man."

Friends. Eagan and Ahearn were friends. *Damn.*

"Faith and isn't that the truth." Ahearn turned his eyes on Nick and smiled. "So, can I be goin' now, Detective?"

"Greaves, do you have an explanation for why Mr. Ahearn is in your office?" asked Eagan.

"I'm asking him some questions about a pair of warnings recently left at Mrs. Davies' house," said Nick.

"I've known Connor since he was in short pants, Detective," replied Eagan, a muscle twitching on his jaw. "He wouldn't have anything to do with that."

"Then he won't mind answering my questions, Captain," said Nick. Taylor slid even farther down in his chair.

Eagan rested a hand on Ahearn's shoulder. "You can leave now, Connor. Give my best to your sister and mother."

"I shall indeed, Mr. Eagan." Ahearn rose and tugged the brim of his cap. "And a fine day to you, Detective. Hope it's better, but I'm doubtin' it will be."

Ahearn strolled out.

Eagan stabbed a thumb onto the papers spilling over Nick's desk. "I want to see you working on these cases I've left you and nothing else."

"You gave me until Wednesday," Nick reminded him. "And you just let my best lead walk out the door."

"Connor Ahearn is not your man, Greaves. And no more attending Chinese prostitutes' funerals or talking to Joseph Palmer or interrogating the sons of my old friends."

"Why did you need to send Briggs to spy on me?"

"I've never needed to order Briggs to spy on you. He's happy to tell me what you're doing all of his own accord." The captain cocked his head to one side and scratched the fingertips of his right hand through his whiskers, a slow, deliberate motion. "The man doesn't much like you, to be blunt."

"The feeling's mutual." Nick gathered both warning notes. "These are the notes Mrs. Davies has received."

Eagan plucked the papers from Nick's fingers and read them. "Doesn't mean anything, Greaves. A piece of mischief after reading her name in the papers." Eagan tossed the notes at Nick. "And make sure you leave Palmer alone."

"Are you protecting Palmer, and Ahearn, too, because you're afraid of them?" Nick asked, skimming close to the thin edge of the ice on a half-frozen pond.

"You'd better watch what you're accusing me of, Detective." Eagan spread his broad hands atop Nick's desk and leaned in close. "Your uncle always said you had a hot head. But you're a good detective, and I respect that. Stop being good, and you'll be sheriffing in some tin-pot cow town."

"Why don't you just kick me off the force right now?"

"I don't know." A muscle in Eagan's jaw flexed. "Maybe I made a promise to a man I admired." He straightened and turned on his heel. "Get back to your own desk, Taylor," he snapped, and stomped off.

Taylor pulled the cigar from his mouth. "What's going on, sir? I mean, Eagan and Ahearn and Palmer. They're all friends?"

Nick stuffed the notes into his desk drawer and slid it shut. "And two of them knew Li Sha. I wonder if Eagan did, as well."

Taylor whistled, and a flake of ash fell from his cigar onto the floor.

"What has happened with the girl I treated?" Celia asked. The old woman crossed her arms into the depths of her sleeves and stared, unmoved by Celia's efforts to get past her.

"You go," the woman demanded.

Closing her fist around the handle of her medical bag, Celia took a step to the side to look down the length of the narrow alleyway, at the line of closed doors flush with the rickety plank pavement. Here and there a prostitute without a customer peeped through a latticed window. Though it was still afternoon, the shadows in the alleyway were lengthening, and lamps flickered inside the rooms behind those windows.

The room her patient had occupied was dark, however.

The other woman continued to shout at her, and one word—*sze*—captured Celia's full attention.

"She is dead? Is that what you are saying?"

"*Sze*," the old woman repeated, and nodded crisply when she saw that Celia understood.

"Didn't the surgeon come and remove her arm? He said he would try to help."

"You go," the woman demanded and strode off, leaving Celia standing alone in the alleyway.

As she turned to leave, a flash of blue caught her eye. The woman who had befriended Celia's patient had exited a door and was hurrying down the alleyway.

"Wait!" Celia called out, dashing after her. She dodged a chicken squawking across her path. "Please! I want to talk to you."

The girl glanced back, skidding in the alley's filthy mud, and fell.

"Let me help you," Celia said, extending a hand. The young woman looked at Celia with suspicion before accepting the offer and allowing Celia to pull her to her feet. Celia didn't release her grip, convinced the girl would bolt again if given the chance. As it was, she looked as alarmed as a hare caught in a net. "You speak some English, correct?"

The girl shook her head, belying the denial. She tried to tug her hand free, but Celia held fast.

"You do just a little. I remember." Celia remained firm. "What happened to my patient, your friend?"

"Man come yesterday. But she dead."

The surgeon had waited an entire day before attending the girl. At least he had finally done what he'd promised.

"What about Li Sha?" she asked. "Tell me what you know."

The Chinese girl stilled at the mention of Li Sha's name, and her eyes welled with tears. "She friend."

Celia released the girl's hand. "The last time I was here, you mentioned some man to my cousin, Barbara. Do you think this man hurt Li Sha?" she asked.

A tear slid down her smooth, high cheek. "He look for her," she said. "Angry."

"This angry man came here, looking for Li Sha?"

Reluctantly, the girl nodded.

"Was he a white man? Pale, like me, with a brightly colored waistcoat and red hair, perhaps?" Celia asked, making a guess as to the man's identity. She gestured at her own face and clothes, mimicking what she hoped suggested flashy attire.

The young woman nodded again and was about to say more when her gaze shifted to a spot beyond Celia's shoulder. Her eyes widened.

"I go," she said, and bolted in the other direction.

A Chinese man had been watching them from a nearby doorway. He was dressed in an immaculate inky black silk tunic and trousers, a black silk skullcap on his head and red silk slippers on his feet. He was an herbalist, based on the sign above the entrance of his shop written in Chinese and English, and on the rows of jars and drawers within the shop itself, the bones and unidentifiable objects suspended from the ceiling.

Skirts lifted clear of the alleyway mud, Celia walked over to the merchant. A nearby laundryman, sweeping a saucepan-shaped iron back and forth over a shirt, watched her with interest.

"You speak English," she said to the herbalist.

"The girl must not talk to you," he answered. "And you must not come here alone. Dangerous."

"But I am not alone. The constable is waiting . . ." Celia glanced toward where he normally stood. He wasn't there. "The constable *was* waiting."

"It best you leave, Mrs. Davies."

He knew her name. Perhaps all the merchants in Chinatown did. "If the girl can help lead the police to Li Sha's murderer, she must speak out," Celia persisted.

"Why?" he asked, his expression opaque except for the pessimism in his dark eyes.

"Tell me who you think killed Li Sha. A former client? Someone from the anti-Chinese groups? A man named Connor Ahearn, perhaps?"

The herbalist shifted his weight to step closer, the rustling of his glossy silk releasing a sweet and strangely medicinal odor.

"There are many who hate us." He let his gaze scan the street, drawing her attention to a shop owner cleaning up broken window glass.

"You might all be in danger," Celia said urgently. "Connor Ahearn and his friends want to burn your shops and your homes."

He considered her. "If the white men want to hurt us, how can a mere Celestial stop them?"

Just then a Chinese customer, her black hair caught up in a fantastic pile secured with a lacquered hair comb and her aquamarine silk tunic rustling, approached the shop and stepped around Celia. The woman issued a command to the merchant in Chinese and tottered into the shop on her high shoes. The herbalist hastened after her without another word.

I must inform Mr. Greaves.

Celia wondered if he could do much with what she'd learned, since the information had come from someone who could not testify in court. It was critical, though, for him to know that Connor Ahearn had recently been seen in Chinatown looking for Li Sha. Because to her mind, the information solidified his role as the most likely suspect.

Medical bag swinging in her hand, Celia rushed across the road, dodging traffic and a freshly deposited pile of steaming manure. Even though the herbalist had been unwilling to confirm that Mr. Ahearn was responsible for Li Sha's death, it simply made sense that he was. According to Mr. Greaves, he despised the Chinese and Li Sha in particular. He owned a knife and lived near where Li Sha's body had been found. Would Li Sha have thought to approach Connor Ahearn for money the night she died? She might have done, if she were desperate enough and also believed he might gladly help a Chinese person leave San Francisco.

"It all fits!" Celia exclaimed to herself just as she collided with a grocer hauling a crate of potatoes from a wagon parked at the curb.

"Hey, watch it!" the grocer shouted, scrambling after the potatoes rolling toward a dirty puddle.

"Pardon me," she murmured, and helped him collect his spilled wares before rushing onward.

The warning notes she'd received continued to mystify her, however. Celia supposed Mr. Ahearn might have come to believe that Li Sha had mentioned him to Celia, perhaps saying she was afraid of him. He might have learned from one of the Langes that Celia had taken Li Sha under her wing, a relationship that would naturally lead to confidences. Had Tessie Lange come to suspect Connor Ahearn as well? Had she gone to the Barbary to get him to admit he was responsible? But why not inform the police of her suspicion? Unless she was too frightened he would kill her, also.

"Mrs. Davies!"

It was Joseph Palmer. He steered his buggy to a halt on the street alongside her.

"Good afternoon, Mr. Palmer," she said. "I apologize for not speaking with you at the funeral. I wish to extend my thanks again for your kind generosity. Although I wonder if my cousin might have already expressed our thanks," she added, a clumsy way of asking what he and Barbara had been so urgently discussing that morning.

"Miss Barbara? Why, yes. Yes, indeed," he replied smoothly. "Do you require a ride home, ma'am? I was headed to my warehouse to meet with Mr. Douglass, but I can make a detour."

"Actually, I was bound for the police station."

His leather gloves creaked as he tightened his fists around the reins. "To visit your brother-in-law?"

"I did see Tom this morning already. No, I wish to . . ." She stuttered to a halt. She found the intense way he was watching her unsettling. She'd known Joseph Palmer for years. She could trust him with what she had learned from the Chinese prostitute. Nonetheless, she decided not to.

Celia smiled politely and said the first thing that came to her mind. "I wish to ask if the police have finished with all of Li Sha's possessions. I would like to distribute them to her friends. Small tokens only. She owned so little."

"She had sold everything she'd been given, hadn't she? A

healthy, clean break from her past life, in my opinion." Mr. Palmer tapped his fingertips to the brim of his top hat. "If you do not require a ride, Mrs. Davies, I must be on my way. I am late for a meeting. Give my regards to Miss Barbara. Good day to you."

"Good day, Mr. Palmer," she replied.

He flicked the reins across the horse's back and steered the buggy away.

She did wonder, though, as she stared after him, how he had learned that Li Sha had sold the gifts she'd received.

"*Y*our daughter never came to the station today, Mr. Lange," said Nick, who'd gone to Lange's store after a failed attempt to find Palmer's associate, Douglass, at the man's office. "Where is she?"

The man blinked at him and pressed a fingertip to his spectacles to straighten them. "I have not seen her since before I left for Miss Li's funeral. She left no message for me. I do not know where she is."

"Not since before the funeral?" That would've been— Nick checked the clock hanging on the far wall of Lange's apothecary store—more than six hours ago. "She hasn't been here for six hours?"

"This is not like her. There has been such trouble since Miss Li died. And now . . . *ma pauvre fille.*" Lange removed his spectacles and wiped his eyes.

Damn, had his daughter run off? "This doesn't look good for her, Lange. It makes me think she's guilty of something."

"Something horrible has happened. This I fear."

"Is there any indication somebody took her against her will?" Nick scanned the main store area. No sign of a struggle in here. "Were either of the doors to this building forced open, for instance?"

"No. They both were locked when I arrived from the

cemetery. She took her key from where it hangs in the kitchen and left." He shuddered and steadied himself against the large table in the center of the room.

Nick eyed him. What the hell did Lange know that he wasn't telling? "Do you have some idea where she might be, or who she might be with? Ahearn, maybe? He came looking for her yesterday."

"I cannot say."

"Your daughter has either skipped town because she knows something about Li Sha's murder, Mr. Lange, or Li Sha's killer has apprehended her. Either way, your daughter's in trouble, and it could be fatal trouble." Nick leaned across the table, and the man cringed. "So, maybe you *can* say where you think she's gone. And while you're at it, why not also explain why she told me she came home last Monday night an entire hour earlier than what you claimed."

Lange, white-faced, stared at Nick. "I . . . I was mistaken."

"What's going on, Lange?"

Beads of sweat popped out on the man's forehead. "There is a man I have seen on the street, an evil-looking man—"

"And you're just telling me about him now?" Nick asked.

"I do not think Tessie knows this man," Lange replied.

"When did you first notice him?"

Lange paused to think. "It has been a few weeks. Not longer."

"And it wasn't Ahearn."

Lange shook his head. "I should have warned her. You must search for her, Detective Greaves. It is most urgent."

"Can I look through her room? There might be a clue to where she's gone."

Lange led him upstairs and opened the first door on the left beyond the kitchen. It was a tiny, dark room with a narrow window looking out at the gap between buildings. Lange went to light the lamp on a bedside table. The room contained a quilt-covered bed, neatly made, a washstand, and a chest of drawers with a mirror on the wall above it and a lacquered wooden box on the polished surface. A handful of pencil sketches of animals, which looked as though they'd been drawn by a child, were tacked to the walls, and a long wool cloak hung from a hook by the door.

The cloak gave Nick an idea. "Have you ever seen your daughter with a set of men's clothing, Mr. Lange?"

"What? No."

The question had been worth a shot. Nick poked through the drawers and examined the items on Tessie's washstand, but there wasn't much to see. "Does your daughter keep a diary?"

"I think not." Lange gazed sadly around the room. "There is nothing here to tell us where she has gone."

Nick crossed back to the chest of drawers and flipped up the brass latch on the lacquered box. The box was lined with purple velvet and, apart from a mother-of-pearl hair comb, was empty. "Is this comb all Tessie keeps in here?"

"*Mon Dieu*, no. She had her mother's jewelry." Lange squinted at the box. "Where did it go?"

"I'd say the jewelry went to a pawnshop, Mr. Lange," answered Nick.

"But her clothing, it is all here."

Nick frowned. She might have left town on her own accord, but without her clothes it was more likely she'd been waylaid. "We'd better find her, Mr. Lange. Before somebody else does."

Nick headed up the street toward his lodgings. The lamps were being lit along the road, and the gas flared and snapped behind the glass. The doors to a saloon hung open, and somebody was belting a bawdy song, making the patrons laugh. Just another night in San Francisco. And somewhere out there was Tessie Lange, possibly with a purse full of money obtained from pawning her mother's jewels. She might've left her clothing behind to hide her intention to leave the city. Or she might've left it behind because she'd planned to come right back home, once she'd finished with her business. But she hadn't come home. And all Nick knew for sure was that Tom Davies wasn't responsible for her disappearance.

Nick turned down a quiet street and realized that footsteps echoing off the buildings had been accompanying him for several blocks. He strolled on casually and started whistling, some tune he remembered from his childhood. He sauntered around the next corner and ducked into the deep entrance to a hardware store, unholstering his gun. A shop boy who'd been washing windows across the street caught sight of the Colt and froze, the scrub brush dripping soapy water onto the sidewalk.

Damn.

Nick gestured for him to go inside, and mouthed, *Go.* The boy blinked at him.

"Go inside!"

The kid grabbed his bucket and bolted through the door, sloshing water.

Nick took a cautious step forward, risking a look along the sidewalk. He didn't see anybody, even though the person following him couldn't have been more than a dozen yards behind him.

The hardware store owner had come to the front window and was staring at Nick over the cans of nails and tools on display. If Nick kept standing there, he'd gather a confounded crowd.

Gun in hand, Nick crept back to the street corner and peered around the edge of the building. He startled a grizzled man tying his horse to a hitching post.

"Apologies," said Nick.

Nick checked that the gun's hammer was resting on the empty chamber and reholstered the weapon, letting his coat flap back into place. He continued on his way home. He might've been imagining he'd been followed, but he didn't think so. His visit to Lange's had made somebody nervous. Was it the man Lange had called evil looking or some other—

The blow to Nick's head came from out of the blue, staggering him to his knees. He reached for his gun and rolled to one side as his assailant swung again, striking Nick's forearm and sending the Colt skittering across the rocky dirt of the alleyway. White-hot pain shot along his arm, flooded his body. His head reeling, Nick struggled to stand. It was too dark in this stretch of the road to make out more than the attacker's general shape, his features obscured by a drawn-down hat and a piece of cloth over his face. The man raised his weapon—a thick bludgeon—and Nick kicked out, losing his balance, but he caught one of the man's knees with his boot heel, knocking him backward. Breathing hard, Nick jumped up, his surroundings swaying.

He pushed off from the nearest wall and kicked out again, but the man fended off the kick with the club. Nick lunged for him, but his assailant was strong and tore away from his grip. The man took off running with long, loping strides.

"Damn!" Nick's stomach heaved from the pain in his arm as he gave chase. "Stop, damn it! Police!" he shouted.

The assailant dashed into an alleyway and Nick followed.

But the alley was deadly quiet and too dark to make out anything more than a sliver of purple sky overhead.

The man was gone.

"*Y*ou did very well with your arithmetic today, Barbara," said Celia, wiping a sponge soaked in a mild solution of creosote water across the oilcloth surface of her examining table.

A patient had been waiting when Celia had returned home from her unsuccessful visit to the police station, where she'd found neither Mr. Greaves nor Officer Taylor. The patient had been a domestic with the measles, and Celia always disinfected her examination room after seeing contagious cases, even though Addie would complain about the smell afterward and Celia's hands would be chapped for days.

"Oh," responded Barbara to Celia's comment, not interrupting her inspection of the darkened streets beyond the clinic's window blinds.

"I have not seen anyone watching the house today." Celia dropped the sponge into the bucket at her feet. "Maybe the person has tired of spying on us and leaving notes."

"Do you really believe that?" asked Barbara.

"Yes," she answered, calmly holding her cousin's gaze. It was a small lie, but worth telling to calm her cousin. In the morning, Celia would speak to Nicholas Greaves about Connor Ahearn, the man would be arrested, and Tom would be freed. Soon they would no longer live in fear.

Barbara let the slats drop into place. "Then maybe we don't need to bother Madame Philippe with our questions tomorrow."

"Addie still wishes to go." Celia decided not to share that she wanted to question the woman about anything Tessie might have said to her about Li Sha or Connor Ahearn. Barbara would only criticize Celia's involvement in the investigation again. "Thank you for helping organize the supplies in here, Barbara. It has been a long day and you look tired. You should go to bed."

"Good night," Barbara said, and shuffled off.

Celia hefted the bucket and pushed through the connecting door between the examination room and the kitchen. Addie was scrubbing the oak worktable, the pots and pans from the day's meal preparation already cleaned and hung on their hooks.

Addie wrinkled her nose. "Och, now you're bringing that concoction in here?"

"I have to dispose of it somewhere," she said, dumping the solution into the wet sink in the corner.

"Smells like the verra devil. Maybe you should take it to the Palmers' for their cleaning." Addie's scrub brush went around in increasingly rapid circles. "I met that new housekeeper of theirs, Rose, at the Washington Market today. Rose talked my ear off about how Mrs. Palmer is following her about, inspecting her cleaning as if the girl doesna ken what's she's doing!" Addie shook her head. "She willna stay with them any longer than the last one, I predict."

"Elizabeth should learn to be grateful for the capable domestics she has been able to hire."

"Perhaps she believes like my father that gratitude is a heavy burden. Only, in Mrs. Palmer's case, it's a burden she'd rather not carry." Addie paused. "Whisht, is that the fire bell?"

Celia lowered the bucket to the kitchen floor and listened for the sound. The tocsin at city hall that alerted the fire stations was ringing.

"Four bells," she said. The Barbary Coast and parts of the Chinese district were in the Fourth Ward.

"The fire should stay south of us, ma'am," said Addie. "Dinna fash yourself."

"I am not worried about the fire reaching us, Addie." Celia removed her apron and headed for the front door, snatching up her half boots on the way. "I am worried that Connor Ahearn and his men have decided now is the time to burn out the Chinese."

"You canna be going there!" screeched Addie, who'd scrambled after her. "At this time of night and with that watcher fellow out there, wanting to harm us!"

"He has not been out on the street today," said Celia, kicking off her soft mules and sitting to tug on her boots.

"And now you're splitting hairs," said Addie, stooping to tie the bootlaces.

"I have to go," Celia responded, and stood. "If any of the Chinese get injured in the melee, who will come to their aid? No one. I must help."

With a loud sigh, Addie untied her apron and tossed it onto the hat rack by the door.

"What are you doing?" asked Celia.

"I'm coming with you."

"We should not leave Barbara alone."

"Then I'll go next door and ask Mrs. Cascarino to come over." Addie fisted her hips. "Because you're nae going to the Barbary at night without me."

Celia grinned and squeezed Addie's hand. "Fetch my bag. Quickly. We must hurry."

CHAPTER 12

The fire glowed orange over the intersection of Jackson and Dupont, and smoke, lit from beneath, billowed into the sky. Nick ran toward the blazing buildings, his sore head throbbing in rhythm with the pounding of his feet. His arm, wrapped in an improvised sling, didn't feel much better. He'd rather be nursing it and the knot on his skull with a few stiff slugs of whiskey. But when he'd heard the city hall bell indicating a fire in Chinatown, Nick had been convinced the anti-coolie hooligans were following through on their promise to burn out the immigrants.

A horse-drawn hose reel clattered past him, its bell ringing to forge a path through the gawkers crowding the cobblestones. It pulled alongside the steam engine from Company One, which had already hooked up to the hydrant at the corner. Firemen, their red shirts soaked with sweat from the fire's heat, trained the water hose on the flames. A laundry was on fire, along with the saloon next door.

"You have to save my shop!" yelled a white storekeeper, gesturing wildly to where sparks and ash were raining down on his jewelry store.

A clutch of Chinese men had collected buckets and futilely tossed water onto the laundry shop even as it dissolved in a wall of flames. The fire created a wind that fluttered their tunics. *Burn them out.* Wouldn't be hard. If the wind picked up, the whole street could turn to cinders in no time.

"You there." One of the firemen, the company emblem attached to his tall leather helmet reflecting the flames, shouted at the Chinese men. "You need to get back!"

Nick paused at the edge of the crowd. Patrons of the gambling dens along Jackson, who had come to see the spectacle, were wagering on how many other buildings would go up.

"And you, too!" The fireman pointed at Nick. "Out of the way!"

"Police." Nick flashed his badge. "How did it start?"

"Sorry, Officer. Not sure. Looks like it might've begun in the alley at the back of the laundry. But it could've started at the saloon next door." He jerked his chin toward a man seated on the curb, cursing in what sounded like German. "He keeps muttering 'kerosene.' Maybe somebody overturned a lantern. But the captain thinks it looks like arson."

"Did you talk to the man who owns the laundry?" Nick asked.

"Him? He won't say anything to us. Not even in that funny English them Celestials speak."

The flames flared up, the roar deafening. A portion of the upper floor of the laundry crumbled and collapsed in a thundering heap of sparks. Hot air fanned over the crowd, making everyone jump back. The firefighters unrolled another length of hose and began to attack the fire from the other side.

"Gad," said a familiar voice at his shoulder. "Is anyone hurt?"

Nick looked over at her. "Everybody escaped the fire, Mrs. Davies."

"Thank goodness. I was expecting a brawl, to be frank. The fire, however, is bad enough." Her fist tightened around the handles of the medical bag she'd thought to bring with her. Beside Mrs. Davies, her housekeeper clung to her shawl and gaped at the flames. "So they have done what they threatened," Mrs. Davies said.

"We don't know that this was caused by Ahearn or any of the anti-coolieites, ma'am," he pointed out.

"Do we not, Mr. Greaves?" she challenged. Her gaze dropped to the old undershirt he'd looped around his neck to cradle his forearm. "And what, may I ask, happened to you?"

"Not sure I want to bore you with that story, ma'am."

"I am not going anywhere soon," she said, an eyebrow arching. "So you may as well."

"Remove the sling and roll up your sleeve," demanded Celia, once she had managed to extract the story of his attack out of Nicholas Greaves. They had moved farther from the fire, which was coming under control. It seemed the rest of the block would be saved. *Thank heavens.*

Mr. Greaves balked, tucking his injured arm closer to his chest. "It's nothing."

"Please do as I ask, because if you are busy being assaulted in alleyways, I want to see what damage has been done." She handed her portmanteau to Addie, who was now gaping more at the firemen, handsome in their uniforms, than at the fire. "Did you see your assailant's face?"

"Not clearly. He had a cloth of some sort wrapped around the lower half. He must've been afraid I'd recognize him." Gingerly, Mr. Greaves extracted his arm from the sling. "And I couldn't tell if he was wearing a red-and-yellow vest, either. He had on a long coat buttoned up over his clothes."

"A duster coat like what the cowboys wear?" she asked. "Because the person I saw watching our house might have been wearing one as well."

"Could've been a duster."

"And now the watcher is after you."

His eyes met hers. "Or maybe it's just one of the many friends I have in the city, ma'am, paying their respects."

"Most amusing, Mr. Greaves."

He took off his jacket, which he also handed to Addie, and rolled up his shirtsleeve. There was a large, swollen bruise on his forearm. Celia prodded the area gently, making him wince.

"Honestly, between you and Owen . . ." She carefully turned over his arm. His hand, long fingered and broad, rested against her sleeve.

"Well?" he asked. He was watching the movement of her fingers over his skin, and his breath whispered across her forehead. Her pulse lifted at the intimacy of the contact.

She released her clasp on him.

"It is hard to see in this light, but I do not think your arm is broken," she said, turning to observe the last of the flames gutter out, avoiding his eyes. He was too observant and would see what she'd felt. "It is a good thing both you and Owen are particularly sturdy."

"I want to meet this Owen kid someday. From what you've said, he's the sort of person I'd like."

"He *is* the sort of person you would like, Mr. Greaves. Courageous and honest and loyal." Celia nodded toward his arm. "Put a cold compress on that bruise when you return home. And are there any other injuries you would like to tell me about?"

"No, ma'am," he replied, taking his jacket from Addie. "None that I'd like to tell you about."

"The firemen have finished, ma'am," said Addie.

They had shut off the water and were coiling their hoses. The laundry and the saloon were smoldering piles of embers and shattered glass, their upper floors collapsed into the ground floors. The crowd dispersed, wandering back to their lodgings or to nearby drinking establishments. The fire would make good conversation over liquor and cards.

"Wonder where the German who owns the saloon went to," Mr. Greaves said as he restored the sling around his arm. "I would've liked to ask him if he saw anybody suspicious."

"Should I speak to the owner of the laundry?" Celia offered.

"That'd be helpful, ma'am."

She crossed the street. At first the man did not wish to talk to her. She managed, though, between English and fragmented Chinese, to explain that she wished to help.

"*Fo.* The fire," she said. "Did you see . . ." Celia did not know the Chinese word for "anyone." "Did you see a man? *Yan?*"

The laundry owner narrowed his dark eyes. "See man. White man. Come today. Yesterday. He look at my store a long time."

"What did he look like?" she asked. "His face. *Min.*"

"White," he answered, and pressed his lips together.

"Did he have on a red-and-yellow waistcoat?"

"You know him, you tell him we not go." He turned on his heel and stalked off. Celia returned to where Mr. Greaves waited and relayed what the man had said.

"Can't say it was Ahearn, then," said Mr. Greaves.

Celia watched the hose-cart driver guide the horse away from the fire. The water had left huge puddles of mud in the road. The owner of the laundry sat on his haunches and stared at the remains of his business. "The Chinese have done nothing to deserve this violence," she said.

"They've come to California and upset the balance of the world for a lot of folks. Reason enough."

The crisp breeze ruffling the fringe of her shawl drifted smoke toward them, and Celia coughed.

"Let's get you two home," the detective said, making a quick final scan of their surroundings before heading up the road.

It would be a steep climb from here. Celia was exhausted and dreaded the hike back to the house, but the streetcars did not run at this hour, so she trudged alongside Mr. Greaves.

"'Tis awful," said Addie, trailing behind them. "Miss Barbara will be asking again to leave the city."

"I hate to tell you this, Miss Ferguson, but you probably won't be able to leave," said Mr. Greaves. "They'll likely subpoena you to be a defense witness for your brother-in-law, Mrs. Davies. You'll have to stay in San Francisco for the trial."

"Och, no," muttered Addie.

"What shall I say to Barbara? This fire, coming so soon after the notes we've received, will terrify her."

"Sorry, ma'am."

"You must arrest Connor Ahearn, anyway," she said, as they left the Barbary behind and headed into the quieter neighborhoods that tumbled down the side of Telegraph Hill. The lights of the houses on the hillside winked among the shadows. "If he did not commit arson himself, he incited someone to."

"Owen Cassidy overhearing his friends claim that a man named Connor wanted to burn out the Chinese isn't quite enough proof to arrest Ahearn. I'm sorry. Truly, I am."

"But it is still possible Mr. Ahearn was involved in Li Sha's death." Celia explained that he'd been in Chinatown looking for Li Sha. "I find it ironic that a man who claims to hate the Chinese makes use of Chinese prostitutes. Although does it not seem sometimes that people most vocally revile what is, in truth, their greatest temptation?"

"He's just scum, Mrs. Davies. I don't think we need to ascribe more thought to his actions than that," said Mr. Greaves. "You need to know that Tessie Lange has sold all her mother's jewelry and taken off without leaving a note. She might've left town, but she didn't take any of her clothes."

Addie gasped. "Her, too?"

"Is Tessie in danger?" asked Celia.

"Taylor's been searching for her. We'll find out what's happened to Miss Lange."

"More to ask Madame Philippe tomorrow, ma'am," said Addie.

"Who's Madame Philippe?" asked Mr. Greaves.

"An astro—"

"Dinna explain, ma'am," Addie interrupted, scowling. "He'll only laugh like his great gowk of an assistant." She tossed her head and stalked ahead of them, Celia's medical bag swinging in her hand.

"I will tell you later," said Celia to Nicholas Greaves.

"Can't wait to hear."

*C*elia lay awake, her eyes attempting to trace the printed vines that twined up her bedchamber's wallpaper. If she did not get some sleep, she'd be of no use to her patients tomorrow. She kept thinking about the fire, though, and Tessie and Connor Ahearn's possible culpability in Li Sha's death.

Tom was reluctant to condemn them, though. Did his hesitation mean he thought they were guilty—or not guilty? But why go to the hangman's noose for a woman he no longer cared for and a friend who had hated Li Sha? Celia understood loyalty, but not at that cost. Unless Tom was reluctant to admit to himself that two of his closest acquaintances had conspired to kill the woman he'd come to love.

"Oh, Tom. What a mess."

Celia had started on the third column of vines to the left of her window when she heard a cry come from inside the house. Scrambling out of bed, she threw open her chamber door. Pale moonlight shone through the window at the end of the hallway. Her cousin's chamber was across the way, next to the room that used to be her father's bedchamber. Celia could hear Barbara's sobs through the closed door. Addie slept in the tiny room on the other side of the staircase. It would take more than Barbara's weeping to awaken Addie; she could sleep through a cannonade.

Celia tapped on her cousin's door. "Barbara? What is it?"

The sobbing halted and silence descended.

"Barbara, I heard you crying, so you can stop pretending to be asleep," Celia said through the closed door. "Let me in."

She heard the sound of feet padding across the floor, and Barbara opened the door. Her cousin clasped her long braid like a lifeline, and her eyes were bloodshot. "I'm sorry I woke you, Cousin."

"Don't worry. I was not asleep." Celia pushed the door wide and entered the room. "What is the matter? Are you upset because of the fire?"

"No. It's nothing."

She tried to turn away, but Celia seized Barbara's arm to halt her. "You can tell me."

Barbara wriggled out of her grasp. "I had a bad dream; that's all." She limped to her bed and flopped onto it, the hair-and-spring mattress sinking beneath her weight.

Celia sat next to her on the bed. "If you tell me about this dream, you might feel better."

Tears collected in Barbara's eyes. "It's about Li Sha. I spend more time thinking about her now that she's dead than I did when she was alive. Why won't she leave me alone?"

"What happens in your dream?" Celia asked gently.

Barbara reached for her pillow and clutched it to her stomach. "It's horrible. I see a man, but not his face. He's wearing all black and Li Sha is wrapped in a white sheet stained with blood. He drives a wagon down to the pier and tosses her out. She lands with an awful thud. He laughs and drives away." She drew in a ragged breath. "It's the same every night."

"Do you think you recognize him?" But what did a dream portend, other than to reveal one's deepest fears?

Tears seeped from the corners of Barbara's eyes to spill down her cheeks, and she grabbed Celia's wrist. "Can't we please leave San Francisco, Cousin Celia? Go out to Healdsburg and visit the geysers for a while? I think we can afford a short trip, and your patients will be fine without you for a few days."

"Detective Greaves has told me I will likely be subpoenaed

to appear as a defense witness in Tom's trial. I cannot go anywhere. I'm sorry."

"Well, maybe *I* can go with Addie."

"Going to Healdsburg will not end the nightmares, Barbara," said Celia.

Barbara released Celia's wrist. "It might."

"We can discuss a possible trip to Healdsburg tomorrow,"
Celia said, conceding in order to calm her. "Besides, who knows?
Perhaps Madame Philippe will have an insight for us that will
resolve all our questions."

"You're not really expecting that, are you? They're all char-
latans."

"No, Barbara, I am not expecting an astrologer to reveal
what actually happened to Li Sha," said Celia. "But it *is* possible
Madame Philippe will say something that will spark an idea and
help me understand what I've learned so far about the murder."

And maybe, just maybe, the woman would have important
information about Tessie Lange.

"We're going there just so you can outwit that detective,"
Barbara said curtly.

"My goal is to help find Li Sha's murderer by whatever
means possible," said Celia. "Not to 'outwit' Detective Greaves."

Her cousin's expression turned dubious. "You might have
convinced yourself that's true, Cousin Celia, but you haven't convinced me."

"*B*et the other fella looks worse than you, sir," said Taylor,
eyeing Nick's sling.

They passed Portsmouth Square. The midday sky was clear,
and it was good weather for a stroll to the Barbary. For once,

Briggs had been in the detectives' office. Nick didn't like having Eagan's toady spying on his every move. Next, Briggs would be rifling around in Nick's desk, reading his case notebooks.

"He's hobbling like an old geezer," said Nick, frowning. The whiskey he'd drunk last night to numb the pain had left him with a worse headache than what the blow to his skull had caused; he was in no mood to explain to Taylor how easily the assailant had gotten away. "He might never walk straight again."

"That's what I figured!" chirped Taylor.

They turned up Dupont. The wind carried the smell of damp, burned wood down the road. At the end of the block, two groups with shovels and brooms—one Chinese, one white storekeepers—were at work cleaning up the debris, tossing soaked and blackened timbers and chunks of brick onto the bed of a hired wagon. The laundry owner and his wife picked through the remnants of their business, salvaging what they could. The German saloonkeeper was still missing.

"Got to work quick, didn't they?" observed Taylor.

A man in a heavy apron, his long queue swinging, was setting crates of vegetables on the sidewalk in front of his grocery. He glanced at Nick and Taylor as they walked by, taking particular notice of Taylor's uniform. His scowl seemed an accusation.

"No love lost, eh, sir?" Taylor asked once they'd gone past.

"Besides the boy I saw in the alley last week and that servant you heard about, I'll bet there have been other Chinese people attacked by white folks recently," said Nick. "They've probably been expecting all sorts of violence. And they also probably blame the police for not preventing the fire."

They came to a stop a dozen yards from the rubble that spilled into the street.

Taylor plucked his cigar, smoked down to a stub, out of his mouth. "I've heard the Anti-Coolie Association's planning a big meeting tomorrow night. Bet there'll be more trouble after that."

Good God, Nick hoped not. "Talk to anybody who speaks English to get a better description of the man the Chinese laundry owner saw. We need to figure out who he is and if he's associated with the anti-coolieites. Track down that German saloonkeeper, too, and get a statement from him."

"You'd think he'd be tracking *us* down, itching to get ahold of the arsonist," said Taylor.

"Then we've got even more reason to find him."

Taylor studied the people clearing the debris, the *plink* of salvaged bricks being stacked for reuse joining with the thump of burned timbers being tossed into the wagon bed. "I can't see that this fire has anything to do with Li Sha's death, though."

"It might not, Taylor, but I want to be thorough," said Nick. "And if there *is* a connection between the fire and the murder, then all the Chinese in San Francisco should worry they'll be next."

"Don't rightly see how we're gonna be able to contain all the anger, if it gets out of hand."

"I don't, either," Nick said. "When you've finished here, go to Lange's to find out if he's heard from his daughter. He gave me the name of a few friends who might know her plans. I'm not expecting much, but talk to them if she hasn't returned." Nick gave Taylor their names. "Also, I need you to question Ahearn again and find out what he was doing in Chinatown recently looking for Li Sha. I'm off to the Douglasses' house."

"Who are they?"

"The woman heads the Ladies' Society of Christian Aid and

knew Li Sha," he said. "Mr. Douglass is Joseph Palmer's business associate. Palmer suggested at the funeral yesterday that I might want to ask Douglass about Li Sha and her search for money."

"Is Mr. Douglass also a friend of the captain's?"

"Wouldn't be surprised to find out he is," said Nick.

"But I thought we were focusing on Ahearn, sir."

"I'm keeping all my options open, Taylor."

"I'll get on those inquiries, then, sir . . . Mr. Greaves," said Taylor, his cigar stub teetering between the fingers of his left hand while he fished in his coat pocket for his notebook with his right. "But I thought we're supposed to be finished with this case. I mean, Davies was indicted by the grand jury this morning."

"I'm taking until Wednesday, and that's tomorrow. Which leaves us the rest of today to get answers." Nick scrutinized his assistant. "And for God's sake, Taylor, whatever you do, don't drop that damned cigar butt onto anything flammable."

"*N*ow then, we'll have to ask a specific question so Madame Philippe can draw her astral chart specially," Addie explained as she, Celia, and Barbara descended the incline of Montgomery Street on their way to the astrologer's lodgings, where she conducted her business. Barbara had surprised Celia by asking to accompany them to Madame Philippe's, even though Celia had given her cousin the option of staying with the Cascarinos instead. Perhaps she was more curious about what they might learn than she wanted to acknowledge.

Celia's stomach grumbled. She hoped the woman wouldn't take long. They'd had to wait to make their visit until after Celia had finished her appointments for the day, and in their haste to leave the house, Celia had forgotten to eat lunch.

"At least," said Addie, looking abashed, "that's what I understand from Miss Lange."

"Addie, have you already been to see Madame Philippe?" Celia asked.

"Weel, ma'am, maybe once."

Likely with the intention of inquiring where to find a husband, thought Celia, concealing a smile. "Our primary question is to ask Madame Philippe where the killer can be found."

"We also have to ask what the man who left us those awful warning notes looks like, so we can tell the police," said Addie. They made their way past the Broadway cut and the houses that had been left stranded high above the roadbed, all in a desire to level the street in the name of progress. The same sort of work that had been done by those Chinese laborers who'd been attacked last month, the first outward manifestation of a hatred that had been long simmering, ready to boil over like a froth of too-hot milk.

"The police won't listen to anything an astrologer has to say," said Barbara.

"The police might listen to her," Addie said defensively, since the visit had been her suggestion.

"I doubt it," said Barbara. "Besides, shouldn't we be worried that Madame Philippe might make us think the wrong person's guilty?"

"Let us simply see what she has to say," said Celia. "A visit to Madame Philippe is no great effort."

They waited at the curb for a horsecar, clipping along the rails at a rapid pace, to rattle past. Barbara was scrutinizing the people on the street, her brow creasing.

"Are you searching for those boys who bothered you last week?" Celia asked her.

"I don't see them anywhere," answered Barbara. "And please don't suggest I ask Madame Philippe about *them*, too."

"I shan't. How much farther is it, Addie?" asked Celia. She dodged a newspaper boy dancing about on the corner, trying to attract attention to the daily he was peddling. Last night's fire in Chinatown was front-page news.

"She's just down the road a wee bit more, ma'am."

Addie pointed out the astrologer's lodgings. Madame Philippe had third-floor rooms in a stucco-fronted building with arched windows and pediments. The building was part of a long line of similar buildings that filled the entire block, all of them far more respectable looking than Celia had anticipated.

They reached the entrance and stopped. Celia looked at Barbara, pale and anxious, and at Addie, high color pinking her cheeks.

"Shall we?" Celia asked, and started up the front stairs.

"*I*'m sorry my husband isn't here to speak with you, Detective," said Lena Douglass, gesturing for her Chinese servant, a bony kid barely into his teenaged years, to depart. She'd been doing needlework in the light of the tall parlor window when Nick had been shown in, and she sounded none too happy to have been disturbed. "But perhaps you can explain to me why you've come."

The servant tiptoed out of the parlor. It was a fine room, if a person liked lots of fringe and floral chintz. Nick didn't.

He cradled his injured right arm with his left, his war wound aching in sympathy. "I have some questions about Li Sha's murder."

"It's my understanding that Mrs. Davies' brother-in-law is being held for that crime," she said. "I don't see what I or my husband can say that could help free the man, Detective Greaves."

"I'm here because of a conversation I had with Joseph Palmer yesterday," said Nick. "I've learned that Li Sha was looking for money the night she died. She hoped to secure enough to leave town. Did she approach either you or your husband?"

"Did Joseph Palmer suggest she had?"

"He thought I might like to ask."

"How dare he accuse Robert of having anything to do with that girl's murder," Mrs. Douglass said, her voice rising. Out in the hallway, somebody drew in a quick breath. Probably one of the woman's servants, eavesdropping.

"He didn't actually accuse your husband, ma'am."

"You are here making queries, aren't you?"

He couldn't deny her logic. "Back to that question—did Li Sha ask you or your husband for money?"

"No. She did not," she answered. "This is insufferable."

He smiled as if he'd heard the comment a thousand times. "That's how the police are, Mrs. Douglass."

"That may be so, but not in my house."

"Can you account for your husband's activities Monday of last week?" Nick pressed. "And last night as well." Was Robert Douglass the man who had taken such pains to conceal his identity before thwacking Nick with a bludgeon? Or the person who'd gone to Chinatown and set a fire?

"Why should I account for my husband's activities? He's done nothing wrong."

"How about you just humor me?"

She was a handsome woman except when she frowned, which she was doing right then. "I shall speak to Police Chief Crowley about this."

Stand in line. "You have the right to do so, ma'am."

Satisfied she'd be able to get Nick in trouble, she told him what he wanted to know. "Robert was at the Men's Benevolent Association meeting last evening and last Monday. He came home from the meetings at the time I expected. He was not out murdering Chinese girls, or whatever he is supposed to have done last evening that you're so interested in."

"He attends the meeting every Monday?" asked Nick.

"Yes. He's there along with Joseph Palmer. They're both members. Of course, last Monday Joseph was away on business, I understand, and didn't attend that night. It was probably the only Monday he's missed in months."

"Can you provide me with the names of other members who can vouch that your husband was in attendance both Monday nights?" he asked.

"Really," she huffed, but offered up the names. Nick recognized a few of them. Prosperous men. Important men. Men who'd protectively huddle around Douglass and Palmer.

"Anybody else?" he asked.

"One of your police captains. A Captain Eagan," she answered, and appeared amused to see the shock on his face.

They were absolutely as thick as thieves, the bunch of them.

*M*adame Philippe greeted them in a soft voice with an even softer French accent and took their wraps. She was a small, brown-haired woman with an honest expression and intelligent eyes, nothing like the wrinkled crones who inhabited bad novels and penny dreadfuls.

"Do come in, please," Madame Philippe said, ushering them into her suite of rooms.

The astrologer had converted her parlor into a consulting

room. It smelled of rose petals and candle wax, scents that reminded Celia of her family's church back in Hertfordshire. The space was tastefully furnished, the spindly-legged fruitwood chairs and settee upholstered in burgundy toile and, to Celia's eyes, very French. The astrologer had arranged four chairs around a circular walnut table, and candles were lit upon the fireplace mantel and on a compact corner table. They could have been in a boudoir in Paris, if not for the framed posters of astrological signs and the sets of books with titles in English that filled a bookcase.

"Thank you ever so much for seeing us," said Addie.

"You require my assistance, and I will help," Madame Philippe answered. She wore an old-fashioned gown of simple black bombazine, which whispered like the soothing rustle of springtime leaves as she guided them to their chairs. "You do not need to thank me."

Barbara mumbled something Celia could not make out, but the girl sat at Celia's left and managed not to appear too dour or too incredulous.

As they settled in their seats, Madame Philippe produced a piece of paper and spread it upon the table. A circle was drawn in its center and split into twelve equal segments, the twelve astrological signs imprinted around its perimeter.

She looked at them expectantly. "Begin."

"Where can we find the killer of our friend?" asked Addie, describing Li Sha. Out of respect for the girl, Addie omitted the detail that Li Sha had once been a prostitute.

"Tell me the day and the time of this horrible act," said the astrologer.

"Monday last week, late at night," said Celia. "Or early Tuesday morning. We do not know precisely."

"Then what I read may not be accurate," Madame Philippe said.

Addie murmured sympathetically. Barbara grumbled under her breath.

Madame Philippe drew a book from the edge of the table over to her. *An Introduction to Astrology* was inscribed on the spine. She flipped it open and began consulting pages filled with tables and written explanations. As she read, she paused occasionally to fill in some of the circle's segments.

At last, Madame Philippe returned her pen to its holder and gazed at them, her eyes moving from one to the next, smiling when her gaze alighted on Addie, a true believer. "The sun is in Leo. Was your friend injured in the upper body?"

"She was," answered Celia. Among them, she was the only one who knew the details of the crime.

Barbara stiffened and stared at the woman. "You're guessing."

"I merely tell you what I see." The astrologer's fingers glided over the paper as if she could feel the symbols she'd drawn there. "Saturn is in the house of friends. She knew the person who killed her. They were cordial acquaintances."

"Besides the three of us, there are very few people whom Li Sha might have considered cordial acquaintances," said Celia.

"The people she used to work with, undoubtedly," offered Barbara. "Or Tom," she added, her voice flat. At least she did not glance at Celia for a reaction to that comment.

Or a client, thought Celia. But not Connor Ahearn.

"Anything else, Madame Philippe?" asked Addie.

"I do not wish to mislead," Madame Philippe said. "The placement of the moon suggests travel, but that is all I can add."

"She wanted to leave town," said Addie. "Och, this is sending shivers across my skin."

"So you can't say anything more particular about the killer?" asked Barbara.

"We need to ask a specific question," said Addie, plunging ahead. "Can you tell us what this awful person looks like, Madame Philippe?"

"I can attempt this." Again, her fingertips caressed the chart, smearing ink that had yet to dry. She frowned and flipped through her reference book again. "Saturn is in conjunction with Mars. The killer is a person of rash disposition."

"Can she mean Tom?" asked Barbara, her hands clenched together in her lap. "He's rash. We've learned he has a terrible temper, haven't we? Maybe he did kill her, after all."

Celia peered at her cousin, who had gone from skeptical to believing in the span of a few short minutes. "I would expect most killers to be of rash disposition, Barbara."

"It is not certain that the killer is a man," said Madame Philippe. "But I cannot say the killer is a woman, either. The chart, it is not clear."

"Then it could be Tessie Lange, ma'am," Addie murmured to Celia.

"Did Miss Lange ever mention Li Sha to you? Or a man named Connor Ahearn?" Celia asked Madame Philippe. "Addie has told me Tessie uses your services."

The astrologer's gaze narrowed. "What is asked within these four walls, madame, is kept in confidence. I cannot discuss what my other clients have asked of me."

"Of course," replied Celia. She should have foreseen that might be the woman's response.

"Maybe you can tell us what's happened to Miss Lange, Madame Philippe," said Addie. "She might be in trouble."

"Do you know the date of her birth? I do not keep the records of my clients, for their privacy, and therefore do not have the information," explained Madame Philippe.

Addie shrugged and looked at Celia, who shook her head.

"Then I am unable to answer your question," Madame Philippe said, politely remorseful.

"'Tis a pity," Addie said, sounding crestfallen. "But you still haven't told us what the person who killed Li Sha looks like, Madame Philippe."

"Given the location of Saturn here," she said, pointing to a spot on the chart, "the killer may be of medium size with dark hair."

Not auburn haired, thought Celia. *And now I seem willing to believe that Madame Philippe possesses extraordinary insights.* It was becoming easy to understand people's fascination with Spiritualists, when she herself was so desperate for answers.

"Dark hair could also describe Tom," said Barbara.

"A description that applies to any number of people, including some of the women Li Sha once worked with," said Celia, not happy that her cousin kept bringing up his name. "It might even describe you, Barbara."

"I didn't kill Li Sha!"

"I know you did not." It was perhaps one of the few things Celia *could* be certain of. "I am simply making a point."

Madame Philippe was observing Celia. "You have been looking for this killer. Do I help in your search?"

"You have given me much to think about, madame."

"I've remembered what else we wanted to ask," said Addie.

"On Saturday and Sunday, someone left warning notes at our door. Who was it?"

Madame Philippe contemplated them. "I regret the request, but two more charts will require more money."

Celia handed over another dollar coin, precious funds when she had decided that the woman had nothing useful to tell them.

"At what times were these notes left at your door?" the astrologer asked, and extracted two fresh pieces of paper from the unseen supply located at her knees.

"One was left at eight or nine in the evening on Saturday," said Celia. "The other, at six in the evening on Sunday."

The ritual of consulting the book was repeated, and signs and numbers filled the segments of the circles on the papers. When she was finished, Madame Philippe exhaled a long, slow breath, her gaze skimming over them.

"There is another," she said. "Not the one who killed your friend. A person seeking to rise in his station. But that is all I can read."

"Two different people?" asked Barbara, her eyes wide.

Was it possible? Celia hadn't considered that could be the case.

Addie muttered unhappily, "Now we've two to be wary of, ma'am. 'Tis dreadful."

"I wish I could tell you more that would help," the astrologer said, her small hands pressed together in a prayerful pose.

"Thank you nonetheless, Madame Philippe," said Celia. The visit had not brought Celia any nearer to identifying a killer—or killers—but it had managed to alarm them all. She stood, and the others did likewise. "The hour grows late, and we need to return home before dark."

Celia gathered her shawl and turned to depart. The astrologer followed, opening the door for them.

Madame Philippe turned her attention to Celia, the expression on her face somber. "You wish to help the ones who are most helpless."

"Yes," replied Celia. "I always have."

"That is good. I see that you are strong for the task." The astrologer gripped Celia's fingers and looked into her eyes. "But you must be stronger, because what I have read tells me this person will kill again. There is danger, Madame Davies. Much danger."

CHAPTER 13

"Taylor, in the office now," ordered Nick.

Taylor jerked out of his desk as though Nick had snagged him with a fishing line, and scurried after him.

Nick strode into the empty detectives' office. Briggs must have found something better to do today.

"Douglass has an alibi for the evenings in question." Nick sat at his desk, the castors on the chair squealing. "On Mondays he's at the Men's Benevolent Association meetings with Palmer. And Eagan."

Taylor whistled. "Whoa, sir."

"Any more news about the fire?"

"Talked to the fire marshal," said Taylor. "His men have determined the blaze was started in two spots, one behind the laundry and another behind the saloon. No idea yet who might be the arsonist, though."

"So the laundry wasn't the sole target, then."

"Guess not. And the saloonkeeper's still scarce as hen's teeth. Maybe he's run off." Taylor chuckled. "One of the local wags suggested the German's wife is responsible. Apparently she was in a temper because her husband likes to visit Chinatown. Don't rightly know what good it does her to burn their own saloon to the ground, though."

"What about Tessie Lange? Anything new on her?"

"Her friends didn't have any idea where she is. And when I was at the shop, Lange kept muttering, 'I should have warned her' over and over, but I couldn't get him to say what or who he should've warned her about. He was pretty drunk," added Taylor.

"I can't blame him. I'd probably be drunk, too." For Lange, the bad news was piling up like turds in a cow pen.

"I went to the ferry offices to ask if a woman who looked like Miss Lange had bought tickets in the past couple of days, but no luck there. I'll keep looking for her."

"See if Mullahey has time to help out. If he doesn't, ask one of the other men. We have to find her." Nick unlocked the desk drawer, wanting to review his case notes. "What about Ahearn?"

"Haven't got to the ironworks where he's employed yet, sir. I'll be heading back out in a bit."

"Let me talk to him. You stick with trying to figure out where Tessie Lange has gone and with digging up that German saloonkeeper." Nick pulled the drawer open, but it was empty. His case notes were missing. "Have you been in my desk, Taylor?"

"I don't have a key, sir . . ."

"One of my notebooks is missing." He eyed Briggs' desk. "Does Briggs plan to come back soon?"

"I dunno."

Nick stood and went over to the man's desk. He rattled the top drawer. Locked. He looked around for a suitable tool with which to pry it open. Grabbing Briggs' letter opener, Nick squatted on his heels and slipped it into the crack between the drawer edge and the desk frame.

"Sir! What are you doing?" Taylor asked. He glanced out into the main office and shut the door. "You can't break into Briggs' desk. Eagan'll string you up!"

The letter opener didn't work. "Do you still have your old lockpicks?" Nick asked.

"Don't involve me, sir! I need this job! I give money to my family to feed my brothers and sisters!"

Nick held out his hand, palm up.

Taylor sighed, rummaged through one of his pants pockets, and pulled out a set of lockpicks hanging from a metal ring. He handed them over. "Gotta say I think this is it, sir. It's been nice working for you."

Nick slid his arm out of the sling to free up his right hand. "I'm just trying to prove something to myself, Taylor. Don't worry."

He wriggled the thickest pick into the lock mechanism, trying to move the levers that would release the bolt. Finally, he got the levers aligned and the bolt slid free.

Just then, Briggs barged through the door. Taylor retrieved his picks and stuffed them into his coat pocket. "What are you doing in my desk, Greaves?"

"Looking for my notebook."

"I don't have your notebook."

Nick hunted through the drawer, encountering the sticky remains of something that might've once been food but not finding his notebook.

Briggs looked smug. "See?" He sauntered across the room and slammed shut the drawer. "Your boss is slipping up, Taylor."

A handful of police officers had collected around the open office door. "I'm betting you can take him, Greaves," one called out. "Even with your bum arm!"

"He's got two bum arms," corrected the man next to him.

"I'm still betting on you!"

The others snorted and Briggs glared. "I don't need to take your case notes to prove you're incompetent, because I already *know* you are. You only got this job because of Asa Greaves, not because you're actually worth a damn."

Just then the wall of men parted as Captain Eagan shoved his way through. "What in hell is going on here?"

The policemen scattered, leaving Nick, Taylor, and Briggs behind.

"I found him breaking into my desk, sir," said Briggs.

"Have you got an explanation for that, Greaves?" asked the captain.

"A notebook's missing from my desk."

"No, it's not." Eagan held up the notebook, then tossed it onto Nick's desk. "I decided to read through your notes and see what you've been doing. You haven't made much progress, have you? Well, this is your last day on this case."

"Even if the daughter of the man who employed that dead Chinese girl has disappeared?" Nick asked. "Tessie Lange is in trouble, Captain. We have to find her."

"Women run off all the time, Greaves," Eagan said, and turned on his heel to leave.

"I've got another question, Captain. Can you tell me what goes on at the Men's Benevolent Society meetings on Monday nights?" Nick called after him. "The meetings you attend with Douglass and Palmer, a couple of men linked to that same murdered girl. How many friends of yours knew her?"

Eagan's shoulders twitched, but he kept on walking.

They headed home, Barbara pensive and Addie preoccupied. Celia had thought she might learn something from Madame Philippe, but her observations had only left Celia with a stew of confusing thoughts and conflicting opinions.

She'd been trained to be logical, her months at the Female Medical College of Pennsylvania having taught her to record her observations, consider possible causes, and tend to patients by following reasoned and methodical steps. A reliance on superstitious sentiment or outdated treatments was to be discouraged, cleansed from her brain like suppuration from a festering wound. An astral chart was not logical, and listening to Madame Philippe was not reasonable.

Nonetheless, Celia didn't believe she could ignore the woman's warning. There was too much truth in it.

"Even Madame Philippe says we're in danger," said Barbara, returning the hostile stare of a boy loitering in the doorway of a dentist's office. "I told you we should leave town. I can't stay any longer."

Celia could no longer disregard her cousin's concerns. "Addie, send a telegram to the hotel in Healdsburg and inquire if they have rooms available."

"We canna go without you, ma'am," protested Addie. "'Tisn't safe to leave you alone. Not with that watcher person."

"Perhaps Elizabeth and Emmeline might like to take a trip to the geysers," said Celia. "What do you think about asking them, Barbara, and leaving Addie with me?"

Her cousin's brow furrowed. "Maybe."

Celia heard a commotion up ahead. A wagon loaded with timbers had broken an axle and spilled its contents onto the street. The pile of wood had tumbled everywhere, scattered haphazardly like a giant game of jackstraws.

"Clean this mess up!" shouted a shop owner whose entrance was blocked.

The wagon driver bellowed back in a mix of Italian and English. A man in the boisterous crowd that had gathered shouted for fisticuffs.

"*Sì!*" the driver agreed, with a broad grin. He peeled off his coat and handed it to a bystander.

"We should go around to the next street," suggested Celia, and they made use of a nearby alleyway. It was quieter here, the occupants all apparently enjoying the spectacle on the main road. They were not taking the path alone, though; Celia heard footsteps behind them.

When they rounded the corner at the end of the alley, she glanced back and spotted a boy several dozen feet behind her. She wasn't certain he was following them; the lad might simply be taking the same route in order to avoid the commotion. But her skin tingled with alarm, and she began to walk faster.

"Here. Let us take this lane." Celia tugged Barbara's arm and guided her to the left. "It parallels Montgomery, and I believe there is another alleyway not far from here that will return us to the main road."

"Why are you walking so fast?" her cousin protested. "My foot hurts."

"I have suddenly recalled some urgent business back at the clinic."

Barbara resisted Celia's attempt to hurry her. "I can't keep up."

"You must try."

"Och, ma'am," said Addie. "I dinna care for these unchancy roads so near the warehouses."

The footsteps behind them doubled in number, and Celia risked another backward glance. Now there were two boys, both grinning. They had turned down the same lane, and they were definitely following them.

Suddenly, the path Celia had chosen felt ominous. The narrow alley was dark and filled with the litter of people's lives—an abandoned shoe with a great crack in its sole, splintered slats from an old crate, shards of glass from discarded bottles. The air stank of refuse and raw sewage, and there was nothing but closed doors and shuttered windows on all sides.

"Are those lads following us?" asked Addie, whispering into Celia's ear, her voice wobbling.

The two boys had become four, gathering mass like a rolling snowball. She was certain one of them was the boy who'd been lounging in the dentist's office doorway. Their voices echoed, and one called out "China girl!" followed by raucous laughter. The end of the lane was so very distant.

"Hey! China girl!" another cried out. "What're you doin' outside of Chinatown?"

Barbara looked over her shoulder at them. "Leave me alone!"

Celia's pulse thudded. They were only boys, the youngest probably ten, but two were carrying chunks of cobblestone and the tallest had found a broken bottle, which he swung menacingly.

"Can you run?" she asked her cousin.

"No!" answered Barbara, close to tears. "I can't!"

A chunk of stone whizzed past their heads, pinging against the pavement.

"You are going to have to try."

Celia took off, dragging Barbara with her. Addie screeched and bolted. The boys started chasing them, their laughter and shouts rising in pitch and fever, like a pack of wolves on the hunt. And they were the prey.

"Help!" shouted Celia, sliding on a patch of kitchen waste. A dog barked from behind a door. No one came to help them. Another chunk of cobblestone landed near her feet.

Barbara stumbled and fell to one knee, pulling Celia down with her. Addie skidded to a halt.

"Go on!" Celia shouted to her. "Get help! The police station isn't far."

Addie hesitated, then dashed through a break between the buildings and was gone.

"Good luck with Ahearn, sir," said Taylor, doffing his policeman's cap and striding off toward Chinatown again.

Nick rounded the corner and headed down Clay. The ironworks that employed Ahearn was located on Front about half a mile away. Nick was looking forward to showing his police badge to Ahearn's boss and causing as much trouble as possible for the man.

He was crossing Montgomery when he heard a woman's shouts. A load of lumber had spilled into the street, and next to the pile, two men were exchanging punches. The neighborhood constable seemed to be entertained by the scuffle and was ignoring the source of the screeching, a woman who jumped about him like a marionette in a show at the Academy of Music, her arms flailing.

Nick was about to continue on when he realized who she was.

"Miss Ferguson!" he yelled, rushing down the road. His injured right arm bumped against his side, shooting pain up to his shoulder.

"Och, Detective Greaves!" she said. "You must come quick. It's Mrs. Davies and Miss Barbara. They're in terrible trouble!"

She ran off, knowing he would follow.

The boys had vacillated about attacking them for longer than Celia had dared hope. Shielding her cousin with her body, Celia faced the boys. One decided the wait had been long enough and heaved a rock. It missed Celia and struck the wall at their backs.

"Leave us alone!" Barbara shouted from behind her.

"What do you think yer doin' 'ere? This ain't yer part of town," said the apparent leader, the tall one.

"Walking like anybody else," Barbara answered, her voice strong.

The boys sniggered. None of them looked older than fourteen. They were hotheaded children who would grow up to become dangerous men.

"You ain't got no business leaving Chinatown," said the youngest, smallpox scars dotting his cheeks. He lifted the stone in his hand but appeared uncertain of what to do with it now that they'd cornered their prey.

"If you leave us alone, I will not report you to the police.

Go home, boys," said Celia, hoping Addie brought help soon. She did not trust her ability to calm this lot.

"Go home?" The tallest stepped nearer and swung the broken bottle. "Hear that, mates? She wants us to go home! Ain't that funny? Why don't you tell your China girl to go home?"

Barbara stepped out from behind Celia's protective cover. "You're lily-livered to pick on women."

Another of the boys, a gap showing in his teeth, had come to the leader's side. "Oh yeah?"

"Yeah," Barbara retorted.

Before Celia could get between them, the boy shoved her cousin hard, and she fell to the ground.

"Barbara!" Celia helped her cousin to her feet. Barbara had cut her palm on a shard of glass, and the wound dripped blood onto her skirt.

"Leave her be!" cried Celia, trying to push the boy away. But he was stocky and strong, and he fought off her efforts.

And then, down the length of the alley, a familiar face caught her eye.

"Owen!" she shouted to him. But instead of coming to their aid, he fled down a side alley. "Owen!" Surely he hadn't joined these wretches.

"You're filth," spat Barbara, and the tall one swung the bottle. It arced close to Barbara and she recoiled. Her head smacked against the brick wall behind her, dislodging her bonnet.

"Hey!" said one of the other boys. "We're not supposed to be hurtin' them, are we? Just puttin' the scare in them, like."

"Shut up!" the ringleader ordered.

Celia kicked his shin as hard as she could. He shrieked like a wounded animal.

"Who ordered you to frighten us?" she demanded. "Who?"

"That's it. I'm goin'," yelled one, dropping his chunk of stone and racing off.

"Come back!" the ringleader shouted, his hand clutching his shin.

A whistle trilled. "Police!" a man shouted.

The remaining boys threw down their broken bottles and stones and scattered. A policeman chased after one of them, and Nicholas Greaves pursued another.

Thank heavens Addie found help.

"How is your head, Barbara?" With a calming smile, Celia knelt at her cousin's side and untied her bonnet, easing it off. There was a lump and the sticky warmth of blood, but the wound did not seem deep.

"Oh, Cousin," Barbara sobbed. "I've never been so scared! They wanted to kill me!"

"No. They wanted to frighten us."

"Miss Barbara!" Addie dashed over and also knelt beside Barbara. She ran her rough fingers over the girl's tear-streaked face. "Are you all right?"

Barbara shuddered but nodded. Celia cradled her weeping cousin against her chest and looked over Barbara's head at Addie.

"What are we to do, ma'am?"

"Find who is behind this attack," said Celia. "And find who is sending us those messages. Because this has got to stop."

$\mathcal{N}$ick sent a policeman to stand guard over the women while he singled out the nearest boy and pursued him. The kid was quick and knew these back streets better than Nick did. He burst onto the main road, darting through traffic and leaping over horsecar-line rails.

Without slowing, the boy ducked down another alley. A street cleaner stopped to gawp at them, managing to stand in Nick's path. Pushing the man aside, he ran past and turned down the alley. The kid had almost reached the end of the passage. If it led to another lane, Nick would lose him.

"Stop or I'll shoot!" he shouted.

It was an outright lie, but the boy looked back to see if Nick had pulled his gun. The boy had forgotten about the curb and tripped over its edge, falling to his knees.

Breathing hard, Nick reached him before he could get up and run off again.

"Hold on, kid," he said, hooking one scrawny arm and hoisting him upright.

"Why're you chasin' me?" the boy demanded, showing a good amount of gumption to pretend innocence. He was shaking, however.

Nick dragged the boy closer. "What did you want with those women? Who put you up to attacking them?"

"We weren't attackin' them!" He was ten or eleven and filthy, and the gap in his teeth made a whistling noise when he spoke. "We was just funnin'."

"Funning?" Nick shook him, and the boy's head jiggled back and forth. "Hurling rocks at them is not *funning.*"

The boy started to cry. "Don't take me to the calaboose. My ma'd kill me." A tear plopped onto his grimy coat.

"You should've thought of that before." Nick's left arm was tingling and he could feel his fingers going numb. He didn't let go of the kid, though. "Tell me who told you to attack those women."

"Nobody did. Honest! My pa's against them Chinese and we thought . . ." The tears started falling more rapidly. "It was just funnin'!"

"What's your pa's name?"

"He's gonna kill me, too!"

The boy twisted his arm and Nick's hand went numb. He lost hold, and the kid jerked free and ran off faster than Nick could chase him.

"Damn!" Nick shouted at the empty alleyway.

Massaging his tingling hand, he hurried back to Mrs. Davies and her cousin. The women were where he'd left them, the policeman close at hand. Nick told the man he could go back to the ruckus on Montgomery.

He bent over Mrs. Davies and was pleased to see she wasn't bloodied. He couldn't say the same for her cousin, whose cut hand had bled onto her skirt.

"Are you okay, ma'am?" he asked Celia. "And your cousin?"

"She will be," she responded, and managed a smile. "And I must say, Detective, you are the finest thing I have seen all day."

Celia folded her skirts around her shins and dropped onto the top step of her rear porch next to Mr. Greaves.

"Don't think I've ever seen a woman manage a maneuver like that so well in a corset and crinoline," he commented. "There are chairs right over there." He nodded to the set of wicker chairs teetering on the garden's lumpy dirt.

"But then I would have to get right back up again, Mr. Greaves, and that would be more than I can manage at the moment." She rested her head against the porch post. She was so very tired. "Barbara is resting. I gave her some laudanum to help her sleep."

She had dressed the cut on Barbara's hand and tended to her head wound. Her cousin would recover from her injuries. Celia would not hazard a guess as to when her cousin might recover from the fright.

"Rest will do her good," the detective said.

Celia released a long breath. "How can the evening be so lovely when it was such a horrible afternoon?" she asked, gazing beyond the clapboard houses at the sky. It was turning a sort of bluish purple, and the smell of food cooking drifted on the breeze, accompanied by the sound of pans banging against stovetops. Next door, Mrs. Cascarino scolded in a stream of Italian, and Angelo, who'd been spying on them around a window curtain, vanished from sight.

Celia glanced over at Nick. "Do not mind Mrs. Cascarino. She is loud but harmless."

He seemed to recognize the name. "Does she have a daughter named Mina?"

"Why, yes. Do you know her?"

"She works at Bauman's. I've seen her there."

He turned to stare at the garden before she could figure out if there was more behind his casual comment than he was revealing.

"Did you recognize any of the boys?" he asked, deftly changing the subject.

"No, and neither did Barbara. They are not the same ones who accosted her in the street last week. How many of these hooligans are out there?"

"Too many," he answered. "Stick close to the house, Mrs. Davies, until I've figured out what's going on."

"Barbara will not be overeager to leave, I can promise you," she replied, tucking her feet beneath the hem of her skirt. "Did the boy tell you anything useful before he broke free?"

The others had managed to elude capture as well, according to Detective Greaves.

"Just that he got the idea to harass your cousin from his father, who dislikes the Chinese," he said.

"Did he say if they were after us specifically?"

He glanced over at her. "He didn't. They might've been waiting for any Chinese person to happen by."

Addie banged open the back door, a tray in her hands. "Och, how am I to serve you some tea when you're perched on the steps like a pair of urchins?" She bent down and plunked the tray onto the floorboards with a rattling of cups. "You are certain you willna stay for dinner, Detective Greaves?"

"Don't want to impose."

"Weel, 'tis good because we've only cold meat and some beans to eat." She straightened, brushing her hands together. "Nae that a one of us has an appetite after today. Horrible town. Women attacked in the street! We should be going back to England. Nothing like this ever happened there. Madame Philippe warned us, ma'am, and she was right." She stomped off, the rear door slamming behind her.

"It's time to tell me who Madame Philippe is, Mrs. Davies," Mr. Greaves said, once Addie's footfalls had receded.

"Please do not laugh," Celia said. "The woman is an astrologer, and Addie suggested that we consult her about Li Sha's murder. I agreed when I learned that Tessie Lange makes use of her services. I was hoping Madame Philippe might reveal that Tessie came to her with concerns about Tom or Li Sha or Connor Ahearn, but she declined to share the confidences of a client. However, she did warn us we were in danger, as Addie mentioned."

Nicholas Greaves hadn't laughed, but he did look cynical. "These days it doesn't take an astrologer's supposed gifts to figure that a Chinese girl, even one who's only half-Chinese, might be in danger, ma'am."

"Don't worry, Detective. I am not proposing that astrological consultations become a regular part of police investigations."

"Good thing, because I doubt the captain would foot the bill."

Celia considered him. Would he say no to what she was about to ask? "Mr. Greaves, I read in the newspaper this morning that a large meeting of the Anti-Coolie Association is scheduled for tomorrow night. The boys who attacked Barbara might be there, along with their fathers."

"Taylor's mentioned the meeting to me. I plan to go."

"Then I wish to go as well," Celia said firmly, daring him to deny her. "The person who has been watching this house might also be there, if the warnings have anything to do with Barbara's ethnicity or Li Sha's murder."

"I thought you said you couldn't tell if this watcher was a man or a woman. How are you going to recognize anybody?" he asked.

"It is worth a try, Mr. Greaves," said Celia. "I insist on attending."

"It's too dangerous for you. If any of those people recognize you and know that you work with Chinese girls, they might turn on you."

"If there is any chance, no matter how remote, that I can bring the threats against us to an end, then I must go to this meeting. I have no other choice," she said, pressing a hand to his sleeve. "I shall attend whether you accompany me or not."

"You're too stubborn for your own good, Mrs. Davies."

"But stubbornness is valuable, is it not?" she asked, her fingers closing around his wrist. "If one is searching for a killer."

Stubbornness is a good way to get yourself killed, Mrs. Davies, thought Nick, bound for home. The woman was depleting his supply of patience, and he hadn't started with much.

After leaving her house, Nick had gone to the ironworks and found Ahearn preparing to leave his station, looking as innocent as the Madonna. His boss explained the man had worked an extra shift last night. Ahearn had an alibi again. He also proclaimed he'd never gone to Chinatown to look for Li Sha, and any Chinese prostitute claiming he had was a damned liar. Nick made sure Ahearn's boss overheard Nick telling Ahearn he'd be hauling him back to the police station for more questioning if he found out otherwise. That might make his life miserable around the shop for a while.

Nick had then stopped at Lange's. The store was closed and had been for a few hours, according to a neighbor who also informed Nick that Lange had gone to look for his daughter. When the neighbor wanted Nick to explain what had happened to Tessie, Nick walked off. The story of the girl's disappearance would probably be all over the newspapers tomorrow, anyway.

By the time Nick got home, the sun had vanished below the western hills. He trudged up the front steps of his boardinghouse and went inside. Mrs. Jewett didn't come out of her ground-floor rooms to greet him, as she usually did when she heard him come through the front door. He didn't mind; he wasn't precisely in a sociable mood.

Rolling his head to work out the kinks in his neck, he climbed the stairs to his rooms. At the landing, the wood planks offered up their customary squeak. He paused to pull out his key, waiting to hear Riley's familiar bark at the noise. Except it didn't come. It was then he noticed the sliver of light beneath the door at the top of the steps. Somebody was in his rooms. And it was too late in the day for that somebody to be his landlady.

He removed the sling, drew out his gun, and sighed. He was getting mighty tired of having to brandish his revolver. Although what intruder declared his presence by lighting the gas lamps? Only a stupid one. And stupid ones were always the most worrisome.

Nick reached for the handle and threw open the door. With a bark, Riley jumped up from where he'd been lying, and the person inside dropped the glass of water she was holding. It smashed to the floor.

"Nick, honestly! What is wrong with you?"

"Mina."

Her gaze went to the gun in his hand. "Can you put that thing away?"

He did as she asked and set his Colt on the table. Riley loped over to greet him. "How did you get in?" he asked her as he scratched the dog's ears.

"Your landlady believed me when I said I was your sister. She's too trusting." Mina retrieved a rag from the basin in the kitchen and crouched to mop up the spilled water.

"Let me do that. You'll get your dress dirty."

"And you've hurt your arm. I'll take care of it." Mina scooped the broken pieces into a pile. He really wished she hadn't dropped the glass; he had only four.

"Why aren't you at Bauman's?" he asked.

"Herr Bauman is trying out a new girl." Her eyes glittered with jealousy and dread, two feelings she quickly smothered. "He thinks he can get someone who can sing as well as I do for less money."

"That's not possible," said Nick. "But you're not here for a social call or to complain about Adolph Bauman's treatment. So what is it?"

Her eyes searched his face, and he felt a rush of the old feelings he'd once harbored for her. But those feelings went no deeper than habit.

"There were men in Bauman's last night talking about that fire on Dupont. Laughing over it," she said, tossing the wet rag into the corner sink inside the storeroom.

"Somebody burned down a Chinese laundry and the saloon next door."

"The fire was started as a warning to the saloonkeeper. It seems he's involved with smugglers, and they've taken a dislike to something he's done."

Nick recalled that Eagan had mentioned a smuggling case; he should've taken more time to read the captain's notes.

"Thanks, Mina." He reached inside his coat and pulled out some coins. "Here."

The twitch at the corner of her left eye revealed her rising temper. Next, she'd be slapping him. "You're going to try to pay me?"

"I appreciate the trouble you've taken to come here and tell me what you've learned."

"You're damned impossible, you know?" She stepped closer,

bringing the scent of tuberose to him. "I'm not here because I want money, Nick. You asked me to find out what's going on. Well, I did, because I thought we were at least still friends."

"Don't get mad, Mina." He returned the coins to his pocket.

"Too late for that." She looked disgusted. Whether it was with him or herself wasn't clear. "Don't worry, Nick. I won't be back to bother you."

With an irate swish of her silk skirts, she swept out of the room and down the stairs. The bang of the front door rattled the house.

*C*elia rested her fingers on the door handle of her cousin's bedchamber. For the moment, Barbara was sleeping quietly, her breathing even. But after what they had endured so far, how could Celia guarantee that there would not be more trouble? *When sorrows come, they come not single spies but in battalions.*

Celia shut the door and carried the kerosene lamp back to her own room, setting it upon her walnut dressing table. She crossed to the window and pressed a hand to the cool glass. Outside, the houses cast in shadows across the street were as indistinct as the answers Celia kept chasing. Why could she not discover who had killed Li Sha? How much more evidence would she or Mr. Greaves require in order to find the murderer and stop the hateful messages, the attacks?

Celia lowered her hand, made cold by the window glass. She was about to close the curtains when a movement outside caught her attention. Someone was coming down the street in the direction of their house, moving from shadow to shadow. The person crossed the road to avoid the light from the lone streetlamp, then crossed back over again.

Grabbing the kerosene lamp, Celia hurried down the stairs and out to the vestibule. She had reached to unlock the front door when she paused. The stairs to the porch had creaked. The watcher was out there, and she had no defense.

"Ma'am?" Addie, her brown hair springing out around her nightcap, leaned over the upstairs banister. "What is the matter?"

"The watcher. He is outside."

"Och!" Addie dashed down the staircase, her slippers flapping against the treads. "Let me get my knife."

"Addie!"

"We've no other protection, now, do we?" She ran through Celia's examination room and into the kitchen.

Trembling, Celia leaned toward the door. What could she or Addie do? Was the watcher going to try to break into the house? She heard a soft thump against the front door followed again by the creak of the stairs.

Addie returned, carrying a cleaver. "This'll stop him."

Celia peered through the door glass; all was darkness. "I think he may have gone."

"Move aside, ma'am. I'll check." Addie unlocked the door and eased it open. She looked down and screamed.

"What? What is it?" Celia asked, peering over her housekeeper's shoulder.

What had once been a rat, its insides gutted, lay on the threshold. Celia kicked it, leaving a smear of blood on the porch. The dead rat bounced off the railing and landed in their front yard.

"Ma'am. Ma'am!" Addie was panting with alarm.

"Take slow, deep breaths, Addie. Before you faint." Celia crept across the porch, the damp air making her shiver. Across the way, a sleepy neighbor peeked around his curtains. Celia descended a few steps.

"Ma'am, be careful!" called Addie, the cleaver held high.

"There is no one out here, Addie." *Besides me, being foolish.*

A lantern appeared in the Cascarinos' upper window, and Mrs. Cascarino drew up the sash, the pulleys squealing. "Signora Davies! What is wrong?" she called down.

Celia looked up at Mrs. Cascarino. Out of the corner of her eye, she noticed a flame snuff out in Barbara's room. Addie's scream must have awakened her, too.

"Addie thought she saw something, but she was mistaken, Mrs. Cascarino," Celia said. "I am sorry to have disturbed you. Good night."

Mrs. Cascarino nodded, yawned into her fist, and closed the window.

Celia retreated to the porch, where Addie scowled from the doorway, the cleaver in her hand reflecting the lantern light. "He's leaving us a gutted rat now! Weel, I dinna care what that detective says about you needing to stay in town for Mr. Davies' trial. You're nae safe here. None of us are."

"I shall send a message to Mr. Greaves tomorrow and ask what he thinks we should do."

"Leave is what we should do," said Addie.

Before Celia rejoined her inside the house, she turned to look along the road again—and saw a hunched figure in a long coat sneaking around a distant corner. He was followed by the shape of a boy, his form merging into the blackness.

CHAPTER 14

Nick sat in the dark, watching the orange glow of coals in his parlor stove grow dim. At his feet, Riley rearranged his position.

"Riley, what is it with women?" He had always stepped wrong with Mina. And Mrs. Davies, who attracted trouble like flypaper snagged insects, was sure to put herself in more danger by attending that anti-coolie meeting tomorrow . . . he listened to the chime of his landlady's hall case clock and counted twelve . . . that meeting tonight. "Don't bother to answer, boy, I know."

Nick took a sip of whiskey and turned to gaze out the window, propped open with a stub of wood, a breeze ruffling the faded curtains. And of course there remained the mystery of who had killed Li Sha. It was Wednesday and he hadn't solved the crime. There were too many pieces, like in one of those fancy dissected picture puzzles sold in emporiums, and none of them were fitting together.

Tessie Lange, in need of money and then vanishing.

Connor Ahearn, who had plentiful alibis as well as friends in high places.

Eagan, one of those friends, who was also cozy with Douglass and Palmer, two others who'd known the girl, possibly better than they'd admitted.

A German saloonkeeper involved in smuggling, who had been the victim of arson. And who also liked to go to Chinatown.

Hubert Lange, who claimed a strange man had been hanging around his store. The same man, maybe, who liked to pummel detectives with bludgeons and send warning notes to Celia Davies.

And a gang of boys, inspired by somebody's hate-filled pa, who'd decided to terrorize Barbara Walford. Except that one of them had gotten the bright idea to send a more serious message with a chunk of cobblestone.

The tocsin sounded at city hall. Two bells. North Beach. Another fire, and only a day after the one in Chinatown. It was either a tragic coincidence or no coincidence at all.

Nick set down the whiskey and stood abruptly, startling Riley. The dog lifted his head. "I'm going to check on that fire, boy. Be back in no time."

Not bothering to light a lantern, Nick collected his gun and holster, pulled on his boots and coat, and left the boardinghouse. He headed west, then started north. At this time of night, the streets were quiet. Every saloon that didn't want to get in trouble with the law was shut down, its windows dark. Behind him, Nick heard the clatter of wheels on cobblestone. A fire engine rattled up the road, and he hailed it. The driver, outfitted in a fireman's uniform, looked ready to drive right past him.

Nick darted into the road. "Stop!"

The man reined in the horses just in time to avoid running him over. "What are you doing, you lunatic?"

"I need a ride to the fire." He flashed his badge and climbed onto the seat next to the driver. "Police business."

They arrived at the fire's location along the shore within minutes. Nick hopped down. A small warehouse near the foot of Meiggs' Wharf was ablaze. A hose wagon was already there, the firemen attaching hoses to the hydrant down the street. Out on the bay, a schooner bobbed alongside the pier, and a handful of boatmen had come on deck to gawk.

Nick noticed a constable across the road from the burning building. He was restraining a crowd, locals in their night-clothes, who were pressing forward for better views.

Nick trotted over and introduced himself.

The constable looked surprised. "That was quick. Didn't know Rodgers had already managed to get to the police telegraph."

"Rodgers," *whoever he was*, thought Nick, "didn't send for me. I heard the bell and thought I'd see what's going on. There have been two fires in two days. Not good."

"Heard about that one last night. Arson, right?"

Nick nodded. "What about this one? Any idea?"

"Looks like an accident to me. There's plenty of tinder around." The constable pointed at the stacks of discarded bar-rels and piles of lumber. "It's worse inside. The warehouse ain't been used for months, but the last owner left a whole pile of junk behind. Empty barrels and crates. God knows what used to be in all of them."

"An accident," Nick said. Just a tragic coincidence.

"I'd guess the fire was started by the drunk who likes to sleep in there, trying to keep warm. Lucky for him, the lodging house owner next door heard the fellow screeching and pulled him outta the building afore he burned to a crisp." The constable scratched the scrap of beard on his chin. "Couldn't save the woman, though."

"A woman?"

"Yep, there's a woman in there, too. Burned up pretty bad." From inside the building a small explosion reverberated. Flames shot higher, and the assembled onlookers gave a collective gasp. "The lodging house owner who saw her body thought she musta been dead afore the fire started, though. 'Cause of the slice across her neck, you see."

"*H*ere is fifty cents, Joaquín." Celia handed coins to the boy from across the street. "Take this note to Detective Greaves or to Officer Taylor. Can you remember their names?"

His dark eyes blinked at her. "I do not like the police station."

"Tell the officers you have brought a message from me. Use my name specifically, and they should not bother you," she said. "Hurry before the rain starts again."

He still looked dubious, but took the note and scurried up the road. At the corner boardinghouse, one of the tenants was smoking on the second-floor balcony, his feet propped on the railing. In Spanish he shouted at Joaquín to slow down, then laughed, curls of smoke spiraling from his mouth and vanishing into the damp air. Joaquín hurried on, and the neighbor looked in Celia's direction, his laughter fading. She felt an uncontrollable shiver. *He* could be the watcher; Celia didn't know everyone on their street, so many strangers coming and going with the rise and fall of their fortunes.

But such thoughts were ridiculous—when had their neighbors ever given them a reason to feel apprehensive?—and she smiled at the man to prove to herself she wasn't afraid before hastening back inside.

Tucking her mother's shawl around her neck, the cashmere comfortingly warm, Celia entered the parlor. She stared at the grinning portrait of her uncle. *What would you do, Uncle? I want to stay and show the person behind the threats that we will not be intimidated. But if we stay, what dreadful business will happen next?*

The previous night, Barbara's peaceful sleep had not lasted long. Her dream had been worse when it had come, even though Celia hadn't told her cousin about the rat. Barbara had cried and cried, forcing Celia to dose her with more laudanum and hold her until exhaustion and the medication took hold. First thing this morning, Celia had gone to each door of her nearest neighbors to inquire if they had seen anyone suspicious last night. All of them had said no.

Addie came into the dining room, a cup of tea in her hand, and noticed Celia standing in the parlor.

"Come and have some tea, ma'am. A nice oolong, brewed the way you like it." She placed the teacup and saucer on the table and pulled out a chair.

Celia went over and sat. "I hope Mr. Greaves can figure out how we can leave the city without jeopardizing Tom's defense." She cradled the teacup in her hands, savoring its warmth and calming aroma. Still, she felt as though her bones were formed of ice.

"The police have to see sense, ma'am. We canna stay here. Not with that . . ." Addie blanched. "Not after last night."

"Why can I not identify the wretch who is responsible?" asked Celia.

"Weel, ma'am, let's both think on that. Because two heads are better than one, now, aren't they?" Addie pulled out another chair and dropped onto it, her eyes shining. Evidently, she enjoyed playing the part of sleuth. "So, let's see. The notes were nae from anyone we know."

"As far as I can tell," Celia answered, taking a sip of tea. It was bitingly strong. "However, that might have been a deception."

"In which case, we do have to account for all the people we know. Who's been acting the most peculiar since Miss Li died? Because guilt always shows in the eyes," she avowed. "They are the windows to the soul, after all. All we need do is look!"

"Oh my goodness, Addie, I believe everyone has been acting peculiar. Everyone except you, that is," Celia added, lowering the teacup to the saucer. "And our neighbors have not changed their behavior, so far as I have noticed," she said, despite her reaction to the man smoking on the balcony of the corner boardinghouse. "Do you think any of them have done?"

"No, ma'am. Other than Joaquín's mother, who's still fearful angry with us after checking his feet against those boot prints." Addie tutted.

"Mr. Lange has been more tense than I can ever recollect," Celia continued. "Although that might simply be his upset over the murder of a gentle young woman whom he knew. And there was Tessie's suspiciously urgent visit to the Barbary to speak with Connor Ahearn, and now she is missing."

"And that bodes ill. You ken it does, ma'am."

"It does indeed," said Celia. "Elizabeth Palmer has been unusually concerned about my work with the Chinese women, and her daughter has been more sickly than usual. Although again, Li Sha's death is stunning to us all, and simply because the Palmers had only met her once does not mean they are immune to the shock. And Mr. Palmer . . ." Celia paused and clasped the cooling teacup again. "The other day he commented on Li Sha having sold her belongings, the gifts she had been given by her clients. I thought it odd that he knew that, although I suppose Elizabeth might have mentioned it to him."

"The Palmers. Hmph," said Addie. "I canna understand why Miss Barbara likes them so."

"Because they have been kind to her, and she has few friends."

"Your uncle, God rest his soul, was always leery of their motives."

"I appreciate anyone who treats Barbara well," said Celia, closing the topic of the Palmers and their relationship with Barbara. "I do not know this Mr. Ahearn, who seems the most likely candidate. And the last people on our list are the Douglasses. I have not seen enough of them to comment on their behavior, aside from how surprising it was that they both attended Li Sha's funeral."

" 'Twas guilt over how they treated Miss Li, and you, too. Dismissing your work with the Chinese girls because of those awful anti-coolie people. Bah."

The bell for the front door rang. "Who could that be?" asked Celia.

Addie got to her feet. "Should I send them away?"

"See who it is first."

Addie went to open the door, and Celia heard Elizabeth Palmer's voice. She stood and greeted her in the entry hall.

"What brings you here, Elizabeth?" Celia asked.

"I saw news of the attack on your cousin in the newspaper this morning." Today Elizabeth wore a day dress in lilac silk with mother-of-pearl buttons. Instead of her voluminous burnous scarf, she had tossed a white cashmere shawl banded in vermillion over her shoulders and carried a silk umbrella, which she deposited in the brass stand by the door. Celia couldn't recall a time she had ever seen Elizabeth in a plain gown. "A gang of boys? What next?"

"Come into the parlor. Addie, bring tea for us there."

Elizabeth accompanied Celia into the parlor and they took seats on the settee. "I have not had an opportunity to read the account," Celia said. "I hope they didn't exaggerate the extent of Barbara's injuries."

"The account was vague." Elizabeth knitted her brows. "Is she well?"

"She has a bump on her head and a small cut on her hand. Nothing serious. She is more discomposed than actually wounded."

"I did warn you, Celia, that you were placing yourself in danger by working with those Chinese women. And this is what happens." The wave of Elizabeth's right hand encompassed the parlor, as if the crime had been committed within the walls of the house instead of in a grimy back alley. "See how violent the anti-Chinese people are? You're fortunate your cousin, so young and fragile like Emmeline, was not seriously hurt."

Addie entered with the tea tray. She gave Elizabeth a wary sideways glance as she set the tray in front of Celia.

"Thank you, Addie." Addie departed and Celia poured out the tea.

"What do the police have to say?" asked Elizabeth, accepting a cup.

"They are attempting to find those responsible for assaulting us and bring them to justice."

"Do they think the attack is related to Li Sha's murder?" Elizabeth. Ever collecting and distributing rumors and tidbits. If gossip could be traded on the mercantile exchange, she would be wealthier than she already was.

"I cannot say, Elizabeth. Detective Greaves is working on uncovering any connections, however."

Footsteps clattered down the staircase and Barbara burst into the parlor. "Mrs. Palmer!" She looked as though she'd just scrambled out of bed, her hair coming unwound from its braid and her wrapper tied loosely over her nightgown.

"Good morning, Barbara." Elizabeth pursed her lips at Barbara's undignified entrance.

"Barbara, what is it?" asked Celia.

"I thought I heard . . ." She blushed. "When I heard Mrs. Palmer's voice, I thought I also heard Mr. Palmer's."

And of course you had to come running. "It is only Elizabeth this morning. She was worried about you, but I have assured her that you are recovering."

"Yes, I am, Mrs. Palmer. Thank you so much for your concern."

"Would you like Addie to bring tea up to your room?" Celia asked her.

"No, I'll just go to the kitchen and have her make me some toast. Good day to you, Mrs. Palmer. I'm sorry for interrupting, Cousin." She hurried out of the room and shut the pocket doors between the dining room and parlor.

"Poor child. She looks unwell," said Elizabeth after a brief pause. "But it's understandable, given the strain of having your brother-in-law accused of killing a girl she knew. I must say, it's curious how long it's taking for Tom Davies to go to trial for Li Sha's death. It must be painful for you all, having to read about the crime nearly every day in the newspapers. I'd imagine you would like the whole messy business finished quickly. I know I would."

"I do not know how long to expect the proceedings to take, Elizabeth. I am thankful, however, because the delay allows—" Celia nearly said "us." "It allows the police more time to find Li Sha's true killer."

Elizabeth tucked her brows into a sympathetic furrow. "Oh, Celia, I know this is hard to accept, but your brother-in-law has to be the person responsible."

Has to be? "Since he has been in jail, a man has been watching our house and leaving threatening notes."

Elizabeth gasped. "Threats? Celia, that's dreadful!"

Bloody hell, thought Celia, instantly regretting the burst of outrage that had caused her to tell Elizabeth. Next she'd be blurting out the entire list of suspects. She would *not*, however, mention last night's gutted rat, now buried in the dustbin for later disposal.

"I did not mean to alarm you, but the reason I mentioned this man is that with Tom in jail, he can be neither the watcher nor the author of the notes. It is possible this person wishes to frighten Barbara because she is Chinese, but it is also very possible he murdered Li Sha and wishes to frighten us into silence. If that is the case, it is not at all reasonable to think my brother-in-law *has* to be responsible for killing Li Sha. Someone else is."

"If there is somebody else out there who murdered her, Celia, then you're all in terrible danger!"

"Elizabeth, please keep your voice down," hissed Celia, mindful that Barbara likely sat in the dining room on the other side of the closed doors.

Elizabeth leaned forward. "You should leave town, you know. You and your cousin. Get away from here, for your own safety. I have been warning you."

Yes, you have. Celia sipped her tea and considered the woman seated next to her.

"Elizabeth," she said, setting her teacup on the saucer, "on Monday when I was returning from a visit to Chinatown, I encountered your husband. He made an interesting comment to me."

Elizabeth's recoil was subtle, the slightest shift of her torso farther away from Celia. If Celia hadn't been watching closely, she might not have observed the motion.

"And what was that comment?" she asked.

"He mentioned the trinkets and jewelry that Li Sha had been given by her former clients. He knew she had sold them. I found it strange that he knew about the items at all."

"What are you implying?" asked Elizabeth, her voice edged with anger. "That my husband knew Li Sha beyond the one time he'd met her?"

Was that what she was implying? Perhaps it was.

Elizabeth read Celia's answer in her eyes. "He made a supposition, Celia. How else could she have escaped the brothel except to have bought her way out? And I presume he knows, like many men know, that prostitutes are given gifts."

"That does seem reasonable."

Elizabeth was not placated by Celia's response. With a frown, she glanced at the clock chiming on the mantel and stood.

"I must leave now for a meeting," she said coldly. "I'm grateful to find Barbara not seriously injured, but you all need to be on your guard, Celia. You've been imprudent to get involved with the prostitutes in Chinatown and now to be asking questions . . . it's simply reckless. Dangerously reckless."

She swept out of the room, charging ahead before Celia could open the front door to see her out. Elizabeth hurried down the steps as heavy raindrops began to fall, her silk umbrella forgotten in her haste to depart.

"*A*re you sure you want to see this again, Greaves?" Dr. Harris wiped his hands down his dark apron, though Nick didn't notice anything on them that needed wiping. Maybe it was a habit.

"I want to be certain it's her, Harris." Nick took a step farther into the coroner's gas-lit examination room. The windows were shut against the rain, and the noxious stink was stronger than usual. "I didn't have much chance last night before you got there."

When a pair of firemen had brought the body out of the building, carrying it on a plank of wood that served as a makeshift stretcher, the crowd had surged forward to gawk. It was all Nick and the constable could do to restore order.

"She might be hard to recognize." The coroner contemplated the sheet-covered form lying on the table. "Last night, a few of my jurors fainted dead away when I asked them to examine the body. One of them declared he was going to decline any request that required him to assess the cause of death on remains as repellently disfigured as hers are."

"You know I don't faint, Harris." Nick gripped the brim of his hat in his right hand and gently kneaded his bruised forearm with his left. He couldn't work out how a man did a job like this. Harris had a nice medical practice. He wasn't coroner because he needed the twenty-five hundred dollars he got paid each year.

Harris eyed his forearm. "I thought it was your left arm that bothers you."

Nick had stopped using the sling, tired of the nuisance. The bruises still ached enough to have kept him awake last night, though. "A small run-in with a man and a cudgel."

"Ah."

The coroner peeled the sheet down to the woman's shoulders. Nick winced. Her hair had been burned off, and the left side of her head and neck looked like a crisped piece of chicken. A deep gash ran from one side of her throat to the other. Her face—what remained of her face—was barely recognizable, her lips and nose and ears shriveled and blackened. But Nick could still identify enough to know who it was.

He swallowed down bile. She should've come to the police; they might have been able to protect her, but it was too late now. "That's her. That's Tessie Lange."

"As you can see," said Harris, "her throat was slit, which was what killed her. Likely done before she was dumped in that warehouse. Undoubtedly the fire was set to cover the killer's tracks, but he must not have known about the drunk who, according to the locals I talked to, has been sleeping there for weeks. If it weren't for the fuss the man raised, the building might have burned around her and we'd never have known who she was."

Nick looked away from the body; his stomach was becoming as weak as Taylor's. "I guess that's something to be thankful for."

"It definitely is, given how many folks come through here who are never identified."

"Was there any money or jewelry on her?"

"Nope." Harris replaced the sheet.

Then she might have met with the person she'd intended the money for.

Nick gestured toward the body on the examining table. "Don't let her father see that."

"I'll do what I can, but the magistrate will prefer that a family member make the formal identification. Do you know who did it?"

"Not yet. But I believe I know somebody who has an idea."

"$\mathcal{D}$on't you think it's time to tell me who you were afraid might hurt your daughter?" Nick asked Lange, who was slouched in a chair in his upstairs kitchen. Rain drummed against the window, and it was cold and dank in the room. Nick guessed nobody had lit the stove since Tessie had run off.

"I need a name, Mr. Lange, if you want me to find her killer."

Lange's head hung slack over his chest, and his spectacles dangled from the fingers of his right hand. "My poor, sweet daughter."

"Your poor, sweet daughter knew a murderer," said Nick. "I'm also guessing she'd gone to meet him with the money she received for pawning her mother's jewelry. Maybe you've got some idea of what she hoped to achieve."

"No. No." Lange sank lower in the chair, the defeated husk of a man who'd failed to protect his only child.

"Who was the man you told me you'd seen around your store?" asked Nick. "The one you needed to warn Tessie about."

Lange sobbed. "Roddy," he said, surrendering up the name. "He said to call him Roddy."

"What did Roddy want?"

Lange slowly lifted his gaze. His eyes were bloodshot. "He wanted me to buy smuggled opium from him. I would then split the profits I would make when I sold my formulations at a higher price. I refused him."

Smuggling. *Damn.* Mina had told Nick that the German saloonkeeper was involved in smuggling, too, but that wouldn't have involved opium. And God only knew how many opium smugglers there were in San Francisco. Probably not a one of whom was actually named Roddy.

"So you refused him," said Nick. "Why didn't he leave you alone after that?"

"He wanted to be certain I did not inform the police of his request."

"Is that why you thought he might've wanted to hurt Tessie? Because she'd seen or overheard something?"

"I did not think she had ever seen him," said Lange. "I did not believe she would be in danger at first. Not until she disappeared."

"But even after she left without a message, taking all her mother's jewelry, you didn't tell me the truth."

"I was very afraid of him. I am a foolish man."

Wasn't *that* the damned truth. "Where can I find Roddy?"

"I do not know."

"You don't know or you won't say?"

Lange held Nick's gaze, possibly the steadiest thing Nick had seen the man do since he'd first met him. "I do not know."

The contents of Li Sha's ragged carpetbag, plus the few items she'd been wearing when she had died, were strewn across the bed in Uncle Walford's unused chamber. Elizabeth Palmer's visit had made Celia more determined to find a clue—any clue—that would reveal who had killed Li Sha. Celia was tired of suspecting everyone, not knowing who was innocent and who might be a murderer. Moreover, she was tired of sensing that the answer lay among Li Sha's belongings, but she hadn't the wits to see it.

While a steady rain pelted the street-facing window, Celia surveyed each object. There was a lovely sapphire-colored silk tunic with an intricate, brightly colored design embroidered along the edges: a remnant of life in the parlor house and an expensive item Li Sha must have been reluctant to discard, no matter the memories that must be attached to it. Underthings and a pair of cotton stockings with a hole in the heel, which she'd probably meant to repair. Two lacquered combs for displaying in glossy hair. A tiny book filled with Chinese characters in red ink. And no jewelry, other than the cheap earrings Celia had given her, the rest sold.

Celia exhaled. She'd hoped for clues and all she saw were the sad remnants of a desperate woman's life.

That's all? Barbara had said. She had expected more. But staring at the contents was not offering Celia any answers.

She was packing away the last of Li Sha's belongings when Addie strode into the room, a piece of paper in her hand.

"Not another note," said Celia.

"This one's from Owen, ma'am." Addie peered at the carpetbag. "Have you discovered anything?"

"No." Celia snapped the bag closed and set it on the floor. She took the note from Addie. "Why did Owen not wait and speak with me?"

"Poor lad. Dripping like a wet dog, he was," said Addie. "He claimed he had something important to do and couldn't stay to visit. So he handed me that note and ran off."

"I did not even realize he could write," said Celia.

"Someone must have helped him."

Celia broke the seal, a ragged lump of wax, and flipped open the paper.

Tell Miss Barbara I'm sorry. I didn't know they wanted to hurt her. I should've stayed to help. I'm sorry. I'll make it up to her and to you, too, ma'am. I'll get that fellow who killed Miss Li and then you'll be happy with me again.

Respectfully yours,
Owen C

Celia's heart constricted. *Then you'll be happy with me again . . .*

"That foolish laddie. What has he gone and done?" said Addie.

Celia tucked the note into the pocket of her skirt. "He is taking a great risk." All in hopes of gaining affection.

"And, ma'am, Madame Philippe has come. She wants to speak with you. I've shown her to the parlor."

Full of questions, Celia headed out of the bedchamber and down the stairs.

Madame Philippe stood in the center of the parlor, appearing even more subdued and small beneath the room's tall ceiling.

"Madame Philippe, may I offer you some refreshment?" asked Celia, gesturing toward the settee.

"Thank you, but no. My visit will be brief."

"Have you more news for us?" asked Addie, hovering in the doorway behind Celia.

"I have been thinking about Miss Lange," said the woman. "I should have told you when you came to visit yesterday. When I saw in the newspaper that Miss Walford was injured, I realized how important what I have to say could be."

"Yes?" asked Celia.

"Miss Lange came to me to ask about a stranger, a man who frightened her. A man who worked with her father. But his visits were late at night, after the store had closed."

Only disreputable men made late-night visits to conduct business. Apparently, there was more to learn about Hubert Lange.

The astrologer's gaze moved between Celia and Addie. "Miss Lange believed this man was pretending to be someone he was not. That he was dangerous. She asked me where he could be found."

"Is he the man who's been watching our house?" asked Addie breathlessly.

"This I do not know," answered Madame Philippe. "I do not see clearly where he can be found. I saw water and told that to Miss Lange. She seemed to understand and was satisfied."

"Did Miss Lange believe that water suggested this man works near the wharves?" asked Celia. Perhaps even the wharf where Li Sha was discovered.

The astrologer inclined her head. "She may have. I cannot say more than that."

Had Tessie learned where this man worked or lived and gone to confront him? It might explain her disappearance. "Thank you, madam."

The woman made a polite bow and followed an excited Addie to the vestibule. "Miss Lange was right about how wonderful you are, Madame Philippe," Addie declared, handing the woman her waterproofed cloak. She opened the front door and peered through the rain. "That Officer Taylor's finally come, ma'am."

Celia stepped through the door after the astrologer and bade her farewell. Madame Philippe tugged the hood of her cloak over her head and descended the stairs.

Down at the street, Officer Taylor hunched in the gray oilskin cape all policemen wore in bad weather. He glanced at the door when he heard Celia's footsteps on the front porch and tipped his hat in greeting, sending a cascade of water down his front. His gaze followed Madame Philippe, who murmured a quiet greeting and glided past him.

"Dinna tell him who she is, ma'am. I dinna wish to hear his opinion again," whispered Addie.

She spotted the deliveryman from the butcher's stall across the road and shot Officer Taylor a quick glance before smiling broadly. "Hullo!" Addie called to the man, who was hurrying up their neighbor's stairs with an armful of paper-wrapped meat.

"Howdy, Miss Ferguson," he called back, grinning.

"You'll catch your death in this rain."

"Why, thanks, miss, for thinkin' of me!" he said. "And don't forget about the Willows. Maybe next Sunday?"

"Maybe next Sunday. Good day to you."

Addie gave Officer Taylor, who'd been watching the proceedings with lifted eyebrows, a parting glance and, with a toss of her head, retreated into the house.

Celia bit back a smile.

"Thank you for coming, Officer Taylor," she said. "I hope you have good news."

"I'm afraid it's not good news," he said, climbing the steps. Rain dripped off the roof, splattering mud onto his legs.

"But we cannot stay in town. Barbara shall be frantic."

"Sorry, ma'am." He joined her on the porch. "Was that a patient?" he asked, looking down the street toward the receding form of Madame Philippe. "She doesn't look like she needs a free clinic, the way she's dressed."

"No, she is not a patient," replied Celia. "Tessie Lange came to her for help in locating a man she was afraid of. A man who had suspicious late-night meetings with her father."

"Why'd she think that woman could find him?"

"Madame Philippe . . . can be very knowledgeable about such matters," Celia prevaricated, honoring Addie's request. "But she could tell Tessie only that he worked near water."

"Water, eh?" he asked. "Mr. Greaves and me think we've heard about this fellow. He's an opium smuggler who goes by the name of Roddy."

"Mr. Hubert Lange was involved with smuggling?" He was not at all the man she'd believed him to be.

"Seems so, ma'am." Taylor pulled out his ever-present notebook. "So, Miss Lange wanted to know where she could find this fellow?"

"Yes."

"That confirms our suspicions about what happened to her,"

said Taylor, jotting an entry in his notebook before putting it away.

"You mean that she did go to look for this smuggler, and he is responsible for her disappearance?" said Celia.

Officer Taylor turned pale. He had freckles like Owen, which she had not noticed before. "There was another fire last night . . . ," he began.

"I heard the tocsin." But since the fire had been far from Chinatown, Celia had been less concerned. She'd also felt she could not leave Barbara and investigate. Not that Addie would have let her step a foot outside the house, anyway.

"Was it bad?" she asked.

He scratched nervously at his neck with the edge of his notebook. "The firemen found a body."

Celia felt a chill like the coldest wind. "It was Tessie Lange, wasn't it?"

The inclination of his head was nearly imperceptible, but Celia required no greater validation of her dreadful guess.

CHAPTER 15

Taylor descended the steps of city hall alongside Nick. "The beat cop says he's certain the saloonkeeper's at his boarding-house right now."

"Then let's see what the German has to say for himself." They strode across Kearney. "Did Mrs. Davies ask to leave town again when you saw her?"

"That rat left on her doorstep upset her pretty bad. And now with Miss Lange dead . . . Do you think it's this Roddy fellow who's behind all that?" asked Taylor.

"I don't understand why a smuggler would be after Mrs. Davies," said Nick. "Unless he killed Li Sha, then learned Mrs. Davies was friends with the girl and got scared of what she might know. Although I don't see how he could've learned of their relationship, unless Lange told him for some reason."

"Hmm," grunted Taylor.

"Any luck at all finding him?" Nick asked.

"There aren't any Roddys in the city directory," said Taylor. "And no one on the force has heard of him, either, so he hasn't been to the station for any reason."

"He wouldn't be the first smuggler to use an alias," said Nick. "He might not be the man who killed Li Sha or who is threatening Mrs. Davies, but he's our best lead for who killed Tessie Lange. We have to find him."

"But what about Mrs. Davies and her cousin? Any chance they can leave town until we close this case?"

They turned up Pacific. "I'll talk to the magistrate and see what he has to say about letting her be questioned by the attorneys before Tom Davies' trial," said Nick. "It's irregular, but given the situation, maybe he'll bend the rules."

"I've asked the cop who makes the rounds in her neighborhood to keep a lookout. But you know if there's trouble in the Barbary, he won't be bothering with her house, sir."

"We should move them someplace safer, like a hotel in town, until she can give her testimony and leave the city," said Nick. "I'll suggest that to her when I see her tonight."

"You're planning on seeing Mrs. Davies tonight?" asked Taylor, the ghost of a grin on his mouth.

"It's business, Taylor. I'm taking her to the anti-coolie meeting to see if she can identify the person who's been watching her house," Nick replied. "And while you're teasing me about Mrs. Davies, I thought you were interested in that housekeeper of hers. You talked about her quite a bit afterward. Maybe you can stop by the house today to see how she's doing."

"Me, sir?" Taylor sounded affronted. "Me interested in a

woman who goes to astrologers? Not a chance. Nope. Besides, she's sweet on a delivery fellow from a butcher's shop."

"Well, then it's good you're not interested," said Nick. He didn't think Taylor noticed his smile.

They arrived at the lodging house where the German saloon-keeper, Uhlfelder, lived with his wife, on Pacific, around the corner from his ruined business. The woman who answered the door showed them into a dark and musty parlor and went to fetch the man.

The saloonkeeper entered the parlor. He wore a heavy traveling coat over his suit of clothes and a nervous expression on his thick face.

"Going someplace, Mr. Uhlfelder?" Nick asked.

"Why do you want to talk to me?" he asked. "Is it the fire?"

Taylor took the lead. "We've been told the fire was started as a warning. To you. Is that why you've been in hiding?"

"I have not been hiding," said Uhlfelder. "I have been away from town. Business matters."

"We've also heard you're associated with some less-than-decent types," said Nick. "Smugglers, in fact. Is that true?"

"I am an honest businessman," he insisted. "I do not open my saloon outside the legal hours. I pay my rent on time. I do not make trouble."

"Do you know a Joseph Palmer? Or a Hubert Lange?" asked Nick, trying to draw connections among a group of men he was beginning to dislike more each day. "How about a Mr. Douglass? Or a Captain Eagan?" he threw in for good measure.

Taylor's pencil made a scratching sound as he blacked out that last name as soon as he'd written it.

"I do not know any of them," said Uhlfelder, shaking his head. "They are not customers of my saloon."

"I didn't ask if they are customers. I asked if you know them," Nick pressed.

Uhlfelder swallowed, his Adam's apple bobbing above his collar. "I may have heard one or two of their names. They are well-known, I believe."

"I think maybe you meet with them every Monday night at the Men's Benevolent Association," said Nick.

"*Bitte?* The what?"

"What about a man with the last name of Roddy?" asked Taylor, looking up from his notebook.

"My shop," Uhlfelder murmured.

"What about your shop? Do you think Roddy set fire to it?" Nick asked.

"He would." The saloonkeeper frowned. "I knew it. I would not help him and this is what he's done."

"Help him with what?" asked Taylor.

"He is a smuggler and a dangerous man. I don't wish to be involved," said Uhlfelder.

"Where can we find him?" Nick asked.

Uhlfelder's frown deepened. "You do not find Mr. Roddy. He finds you."

*C*elia and Mr. Greaves were late to the Anti-Coolie Association meeting, arriving at the American Theater among other stragglers who were pushing through the front doors.

"I confess, Mr. Greaves, that I did not realize the sort of man Mr. Lange was," said Celia as he held the door open for her. "'God has given you one face and you make yourselves another.'"

"What's that?" he asked. "Another quote from that Pope fellow?"

"A quote from Shakespeare expressing how we are not always what we seem."

But perhaps all people wore impenetrable facades, the faces they showed to the world, while behind the exteriors swirled dark longings and terrible secrets. She hated that she may have been misled by Lange, a man she'd trusted. However, she had also misjudged Patrick and Tom—and she had misjudged her own heart.

"We haven't established the extent of Mr. Lange's association with smuggling yet, ma'am," said Mr. Greaves as they climbed the sweeping stairs to the second floor. As was usual for him, he scrutinized every person they encountered. "He might be as innocent as he claims. Just another victim of this tragedy."

They crowded into the rear of the upper circle, taking seats on chairs with fading upholstery. The gas lamps along the walls flickered, their light dancing off white walls embellished with gilded carvings. Undoubtedly at one time the theater had been quite grand, but now the velvet curtain surrounding the stage looked worn, and the parquet floor was scuffed and dirty.

Celia arranged her skirts and looked around her. The air was warm and humid from the crush of men—and some women, she noted—seated in the gallery and the upper circle, hats in hands, nodding as the speaker expounded his points against the Chinese. She felt the first trickle of sweat beneath her collar.

"By the way, I spoke to the judge this afternoon," said Mr. Greaves in a low voice. "He wants you in the courtroom during the trial and won't budge."

"Barbara will be distressed to hear that."

"I think it best that you and your cousin move to a hotel in town as soon as possible, Mrs. Davies," he said. "Tomorrow morning, first thing. You'll be safer where there are a lot of people around."

"I suggested to Barbara that she go to Healdsburg with Mrs. Palmer and her daughter, but Emmeline is too ill to travel."

"Then your cousin will have to stay in town with you."

Celia preferred to keep Barbara, as anxious as her cousin had been lately, close at hand anyway. "As soon as I return home, I will tell Addie to pack our things."

He nodded. "Now, let me know if you see anybody you recognize."

Celia scanned the audience. Beneath her, all she could see were the tops of heads. How could she ever hope to identify the person who'd been watching the house in this mass of red-faced, angry people?

"Not yet." Celia searched among those occupying the upper levels that curved around the walls, their faces hidden in shadows. "I may have been overly optimistic to think I might spot the watcher. This seems rather pointless."

"Let's try anyway, okay?" he encouraged her.

Celia examined the people seated nearest to them, but none looked familiar. Although she did recognize a man halfway along the back row; he was the son of her grocer and employed at the Mission Woolen Mills. Or perhaps, if he was here, he was no longer employed and blamed the Chinese.

"As the Chinaman progresses, the white man will retire before him. One by one, three by three, men from each of the living branches of California employment will go!" said the speaker, whose name was Mr. Mooney. For added emphasis he pounded a fist on the podium. "This vast and fair country will be handed over to the Chinese—will become a colony of the emperor of the Celestial Empire!"

Audience members jeered and hooted, cheering him on. Mr. Mooney was dressed like a banker in his dark suit, a watch suspended from a fob chain. He had paused to mop his brow with a handkerchief. She doubted his occupation was endangered by the Chinese.

"Admit the Chinese to take possession of your vocations, labors, and business, and those who now are wedded to California will soon change their mind, finding that they must leave!" He'd been well chosen for the task—he had a carrying voice and no end of arrogant self-confidence.

There was more jeering and stomping of feet, hundreds of boot heels thudding against the worn floor.

"Are your men in attendance, Mr. Greaves?" she asked, searching for anyone who might be a police officer.

"Mullahey's up against the left wall," he said with a jerk of his chin. "And Taylor's sitting beneath us on the aisle there."

Neither of them wore their uniforms.

"Why, there is one of the boys who attacked Barbara," she said. "Standing very near Officer Mullahey with a man whom I suppose could be the boy's father."

Mr. Greaves signaled to Officer Mullahey, who had been watching for the cue. "Mullahey will wait until they leave to arrest the kid. If he confronts them here, we'd probably have a riot on our hands."

"Is Mr. Ahearn here?" she asked. She wondered, too, if Owen was hidden among the throng.

"Taylor would've pointed him out if he'd seen him in the gallery." He looked around. "Ahearn must be lying low."

The speaker took a drink from a glass of water at his elbow and continued. "But is there any remedy for this threatened pestilence? Yes! Let us all unite—every white man of every creed and political hue! Send a deputation from this meeting to the Chinese merchants, intimating our warning to them against bringing any more of their countrymen!"

A man off to one side of the gallery stood and shouted his support.

"And there's our Mr. Wagner singing out," said Mr. Greaves. "He must've decided he's not fine with the Celestials after all. Does he look familiar?"

She squinted. "No. Not really."

Just then, the man turned toward them. He glared at Mr. Greaves. "Who is he?" she asked.

"He's the man who found Li Sha's body," he explained. "A customs officer and a tough customer."

"Oh."

"I wouldn't mind having another conversation with him, though." Mr. Greaves repeated to Officer Taylor the signal he'd given to Officer Mullahey. "It's going to be a busy night at the station."

"We must make a vow against employing them in any shape or way," Mr. Mooney continued. "A vow against dealing with any establishment that employs them or any one of them!"

People jumped to their feet and punched fists into the air. Others grumbled, their discontent flowing across the rows of seats like a wave.

The speaker was winding up his address. "We shall not surrender this vast, fertile land—the richest prize of the Caucasian family—to a nation of serfs whose presence is a nuisance, a pestilence, a calamity, and a curse!"

Men bellowed their assent. The crowd poured into the aisles and pushed toward the stage to congratulate the speaker on his rousing talk. Against the far wall, Officer Taylor had cornered Mr. Wagner and a middle-aged woman who clung to Mr. Wagner's arm.

Mr. Greaves let out a breath. "We should go."

"Mrs. Davies!" called a male voice. "What are you doing here? Have you come over to our side all of a sudden?"

Oh no. It was the grocer's son, descending on her like a frigate bearing down on an enemy ship. He glanced at Nicholas Greaves, who had taken a protective stance in front of her.

"Why, hello," she responded, feeling the detective's pressure on her arm, tugging her toward the exit. "It was a most interesting speech, but I am afraid I do not have time to talk. We are expected elsewhere."

Celia turned and Mr. Greaves propelled her toward the doors leading to the stairs that would take them to the ground floor.

"Are you and him spying on us or somethin'?" The man's voice echoed off the walls.

"A friend of yours?" the detective asked, shoving through the crowd of people clogging the steps. A burly man with auburn hair grumbled at them to watch where they were going.

"He is the son of my grocer." She gathered her skirts higher to avoid tripping over them in their mad rush to leave the theater. "Is he following us?"

"I'm not stopping to find out," answered Nick as they reached the theater's entry hall.

"Hey! Wait!" He *was* following them, pushing people out of his way. "You support the Chinese, don't you? Don't you?"

Nicholas Greaves cursed, seized Celia's hand, and picked

up the pace. He plunged through the front doors and pulled her out onto Sansome Street. They dashed across the road, splashing through puddles.

An empty hack waited across the street, the driver slouched beneath a turned-down hat. Mr. Greaves reached the carriage and threw open the door.

"Hey, what do you think you're doing?" protested the driver. "I'm taken."

"Not anymore. Unless you like trouble with the police."

Mr. Greaves shoved Celia through the doorway. She clambered onto the seat and dragged her skirts out of the way. He climbed in behind her and slammed the door. The driver whipped the horses, flinging Celia back against the cushions. It wasn't until they were two blocks distant that Mr. Greaves appeared to relax.

"I'm afraid you've lost yourself a grocer, ma'am," he said.

She took a deep breath and smiled. "That is quite all right, Mr. Greaves. I shall find another."

"Are you okay?" His gaze scanned her face.

"'Blythe as a bird on the wing,' as Addie might say," she said, attempting to jest. And then exhaustion hit, and she sank into the seat. "I am tired of being afraid, Mr. Greaves. Very tired indeed."

"I'll come and check on you at the house once I'm finished at the station tonight."

"There is no need to go to the bother. We will bar the doors and windows and be fine." Nonetheless, the concern she read on his normally impassive face touched her.

"There's every need, Mrs. Davies," he said. They passed a streetlamp, and the flames lit the angles of Mr. Greaves' face. A muscle flexed in his jaw. "I don't want to lose another woman because of my stupidity."

"Do not worry about me, Mr. Greaves."

"Ma'am, it seems that's about all I do."

The hack stopped and they alighted. Addie threw open the front door. "You made it home, then!"

Celia turned to Mr. Greaves. "Thank you. I shall be safe from here."

"Lock every door tight, ma'am. I'll return as soon as I can. Miss Ferguson," he said, nodding at Addie before climbing back into the hired carriage.

Celia ascended the steps and went into the house. "Pack to leave tomorrow morning, Addie. Mr. Greaves has recommended that we find accommodations at a hotel. I suggest the American Exchange."

" 'Tis expensive," said Addie, taking Celia's wrap.

"We shall not be staying long," she said. "I shall take the money out of the funds Uncle Walford left for the clinic."

"I'll pack as soon as I fetch you some tea," said Addie, tea being the solution to every problem. "Miss Barbara will be happy to hear we're leaving this house for a while."

"I hope so, Addie."

*C*elia awoke with a start, her neck stiff from her awkward position. She must have fallen asleep at the dining room table. The candle Addie had left lit on the sideboard had guttered out and the fire in the kitchen stove had dwindled, plunging the dining room into darkness. She'd sat at the table for a long time, long after Addie had finished packing upstairs and the house had gone quiet. Celia had been so weary, she hadn't been able to convince herself to stand and go to bed. But she *had* managed to doze off and leave a crick in her neck.

She stood and shuffled toward the kitchen with the cold tea things, skirting the dining chairs. She had walked this path hundreds of times; she needn't bother to rummage about to find the matches and light a candle.

She yawned and wondered if Mr. Greaves had ever come by to check on the house. Celia felt sorry for him, though she supposed he would not care for anyone's pity. But the look on his face when he'd mentioned the woman he had lost had reflected the deepest pain. He had to have meant his younger sister. Celia hoped that one day he would entrust her with the story. Because Celia understood his suffering more than he might believe.

With another yawn, she crossed the threshold between the dining room and kitchen. She heard a sound, the faintest rustling, and paused. Barely able to make out the table that she knew was directly ahead of her, she felt her way forward and set down the heavy tray. Her pulse hammering, she peered into the room's black shadows.

"Hello?" she said, her voice wobbling.

The noise did not come again. It had probably been a mouse.

It was then she noticed a chink of light between the back door and its frame. The door was open. Addie would not have left it ajar.

Celia turned to flee just as a hand grabbed her from behind. The other clapped over her mouth, silencing her scream. The hard end of a blunt object jabbed into her stomach where her assailant clutched her. A knife? It had to be the butt end of a knife.

She fought against him, flailing her legs, her stocking-clad feet hitting his shins. He grunted and she struck out again, as hard as she could, and knocked him off balance. She flung back an elbow, connecting with his arm. The collision broke his hold on the knife, which clattered to the floor and skidded across it.

"Help!" she screamed, and he slapped his hand over her mouth again.

She bit down on his fingers, tasting blood. He cursed and started dragging her toward the rear door. She had to get free. The more she struggled in her assailant's grasp, the tighter he held her, his fingers digging into her cheek and chin. He stank of liquor and cigar smoke.

Celia tried again to scream, but the sound didn't make it past his fingers. He butted her head with his, sending her senses reeling, and she stumbled.

Grumbling, he yanked her to her feet and continued to pull her toward the door. But he was not headed outside. He was trying to recover the knife, which must have ended up between the pantry and the doorway.

Celia clutched his arm and lifted herself, kicking out, trying to knock over the stool she knew was somewhere nearby. He angrily jerked her backward. They were almost at the door now. She had to find a weapon. One hand was free, but she couldn't reach far because of the way he held her. They reached the pantry, and he turned to search for the knife. His hold slackened, and Celia hastily groped along the edge of the small table near the wall, looking for something, anything. Her fingers connected with a heavy pan, and just as he eased his grip on her arm to crouch and hunt for the knife, she lifted the pan and swung backward. The blow glanced off his head, and he bellowed with rage. He seized the knife and swiped it at her. Free of his grip, she flung herself out of his reach, falling to the ground.

"Addie! Help!"

The outside door burst open, and a boy, silhouetted in a hazy shaft of moonlight, shot through the doorway and into the kitchen.

"Oy, there!" he yelled.

Taken by surprise, her assailant lashed out with the knife, connecting with the boy's arm. Owen recoiled, his back smacking against the hard edge of Addie's oak prep table.

"No!" Celia screamed.

Again the man swiped at Owen with the knife and lunged for the open door. He ran outside, his heavy boots thudding down the stairs. Celia dropped to Owen's side. She felt for his arm and found warm, sticky blood, a great quantity of it. The assailant had sliced through more than just the boy's arm.

"Owen?" she said, wishing she could see more than the dim outline of his face and the darkening pool spreading across the floor. *No. No!*

Overhead, footsteps pounded along the hallway and down the staircase.

"Addie! Addie, come quick! To the kitchen," she shouted.

"I saved you, ma'am," Owen said, gasping for breath. He attempted to sit up and slumped against her arm.

"Owen?" He did not respond. "Owen!"

Light bobbed through the dining room, and Addie rushed into the kitchen with a candle. "What's happened?"

"He's fainted, Addie." Now that there was light in the room, Celia could see how badly Owen had been cut. There was a deep wound on his arm and across his chest as well. "Light the lantern in my examination room and gather my supplies."

Addie hurried through the connecting door to the clinic, the desk lamp flaring inside.

"You were very foolish, Owen," Celia said, gathering the

hem of her petticoat and pressing it to the gash in his arm. The cotton quickly turned red.

Addie returned and gathered Owen's legs while Celia clambered to her feet and lifted his shoulders. Together, they carried him to the clinic, Owen's blood trickling to the floor, and lowered him as gently as possible to the examination bench.

Addie collected what Celia required. "Your carbolic, ma'am. And your silk thread and needle," she said, handing the items over. She held the lantern aloft. "Oh, poor wee bairn. What have you gone and done, Owen Cassidy?"

"He saved me, Addie." Tears pooling in her eyes, Celia swabbed the wounds with the carbolic solution. "He saved me," she said, threading the needle and starting to sew.

"*You* were damned lucky," said Nick, staring at Mrs. Davies, who was scrubbing blood off the oilcloth-covered floor of her kitchen, seemingly every lantern she owned called into service to illuminate the room.

Earlier that evening, they hadn't been able to pin anything on Wagner and had been forced to let him go once again. And by the time Nick had finished interrogating the boy who'd earlier assaulted Mrs. Davies and her cousin, along with the kid's father, and drawn up assault charges, it had gotten late.

He'd gone to Celia Davies' anyway, even though he'd been in a foul mood, because he'd made her a promise. His mood had gone from foul to panicked when he'd been forced to pound on the front door to get anybody to open it. By the time Addie Ferguson had shown him into the house, Mrs. Davies had just finished stitching up a scruffy Irish boy while a hysterical Barbara Walford sobbed from her perch on the staircase.

The watcher had finally escalated his attacks from cryptic messages and disemboweled rats to a direct assault. And Nick hadn't been there to stop the man. He could've lost Celia, too.

"I am aware of how fortunate we are, Mr. Greaves," said Mrs. Davies, dipping the rag into a wooden bucket, the water inside red with Owen Cassidy's blood.

Addie Ferguson dumped a second bucket of water into the corner sink. "'Twas Owen who saved us," she said with a frown, pumping the tap handle until fresh water splashed into the bucket. "And now he's upstairs, clinging to life!"

"He should recover, Addie," Mrs. Davies said, the rag swirling across the floor. But to Nick she didn't sound all that certain.

"You need to move to the hotel in the morning, ma'am," he said. "That fellow tried to kill you. He might try again."

"That was my intention, but now I cannot leave Owen."

"Then bring him with you."

"He lost too much blood and is very weak." She gazed at the damp encircling where she knelt. Blood had splattered everywhere, and a trail of it led through a nearby doorway. The iron pan Mrs. Davies had used to thump her assailant on the head lay against the baseboard where she'd dropped it. The Cassidy kid was asleep in an upstairs bedroom, probably resting in a soft bed for the first time in years, Barbara Walford assigned the task of sitting watch over him.

"It appears Owen also bruised several ribs when he fell against the table there," she said. "It would be dangerous to move him now. I simply will not consider doing so."

"Then pay somebody you trust to watch him," he said. Why in hell did she insist on being so stubborn? "You've *got* to leave this house and go someplace safe until we catch the man who assaulted you!"

Celia Davies looked over at him. Her pale eyes were red rimmed, and strands of hair straggled down one side of her face. The boy's blood was a rusty streak across her skirt and on her cheek where she'd accidentally wiped some. Her attacker had left a bruise along her chin. He'd kill the man. Honest to God, he'd kill the man.

"You do not need to shout at me, Mr. Greaves," she said with more calm than *he* was feeling. "There is no one I trust to tend to Owen. He saved my life, and now I shall save his. It is plain and simple."

"'Tis no use trying to change her mind, Detective," tutted Addie, sounding resigned to her mistress's pigheadedness.

Nick drew in a deep breath and then released it. "At least tell me what you remember about your assailant, ma'am."

"All right." Mrs. Davies dropped the rag into the bucket and moved to stand. Nick helped her to her feet. "I cannot recall much. It was dark in the kitchen. Far too dark to see."

Her housekeeper moaned. "'Tis my fault. I must have forgotten to lock the door afore I went to bed."

"You did not forget, Miss Ferguson," Nick said. "The door was forced." The lock on the side gate had been broken as well, the hasp yanked off the hinge.

"Perhaps that was the sound that woke me, then," said Mrs. Davies.

"Can you remember anything about the man?" Nick asked. "His height, weight? Any smells that might suggest a line of work? What about his clothes?"

She mulled over his questions. "He was taller than me, given that when he struck my head with his, he hit the crown of my head. It seemed he was stocky, but that might have been the thickness of his clothing. He did not speak, so I cannot tell you what his voice was like, or if he had an accent of any sort. As for aromas . . . the smell of a cigar was distinct. And alcohol. Also, he wore heavy boots. I heard them against the floor."

"He had to be the man who's left the notes and that rat, Detective Greaves," said her housekeeper.

"There will also be a sizable bruise on his forehead from where I struck him, Detective." Mrs. Davies' glance took in both him and Miss Ferguson. "If the bruise does not identify him, I do not know what will. I only wish I'd landed a better blow and knocked him senseless."

"Taylor and I will visit everybody we've come to suspect and see if they have signs of the injury you caused," he said. He pushed away from the table he'd been leaning against and gathered his hat. He pointed it at her. "And, Mrs. Davies, if you still refuse to go to a hotel, then don't even think of leaving this house until I've caught the man."

She didn't blink or cringe. Worse, she didn't agree. He could tell she wasn't going to listen to him. *Damned woman.*

"He attacked me in my own kitchen, Mr. Greaves. Which makes me question if there is much difference between the security of the street and that of my home," she replied soberly. "If I am called to tend to a patient, I shall leave."

He slapped his hat atop his head. "Then, go buy a gun." He turned to the housekeeper, her mouth agape. "Don't let her out of your sight. You got it?"

"I'll do what I can, Mr. Greaves," she said, which didn't sound like much of a promise at all.

"*H*ow is he?"
Celia looked up to see Barbara standing in the doorway to her father's bedchamber, her fringed shawl wrapped around her shoulders.

"I am glad to see you looking better this morning, Barbara." Celia placed Owen's bandaged arm beneath the covers and considered his sleeping face, the long lashes on his closed eyes, the freckles sprayed across his nose and sallow cheeks. His forehead glistened with sweat and his pulse raced, but his condition had greatly improved from last night. After Mr. Greaves had departed, Celia had been able to feed Owen some broth, but the lad had taken only a few sips before falling back asleep.

Celia stood to leave the room. "As for Owen, his wounds have not become inflamed, so that is good news. But he is still very weak."

"So you won't leave him," Barbara said.

"No." She shut the door and considered her cousin. "I sent a note to the Palmers first thing this morning asking if you can stay with them. Elizabeth has already responded that since Emmeline has been feeling better lately, she will send someone to collect you this afternoon."

"Oh. The Palmers." Barbara's grip on the shawl tightened.

"I thought you would be happy to go to them."

"Yes, because I'm sure he wouldn't hurt me . . ." She blanched and looked away.

"*He?* Who do you mean, Barbara?"

"The watcher, of course." She tried to smile. "I'm tired, and I have a headache. I think I'll go back to bed for a while."

She tried to walk off, but Celia grabbed her arm and halted her. "You do not mean the watcher, Barbara. You mean someone else in particular."

"You're hurting me, Cousin. Let go."

"All along, you have known something critical and held back," Celia accused her. "I was nearly killed last night, Barbara. You cannot have wanted that to happen."

"He wouldn't do that!"

"Who, Barbara? Who? You must tell me!"

Barbara was trembling. "I thought I saw him. The night Li Sha died. When he wasn't supposed to be in town . . ." Her voice trailed off.

Days ago, Barbara had mentioned someone being out of town . . . Mr. Palmer. That was whom she'd mentioned. Her cousin had even asked Celia if she knew if he was back after attending to business outside the city.

"You mean Mr. Palmer, don't you? Elizabeth told us he was looking at farm property the night Li Sha died and did not return until Tuesday." But here was Barbara saying quite the opposite. "Did you see him, though?"

"I can't be certain. It was late—we were returning from the society meeting and I was upset because of the ladies. You remember. But I looked out the carriage window and I thought I saw him riding along Kearney. His roan horse is so distinctive. But it couldn't have been him, could it? Mrs. Palmer wouldn't lie about her husband being away from the city. So I've got to be wrong, don't you think?" Barbara asked, wanting Celia's reassurance of his innocence. She could hardly give it. "Besides, he didn't have any reason to hurt Li Sha."

"Not one that we understand." Celia could think of a

possible reason, however, and it involved the baby Li Sha had been carrying. Although Dora had been certain the child was Tom's.

"But the Palmers were good to her," continued Barbara. "Despite what she'd been, some fancy prostitute who got enough gifts to buy herself free. They paid for her funeral, after all."

"If he is so innocent, then why did Mr. Palmer lie about his whereabouts?" Celia asked quietly.

"He didn't lie. I must be wrong about seeing him. I knew I shouldn't have said anything. I knew you'd misunderstand." Her cousin's chin wobbled, and tears started in her eyes. "You've got everything all wrong, Cousin Celia. All wrong," she cried, breaking free of Celia's grip and rushing down the hallway as quickly as she could, seeking the solace of her room.

CHAPTER 16

Taylor intercepted Nick on his way to the station after another visit to Uhlfelder's lodgings.

"Figured out why we haven't seen hide nor hair of Ahearn, sir . . . Mr. Greaves," said Taylor, trotting alongside. "And why he wasn't at the meeting last night. For the past two days he's been locked up in the Santa Cruz County calaboose for brawling. Don't know what he was doing down thataways, but I guess it means he didn't attack Mrs. Davies last night."

"And he couldn't have thrown that rat onto her porch Tuesday night, either," said Nick, halting on the street outside city hall. "He still might've killed Tessie Lange, if she was murdered on Monday."

"Suppose so."

"What about Lange or Palmer?" Nick asked. "Have you had a chance to check on them?"

"Both of them were out earlier when I went looking for them. Lange's neighbor says he's at the undertaker, making arrangements for his daughter's funeral. Palmer's clerk claimed he was in a meeting too important to be interrupted. Consulting with our Mr. Douglass, apparently. But wasn't there something in the paper about Palmer and his wife hobnobbing at a fancy party last night?"

"Which would mean he didn't attack Mrs. Davies, if it's true," said Nick, tipping his hat to a pair of ladies strolling past.

"Guess not, sir," said Taylor. "Did you talk to the saloon-keeper?"

"Uhlfelder was out as well, but his landlady saw him this morning. Not a bump or bruise on him." One suspect down, too many to go.

"I'll go find Lange," said Nick. "What's the latest on Wagner?" They might have released the man last night, but he was still a suspect.

"Wagner wasn't at the customhouse this morning. His boss says he fired him last Friday. Apparently, Wagner was missing a lot of work, and his boss had had enough, but now they're short-handed. The man was hopping mad, needing to inventory some smuggled opium they'd apprehended off a merchant vessel fresh in from China. Something like two hundred or more five-tael boxes." Taylor shook his head over the amount. With a one hundred percent tax on opium, there were plenty of people out to make money by sneaking it in beneath customs' noses. "Wagner wasn't at home, either. But his wife was there, as ready as ever to tell us he was with her last night after the meeting."

"I'll give her credit for being loyal."

"Oh, and Eagan looked fine this morning when I saw him, sir," added Taylor.

Two suspects down. But the mention of Eagan brought the Men's Benevolent Association to mind.

"I keep wondering how many men are in that Monday night association, Taylor, and if the group includes our smuggler." Now, *that* would give Eagan a reason to discourage Nick from investigating Palmer. "I need all their names."

"I'll get them. And how about I poke around down by the wharf again, sir, rather than go back to have a look at Palmer right now? Maybe, with a little financial help, somebody'll know who Roddy really is and where we can find him." Taylor jingled coins in his pocket and grinned.

"Do I want to know how you managed to get extra money to throw around?" If Taylor were caught in a gambling den, he'd be thrown off the force.

"Nope, sir. You definitely don't."

"*Y*ou will tell Mr. Greaves that my cousin believes she saw Mr. Palmer the evening Li Sha was murdered?" Celia asked the detective, who'd introduced himself as Tobias Briggs. She'd left the house despite Mr. Greaves' admonition that she stay put, wanting to deliver her message in person, only to have her plans derailed by his absence from the police station.

"It is critical for Mr. Greaves to know that Mr. Palmer may have lied to him," she said.

Detective Briggs eyed her. She'd seen him, briefly, at Li Sha's funeral and did not care for his manner. At least he hadn't stared too long at the bruises on her face.

"Will do, ma'am."

"Thank you."

She left the station and decided to walk home. People were out and about, enjoying the sunshine after yesterday's rain, and she strolled among them up the road's incline. Walking might help her reason more clearly over Barbara's information.

Did Joseph Palmer's claim he was not in San Francisco the night Li Sha died mean he'd killed her, or was there another explanation? Perhaps he'd been engaged in some other illicit activity that evening.

Celia moved out of the path of a shop boy wheeling a handcart as she continued up the hill. There was also what Madame Philippe had told her yesterday. Tessie had been looking for a suspicious man who worked near water. Mr. Palmer owned a warehouse near the harbor. But if Joseph Palmer was the smuggler who called himself Roddy, Mr. Lange would have been alarmed to spot him at Li Sha's funeral.

Celia paused in front of a pawnshop. The usual items were on display—watches and guns and pieces of jewelry. She squinted. The locket on the topmost shelf looked like the one she had given to Mr. Smith, the locket containing the picture of Patrick so the man could show it while looking for her husband. *Oh dear, Mr. Smith. You did pawn the locket, as I'd feared.*

Suddenly she recalled another locket and realized she'd captured the memory that had been eluding her. She knew what was missing from the pile of items Mr. Greaves had handed over at Li Sha's funeral—a silver locket. Celia had seen the necklace only once or twice, since it was usually hidden beneath the high collar of Li Sha's dress. Li Sha might have sold the necklace in the days before she'd died, but Celia believed she wouldn't. For some reason, the girl had been very attached to it. But what was so significant about the locket that Barbara had chosen to keep secret its absence?

Celia had never learned who'd given the necklace to Li Sha. It had been too costly for Tom Davies to afford. Mr. Lange would not raise unseemly questions by providing his employee with such a handsome present. Mr. Douglass? Mr. Greaves thought he was connected to Li Sha, but Celia's observation of the man only ever indicated that he possessed disdain for the Chinese race.

Would Connor Ahearn have given a lovely necklace to a Chinese prostitute? He'd known Li Sha, but Mr. Greaves had claimed Mr. Ahearn hated her. And Celia could not speak for the mysterious smuggler called Roddy.

Which left one man. Joseph Palmer could certainly afford a fine locket. Barbara must have suspected Mr. Palmer had given it to Li Sha, or perhaps Barbara knew that he had. She might also have reasoned that its absence somehow connected him to the girl's death.

Had Li Sha come to ask Joseph Palmer for money the evening he was supposed to be miles away? Had he wrenched the necklace from her neck, to remove the clue linking him to her, after he'd killed her in a rage? And the afternoon that Celia had encountered him on the street, he'd made certain to comment that Li Sha had sold all of her valuables. Had he done so hoping that if Celia had noticed the necklace was missing, she wouldn't conclude the murderer had taken it off the girl's body?

"And Tom," she muttered, "told me plainly Li Sha had not sold all her gifts."

He'd known, too, that Li Sha had held on to one item, but

Celia had been unable to fit the various comments together. Until now.

Celia gripped the straps of her reticule. Had Joseph Palmer killed Tessie as well? And had he left those terrible warnings for Celia's own family? He might have cleverly disguised his hand-writing and left the notes, but to terrify Barbara so thoroughly and then to attack Celia . . .

But what if he hadn't been after her, but after Barbara? Had he come to their house last night in a failed effort to silence her cousin, who knew too many of his secrets? No wonder Barbara had balked at the idea of going to the Palmers' today. She must have come to fear him at last, and knew she was no longer safe from him.

Celia started to run toward home.

*C*elia hurtled through the front door. She threw down her reticule and sprinted up the staircase, her many layers of skirts tangling around her ankles.

"Ma'am, what is it now?" asked Addie, hastening into the entryway.

"I've remembered," Celia called out, breathing hard from the dash up Kearney.

She rounded the banister and hurried down the hallway, pausing to catch her breath before tapping on the closed door to her cousin's bedchamber.

"Barbara? May I come in? I need to speak to you urgently." There was no reply. "Barbara?" she asked again, and opened the door. The bedchamber was empty.

Celia rushed back out into the hallway and down to the room Owen occupied. He lay deeply asleep and quite alone. She leaned over the balustrade. "Addie! Where is Barbara?"

Addie looked up at her. "She isna upstairs?"

"No. Did the Palmers come to fetch her?"

"No, ma'am. But there was that message that came for her right after you went to the police station," said Addie. "Very secretive about it, she was, and wouldna say who'd sent it. She must've slipped out without my knowing."

"We have to find that message, Addie. It might tell us where she's gone."

Celia returned to her cousin's bedchamber as the housekeeper's footsteps sounded on the staircase.

"Help me look, Addie. I am hoping she left that note here."

Celia rummaged around in drawers and atop her cousin's dressing table, pushing aside brushes and mirrors, a photo of Barbara's father. Celia searched her cousin's wardrobe, shaking out boots and slippers and hunting through pockets. Addie turned down the covers on Barbara's bed and looked beneath the pillows, lifted the hair-and-spring mattress.

With a sigh, Addie let the mattress drop back into place. "Nothing, ma'am."

Barbara had likely taken the note with her.

"Wait, is this it?" Addie bent to retrieve a crumpled scrap of paper from the dustbin. She smoothed out the creases.

Celia took the paper from her.

B—

You and your cousin have nothing to fear from me. Meet me at Union Square at two and I shall explain.

J

Barbara had gone to meet Joseph Palmer, who called the girl by her Christian name. A man with secrets whom Barbara had willingly protected in a naïve display of loyalty and affection.

Addie stared at the note Celia handed her. "What does it mean, ma'am?"

Celia glanced at the watch pinned to her waist—half two. She might already be too late to intercept them.

"I am going to Union Square to look for Barbara, and if she is not there, I will head to the Palmers' house."

"Now you're off, too?"

Celia rushed back downstairs, Addie on her heels.

"I need you to go to the police station and tell Detective Greaves or Officer Taylor—gad, I hope they are there now—that Miss Barbara has gone to meet Mr. Palmer at Union Square. She saw him here in town the night Li Sha died, and I am very concerned. Mr. Greaves will understand. Tell him where I'm going, as well." He would be angry with her, but she could not wait for either his approval or his assistance. "And while you are there, also tell him I have remembered what was missing. A necklace."

"But I dinna understand! Is Miss Barbara in danger?"

"I pray not, but she very well could be." Celia collected her bonnet and shawl. Her silver letter opener winked at her from a parlor side table. She had left it there that morning after Addie had fetched the mail from the post office and Celia had separated private correspondence from the bills. Before events had begun to spin toward an inevitable conclusion, sucking Celia in like a maelstrom.

On a whim, she picked up the letter opener and tucked it into her pocket.

"And what are you thinking of doing with *that?*" Addie's voice was growing strident.

"Nothing, I hope. But since we do not have that gun Mr. Greaves recommended and your cleaver's too cumbersome—"

"Och! What is this world coming to?"

"Dangerous and dark things, Addie. Dangerous and dark," Celia answered. "Now, please hurry."

"Aye, I'll fetch that detective. And pray for your fool head while I'm about it," she said, and stormed off.

Celia closed her fingers around the narrow silver blade in her pocket.

Dangerous and dark things, indeed.

*C*elia leaned through the window of the hack and searched the paths and benches of Union Square. "Circle again," she demanded of the driver.

"It's your dime, ma'am."

Dust scuttled across the square's intersecting paths, and the chime of church bells echoed. A man and woman rose from a bench, and Celia's hopes lifted for a moment until she realized they weren't Barbara and Mr. Palmer.

"I would like to make a stop on Sutter, driver," she said, giving him the address of Joseph Palmer's office. It wasn't far and Barbara might have decided to head there, if he had not shown up for their meeting.

"Yes, ma'am."

Celia settled back against the seat and looked at her watch. Ten minutes had passed since she'd hailed the cab. Ten more precious minutes.

"Hurry, driver!"

*A*fter returning to the station from Lange's, where he'd found no incriminating lump on the man's forehead, Nick had just pulled out his desk chair and dropped onto the seat when Taylor charged through the door.

"You'll never believe what I learned down at the Vallejo Street Wharf, sir."

Nick raised his brows, waiting.

Taylor dragged over a chair and sat. "I was asking 'round about Roddy when I found a warehouse worker who'd been checking on a shipment that arrived the night Li Sha was killed. Well, he *claims* he was checking on a shipment. I'm thinking he was planning on adding to his income by pinching some of the goods and reselling them. Especially as happy as he was to take the coins I was offering—"

"What did he see, Taylor?" Someday his assistant would learn to get to the point.

"He saw a buggy that Monday night. A nice buggy with shiny red wheels, which was what made him notice it. It was nicer than most of the traps and wagons that come around the wharf."

Red wheels. Where had Nick seen a buggy with red wheels before? He sat up straight in his chair. At Li Sha's funeral.

"Even better, I got names of all the members of the Men's Benevolent Association. And you'll never guess who's on it." Taylor's eyes shone with giddy excitement.

"I'm not in the mood to guess, Taylor!"

"Right. Well, Uhlfelder is a member, like he told us. But get this. Wagner's a member, too. How 'bout that!"

Damn. Palmer. Eagan. Douglass. Uhlfelder. Wagner.

Knuckles rapped on the office door, and Mullahey poked his head in. "There's a woman to see you—"

Addie Ferguson shoved past him. "I dinna have time for politeness, Detective Greaves, because you've got to help the mistress. She's gone to Union Square, or maybe the Palmers', to chase after Miss Barbara, who's involved in some foul dealings with that Joseph Palmer."

Nick stood and so did Taylor.

"She says I'm to tell you Miss Barbara has gone to meet with Mr. Palmer, and she's worried because Miss Barbara saw him that evening and that you'd ken what she meant. Do you ken what she meant?" She wrung her hands while her gaze shot from Nick to Taylor. "And Mrs. Davies has gone on this chase all by herself, with nothing more than a letter opener as a weapon! And she said, she said she's remembered what was missing. A necklace."

She hiccuped a sob.

"Now, now, Miss Ferguson," said Taylor, patting her shoulder.

Briggs strolled through the doorway behind them. "There you are, Greaves. Forgot to give you a message from a Mrs. Davies. Something about Mr. Palmer lying to you." Miss Ferguson bawled louder and Briggs looked over. "What's wrong with her?"

"Taylor, take Miss Ferguson back to the house," Nick ordered, exiting the office. The Palmers had a buggy with red wheels. So long as Celia Davies and her cousin stayed out in the open, where there would be other people about, they should be safe. But if they both took it into their fool heads to go to the Palmers' house, there was no telling what might happen.

"Don't you want me to come with you, sir?" Taylor called after him.

"Don't worry. I've got a lot more than a letter opener with me."

*N*ick climbed the office building staircase, taking the stairs two at a time. He'd borrowed a horse and gone to Union Square, but neither Barbara Walford nor Joseph Palmer had been there. The next location to check was Palmer's office.

He strode down the hall. Palmer's clerk stood on guard outside the man's office.

"Mr. Palmer is not in."

"I think I'll just check," Nick said, pushing past him.

"Detective!"

The handle to Palmer's office door turned in Nick's hand, and he barged into the room. The smell of cigar smoke hung in the air, but the room was empty.

Nick turned to Palmer's lackey. "Did a Miss Walford come here?"

"Her again? That woman who was here earlier was looking for her, too."

"Do you mean Mrs. Davies?" Nick asked.

"She didn't leave a name."

"Where is Palmer, then? Where'd he go?" He was wasting valuable time here.

"He didn't say. He got a message and went out. Two messages, actually. But Mr. Palmer didn't tell me his plans. Just left."

Nick bolted out of Palmer's office and ran back down the hallway.

*B*arbara had not been at Mr. Palmer's office, and Celia had directed the cabdriver to take her to the Palmers' house.

The carriage rolled to a halt, gravel crunching. Celia had always admired the Palmers' quiet location on the western edge of Clay Street Hill, with space—such a luxury—between their home and their neighbors'. She hopped down from the carriage and turned to stare at the Palmers' house, with its broad pillared porch and deep eaves. If Barbara had decided to look for Mr. Palmer here, the isolated setting went from being admirable to being sinister.

"Please wait for me," she told the driver, who sat hunched on his seat. She had no idea where else to search, though, if Barbara wasn't here.

"You're costin' me fares, lady."

"I shall pay you for your time."

"Expectin' you will." He paused to pucker his lips and spit an arc of tobacco juice onto the ground near her feet. "'Cause it's a long walk back from here."

Celia passed through the gate. There didn't appear to be anyone about, and that included Barbara. The lace curtains at the parlor window were drawn open and the room looked empty.

Celia climbed the front steps and knocked on the door. "Mr. Palmer?" she called out, knocking again. "Barbara?"

There was no answer.

The cabdriver perked his brows when he saw her descend the porch steps.

"A few more minutes," she shouted, hurrying over the flagstone path that flanked the side of the house.

No one was out back, either, not even the Palmers' maid, Rose. Celia looked up at the house. Perhaps Barbara hadn't come here after all.

Her gaze settled on the kitchen door and she noticed it had been propped open. "How odd."

Inside, might she find conclusive evidence linking Joseph

Palmer to Li Sha's death? Or might she find Barbara, unconscious or worse?

I'm sure he wouldn't hurt me. Celia hoped her cousin was right.

Celia drew in a breath. She'd need an explanation for what she was doing in the house. If she'd known she was going to be snooping around inside, she could have brought the umbrella Elizabeth had left in Celia's vestibule stand and claim she'd wished to return it. Perhaps she should say she'd mislaid one of her tortoiseshell hair combs at the luncheon Elizabeth had hosted a few weeks ago. And she could claim that, when no one responded to her knocking, she'd decided to search for it on her own. The next reasonable question would be why she had waited so long to recover the hair comb. Perhaps no one would ask.

With a hasty glance around and seeing nothing more than a pair of finches fluttering among the shrubs and a pony cart wheeling by on a distant road, Celia sped across the veranda and through the door before she could change her mind.

"Hullo? Is anyone at home?" She rested a hand on her reticule and felt the comforting shape of the letter opener, transferred from her pocket, where it had managed to jab her thigh despite her crinoline. "Hullo? Barbara? Rose? Mr. Palmer? Anyone?" She listened for a response and got none.

Celia hastened through the kitchen and up the servants' stairs to the main bedchambers. Hastily, she opened and shut doors to rooms rich with Brussels carpets, rosewood furnishings, and silk curtains.

"Barbara?" she called out.

The door to the largest bedchamber stood open. Celia stepped through. It had to be Elizabeth and Joseph's room, large and airy, with a lovely view toward the western hills. Celia darted from chest to wardrobe to bedside tables. Every door and drawer was locked.

"I guess you don't trust Rose, Elizabeth, do you?"

Celia retreated to the ground floor via the main staircase. She quickly searched the parlor, library, and dining room and was relieved when she didn't stumble over Barbara's inert body.

She hurried back to Mr. Palmer's library, its blinds open to let in the light, the room filled with bookshelves and leather chairs, a mahogany desk and walnut tables. It smelled of lemon wax and cigar smoke. No weapons hung on the walls, but then the Southerners had been forced to give up their weapons after the war. She shouldn't expect to find a bayonet dangling from a silk cord or stashed behind the cushions.

A flash of color outside the window caught Celia's eye. Rose was leaning against the property's far fence, chatting with a neighbor's servant, which explained why Celia hadn't noticed her. Rose was standing perfectly out of sight from both the backyard and the front. At some point, though, she would return to her duties. And find Celia in the house.

Celia scanned the room. Mr. Palmer was just as orderly as his wife, not a pen out of place, every piece of paper neatly stacked. She rattled the desk drawers. They were locked, too, meaning she wasn't going to find clumsily penned love notes from Li Sha or a bill of sale for the silver locket.

She crossed the floral Royal Wilton carpet and thumbed through the books on the shelves. People did hide confidential papers inside books.

Celia heard a creak and halted, holding her breath, but the sound wasn't repeated.

Moving more hastily now, she entered the parlor to continue her search. Expensive textiles covered tables and upholstered chairs. Freshly cut salmon-colored peonies spilled from ceramic vases. The Palmers had done well in this world, which begged the question why Joseph Palmer would ever endanger that success by murdering a pregnant Chinese woman. Even if he were never prosecuted for the crime, the gossip would irrevocably damage his reputation.

Still, if Li Sha had threatened to reveal their relationship if he did not give her money, he might have become angry enough to kill her. Perhaps they'd arranged to meet that Monday, Joseph Palmer possibly anticipating a resumption of their liaison. Only to discover Li Sha had bribery in mind.

"Was that what happened?" she murmured.

"What did you say, Celia?"

Celia spun around.

"Gad, Elizabeth, you startled me!" she squeaked, her voice pitched as high as if she'd been pinched by corset strings. "Emmeline," she added, as the girl stepped from behind her mother. "Good afternoon. You are both looking well."

Elizabeth Palmer stood in the doorway to the parlor, dressed for afternoon visits, her daughter gaping at her side. In truth, Emmeline did not look well at all but had turned particularly ashen.

"What are you doing in our house?" Elizabeth asked. "And whatever happened to your face?"

Celia touched the bruises along her chin. "I fell last night. I am so clumsy."

Just then, Barbara entered the room. Alive and well. *Thank heavens.* "Why, Barbara, there you are! I was worried when I discovered you'd left the house without telling anyone."

"We were on our way home from our daily visits," explained Elizabeth, looking put out, "when we spotted your cousin seated alone on a bench in Union Square. I was confused to see her there, wasn't I, Emmeline? I thought she was coming this afternoon to stay with us."

"I explained that I'd needed some air and left the house. I'm sorry I didn't tell you, Cousin Celia," said Barbara, her voice unsteady. "Mrs. Palmer suggested that I come with them right then and send you a note asking Addie to have my bags sent. I couldn't refuse."

"Ah yes," said Celia, calling forth a smile. "So sensible, Elizabeth."

"I insist you tell me why you're here, prowling through my home, Celia," she said.

"I am quite embarrassed to say that I've misplaced a hair comb. I thought it might have fallen out when I was here for your luncheon the other week. Do you recall?"

"Of course I remember my luncheon."

"It was not until this morning that I remembered where it might be," said Celia, warming to her story. "So I came to the house, found the rear door open, and decided to search for it. I am sorry for the intrusion, of course."

"Emmeline, have you seen a hair comb anywhere?"

Her daughter, who appeared struck dumb, shook her head.

"I didn't expect so," said Elizabeth.

"I was so certain it had fallen out here," Celia replied, glancing around the room.

"And I am certain Rose hasn't found one," insisted Elizabeth. "She is very thorough."

And then suddenly there was that other thought, the one

that had been so elusive until that moment. "How long have you had Rose?"

"Celia, I don't see what this has to do with anything," said Elizabeth. "I'm sure your cousin would like to get settled into her room. She'd probably appreciate that you return home immediately and send her things here. Wouldn't you, Barbara?"

"Why, yes, Mrs. Palmer."

"You hired Rose only last week, didn't you?" said Celia. "Tuesday or Wednesday, correct? Which means . . ." Rose was not in the house the night Li Sha died. The Palmers had been between servants that evening, and if Li Sha had come to the house, only the Palmers would know.

Celia felt her breath whistle between her teeth and wondered when the parlor had turned so very icy. "Li Sha did come here to ask for money that evening, didn't she? Which is why Mr. Greaves has been unable to find whom she approached. Because she came *here* and asked *you.*"

"Mama, she knows," said Emmeline.

"Hush, Emmeline," hissed Elizabeth. "She's asked this before, and I will give her the same response. My answer remains no, Celia. Li Sha did not come here that evening."

"But I think she did," said Celia. "She came here wearing the silver locket, the one your husband had given to her as a present, and she asked for money."

"My husband would *never* give that woman a gift."

"But he *was* in San Francisco the night she died, wasn't he, Barbara? Because you saw him here." Her cousin nodded mutely. "Why, though, did he lie and tell everyone he was elsewhere? Unless he feared the police would start to ask too many questions about that night."

"He did not lie," Elizabeth insisted, but her protests were growing more feeble.

Celia continued, "I'd begun to believe that Li Sha had met him in the city somewhere, but she could have come here. And, of course, neither of you would admit that." Celia had no proof of her hypothesis. Only the agitated look in Emmeline's eyes, the startled stare of a deer before the gun is fired, told her she had guessed right. "She would get money in exchange for not telling the world the baby she carried was his. The locket was proof of his affection. Rather embarrassing, I would say."

"And my husband *never* got some prostitute with child!" A flush covered Elizabeth's cheeks. "I demand you leave. Now! And take your cousin with you!"

Rose scurried into the room from the direction of the kitchen. "Mrs. Palmer, whatever is the matter in here?"

"The necklace," said Barbara. "Do you think Li Sha's necklace is here someplace, Cousin? I thought he must have thrown it away."

"Mama!" Emmeline pressed her gloved hands to her face, trembling so hard her knees buckled. Her mother caught her before she collapsed to the floor. Celia rushed over to help.

Elizabeth pushed Celia away. "We don't need your assistance," she said, leading Emmeline to the settee beneath the front window. She fanned her daughter with her hand. "Rose, please fetch the police. This woman is deranged and is upsetting my daughter. And she has trespassed in our house."

But Rose didn't move. She was fumbling through the pockets of her plain russet dress.

Barbara continued, "I told Joseph . . . Mr. Palmer . . . I wouldn't say anything about the necklace. At the funeral." Emmeline let out a moan. "I let him know that I wouldn't tell anybody he'd given it to Li Sha, or that I thought he'd later taken the necklace from her, to keep the gift a secret. But when I said that, he looked so confused . . ."

"Are you meanin' this necklace?" asked Rose, retrieving what she had been searching for in her pockets. She pulled out a silver chain and locket. "I found it beneath the stove this mornin'."

The moment froze like a photographic portrait captured on albumen paper: the necklace suspended from the maid's fingers, glinting gold; Emmeline, her hand covering her mouth, staring at the locket as though it might lunge and bite; Elizabeth's face a livid shade of red; Barbara's eyes wide.

"It's Li Sha's," said Barbara, breaking the spell. "The one he gave her!"

Celia stared in horror at Elizabeth and Emmeline as full realization dawned. It all made terrible sense. She had suspected the wrong Palmer.

CHAPTER 17

"She does know, Mama!" Emmeline cried out.

"Emmeline, calm yourself," snapped Elizabeth.

Emmeline struggled up from the settee and crossed the room to grab Celia's arm. "It was an accident. Li Sha came here looking for Papa. She wanted money, just like you said, and Mama got angry. So very angry."

"Emmeline, you don't know what you're talking about." Elizabeth, too, rose from the settee. "You're confused. The laudanum you take makes you imagine things. And you were ill that evening—"

"I didn't imagine what happened, Mama. How can you say that?"

Celia focused on Emmeline, who was trembling and struggling to breathe. "What happened that night, Emmeline?"

The girl tightened her grip on Celia's forearm, cutting off her circulation. "Mama didn't mean to hurt Li Sha with Papa's sword bayonet from the war. It just happened."

"Emmeline, come sit down and rest." Elizabeth spoke sharply and came to her daughter's side. "You'll have another of your attacks if you do not calm down. And stop telling Mrs. Davies your fancies."

"But they're not fancies!" she shouted, causing Rose, who'd been watching in shocked silence, to gasp. "I'll confess to killing her, Mama. You know I didn't mean to, but I can say I did."

"Em, no," said Barbara, her voice breaking.

"You did not kill Li Sha, Emmeline dearest," said Elizabeth, slowly. She stroked her daughter's cheek with the back of her fingers. "You're talking nonsense."

"But, Mama, it *is* my fault! I can make the police understand it was an accident," she said, wheezing. "We should've told them right away."

"Emmeline, honestly!" Elizabeth dragged her daughter away from Celia, the girl releasing her grasp only at the last second, jerking Celia's arm. Celia's fingers prickled with the sudden return of blood. "You know the laudanum makes you have strange dreams sometimes. That's what you're remembering."

Behind the two Palmer women, Barbara had started to inch toward the hallway leading to the front door.

"She was here, Mama," exclaimed Emmeline, her cheeks spotted with color. "You have to say she was. Please. She'd come to see Papa, but she found us instead. Because we didn't go to the society meeting that night."

The expression on Elizabeth's face changed, her eyes taking on a look of calculation. Assessing, Celia supposed, how readily

Celia would accept what Elizabeth was about to say. More lies. Who *hadn't* been fabricating falsehoods since Li Sha's death?

"It's true she came here, Celia," Elizabeth said, her gaze unwavering. "I admit that. She'd come to ask for money—we'd been generous to her before and since, as you know—but I refused. Neither of us hurt the girl, and she was very much alive when she left this house."

"But that's not what happened at all. Tell the truth," pleaded Emmeline, clinging to her mother. "Li Sha was going to tell everybody that Papa went to the Barbary Coast every Monday night to visit Chinese prostitutes and that he was the father of her child!"

"Holy saints!" murmured Rose.

Hatred flashed across Elizabeth's face. "It was an utter lie."

Dora had insisted that Li Sha had been true to Tom. Celia still wanted to believe Dora, and she wanted to believe in Li Sha. But the girl had made a dangerous claim in order to persuade Elizabeth to give her money, and she had paid a terrible price.

"I was upset by the gossip such talk would cause," said Elizabeth. "Do you understand what it's like to scratch a living from a parched farm, Celia? I suspect you don't. But that is what I came from."

At the parlor doorway, Barbara bumped into the large vase Elizabeth used to hold gentlemen's canes and umbrellas. Elizabeth, engrossed in her account, apparently did not hear the tiny clink of porcelain against the oak floor.

"I dragged myself up from poverty," Elizabeth continued. "I escaped my family, who are still digging in the dirt back in Missouri like there's gold in the mud instead of sorrow. I found a husband who would make me rich and provide a comfortable, respectable life. Who'd take me away from that hell. Away from my father." Elizabeth's expression hardened. "I didn't want Li Sha to ruin the life we have here. I was terrified of gossip and tried to get her to leave before the neighbors spotted her. You understand, don't you, Celia?"

Should she agree? Should she try to placate her? Celia glanced over the woman's shoulder and noticed Barbara moving deeper into the entry hall as unobtrusively as she could. Where was Mr. Greaves? Had Addie failed to find him?

Off to Celia's right, Rose muttered a string of prayers.

"Rose, please hush. You're giving me a headache," said Elizabeth, and with a snivel the maid fell quiet.

"But Li Sha didn't leave," Emmeline said, stepping between her mother and Celia. "I have to tell her everything, Mama. I can't bear the guilt anymore."

"Stop, Emmeline," warned Elizabeth.

"Mama only wanted to scare her. I saw it all," Emmeline continued, undeterred by her mother's efforts to silence her. She pressed a hand to her chest as if to help her lungs move air. "I was upstairs, trying to sleep," she said slowly, "but I heard them shouting at each other in the kitchen, and I came downstairs to see what was going on. Mama had the bayonet in her hand, and she swung it at Li Sha. She didn't hit her with it, and Li Sha didn't look scared at all, which made Mama angrier."

Emmeline's brow furrowed. "And then I saw that Li Sha was wearing the necklace. *That* one."

She pointed at Rose. The maid goggled at the necklace, forgotten in her grip.

"The necklace was meant to be mine, Mrs. Davies," Emmeline said. She'd turned an alarming shade of red as her breath hissed through her lips. "Papa promised it to me. I saw it one afternoon in the jewelry shop, and he told me I could have it. But he never gave it to me. Instead he gave it to *her*."

Elizabeth squeezed her eyes shut while her daughter spoke.

Emmeline's gaze was glassy, distant. "I ripped it off her neck, breaking the chain. I must have scratched her, because she hollered like a cat and then tried to grab it out of my hands. She was quick, and she managed to slap me. And then Mama . . ." She looked back at her mother, who had turned her face aside. Tears fell down Elizabeth's cheeks. "And then Mama slashed at her. She was only trying to defend me. Weren't you, Mama, weren't you?"

"Emmeline," Elizabeth sobbed.

"It was awful. There was blood everywhere, splattered on the floor, on the table, on the stove. Red, bright red, like the banners in Chinatown."

Rose screeched, dropped the necklace, and crumpled to the floor, moaning between bouts of tears. The rest of them were transfixed like insects trapped in tar. Celia had stopped watching Barbara's progress, and her cousin had disappeared from view. Had the front door opened? She hadn't heard.

"And Mama . . . Mama cut her again. I tried to stop her. I dropped the necklace and pushed Li Sha out of her reach," said Emmeline, her eyes widening, her breath coming in asthmatic gulps. "And then Li Sha tripped, I don't know why, and tumbled backward. She must have hit her head on the edge of the stove, because after she fell to the floor, she didn't move. There was blood coming from her nose and everywhere and she stopped breathing and then she died! It was awful!"

A blow to the head in the right location could be quickly fatal, thought Celia, causing the brain to swell.

"That prostitute attacked my daughter," said Elizabeth, her voice so much smaller than usual, tight and choked.

"I never thought somebody could die so easily," said Emmeline, shuddering. "Mama panicked and told me to fetch an old blanket from the attic. I brought it down and we wrapped her in it. Mama brought out the buggy, and I helped her put Li Sha in the back. It was so hard, she was heavier than I could carry, and the rain made everything slippery. Then we drove her into the city."

She paused. Celia wondered if Emmeline had felt forced to help her mother. The girl, always frail and quiet, had likely never thought to refuse Elizabeth's demands.

"We didn't know where to take her," Emmeline said. "But eventually we found a quiet wharf and dragged her out of the buggy, unwrapped her, and rolled her into the bay. I was so certain somebody would see us and stop us, but nobody did. We came home and burned the blanket and cleaned the kitchen as best as we could before Rose arrived for her first day of work the next morning."

"All that cleanin'," murmured Rose, apparently aghast to have helped scrub away the evidence of a crime.

Emmeline stared at the necklace where Rose had dropped it. "I searched for the necklace whenever Rose wasn't in the kitchen, but I couldn't find it. It must have gotten kicked beneath the stove deeper than I could see. I tried to explain to Papa what had happened, but he didn't want to hear. He said to let Tom take the blame and that I wasn't to speak about that night ever again."

Except for the ticking of the clock on the mantel and Emmeline's labored breathing, silence had descended on the room. Rose had ceased bawling and held a handkerchief to her face, her eyes as wide as a pair of English crown pieces.

Mr. Greaves had asserted that jealousy could be a violent emotion. But it had not been Tom's jealousy or Tessie Lange's jealousy that had snuffed out Li Sha's life. It had been Elizabeth Palmer's seething hatred.

"You were so happy to cast the blame on my brother-in-law and let him hang for what you'd done," Celia said to her. "And there were those times when you suggested we leave town. Why, Elizabeth? Were you afraid that Li Sha had told me about her relationship with your husband? Or did you come to think that Barbara, who'd spent so much time in this house, had to know about it? Were you afraid she or I would see that *you* had the greatest motive to kill Li Sha? Is that why you dressed up like a man and left those warnings at our house?"

But it hadn't been Elizabeth or a frail Emmeline who'd attacked her in the kitchen the other night. Was Joseph Palmer still somehow involved, perhaps helping to hide their crime?

And where *was* Mr. Greaves?

"We had *nothing* to do with any warnings, Celia," insisted Elizabeth.

"What about Tessie?" Celia asked, her heart knocking in her chest. "Did she know about Joseph and Li Sha, and need to be silenced as well?"

Emmeline turned to her mother, a look of alarm on her face. "Mama, is that what happened?"

"Of course not!" Elizabeth glanced around. "Where is your cousin, Celia? Where has she gone? To fetch the police?"

Out in the hallway, Barbara yelped and flung open the front door.

"No! You can't leave!" shouted Elizabeth as Celia sprinted for the door. Barbara had stumbled over the doorstep and fallen forward onto the porch.

Celia helped her cousin to her feet.

"Stop!" Elizabeth held a heavy iron poker from the parlor fireplace. She swung it wildly, the pointed end swishing past Celia's shoulder. The woman struggled with its unwieldy weight, and it clanged against the floor.

"Elizabeth!" Celia shouted, her arm lifted to shield Barbara, who had fallen again and was on her knees in the doorway. "Put it down! We can get the police to understand it was an accident!"

"Mama, don't hurt them, too," cried Emmeline, pulling on her mother's arm.

Celia groped through her reticule for the letter opener and pulled it out. It made a paltry weapon, but she pointed it at Elizabeth anyway.

"Put down the poker, Elizabeth," said Celia with as much calm as she could muster. "Please put it down."

The woman's eyes were wild. She was no longer the beautiful and poised woman in sumptuous attire, with the box at Maguire's Opera House and the regard of San Francisco society. She was that young woman who'd been desperate to escape a Missouri farm.

"You don't want to hurt them, Mama," said Emmeline.

She moved forward just as her mother hefted the poker and swung as hard as she could. Celia turned aside, waiting for the blow, and heard Emmeline scream as the poker struck her.

"Emmeline!" shouted Mrs. Palmer, the poker falling from her grip. Barbara dragged it out of the woman's reach. Celia hurried to Emmeline, who lay crumpled against the entryway wall, moaning and clutching her arm. Celia helped her into a sitting position.

"Emmeline! I didn't mean . . ." Elizabeth Palmer collapsed to the ground, her skirts pooling around her, her voice breaking on sobs. "I didn't mean . . ."

"Mama," Emmeline said between clenched teeth, her skin pasty.

"Rose," Celia called to the maid, who remained motionless in the parlor, "bring lengths of cloth so I can immobilize Miss Emmeline's arm."

Rose stood and hurried off.

Elizabeth extended a hand to caress the hem of Emmeline's skirt. "I will take all the blame, dearest. You mustn't suffer."

Discomfort creased the skin around Emmeline's mouth as she looked over at her mother. "We should've given her the money, Mama. And then she would've gone away, and we could've continued on like always."

"A girl like that would never have left us alone, Emmeline. It never would've ended, don't you see? She would've ruined us."

"We're ruined anyway," said Emmeline.

Barbara, who continued to hold on to the poker, had gotten to her feet and was staring out the open front door. "Detective Greaves!"

"Do not move, Emmeline." Celia clambered to her feet and hurried to her cousin's side in time to see Nicholas Greaves vault over the picket fence surrounding the Palmers' house.

"There was no need for that, Mr. Greaves," she said with a relieved smile. "We are unharmed."

He bounded onto the front porch, took hold of her arms, and ran his hands down them as if he did not believe her claim. "Is Palmer here?"

"No." Celia looked back toward Elizabeth, who was hunched over her daughter. Emmeline refused to meet her mother's gaze. "I was mistaken that he might have killed Li Sha. She died in this house, Mr. Greaves. Elizabeth and Emmeline are responsible."

"Here, ma'am, here!" shouted Rose, scurrying into the entry hall with strips of cloth.

"I have to tend to Emmeline. I can explain later," said Celia, returning to the girl.

Nicholas Greaves entered the house, and Elizabeth started sobbing.

"It was an accident," she whimpered. "She tried to hurt Emmeline. An accident . . ."

"If it was an accident, Mrs. Palmer, why'd you try to hide the crime? Was that your husband's idea?" he asked. "I'd like to talk to him. Where is he?"

"He's not been here all mornin', sir," said Rose. "He's probably at the company warehouse down by the Vallejo Street pier. 'Cause of that man this mornin'. He came by looking for Mr. Palmer while Mrs. Palmer and Miss Emmeline were out visitin'. A fright he was, all banged up around the head."

Celia glanced up. "Mr. Greaves!" She shivered, the feel of her assailant's hand on her mouth fresh in her mind, the bruises beneath her chin a painful memento.

"What did he want?" he asked Rose.

"He wanted me to tell Mr. Palmer to meet him at the warehouse. I told him Mr. Palmer was probably at his office, and I was pure happy to shut the door on his ugly face!"

"Go to the police station at Jones and Pacific and have them telegraph the central police office," Nick ordered Rose. "I need Officer Mullahey here, and Officer Taylor at the Vallejo Street pier. Can you remember those names?"

"Aye," she said, and dashed through the front door and down the steps.

"Don't anybody else leave, especially you, Mrs. Palmer. Mrs. Davies, I'll need you to tell Mullahey everything once he arrives. I'm headed to the Vallejo pier." He followed the maid out the door.

"Nick!" called Celia. He looked back over his shoulder. "Be careful."

He nodded and was gone.

By Nick's estimation, Palmer had been down at the warehouse for at least an hour. Nick didn't know the nature of his business with the man who'd attacked Celia Davies, but he'd wager any sum that the man would turn out to be one of Palmer's friends from the Men's Benevolent Association.

Two ships were docked along the pier, a paddle-wheel steamer and a three-masted schooner with a load of timber. The rattle of logs being rolled over to the ship's crane echoed off the water, and men aboard ship shouted orders to the longshoremen below. It was a busier day than it had been on the morning Li Sha's body had been found in the bay, her clothing tangled on a piling. The type of busy day that meant nobody would pay much attention to a meeting between two men, at least one of whom was often seen down at the Vallejo Street Wharf, checking on his warehouse.

Nick hopped down from the horse he'd borrowed and tethered it to the nearest post.

"Which of these warehouses belongs to Palmer and Company?" he asked the wharf toll collector, who was seated inside the small tollhouse at the pier's entrance.

The man looked up from his books. "Who wants to know?"

Nick showed his police credentials.

"That one over there." He pointed to a brick building half a block away.

Four arched openings filled one side of the two-story building, their massive doors closed.

"Have you seen Mr. Joseph Palmer down here with another man?" Nick asked the toll collector.

He scowled and gestured at the books and papers piled up on his narrow desk. "Do I look like I've got time to be noticing who's coming and going every second?"

Nick headed for the warehouse. He tested several doors before finding one that was unlocked. Slowly, he pushed it open and edged his way inside.

Sunlight streamed through the tall windows, and the space smelled of sawn lumber. Rows and rows of tall shelves, some piled with timber, filled half the main room. The other half was empty except for several towering pallets of bricks. The place looked and sounded deserted. But somebody's passage had disturbed the film of dust on the wood floor, and not that long ago, if Nick was any judge.

Unholstering his gun, Nick moved forward, mindful of where he planted each foot to avoid making a floorboard creak.

There was a commotion above his head, and he spun around, gun raised. It was only a bird flapping in the rafters. Getting his breathing back under control, Nick resumed his slow progress across the space, scanning every inch for movement.

A section of the main floor had been divided by two walls that reached the ceiling, forming a separate room. As he crept toward it, Nick heard voices coming from the interior. A door stood ajar, and Nick padded over, stopping just out of sight of the men inside.

"If you leave town now, the police will suspect you. Calm down."

That was Palmer, his Southern drawl thick and sounding strained.

"But I got to get outta town. That kid, he saw me." The voice was familiar, but Nick couldn't place it. "And I don't think he's dead."

"He saw you doing what?" asked Palmer.

"Doesn't matter. I just gotta get out of here and you've gotta help me."

"I do not 'gotta' help you. You are a risk to our operation. I am ending our association."

Somebody took a step. Nick looked hastily around. The nearest place to hide was a hundred feet away; they'd find him if they came out here.

"No, you can't go!" the unidentified man yelled. Heavy booted feet stomped across the floor. "I'll tell the cops you killed Li Sha. I saw you in town that night. Saw you at the parlor house. Bet you didn't know."

A deadly silence followed the declaration.

"Scared, Palmer? As scared as when that detective came snooping? Afraid he'd figure out what we were doing if he poked around enough?" He grunted. "I would've taken care of him, too, if he didn't have such a hard head."

Well, well, thought Nick. The man who'd attacked him.

"I could just as easily accuse you of killing Li Sha. You assaulted her last summer when she tried to turn you out of the parlor house. Maybe you decided to finally get revenge for the insult." Palmer was sounding confident. A bit too confident, in Nick's opinion.

"You're gonna lay the blame on me after all I've done to keep your part in our operation quiet? You're a louse, Palmer."

"I suppose you set fire to Uhlfelder's saloon." Palmer exhaled loudly. "That was not necessary. He would never have drawn attention to us, because then the police would begin looking at him and all that low-cost liquor he's been dispensing."

"Anybody ever tell you you're almighty trusting? And I'm just plumb sick of Uhlfelder. Never did cotton to him."

"And those notes . . . what was that all about?" asked Palmer. "Did you think Mrs. Davies knew about the smuggling? How ridiculous."

"She saw me with Lange!" the other man shouted. "And she was with that cop last night, looking for me. Apparently, the notes weren't enough to get her to mind her own business. I thought the rat would work, but it didn't, either." He cursed. "If only that kid hadn't shown up."

"What did you do?" asked Palmer, seeming concerned for the first time.

"Don't worry. She's not dead, either." He sounded regretful.

Palmer exhaled loudly again, the noise turning into a groan. "Lange's daughter. You killed her, didn't you?"

"She'd figured out that we'd been selling opium on the cheap to her pa. Damnation, Palmer, didn't you realize that would happen?"

Nick released a breath. Opium and cut-price liquor. And Palmer, adding to his wealth.

"But to kill her—"

"She wanted me to let Lange alone. I don't know how she found me. She must've followed me," the other man said. "She thought she could pay me off, and I'd be happy to leave her pa alone!" He scoffed. "And all she had on her was a hundred dollars. Stupid woman. It's her own fault she's dead."

"So, what now, Wagner?" asked Palmer. "If I don't help you evade the authorities, am I next?"

Wagner. Of course. No wonder he'd been able to afford his fine black suit.

"Hey, there's an idea!" Wagner said, chuckling.

Nick heard the thud of a fist connecting with flesh, followed by a grunt and the sound of scuffling. Gun extended, Nick crept forward and peered around the doorframe. Palmer had pulled a pistol and Wagner was trying to pry it out of Palmer's hand.

"Stop!" Nick fired a bullet into the ceiling, the shot's echo deafening in the small office.

Palmer jumped back and Wagner wrenched Palmer's revolver out of his hand. He shot at Nick, the bullet going wide, and Nick leaped behind a desk. His shoulder burned and he looked down. The bullet hadn't gone wide enough.

Wagner fired at the desk, bullets ricocheting and splinters of wood flying over Nick's head. He lurched to his knees and shot at the man's feet from beneath the desk, missing but making him pause.

"Damn it, Wagner!" yelled Palmer. "You're going to get us both killed!"

A piece of furniture fell with a bang, skidding ledgers across the floor.

There was another shot and then a click as the cylinder of Palmer's pistol reached an empty chamber. Here was his chance. Nick jumped up from behind the desk and leveled his gun at Wagner, whose spent weapon dangled from his hand. The man's left eye, discolored black-and-blue, was almost swollen shut from the clout Mrs. Davies had landed.

Nick cocked the hammer and aimed the Colt at the man's chest, thinking of Tessie Lange, killed because she'd tried to save her father, and of Owen Cassidy, who might still die from his wounds. Thinking of the bruises on Celia's chin and neck. Wagner stared defiantly back at him. Nick had never shot a man in cold blood.

"Thank God you've come, Detective Greaves." Palmer stepped out from behind the bookcase he'd knocked over, his hands raised at his shoulders. "That man is a violent criminal. I'll tell you everything I know about his illegal dealings."

"Oh, shut up, Palmer," said Nick, carefully easing the hammer back into place. He wouldn't shoot now and make it an easy death for Wagner. Better the misery of the hangman's noose.

"You aren't gonna shoot, Detective?" Wagner snickered.

"Guess it's your lucky day." Nick heard the sound of running feet reverberate through the warehouse, and he lowered his gun. "But I won't speak for my men. They might not be so generous."

"You should have immediately told Detective Greaves that you'd seen Mr. Palmer that evening, Barbara," Celia said to her cousin, who was standing quietly at her side as they watched Officer Mullahey help Elizabeth climb onto the police wagon. All around, neighbors were lined up against their fences, hoarding observations to be distributed as gossip later.

"I wanted to believe it wasn't him," Barbara responded. "I'd convinced myself I'd been mistaken. And even when that girl in Chinatown told me a man had been looking for Li Sha just before she'd died, I managed to tell myself she didn't mean Mr. Palmer, and even if she did, he'd have a good explanation."

"The man she mentioned wasn't him, Barbara. It was a man named Connor Ahearn."

"Oh," said Barbara.

"Which does not mean it was perfectly fine for you to lie to me about what the prostitute said." Celia wondered how long it would be before she trusted her cousin again.

"I see that now," said Barbara. "But when we got that first warning note, I was certain she'd meant Mr. Palmer. I was afraid he'd left us the note because he thought I'd reveal what I knew about him and Li Sha and the necklace. I was so confused about what to do."

"What you should have done was tell me the truth. I would have helped."

Barbara lifted her chin. "But he *didn't* kill Li Sha, Cousin. I was right not to believe he could."

"Barbara, please do not claim any of your deception was justified."

"I'm sorry," she mumbled. Celia sighed and wrapped an arm around her cousin's shoulders.

At the police wagon, Officer Mullahey said a few words to Emmeline, who looked over at Celia and Barbara before climbing up after her mother. Elizabeth reached for her daughter, but Emmeline shook off her mother's hand and sat as far from Elizabeth as possible. Officer Mullahey took a seat up front, alongside the policeman who was driving.

"For how long were you aware of the relationship that had once existed between Mr. Palmer and Li Sha?" Celia asked Barbara as the wagon drove away.

"Do we have to talk about this now?" she asked, stepping out from beneath Celia's protective clasp. "I'm tired."

"It is time for there to be candor between us, Barbara."

Her cousin bit her lower lip. "Li Sha told me about him and his gifts. I think it was right before last Christmas. She trusted me," Barbara replied, making Li Sha's faith sound misplaced. "Li Sha had a lock of hair from her dead sister, did you know?"

"I didn't."

"They came to San Francisco together, but her sister passed away within a month of their arrival. Mr. Palmer found out about the lock of hair and how much Li Sha treasured it. He bought that necklace for her—probably two or three years ago, now—just so she'd have a beautiful place to store her sister's hair. He's kind like that."

Barbara's face was shining; Celia realized it might be some time before her cousin saw Joseph Palmer for the man he really was.

"She'd sold all of her jewelry to pay off her debt to the brothel owner," Barbara continued, "except for that locket.

She'd never sell it. So when Mr. Greaves didn't return it with her other belongings, I wondered if the murderer had taken it."

"And that murderer *could* have been Mr. Palmer, Barbara," said Celia, firmly. "But you decided to protect him anyway. You went too far."

"I didn't want to lose him." Tears swam in Barbara's eyes. "He's the only man who's been kind to me, Cousin Celia, besides Papa."

"He could *never* have replaced your father, Barbara, if that's what you were hoping from him." No one could replace Lloyd Walford, thought Celia, and that apparently included her. "You should have realized that the moment you learned he'd been lying."

Chastened, Barbara dropped her gaze and prodded at the gravel walkway with her toe.

Celia studied her cousin. "I was terrified when I found that note from Mr. Palmer in your room, Barbara. I thought it meant he'd lured you to a meeting in hopes of hurting you."

"He never showed up. And then Elizabeth saw me and I had to go with her, since I couldn't explain what I was really doing in Union Square. He wouldn't have hurt me, though. I know he wouldn't have," she declared, and turned away.

Rose, who'd been standing near the gate, walked over to them. "What should I do now, ma'am?"

"We should wait until Detective Greaves returns with news of Mr. Palmer to decide that, Rose," Celia answered, worried by the delay in his arrival. "It should not be long."

"Aye, ma'am," Rose replied. "But I'll not be stayin' in that house another night. Not where there's been a murder!"

The maid turned briskly on her heel and strode back to the house.

Celia squinted up the road and spotted a swirl of dust coming off a horse's hooves. She shielded her eyes with her hand. It was him. She ran to the gate. His face was grim, and there was blood on his sleeve.

"What happened?" she asked as he reined in his mount.

"Is Mr. Palmer okay?" asked Barbara, hurrying over to join Celia.

"Palmer's fine, Miss Walford." Mr. Greaves stared down at Celia from the saddle. "I found the man who attacked you, Mrs. Davies. Wagner. But I'm sorry to say I didn't kill him."

"I know you, Mr. Greaves. You are too good a man to take justice into your own hands."

He pressed a hand to his wound and let a grin lift a corner of his mouth. "For him, ma'am, I might've made an exception."

"You may stop cringing, Mr. Greaves," said Mrs. Davies, apparently doing everything she could not to laugh at him outright. She'd spotted the blood on his sleeve and marched him into the Palmers' kitchen to tend to his arm.

She made another swipe across his bullet wound with the concoction she'd found among the Palmers' store of medications. Whatever the stuff was, it hurt like hell.

"I'll stop cringing as soon as you're done torturing me," he said.

Smiling, Mrs. Davies tossed the rag into the nearby kitchen sink and set about placing a linen compress over the wound. She then wrapped a strip of cotton around his arm to hold the compress in place. The brush of her fingers against his skin warmed him in a way that wasn't proper.

"At least I did not have to take you back to the clinic in

order to use my bullet forceps," she said. She'd not only been doing a good job of not laughing at him; she'd also been doing a good job of keeping her eyes fixed on his injury and away from his bare chest. "We shall be thankful Mr. Wagner is not a better marksman, and the ball passed cleanly through the muscle." She surveyed her handiwork. "That should hold you for now, but you should visit your physician as soon as possible to cleanse the wound more thoroughly. I would not care for you to survive a shooting only to perish from inflammation."

"Neither would I, ma'am."

"And you may put your shirt back on."

"Yes, ma'am." He slipped it on, bloodstained sleeve and all, and buttoned it up. He watched her as she returned the bottle of antiseptic to the pantry shelf. "You took a foolhardy risk coming here alone, Mrs. Davies."

She'd made him worry more than he liked.

"I thought my cousin was in danger, Mr. Greaves. Her safety was worth the risk," she said, collecting the squares of linen she'd instructed the Palmers' maid to cut for compresses. "What I do not understand is why Joseph Palmer ever took up with a man like Mr. Wagner."

"They've known each other since the war. Served together, apparently," said Nick, putting his vest on over the shirt. Palmer had been willing to talk, probably hoping that if he confessed everything, he'd shoulder less blame. "When Wagner moved to San Francisco, they resumed a partnership that had begun back then. Liquor smuggling."

Mrs. Davies pressed the squares of linen she'd been stacking to her chest. "Surely Mr. Palmer did not need the money."

"Some men are simply greedy. And some men enjoy the thrill

of operating outside the law. And some men enjoy both," he explained. "Taylor's combing through Palmer's warehouse for evidence of the extent of the operation, which also included smuggling opium. Some of which went to Hubert Lange, who made a small profit when he sold the untaxed opium to his customers."

"I trusted Herbert Lange." She shook her head. "No wonder he has been acting so strangely. He must have thought Mr. Wagner killed Li Sha and would come for him next."

"I think at first Lange believed Ahearn was responsible. Just like we did."

A smile darted over her lips. "*We*, Mr. Greaves?"

He inclined his head. "I think it wasn't until Tessie disappeared that Lange really began to suspect Wagner, whom Lange knew by the name of Roddy. Lange must have realized his daughter had learned about the smuggling."

"Is that why she was killed?" she asked.

"She tried to pay Wagner to stop involving her father," he said. "Her efforts got her killed."

"And I suppose he sent us those warnings for some reason." She was squeezing the scraps of linen as if she wanted to choke them. "And set those boys on us."

"From what I've learned, the boys who attacked you had nothing to do with Wagner. He was responsible, though, for the rest, including the knot on my head," Nick said. "Finding Li Sha's body, and seeing that she'd been murdered, made him jumpy. Evidently, both he and Palmer had been her customers at one time. Wagner must've thought we'd find out about that—not that I've ever met a brothel owner who'd tell a cop the name of a client—and start nosing around them in connection to the murder. By the way, it seems Wagner was the customer who assaulted Li Sha last year."

"It all comes around in a circle, Mr. Greaves, doesn't it?"

"I suppose so." He grabbed the squares of fabric from Mrs. Davies' hands before she shredded them, and set them aside. "Wagner's wife gave him an alibi for the evening Li Sha died, and he must have thought he was in the clear until you spotted him with Lange one day and he got panicky all over again."

Good old Lange. Taylor was probably at his store right then to take him into custody.

"I do recall seeing a man talking with Mr. Lange the day after I went to Mr. Massey's with you," said Mrs. Davies. "But I thought nothing of their interaction. Mr. Wagner had no cause to threaten me."

"I'd say Wagner's not a reasonable man."

Nick stood to gingerly pull on his coat, then leaned a hip against the table. From the direction of the parlor came Miss Walford's voice, thanking the maid for the tea she'd brought to the girl.

Mrs. Davies heard her cousin's voice, too. "Barbara is not blameless. Foolish child."

"She'll have to answer questions, ma'am, but I doubt the magistrate will charge her with a crime. He'll probably just give her a stern lecture. It would've been different if Palmer had actually murdered Li Sha or if your cousin had known about the smuggling."

"I do not think she did, but after all the mistruths my cousin has spun lately, I make no guarantees," she said. "Do you think that if Barbara had admitted she'd known that Mr. Palmer was in San Francisco on that Monday night . . . wait. Why *was* he in town that night?"

"He was in Chinatown enjoying the sights," Nick answered

with a smirk. "He didn't want his wife to find out. He'd promised her he'd stay away from the prostitutes and the gambling houses. Apparently, he's not good at keeping promises."

"I see," said Mrs. Davies. "But what I need to know, Mr. Greaves, is do you think Tessie would still be alive if Barbara had told us right away that she'd seen Mr. Palmer the night Li Sha was murdered?"

Here she was, asking him again to tell her she couldn't have prevented what had happened. "I have no way of knowing, ma'am. I wish I could say I did. It's best not to think you're to blame, though."

And isn't that hypocritical, he told himself, *telling somebody else not to feel guilty?*

"I shall try, but I will make no guarantees about that, either." She gazed at him. "At least tell me that Mr. Palmer did not know of Mr. Wagner's plans to come to my house. I can see how Mr. Palmer might be greedy, but I cannot see that he would wish me harm."

"From what I overheard, he didn't know of Wagner's threats."

She drew in a long breath and let it slowly out again. "It is all over, isn't it, Mr. Greaves?"

"It's all over but the shouting, Mrs. Davies," he said.

"I believe that means yes?"

Nick grinned. "Yes, ma'am. It sure does."

CHAPTER 18

Celia stared out the window of the hired carriage as it rattled along Stockton and passed the lovely Grace Cathedral, its tall lancet-arched windows glimmering in the sunlight. Outside the grand brick home next door, an ice wagon had paused to make a delivery. She watched the man lugging a block through the servants' access door cut into the six-foot-tall retaining wall that held up the front yard. Another normal day for the iceman, life proceeding as it ever did, without pause or reflection upon a tragedy that had left two women dead, one with an unborn child, and a family destroyed.

The service door closed behind the iceman, and Celia lifted her gaze to the church's bell tower, soaring into the overcast sky. The world might forget Li Sha, might not care at all about a reformed Chinese prostitute, but Celia would not forget her. Nor would she ever again marvel at how vast and deep and dark were the many secrets the human heart could hide. They were plentiful. And frightening.

The road descended and they left the church behind.

"Are we almost home?" Barbara asked, rousing, covering her yawn with a hand. She had dozed for most of the ride, leaving Celia alone with her thoughts.

"A few more blocks."

"Thank goodness, because I'm so exhausted," her cousin said and yawned again. She slid a glance at Celia. "Did Detective Greaves say what will happen with the Palmers?"

"Elizabeth will likely be tried for manslaughter, since he believes the magistrate will consider Li Sha's death to be a crime of passion and not premeditated," Celia explained, recalling what he'd told her. "If so, Elizabeth will not hang if she is found guilty. Emmeline's fate will rest on whether, given her youth and frailty, the magistrate believes she is fully responsible for her actions."

"I hope he's lenient. I like Em."

"I know you do," said Celia. "I do wonder where she will go, however, if she is released but both of her parents remain in jail for any length of time."

"Maybe she can come and stay with us," Barbara suggested. "Until everything is settled."

Emmeline Palmer in their house? A girl who had played a part in Li Sha's murder? Celia felt sorry for Emmeline, but she was not ready to forgive her.

"I expect she has family that will want to take her in," Celia said sternly, and saw that Barbara understood she wouldn't back down on the subject.

"Do you think Mr. Palmer will be in jail long?" Barbara asked quietly.

"He is an accessory to their crime, and he also helped smuggle goods into the city," Celia answered. "I expect he will be charged accordingly, but I don't know what that will mean for him."

"Oh." Barbara leaned into the corner of the carriage and stared down at her hands, pressed flat upon her lap. "Where do you think Li Sha wanted to go with the money she was looking for?"

"Back to China, perhaps." Celia glanced out the carriage window as they turned up Vallejo. "I doubt, though, she ever would have made it home."

Not a young Chinese woman alone and without protection. She likely would have found herself a victim again, returned to the sort of life she had escaped in Chinatown.

"That peculiar Madame Philippe guessed right," said Barbara, "when she told us there were two different people involved and that a close acquaintance had killed Li Sha. And I was so worried that she would mention Mr. Palmer."

"Now that we know what happened, I would hardly call either Elizabeth or Emmeline Palmer close acquaintances." Their culpability explained why they had been so eager to pay for Li Sha's funeral. "And, Barbara, why don't we both agree never to mention the Palmers again?"

Barbara nodded and appeared contrite. "I'm sorry. I truly am. I know I made a mistake."

"I accept your apology, Barbara. And please, the next time . . ." *Please, God, let there not be a next time.* "Come to me immediately, all right?"

"Yes, Cousin."

Their house came into view, and the cab slowed.

Addie, watching anxiously from the porch for their return, sped down the stairs. "You're alive!" she exclaimed.

"And unhurt, Addie." Celia climbed down and helped Barbara to the curb.

Her housekeeper crushed Celia in an embrace. "Dinna ever do anything so foolish again, ma'am."

"I shall try not to," she answered, her voice muffled by the sleeves of Addie's dress.

Addie released Celia and set her at arm's length. "Weel, you can be certain I'll be asking Madame Philippe what are the chances you'll be staying out of trouble. Now that you're friends with that detective."

Celia smiled. She would expect the chances were not good.

"You are looking better, Owen," said Celia the next afternoon, pushing wide the door and stepping inside the chamber where he sat propped up in bed. Owen looked tiny, swamped by an old nightshirt that had belonged to Barbara's father, the massive carved walnut headboard rising like a wood leviathan behind his back. He needed a good head-to-toe scrub, but that could wait.

"Don't hurt so bad." Owen patted the bandage covering the upper half of his arm. Another bandage, hidden by the nightshirt, covered his side. "But I'm dreadful tired. D'you think you could send Addie up here with some more broth?"

"I will most certainly do that," Celia promised, and sat on the bed.

"Addie told me they caught the fellow."

"Mr. Wagner has been charged with murdering Tessie Lange." That, among other crimes, which included assaulting Celia with intent to commit murder.

"I woulda been able to tell the cops where he lived, if he hadn't given me the slip."

"So you were the boy I saw trailing him the other night," she said.

"That was me." Owen peered at the bruises on her face. "But I spotted him again Wednesday night and followed him here. I tried to stop him from hurting you, ma'am, but he was too big for me to knock down."

Celia touched Owen's hand, resting atop the coverlet. "You saved my life. At considerable cost to yourself."

"Takes more'n a couple knife cuts to keep Owen Cassidy down!" he exclaimed. "But I am right sorry about that whole thing with Miss Barbara. That bunch were worthless. They got it into their heads it'd be fun to beat up some Chinese. Shoulda figured they weren't kidding. Miss Barbara, she just came along at the wrong time." He picked at a loose thread poking up from the weave in the blue-and-white coverlet. "I ran off to find the police, but then I started thinking they'd blame me for being with that bunch and I'd get put in jail. So I turned tail and ran. I'm sorry, Mrs. Davies. That was chickenhearted of me."

"You are no coward, Owen Cassidy. And I am proud of you."

The eyes he lifted to her were full of happiness. "And I'm gonna get Addie a husband. Just you wait and see!"

"I believe she is interested in that fellow who delivers meat from the Washington Market." Although, for all that Addie spoke about urgently wanting a husband, she didn't act eager to claim one.

"Him?" Owen scoffed. "You mean the one who's always grinning at folks?"

"You could describe the man that way."

"Pshaw, he's not half as good as my mates," declared Owen. "I mean, my mates that don't try to beat up Chinese folks, that is. I ain't with *them* anymore, ma'am," he added solemnly. "I promise."

"Oh, Owen." She leaned down to hug him close.

His injuries made him squirm only a little.

"*A*hearn's back in town, sir." Taylor closed the detectives' office door behind him, and Nick heard him settle into his usual chair. "He made a visit here to point out how wrong we were about suspecting him. Mullahey gave him an earful."

Outside, clouds hung low, and a spurt of sandy dust rattled across the street, spooking a cab horse waiting on the corner. Nick had made his report to Eagan that morning, and Tom Davies had been freed within half an hour. Meanwhile, both of the Palmers had returned home, two of Mr. Palmer's business partners—loyal men who'd soon be going down with that sinking ship—having posted bond the minute the magistrate had leveled charges. Joseph Palmer had been charged with violating revenue laws as well as being an accessory after the fact for concealing his family's role in Li Sha's death. His wife had received a manslaughter charge, and not the involuntary kind. The judge hadn't been impressed by her pleas that she had been defending her daughter against the attacks of an unarmed, pregnant Chinese girl.

The lawyers, however, had yet to get ahold of her case. God only knew, the woman might still walk free.

As for Emmeline, given her age, poor health, and repeated dosing with laudanum, the judge had decided she was of weak mind, weaker than her fourteen years. He had decided not to charge her as an accomplice and had let her go.

Nick shoved away from the window and turned to face

Taylor. "Did Harris think the knife we found on Wagner could have been used on Tessie Lange?"

"Yep, he thinks it's possible," said Taylor. "And I'm convinced Wagner's boots match the prints at Mrs. Davies' house. He even likes to smoke the occasional cigar, courtesy of Mr. Joseph Palmer's supply." He cocked an eyebrow. "Wagner won't be going back on the confession he gave you, especially since his wife's singing a new tune about where he was all those evenings."

"Good work, Taylor." There would be justice for Tessie. He should feel better about the outcome, but Nick had learned that the satisfaction of successfully closing a case never lasted long.

I'm trying, Meg. I'm trying to make it up to you.

Taylor was grinning over the compliment. "Mullahey brought Uhlfelder in this morning, too. Caught him trying to board a steamer headed for points north," he said. "He knew, all right, that Roddy's real name was Wagner. He'd met him at one of the Men's Benevolent Association meetings. Wish he'd decided to share that bit of news with us."

Nick hadn't been able to get Captain Eagan to admit that he'd ever suspected Palmer and Wagner and Uhlfelder, fellow members of that association, of being criminals. Maybe Eagan hadn't.

With apologies to his uncle Asa, who'd practically worshiped the captain, Nick would be keeping an eye on Dennis Eagan from here on out.

"And you were right to be suspicious about Palmer, sir," Taylor went on. He'd discovered false-bottom barrels in Palmer's warehouse, their only purpose to conceal contraband. "Once Lange's done squealing on Palmer to try to save his own neck, and Palmer's finished doing time, he's gonna have to skedaddle for sure. He won't have a lick of reputation left."

"I got distracted by Ahearn, though," said Nick, massaging the old ache in his left arm. "That was a mistake."

"Well, in the end we found Li Sha's killers and got the men responsible for Tessie Lange's death, sir . . . Mr. Greaves. Sir."

All's well that ends well. Wasn't that something Shakespeare had written? Nick decided he'd have to ask Celia Davies.

He considered his assistant. "Why don't you take the rest of the day off, Taylor? I think we both deserve a break."

"But I've got that jewelry-theft case to look into for the captain."

"Well, get on with it, then." Nick lifted his hat off the office's oak hat rack. "But if anybody asks, *I'm* taking the rest of the day off. I've got a visit to make."

"To Mrs. Davies?" asked Taylor, winking.

"Yes," he confirmed. Why not admit it? "To Mrs. Davies."

*C*elia stepped onto the porch just as a wagon trundled up and stopped behind the hack she'd sent for.

Excellent timing. "Addie, there is a delivery here for us. Please attend to it," she called through the open front door.

Addie, wiping her hands on her apron, walked into the vestibule. "A delivery?"

"Yes. From that butcher's stall at the market. Doran's."

"What?" Addie strode out onto the porch. Her brows shot up her forehead as she stared at the wagon. "You're having us get meat from the grinning galoot now?"

The man in question turned toward the house at that moment and, with a tip of his cap, grinned broadly. At least, thought Celia, he looked to have all of his teeth.

"Good morning, Miss Ferguson!" he called out.

"What have you done, ma'am?" Addie asked, her hands a whirlwind of agitation across her apron.

"I have given your husband hunting a nudge, Addie," she replied, descending the steps toward the hack. "And have him come around to the back, please."

"Aye, ma'am, but . . . but, ma'am!" Addie cried.

"Good day," said Celia to the deliveryman. "Mr. . . ."

"Michael Knowles," he replied, tipping his cap again. Actually, he wasn't bad looking at all.

Up on the porch, Addie scowled down at them. Celia chuckled, gave the hack driver the name of her destination, and climbed aboard. She set down the bouquet of tulips that she'd received from the garden of an apologetic Mrs. Douglass. The chairwoman might never recover from the revelation that her husband had attended Men's Benevolent Association meetings with three criminals. Celia leaned against the cushions with a contented smile. As the carriage wheeled away, she heard Addie bellowing instructions at Mr. Knowles. Perhaps not the best way to begin a romance, but not the worst way, either.

"Driver, I shall only be a few minutes," Celia said to the man. He nodded and tugged his hat down over his eyes, propped his boots on the dashboard, and proceeded to snooze.

Celia opened the gate and walked toward the Chinese section of the cemetery. She stopped before the nearby grave that had been dug just a few days ago.

She turned her back to the city sprawling over the low hills beneath Lone Mountain, to the bay and its ships, to the lands looming beyond the water. A small wooden headstone, painted white, marked the head of the plot and already tilted slightly in the sandy ground, as though it had been hastily and carelessly placed. Celia straightened it and read the brief inscription. *Li Sha. Friend.* And the date of her death. Nothing more, but what else was there to say?

"I have brought you flowers," she said, resting the tulips atop the grave's bare earth. They were a lovely mix of yellows and reds. "And a few pieces of Addie's wonderful shortbread. It is a tradition for your people to bring offerings of food, I believe."

She retrieved the carefully wrapped shortbread from her reticule and set it next to the flowers. "You should have come to me for the money, Li Sha."

But perhaps the girl had sensed that Celia, knowing the futility of any attempt to flee, would have succeeded in talking her out of leaving San Francisco. Perhaps she hadn't wanted to explain to Celia why she needed to leave in the first place— because Tom, Celia's own brother-in-law, possessed an abusive streak that Celia had never suspected.

Patrick's brother was not a murderer, though, and she could rest content in the assurance that she'd done what she could to clear his name.

Celia smiled down at the grave. "I shall come back every year, Li Sha, as your family would do if they were here to remember you. I shall come with offerings."

She would come because she could not visit the grave of her brother, Harry, who'd been buried thousands of miles away, outside of Sebastopol. And because she had no grave for Patrick, possibly drowned, possibly not, the weight of uncertainty a heavier burden on her than a confirmation of his death would have been.

After a farewell, she turned and noticed the man waiting at the gate.

"I didn't want to disturb you," said Detective Greaves when she reached him.

"Your presence would not have disturbed me," she answered truthfully.

"Addie told me you were out here. I wanted to let you know that your brother-in-law has been released from jail."

"I wonder what Tom will do now," she said. "I wonder if he will leave town."

"Probably," he said. "For all its great size, San Francisco can be a small place. Too small to hide in." He nodded toward Li Sha's grave. "If the preachers are right and she can see us here on earth, ma'am, I'd guess that she's pleased you're honoring her."

"That is my wish, Mr. Greaves." Celia gazed up at the face that had become so familiar to her. "I suppose this is good-bye for us."

"I wouldn't say that, ma'am."

"Then I will see you again?" she asked, the question sounding needful, which she never wanted to seem.

A strand of hair, loosened by the wind, fluttered against her cheek, and he tucked it behind her ear. The touch of his fingers made her shiver.

"Don't worry, Mrs. Davies," he answered with a lazy smile. "To quote a blond-haired Englishwoman we both know—you're not going to be rid of me so easily."

He tapped fingertips to the brim of his flat-crowned hat and strode off toward his waiting horse.

Leaving her to smile after him.

AUTHOR'S NOTE

On the morning of February 12, 1867, a "disgraceful riot in San Francisco" occurred, as the headline in the *Sacramento Daily Union* blared two days later. On that day, approximately thirty Chinese workers were grading lots in the South Beach area when they were attacked by a gang of white laborers. Predominantly Irish and unemployed, the laborers blamed the Chinese for taking their jobs. When the police finally quelled the riot, dozens of Chinese workers had been severely beaten and the shacks they'd erected to live in had been burned to the ground. Justice was swift, and each rioter was fined five hundred dollars and sentenced to ninety days in jail. Rather than discouraging further hostile acts, however, the men's punishment added fuel to the fire, and the Anti-Coolie Association sprang to life. In the coming years, the violence would swell far beyond riots.

Anti-Chinese sentiment had been riding high for years before that February day in 1867, and the Irish weren't the only ones who resented the Chinese presence in California. The meeting that took place at the American Theater in early March, which called for the cessation of Chinese immigration, was only one of many meetings that would follow. Ordinances and laws against the Chinese culminated in the Chinese Exclusion Act of 1882. For the first time in United States history, a federal law prohibited immigration based upon ethnicity. Although the law was ultimately repealed in 1943, negative attitudes toward the Chinese would take far longer to subside.

My descriptions of the city and of the Chinese quarter are based on descriptions from the time; not every observer was a reliable one, however, and prejudices of the period color the accounts given. The snippets of the speech given at the American Theater were taken from a report in the *Sacramento Daily Union*. Also, for the bits of Cantonese dialogue included in the book, I have chosen to use the spellings found in John Chalmers' 1907 *English and Cantonese Dictionary*. Interpretations have changed over time. Lastly, whereas the majority of the characters in this book are fictional, Atkins Massey and Dr. Stephen Harris were real people. My characterization of these prominent citizens of San Francisco is my own creation, though.

ACKNOWLEDGMENTS

I could not have written this book without the help and encouragement of many people. First off, I must thank the amazing editorial staff at New American Library, especially Ellen Edwards, who worked tirelessly to whip my manuscript into shape. Your insight made all the difference. Also, I have to thank my agent, Natasha Kern, who has weathered many a storm with me. You have my eternal gratitude for your sage advice and endless support. To my author sisters at Serious Writers—Donna, Jane, Pat, and Robin. Monthly desserts, laughter, and writing talk; what else could a girl ask for? Also, I extend my appreciation to Peter Leavell, historian and author, who cheerfully answered even my stupidest questions about the Civil War. I'm fortunate to call you a friend. And to Sarah Log, who aided my research of the Cantonese language. Any errors are mine and

ACKNOWLEDGMENTS

mine alone. Furthermore, I would be remiss if I didn't mention my critique partner, the fabulous author and former ER nurse whose medical expertise has saved my butt numerous times, Candace Calvert. You have been with me since the beginning and have kept me from quitting more times than I can count. I give thanks for you every day. Lastly, to my family—thank you for understanding why we're ordering takeout for dinner again. Love you all.

{ 362 }

The grisly discovery of a decaying body in a cellar places Celia Davies' young friend Owen in danger and draws Celia and police detective Nicholas Greaves into a complex murder investigation in the next intriging Mystery of Old San Francisco from Nancy Herriman,

NO PITY FOR THE DEAD

Available in print and e-book in August 2016.
Turn the page for a brief excerpt . . .

San Francisco, June 1867

I'm in for it for sure. Dan and his buried treasure. Dang it all.

Owen Cassidy glanced over at Dan as the lantern sent the man's shadow dancing over the cellar wall. He didn't know how long they'd been digging, but they were both down to their sweat-soaked shirtsleeves, and Dan had been cursing under his breath for at least the past quarter hour.

Dan Matthews swore again as another hole revealed only sand and rocks and bits of broken construction rubble used to level the building lot. "Anything there yet, Cassidy?"

"Nope," Owen said.

Soon. Dan would give up soon, and they could stop and pretend they'd never been looking for gold. It *had* to be soon. Owen was tired of breathing in the dust they'd stirred up, most of it from the coal heaped in the corner, and his left palm had an ugly blister that was sure to burst. Plus, he was scared that Mr. Martin would discover that two of the workers he'd hired to refurbish his offices had been down in the cellar poking around. They'd lose their jobs for sure.

Worse still, if Mrs. Davies found out what he was doing, she'd scold the skin plumb off him. And Owen never wanted her mad at him. She was as close to a parent as he had left.

"You sure Mr. Martin would bury gold down here?" Owen asked. "I mean, beneath his offices and all?"

"Where better? His house, where some nosy maid might find it?" Dan replied. "Who'd ever come looking down here? And why do you think he's in an all-fired hurry to have this cellar bricked over, when it's been fine as it is for so long, huh? 'Cause he wants his money covered over for safekeeping and none the wiser, that's why."

Dan sealed his commentary with a nod. It did make sense. Sort of.

And then it happened. If only Owen hadn't shifted to his right and begun a new hole.

The sound his shovel made was suddenly very different from the clang of metal on stone. "Dan?"

Dan almost fell in his haste to reach Owen's side. "You've found it!" he crowed. "It's old Jasper Martin's bag of gold!"

He dropped to his hands and knees and started clawing at the ground, forgetting about his own shovel in his haste to reach the wealth he was certain they'd found.

"What the . . ." Dan drew back, his face going as white as a lady's fine handkerchief. "Shit!" he shouted, jumping to his feet. "Why won't he leave me be?"

"Who, Dan? What?" Owen asked, trying to get a look past

the man's broad shoulders. He couldn't believe what he saw peeking around the peeled-back edge of a length of oilcloth.

Owen felt his stomach churn, and he clapped a hand to his mouth. Because what he saw sure did look like a blackened, rotting arm.

"Shit!" Dan shouted for good measure before bolting for the steps, Owen hard on his heels.

"*M*rs. Kelly, you must stay off your feet if you do not want this baby to come too soon."

Celia Davies sat back, the cane-seated chair creaking beneath her, and clasped the hand of the woman grimacing on the bed. Maryanne Kelly's skin was clammy and her pulse rapid. In the adjacent room, the Kellys' infant bawled, adding to the tension. Twelve months since that child had been born and already another was on the way, and more quickly than it should have been.

"But I've nobody to help, Mrs. Davies." Maryanne pressed her lips together as beads of sweat popped on her upper lip. She'd been experiencing night pains off and on for the past week, and Celia worried for her and the baby. From what Celia's examinations had revealed, the fetus was small and not particularly energetic; an early birth might threaten the child's survival.

Maryanne exhaled as the current pain passed. "John leaves early and gets home so late from supervising that crew at Martin and Company," she said. "He can't help with the baby. And he can't help with the cooking and the cleaning, either."

If Celia had a penny for how many times she'd heard the like from her other patients, she would have been as rich as Croesus by now.

"And don't tell me to hire a nurse," Maryanne added. "You know we've little money."

A situation that was easily observed by a quick scan of the cramped and gloomy bedroom where Maryanne lay. The meager contents consisted of a rope-strung bed topped by a straw mattress, the chair Celia occupied, and one chest of drawers that looked as though it had been rescued from a rubbish pile. The linens were clean, however, and the damp air coming through the window was fresh and smelled of the ocean. Celia had seen worse lodgings. Far worse.

"Yes, I know." Celia released Maryanne's hand and stood. She folded away her stethoscope, returning it to the black portmanteau that served as her medical bag. "But you must spend more time resting. Ask a neighbor to help. Surely there is someone nearby who can stop in for an hour or two."

"To help a Mick and his wife?" Maryanne asked, cynicism in her light brown eyes. "We should've moved to the South Beach area among our own kind rather than live near the Italians and the Spanish and their endless guitar playing. But no, John had to move up here."

Her infant daughter's bawling increased in pitch and volume, and Maryanne looked toward the door. "And that one with the colic. What am I to do? Some days I think you're a lucky one with no children, ma'am."

Celia would not call it luck. And she expected she never would have children, especially given her singular lack of a living husband.

"You will feel more cheerful after the baby is born, Mrs. Kelly."

"That's what John says, too." Maryanne managed a smile, and Celia helped her sit.

"Take some sage tea to ease your pains or a teaspoon of paregoric if the tea does not work." Celia snapped shut the portmanteau and gathered up her wrap. "For your daughter's colic, you can try some ginger tea, if she'll have it. Otherwise, a warm compress on her belly might help."

"Thank you," the other woman said. "I just wish John could be here more often. I'm worried he won't be with me when the baby finally does come. But I wouldn't want him to lose his job because he's tending to me. Not when he's had such poor luck at the other work he had before we came to San Francisco. He won't go back to being a ranch hand or a miner."

"Do ask a neighbor for help, Mrs. Kelly. You might be surprised who is willing to assist a woman in labor." It was a common enough condition among the women who lived in the lodgings that spilled down the hills toward the Golden Gate, and many would be sympathetic.

"I *would* be surprised," said Maryanne, hauling herself to her feet, a hand on her protruding belly.

"There's no need to show me out," said Celia. "Good night."

"Do you need a candle to light your way home? The fog's come in thick tonight."

"I've only a few blocks to walk, Mrs. Kelly." Celia fastened her navy wool wrap atop her crimson garibaldi and grabbed her bag. "I will be fine."

"You've more courage than I do to walk these streets alone at night, ma'am."

"They are not so bad." Which was what she always told her

housekeeper as well. Addie Ferguson tended not to believe Celia either.

Mrs. Kelly thanked her, and Celia let herself out the front door. The fog was indeed thick, the corner gaslight a fuzzy spot of yellow. The mist swirled around a horse and rider passing on the intersecting street, a shadow moving through the blanketing white like a specter. After an anxious inhalation of breath, Celia descended to the street, clutching her portmanteau close.

It was only a few blocks to reach home, she reminded herself. She was well-known in the area and would be perfectly safe. Better still, she was a very fast walker.

Aside from a momentary fright caused by a cat darting across her path, Celia arrived home without incident. Next door, their neighbor was scolding one of her children in a burst of Italian, and the dog across the street found something to bark at. Life was normal, safe and sound.

Rolling her tense shoulders, Celia climbed the steps to her comfortable two-story brick home. She had just reached the porch when the front door swung open.

"You've missed dinner, ma'am," said Addie, her hands fisting on her hips.

"I trust you have a bowl of mulligatawny at the ready for me." Celia stepped past her housekeeper into the warmth of the entry hall.

"I ought to let you starve, if you canna keep normal hours like other doctors."

An idle threat, coming from a woman who enjoyed mothering Celia, even though she was three years younger and, moreover, a servant. "I am not a doctor, Addie—only a nurse, as you well know. And as my patients do not keep normal hours, neither can I."

Piano music drifted through the closed doors to the parlor off to her left, followed by peals of girlish laughter. Barbara was entertaining a friend that evening, something Celia had sometimes feared would never happen for her half-Chinese cousin.

"Have the girls eaten?" she asked, dropping onto a chair to remove her boots and slip into the soft leather mules she kept in the entry hall.

"Two hours ago, ma'am," said Addie. "And that Grace Hutchinson, for all she's as skinny as a reed, has a healthy appetite. Maybe they dinna feed her at that fancy house of theirs."

"I am certain her mother feeds her, Addie," Celia replied, smiling as she thought of Jane Hutchinson, the woman who'd become as dear of a friend to her as Grace was to Barbara. Though Grace was only her stepdaughter, Jane doted on the girl. "But who else makes a mulligatawny like you do?" Celia added.

Another burst of giggling erupted in the parlor.

"Och, those two! They're like as not still laughing over their little joke about Mr. Knowles from the butcher shop." Addie snatched up Celia's boots and collected her wrap. "Asking me if we're to get our meat delivered for free if I marry him."

"It is a reasonable question. I hope we do," teased Celia.

"Me, marry that galoot? Och, ma'am. What a thought."

With a harrumph, Addie hung the wrap on a wall peg and marched with the boots into the kitchen at the end of the hallway. Smiling, Celia slid open the parlor doors and went through to where the two girls, both seated at the rented piano, had their heads bent close together.

Barbara sat bolt upright at Celia's arrival. "Cousin, you're finally back."

Grace Hutchinson rose to her feet. "How is your patient, Mrs. Davies?"

Barbara followed her friend's example and stood, too, wavering on her disfigured left foot before she regained her balance. The girls could not be more different—Barbara, black-haired and dark-eyed, her features an echo of her deceased mother's Chinese heritage; and Grace, her hair a paler blond than Celia's, with eyes a snapping hazel, willowy and already taller than Barbara although she was a year younger. Grace was a polite, cheerful girl, and anyone who could make Barbara laugh was welcome in their house.

"Well enough. Thank you for asking, Grace." Celia consulted the Ellery watch pinned at the waist of her brown holland skirt. Nearly nine. How had it gotten to be so late? "I did not expect to see you two still up at this hour, however."

"We were both hoping to sit with you by the fire and read before we retired," said Barbara, and Grace nodded in agreement. Grace was staying the night; Celia expected there would be more giggling and whispering before they finally fell asleep.

"If you are exhausted tomorrow, Grace, your mother will not be happy with me."

"My mother would never be unhappy with you, Mrs. Davies. She thinks you're so strong and brave, and I can't tell you how much she admires you," Grace insisted. "I mean, who else would've been so daring as to go out and discover her friend's killer?"

Celia heard Addie, setting the bowl of stew on the table in

the adjoining dining room, clear her throat in disapproval. The story had been in every newspaper in the city, as the reporters in San Francisco loved to write about the sensational or the merely strange. A nurse finding the killer of a Chinese prostitute had apparently fit both categories.

"Yes, that," said Celia sternly, dissuading any further conversation on the topic. It was best left buried in the past.

"So, can we stay up for a little while longer?" pleaded Barbara.

"I suppose so," Celia replied.

"Should I bring in some milk and shortbread?" Addie asked. The girls grinned.

"Yes, Addie, please do," answered Celia, and went to sit at the dining room table.

Barbara and Grace ran back to the piano and plopped onto the bench, and Grace began singing to Barbara's tentative accompaniment. Celia smiled. *Two friends, two bodies with one soul inspired.*

"Indeed so, Mr. Pope," she murmured to herself.

She'd taken only a bite of the mulligatawny when someone pounded on the front door.

"Och, not another patient at this hour!" Addie called out from the kitchen. She leaned through the dining room doorway on her way to the foyer. "I'm turning them away, ma'am. You're closed."

She bustled off. Celia heard Addie release the front door lock, then give out a screech. Celia jumped up and hurried through the parlor.

"Stay there, girls," she told Barbara and Grace, shutting the doors on their startled expressions.

Owen Cassidy stumbled across the threshold, gasping for breath. He was covered in coal dust and dirt from head to toe; the only pale part of him were the whites of his wide green eyes.

"Och, lad," chastised Addie. "Dinna even think of coming inside—"

"Ma'am! He's dead!" he cried, gaping at Celia. "He's dead!"

"What nonsense are you blathering?" asked Addie.

"The fellow in the cellar! He's dead!"

Nancy Herriman received a bachelor's degree in chemical engineering from the University of Cincinnati, where she also took courses in history and archaeology. She's a past winner of RWA's Daphne du Maurier Award for Best Unpublished Mystery/Romantic Suspense, and when she isn't writing, she enjoys performing with various choral groups. She lives in central Ohio with her husband and their two teenage sons.